UNFAITHFUL COVENANT

UNFAITHFUL COVENANT

OPUS X™ BOOK TEN

MICHAEL ANDERLE

DISRUPTIVE IMAGINATION

LMBPN Publishing
PMB 196, 2540 South Maryland Pkwy
Las Vegas, NV 89109

First US edition, November 2020
Version 1.02, February 2021
eBook ISBN: 978-1-64971-091-8
Print ISBN: 978-1-64971-092-5

THE UNFAITHFUL COVENANT TEAM

Thanks to the JIT Readers

Jeff Goode
Dave Hicks
Deb Mader
Dorothy Lloyd
John Ashmore
Peter Manis
James Caplan
Kelly O'Donnell

If I've missed anyone, please let me know!

Editor
Lynne Stiegler

To Family, Friends and
Those Who Love
to Read.
May We All Enjoy Grace
to Live the Life We Are
Called.

CHAPTER ONE

September 3, 2230, Gliese 581, New Samarkand, Sogdia

The slightly misshapen Army hovertruck cruised through the narrow and mostly empty streets with a light hum.

Despite all the complaints from locals when the curfew was issued, almost nobody challenged it. In the last week, the only curfew violators the soldiers had caught were stupid kids doing it on a dare.

A stern warning was enough to correct them. Some local teens might shout insurrectionist slogans, but they weren't any different from bored kids anywhere else in the galaxy.

People's respect for the curfew made for easy, if boring, control. When boredom set in, thinking followed, and it was the thinking that often led to trouble. Such was the case for Corporal Chris Donnelly as he stared out of the front passenger seat of the truck.

There weren't enough streetlights in Sogdia. He'd always felt that way. It was sinister at night, with too many pockets of darkness where stupid teens could hide and cause trouble.

He wasn't afraid of the dark. No one lasted long in the Army with a basic and primal fear like that. No, what he felt was annoyance tinged with a different sort of fear.

Chris didn't care for domes. Claustrophobia wasn't a problem for him, so that wasn't it. He'd spent a good chunk of his modest Army career in tight quarters aboard military transports, but there was something about being on a planet or moon and having to remain underneath an artificial dome that reached into the lizard part of his brain and screamed "unnatural."

Maybe the Purists should say something about terraforming.

Sometimes he wondered why humans bothered. He'd yet to step foot on a planet half as beautiful as Earth, and it would take centuries for the terraforming to make this planet remotely approach the less pleasant parts of the human's homeworld.

The partially transparent dome above gave him a good view of the red-tinged sky. The system's star, Gliese 581, was massive in the sky, a constant reminder they weren't on Earth or even in the Solar System.

The expansive dome was a reminder, one of the many connected structures on the surface of the planet that formed the capital city of Sogdia. Densely-packed squat buildings stretched out to the edges of the domes. No one built up on this world, only out until they quick-fashioned a new dome.

Unnatural.

That was what it all came down to. It was easy to ignore when he was on a ship, harder on a planet.

Chris glared at a nearby closed shop, his rifle clutched in his hand. This wasn't where he was supposed to be, not twenty light-years from home, wandering around some asinine dome and accomplishing a great amount of nothing. Annoyance fed his discomfort in a vicious loop.

Too bad there was every indication he'd be sticking around for a while for ridiculous reasons.

He snorted, drawing the attention of the driver, Corporal Kruenig.

The other corporal gestured to the half-dozen data windows open in front of Chris. All contained visual feeds from low-flying drones.

"Don't be staring out the window," Kruenig jerked his thumb towards those data windows. "You're supposed to be watching the feeds and looking for trouble."

"What, more kids making rude gestures?" Chris scoffed. "I was an asshole when I was their age too."

"I'm talking about real trouble," Kruenig replied. "But kids shouldn't be on the streets at this hour anyway. It's not safe."

"Why are we even here?" Chris replied. He gestured around. "What's the point?"

Kruenig eyed him like he'd lost his mind. "We're here because we were ordered to patrol this neighborhood. Just like the night before and the night before that, and the last whole damned week, Donnelly. We're here because there is a curfew in place."

"That's…not what I mean." Chris glanced at the data windows, then out the window again as they approached a narrow alley and peered down it. Then he spoke up again, continuing his train of thought. "I mean, why are we even on damned New Samarkand doing patrols instead of somewhere we could be doing something useful?"

The answer was so basic, Chris wondered if it was tattooed on his left eyelid. "Last time I checked, part of the Army's mission was to stop rebellions. We're supposed to protect humanity from all enemies, human and inhuman." Kruenig frowned. He leaned forward and sniffed near Chris. "Did you get into that brandy already, Donnelly? You sound drunk."

Chris jerked away from him. "I'm sober, Kruenig. Don't you think you would have noticed before this if I wasn't?"

The driver shrugged. "I don't know. You tell me. What's with all the questions? You're acting like you got hit on the head and woke up to the news of a rebellion."

"There's no insurrection here." Chris narrowed his eyes at someone frowning at him through a window one level above the street. "It's just a bunch of assholes with too much time on their hands."

"The government thinks one's coming."

"Based on what? Ghosts make up a lot of shit so they can sound important. That's all this is." Chris grunted in disapproval. "Some ID bastard trying to justify why their budget shouldn't be cut.

Kruenig slowed the hovertruck to a crawl and stopped in front of an alley. He inclined his head toward it. "If there's no rebellion, what's that?"

He opened the door and jumped out of the truck before pulling his slung rifle off his shoulder. Chris followed. Even from a distance, he knew what they were in for—more signs that some of the locals didn't want them here.

Chris marched through the alley and approached the far wall capping it.

A large brightly colored mural covered the expanse, a stylized cartoonish representation of demonic-looking humanoid dog-men with exaggerated muzzles and open mouths filled with long, sharp teeth. Dark saliva dripped from their slavering mouths. The dog men wore UTC Army uniforms and were depicted stomping on cherub-like children complete with golden wings. The cherubs covered their heads in a feeble attempt to defend them-selves. A mushroom cloud blossomed in the distance.

The building design, the multicolor bracelets, and the star in the image made it clear where and what it was depicting, but if that wasn't enough, large blue letters spelled out the message.

End the oppression of New Samarkand! Go home, UTC dogs!

"Oppression," Kruenig read with a snort. "Without UTC funding and backing, this colony wouldn't *exist*. Now that they have the cities set up and the terraforming going on, they suddenly decide they're oppressed." He gestured with his rifle toward the mural and looked over his shoulder. "This is why we're here. Because some idiots don't know their colonization history."

"It's just graffiti. Stupid and rather childish graffiti at that. Besides, at least in this one, they aren't making us look like space raptors."

"You'd rather they make us look like weird killer dog soldiers?" Kruenig asked.

Chris shrugged. "They're just blowing off steam. I'm

more impressed that they got this up overnight without us noticing."

"Don't be. They have preprogrammed painting drones." Kruenig scanned the mural. "It's not like that takes bravery." He glanced at his partner. "Didn't you pay any attention during the briefing this morning?"

Chris shrugged. "I might have spaced out for a couple of minutes. I can't help it if the commander can't talk without putting me to sleep. We should just have put him on a loudspeaker for the whole city; he would bore everyone into submission. If the worst thing we have to worry about is rude paintings, I think the UTC will survive."

Kruenig snickered. "The insurrectionists have gotten wise to using only paint for this kind of thing. Otherwise, it's too easy to trace them in the system and arrest them. These murals," he waved at the wall, "are signs of more trouble, not less."

"Insurrectionists?" Chris eyed the mural like he was judging it for concept and implementation.

"I bet it's nothing more than bored, stupid kids. You're acting like we're going to end up getting shelled any second. You need to pull the rifle out of your ass, Kruenig."

"What about what happened with the 355th?" Kruenig looked smug. "They got ambushed. You want to be ambushed?"

"They got pies thrown at them." Chris chuckled. "This is what you're worried about? Graffiti and pies? Is that what you thought you'd be fighting when you joined the Army?"

"That's how it starts." The other corporal stood right in

front of the mural. "It's probably only five percent of the population, rich assholes who want to set themselves up as kings. I heard that was what it was like on Diogenes' Hope, a few bastards leading a bunch of people into a war they didn't want."

"I don't know." Chris knelt and tapped the wall, tracing a line in the drawing with his finger. "It makes sense, you know."

Kruenig glared at him and muttered something in German Chris didn't understand, but he was sure it wasn't nice.

"How does it make sense? You're in the Army, and you're supporting insurrectionists?"

Chris shook his head. "Understanding something isn't the same thing as supporting it." He stared at the mural. "The reality is they send criminals out to colonies, so it only makes sense that sometimes you have trouble. I've always thought transportation was dumb. Just make more prison stations and stick 'em there."

"You're the one who said we don't need to be here."

"Yeah, because cops and militia can handle criminals. They don't need Army regulars." Chris patted his rifle. "They don't need infantry patrolling the streets or martial law."

"Maybe. But the militia here is all but non-existent, and it's infested with sympathizers anyway." Kruenig stepped away from the wall and tapped his PNIU a couple of times before declaring, "Direct command, mark coordinates. Insurrectionist propaganda detected, schedule for cleaning."

"Graffiti sympathizers?" Chris asked, incredulity in his voice.

"It's not graffiti," Kruenig insisted. "It's proof this place is *ready* to blow. It's a warning. What did you think, they just send soldiers to random planets because some junior bureaucrat gets a hard-on for a promotion? After that shit on Diogenes' Hope, I bet every hick frontier colony has decided they love all the UTC money and tech but don't like being told what to do. If you don't like it *here*, get used to having to deal with crap way farther out."

Chris tilted his head, admiring the artistry of one of the dog soldiers. "This isn't a frontier planet."

"How the hell is this not a frontier planet?" Kruenig laughed. "Does this look like a core world to you?"

"It's kind of in-between, I think." Chris shrugged. "It's too far out to be a core world, but it's too old and not far enough away to be a frontier colony. I think of frontier colonies as places with a handful of domes and a low population. This might not be Earth or Chiron, but they're doing all right."

Kruenig glared at him. "I thought you hated it here. You bitch about it every night. First sergeant even chewed you out for complaining too much! Suddenly, you're defending their colonial honor?"

"I bitch because we shouldn't be here." Chris grunted. "If the Army needs troops everywhere someone complains about the government, we should have billions of soldiers back on Earth kicking people's heads in. I never thought I'd have to deal with this when I joined the Army."

Kruenig pulled his combat knife out of its sheath and walked toward the wall. "Huh? This is exactly what I figured I'd have to deal with. What the hell did you think you would do in the Army? Build domes? Or are you one of those guys who thought he was going to bring himself home a space raptor tooth?"

Chris looked away, not wanting to admit he had joined because he'd thought a war with the Zitarks was coming.

The damned lizards hadn't had the balls to attack the UTC back then. He'd dreamed about standing in front of domes, bravely defending civilians from rapacious reptilian hordes, not hanging out staring at graffiti.

He might as well never have joined up.

"You're missing my point," Chris replied. "It'd be different if it was like Diogenes' Hope. That was an actual rebellion backed by dangerous people, not someplace with a bunch of wannabes painting murals at night." He inclined his head toward the wall. "Some people don't want us here but aren't going to do anything much, which means we don't need to be here. If they would just shut up and stop causing trouble, we could leave and go somewhere with real problems. I'm willing to bet you right here and right now this rebellion will never escalate. We'll rot here for a year until everyone finds something else to obsess over, and we'll have nothing but stupid stories about murals to share, while other guys are off earning the Medal of Valor and Sacrifice for single-handedly stopping a Leem invasion. Mark my words."

"I don't know which is more ridiculous." Kruenig slung his rifle over his shoulder and lifted the knife. "The idea that the Leems are going to invade, or that one ground pounder's going to single-handedly stop them." He drew his blade across the wall slowly, scratching a rough line through the center of the mural. "If we weren't here, they'd shoot people left and right. I guarantee it. That's the whole point—armed deterrence. Peacekeeping. First, it's pies, then it's sabotage, and then it's missiles during patrol."

"I'd rather be somewhere people liked us or hated us enough to shoot at us. At least then we'd get some action."

Kruenig continued his artistic enhancements. After he finished, the mural was still clearly understandable, but there was a new message in large, rough letters in the center.

UTC FOREVER.

"You're going to be in trouble when they show up to get rid of the mural," Chris commented.

Kruenig shook his head. "Nah, they'll erase that too. For now, it gives us a couple of hours of propaganda. I'll *take* that over your ridiculous alien firefight dream. If I can get through this whole deployment without shooting at anyone or getting shot at, I'll be plenty satisfied."

"I don't know—"

A loud hiss preceded a massive explosion. Their hovertruck flew into the sky in a fireball, like a phoenix being reborn into a flitter. The burning wreckage pelted the street, earning dumbfounded stares from the two soldiers.

Chris was too surprised to be scared.

"If we'd been in there..." Kruenig swallowed and tapped his PNIU. "This is Patrol Lima 2-3-2. We are under attack. I repeat, we are under attack. Our vehicle has been destroyed, most likely by missile attack. Requesting reinforcements at our current coordinates."

Chris flipped the safety off his weapon, his heart

pounding. The deadly reality of danger on this planet had made it past his disdain.

His stomach clenched as he assessed their position. The wall with the mural made the alley a dead end, surrounded by buildings on three sides, with no obvious way to climb out. Their only other exit took them toward a burning flitter and rebels with missiles.

"It's a trap," he muttered.

"You think, Donnelly? You're a damned strategic genius. I don't know why they don't promote you to colonel tomorrow." Kruenig ground his teeth together. "And we're being jammed."

"Jammers?" Chris' eyes narrowed. "That can't be right."

The other soldier shoved his knife into its sheath and pointed his rifle down the alley, his expression grim.

"Wishes aren't a strategy."

"This can't be what you think," Chris insisted.

"I told you they'd escalate. These damned—"

A loud crack barely preceded the bullet hitting Kruenig's face. He collapsed in a spray of blood. Chris jumped to the side, avoiding a follow-up shot that sparked off the back wall and knocked out a chunk. He had a small section of wall as his only cover, but he still had no way to get out.

Loud, heavy footfalls echoed in the alley, along with shouts. The rebels were coming to kill him. He couldn't even look at the fallen soldier. They shouldn't have entered the alley.

They should have used a drone to check.

The corporal didn't hesitate when a rebel came into view, nor did he fire wildly. The first enemy wore a tactical vest and a helmet, so Chris waited a precious couple of seconds to line up a neck shot before loosing a burst into the man. The insurgent gurgled out an attempt at a scream before collapsing.

Two other men skidded and turned. Chris downed one with a headshot and forced another back with a burst into his vest. The rebel groaned in pain and then screamed when Chris blew his knee out.

This was what he'd been taught. This was what he'd been drilled on. Discipline under fire. Discipline under terror.

That was what separated a soldier from any random fool with a gun.

Chris moved too far from his wall, which exposed him to a half-dozen other rebels. The hail of bullets nailed his arms and legs and he collapsed in fiery agony, angry at government bean counters who felt that vests were sufficient and "cost-effective" for most soldiers rather than issuing everyone a full tactical suit upon deployment.

His vision swam. He reached for his rifle, which had fallen a few feet beyond his hand, but a tall rebel with a sneer kicked the weapon away. Chris wasn't supposed to die so far from home.

"You don't have to die today, soldier boy," the man taunted. He crouched and pulled out a med patch. "We're going to keep you alive and ask you a few questions. If you're a good POW, you can get out after the war's over with all sorts of interesting stories to tell your grandkids about the time you got your ass kicked on New Samarkand."

Chris tried to spit in his face but mostly drooled blood

on himself. "This isn't a war. This is stupid. You're not an Army, you're just terrorists."

"No, no, no." The rebel shook his head. "This isn't terrorism, it's a rebellion. It's the beginning of a brave new *independent* world, free from the tyranny of people who are arrogant enough to rule from so far away it takes weeks for a message to arrive."

"Screw you. No soldier has killed anyone on this planet, and you just murdered one."

The rebel shot an uneasy look at Kruenig's body before glaring over his shoulder at a tall man with a pinched face. "That wasn't supposed to happen, but now that it has, certain things have been set in motion. That's where you're going to help us. You don't have to die. If you cooperate, I give you my word you'll receive medical attention and be held in humane conditions."

"You can't win." Chris hacked up blood, every part of his body on fire. "They've been reinforcing the garrison. Just because you blew up one truck and ambushed two soldiers, it doesn't mean you're going to pull off an insurrection. This is hopeless. It'll be a waste of lives."

The pinched-face man stepped forward with a sinister smile. "That was before we came. With the weapons we are providing, they'll not only win, but they'll also prove what a pointless, impotent force the UTC is. A new order will arise upon its ashes."

"Who the hell are you?" Chris blinked to try to stay awake. It didn't matter if they'd been jammed, the explosion would be detected and reported. He just needed to survive until reinforcements arrived.

No way in hell was he going to become a POW.

"Who am I?" The pinched face shoved his rifle against Chris' forehead. "The future."

"No," the rebel leader shouted. "This wasn't the plan. It's not right." He shook his head. "He's already down. He's no threat, and we need him for intelligence."

Pinched-Face looked at the leader. "No one wins their freedom without sacrifice, and a low-ranking piece of trash like this will have limited intel. You think you can win your freedom without killing?"

"I'm giving you an order," the rebel leader stated. "Stow that weapon. We'll kill when necessary, but only then."

The pinched-face man smiled. "You forget our agreement. We'll work with you, but we don't work *for* you."

"You mercenary piece of shit." The rebel spat at his feet. "You don't even care. This is nothing but a payday for you." He pointed at Chris. "At least that soldier is fighting for something more than his bank account."

"Hate me all you want. We'll help you win your little war." The pinched-face man clenched his finger over the trigger.

Chris closed his eyes and waited, calm settling over him despite his pain. His execution was over before he felt it.

CHAPTER TWO

September 3, 2230, Solar System, Earth, Victoria Falls

Spreading out into the galaxy and the terraforming that came next were impressive accomplishments.

In just over two centuries, humans had conquered the air and the stars. If it weren't for the Local Neighborhood races, there would be nothing to stop the species from sweeping across the entire galaxy, defying all those who doubted they would prosper.

That was before one considered the advances in medicine and genetics. Although terrifying *yaoguai* reflected the dark side of biological science, de-aging treatments and medicine had pushed back the specter of death.

No one lived forever, but humans were finally living to their true potential.

These feats were the products of humanity's primary advantage over other animals on Earth. Humans were neither the strongest nor the fastest animal.

They didn't have the sharpest teeth, nor could they hold their breath the longest. Their minds set them apart from anything that might prey on them and led them to the inventions and tools that assured humanity need never again fear extinction because of a threat to a single planet.

FTL travel via either the HTPs with their Navigator head start or the jump drive displayed humanity's technology prowess and assured the species' continuity. However, as Erik stood on the rocky outcropping, staring at hundreds of meters of water cascading over the lip of the massive gorge, he didn't care about technological achievements. Nature was power in its most primal form, and that was on display.

A man had to respect that.

Victoria Falls was over a kilometer wide, but Erik was unsure of whether to think of it as one waterfall or a set of close waterfalls. In either event, it ignited more than a smidgen of humility before nature in him. His awe at the impressive display kept him quiet and contemplative. How long had water flowed from the falls into the river below? How long would it continue?

Jia stood beside him, smiling at the waterfall at the edge of an outcropping. The Zambezi River churned below like a hungry god waiting for sacrifices.

"It's beautiful. I'm glad you talked me into coming to see it in person. It wouldn't be the same in a simulation."

Her dark hair fluttered in the breeze. It was a perfect sight: a beautiful woman in front of gorgeous scenery. Erik could get used to this.

Was this a small preview of his future?

"It's pretty nice," Erik replied, "and I figured we should take the chance before Alina makes us jump into Zitark territory to steal a blessed piece of meat from them or something."

Jia laughed. "I don't think they have blessed meat, but I'll admit I'm not an expert on alien religions."

"Wait, are you admitting Jia Lin doesn't know something?"

"There are a lot of things I don't know."

"I'll alert the news reporters."

Erik's left arm itched. He might be fully healed and his replacement installed, but his brain hadn't gotten used to it yet. The doctors had promised him it was temporary. They could tweak the hardware, but there was only so much they could do to his brain.

He shook out the arm and chuckled, gesturing along the length of Victoria Falls. "I wonder if we could fly a flitter through that? Might be fun."

"I don't think the locals would appreciate it." Jia glanced his way, appreciating the joke.

It'd been a while since they'd taken anything approaching a vacation. Playing in nano-AR and VR could be relaxing, but it wasn't the same thing as putting thousands of kilometers between them and the *Argo*.

They'd brought along the MX 60 with the standard gear in its storage compartments, but that wasn't because they anticipated trouble. It would have been too much work to empty it.

Besides, it never hurt to have extra gear on hand in case they bumped into a killer cyborg in a spider-bot body, an insane Leem-human hybrid, or a monstrous *yaoguai*.

At Erik's request, Emma was leaving them alone so they could appreciate the grandeur of nature without her running commentary. He almost found that more relaxing than not having to worry about a firefight with the Core's minions.

"I wonder..." Jia crouched, her eyes narrowing. "I'm pondering its defensive capabilities."

"Huh?" Erik's brows lifted as he tried to figure out where she was looking. "Defensive capabilities of what?"

Jia gestured at the waterfall. "Using that as a defensive position. The sheer volume of water heading down has to help. If you could pop us between the water cascades and fire..." She tapped a finger on her lips. "Maybe stay behind the denser portions."

"I honestly don't know." Erik thought for a moment. "I've never fought someone from behind a waterfall, let alone one that big. Somehow I doubt it'll be a problem."

Jia stood and dusted off her pant legs. "You're probably right. Just curious, like you and the flitter."

"It wasn't like..." Erik looked away. "Now that I think about it, I imagine if we were being chased, we *could* try to use the falls against other flitters. You could crash them if you did it right, or get them down to the river for easy shooting."

Jia gestured around at the nearby trees and slowly turned. "This isn't the greatest tactical environment. They've got a lot of trees, but they're not very dense." She pointed at a thick copse that would require an impressive jump or a flitter to get to. "That's decent—good coverage of most of the area. Sniping, maybe?"

"Thermals would make the trees useless. You'd get picked off easily." Erik scratched his eyelid, trying to visualize what a good close-air support craft like a Dragon might do to the area. "But a big-ass Elite wouldn't do well there."

Jia groaned and rubbed her temples. "What are we doing?"

"Looking at a waterfall, I thought."

"No." Jia folded her arms. "Don't you see?"

Erik inclined his head toward the water. "Kind of hard to miss. It's huge."

"*No.*" Jia walked over to him, took his hands, and looked up his eyes. "You and me."

"What about you and me?" Erik asked, confused by the quick change in the direction of the conversation.

"We're here at a beautiful natural wonder, and we're both thinking about how to fight the Core in this location." Jia let go of his hands and stepped away, waving a hand at the water. "We've got no reason to think they'll ambush here. We even traveled using fake identities."

Erik didn't smirk. It wasn't all that long ago that Jia balked at breaking laws or regulations, but now she had no problem asking Emma for help should they desire to travel without leaving a trail. It made sense during missions, but this was vacation.

"I'm not seeing the problem," Erik replied with a shrug. "It doesn't hurt to think about it."

"Doesn't it?" Jia tromped over to a tree and leaned her back against it. "I see my friends less and less these days. We didn't go to many sphere ball games last season. We spend most of our time training."

"Yeah, I suppose. The new season's starting soon. We can hit more games this season if that's what this is about."

"No." Jia sighed. "Yes, I'd like to go to more games, but

that's not what this is about. It goes deeper than that. It's about you and me."

"What about you and me?" Erik frowned. If there was an alarm for relationships, it'd be screaming right about now. His mind raced, trying to spot the hole so he wouldn't step in it. "Is this about making me go to that freaky restaurant?"

Jia offered him a quizzical look. "No, nothing like that. I'm just saying, patterns become habits, and habits are hard to break. I'm thinking once this is all over, we're going to need to deprogram ourselves. Learn how to be something other than…what was it he called us? That's right, the Last Soldier and the Warrior Princess."

Erik grinned. "I kind of like those names, though it was cool being the Obsidian Detective and Lady Justice."

"This isn't about nicknames." Jia pinched the bridge of her nose, eyes shut. "Erik, we're too alike. We both throw ourselves into our work. Before, it didn't consume me because my lazy captain wouldn't let it, but now…" She opened her eyes and gave Erik a concerned look. "We're people, too."

"Jia, you're letting this work you up." Erik walked over to the tree and patted the trunk before leaning against it. "We're at war with the Core. Of course we're going to spend most of our time on duty or thinking about combat or training. That's what war means."

"Is that how it's always been for you?" she asked. "From what you've told me, you were on when it was time to fight and relaxed when you weren't."

"Sure." Erik stuck his hands behind his head and rested his skull against them. "But during wars, there was a lot less relaxation. That didn't mean I didn't take time off now and again, but I never forgot what it meant to be a soldier and that mindset sticks. You're right, though. It's different now."

"Different?" Jia asked, a touch of fear in her voice.

"Yeah. It was easier to shut off, but I think that's because we're not part of an Army. We're not even part of the Intelligence Directorate. We know they're doing things, and they have people helping us—sometimes a lot of people—but it comes off like we're trying to handle all this ourselves. I think that's what's programming us, if you want to call it that."

"Are you worried about what happens after it's all over?"

Erik shook his head as he stared at the mesmerizing tons of water flowing in front of him. He was grateful for the audio filter Emma had suggested before their arrival. Sometimes a man wanted to appreciate nature without it roaring at him the entire time.

"Once we take out the Core, I'll have my revenge and the UTC will be safer," he replied. "Will it be safe from everyone and everything? Nah. Of course not, but I don't think it's my responsibility to worry about the rest. If those bastards hadn't been involved in killing my unit, I might have retired and been content to live in some frontier colony watching months-delayed sphere ball recordings from Earth."

"It's weird for me to even think about now." Jia stepped away from the tree and back toward the edge of the cliff. "I want to see a lot more of the UTC, and not just when we need to show up to blow up people."

"Then I'll have to make sure we have a good ship. We're going to miss the jump drive when it's gone, but it won't be so bad if we're not rushing to some system looking for trouble."

Jia didn't speak for a good half-minute.

As she continued looking down at the water, a small smile grew on her lips, and the tension on her face and her neck slowly eased. When she broke her silence, her voice was low.

"I'm worrying too much."

"You always do," Erik replied.

Jia glanced at him. "Well, if we're both able to think that far ahead, we won't have a lot of trouble adapting to the future. I like the idea of flying through the galaxy with you."

"Until we run into a Leem with a death wish." Erik grinned.

She shook her head. "Even your Lady isn't that much of a bitch."

"Do you *honestly* believe that after everything we've been through?" Erik offered her a healthy grin.

Jia barked a loud laugh, before she doubled over, mirth was spilling out of her like it'd been desperate to escape. Tears welled in her eyes, and she straightened and wiped them, her huge smile aimed at her favorite part of him.

His heart.

The clouds were gone from her face. "Good thing we did that anti-Leem training then."

CHAPTER THREE

<u>September 4, 2230, Gliese 581, New Samarkand, Sogdia</u>

Loud booms shook the area, rattling the building and windows. Not thunder, explosions.

Bright flashes erupted all over, barely obscured by the short buildings dominating the skyline. Columns of smoke drifted upward and spread out as they hit the top of the dome, forming low-hanging dark clouds.

It was a storm of death.

Agent Lau hoped someone somewhere was increasing the power to the air-handling systems. The Intelligence Directorate agent slowed as he passed a small building with an open garage. There was a blue flitter sitting inside.

Bullet holes riddled the walls. A missing chunk and the blackened ground marked recent explosions.

He jammed his hand into his pocket, nervously confirming his data rod was still inside before glancing at the flitter. Taking the vehicle might get him across town quicker, but he couldn't risk aerial flight without getting shot down. The staccato beat of machine-gun fire shocked him into action, and he continued sprinting down the street.

The ID needed the information on his rod so the government would know the truth about the situation.

He assumed the Army garrison commanders were overwhelmed by trying to get a handle on the rebellion. What had been nothing more than angry protests and graffiti had turned into hellish urban combat so close to overnight he wasn't sure the difference mattered.

Lau slowed as he neared an alley but didn't enter. The last thing he wanted was to be trapped by the mercenaries hounding him. He kept close to the buildings and continued his run.

Ahead, a weeping woman knelt next to a man lying dead. Lau gritted his teeth. There was nothing he could do for her. The rebels and their pet mercs weren't showing restraint or mercy, and if he waited around, he would not be able to help anyone.

"You need to run!" he shouted at the woman. "They're coming. Wouldn't he have wanted you to live?"

Lau didn't wait for her response. He continued down the street, heart pounding, face drenched in sweat. The best thing he could do for the innocent victims in Sogdia and the other cities in the colony was to ensure the ID and the DD got this information. One had to know the enemy to fight them.

Right now, they needed to understand their enemy wasn't who it looked like.

A flitter flew overhead, its movements wobbly. There were no military markings, but it could be a rebel.

Trying to get their attention might prove fatal.

It didn't matter. Seconds later, a missile screamed through the air and struck the flitter, consuming it in an orange-red fireball. Chunks of the vehicle rained onto the street, and a large section plummeted, crashing into the side of a nearby building. Parts of the building cracked off and slammed into the pavement.

"No wonder the military avoids flitters," Lau whispered as he shot a glance over his shoulder.

Had he lost his pursuers? He was sure he'd hit a couple of them, but he couldn't tell if they'd given up or were attempting to trap him another way. The missile could have been fired from kilometers away. Aerial vehicles were easy to hit without towers or mountains.

Lau tapped his PNIU to try to connect on one of the local ID backup frequencies, but an error code flashed in his smart lenses. The bastards were still jamming him, but it was getting weaker. All he needed to do was keep moving. The rebels didn't control the dome, much less the whole city.

It'd be a risk to transmit any information openly. The people after him were obviously a lot more than local rebels, even if the locals were helping them. Encryption might not be enough.

At least there weren't any drones above him. He'd been worried his pursuers might use a chain of laser-comm-linked drones for surveillance, but as he'd witnessed, anything that was flying right now was getting shot down, if not by the rebels, then by the military. Nobody had eyes on anything. That would eventually be sorted out, but not in the coming minutes.

Lau briefly considered the insane idea of purposely

running toward heavy gunfire. Its presence would imply both military and rebel forces. He wasn't prepared to hand over the rod to any random soldiers he ran into, but they could protect him from his pursuers.

A couple of rifles pointed in the opposite direction and grenades tossed towards the enemy would be welcome.

A handful of rebels, a tiny percentage of the population, suddenly had an Army with heavy weapons and government-grade jammers. He let out a hysterical laugh. The external manipulation was obvious even without the intel on his rod.

Everyone had miscalculated, assuming trouble like this would only happen in a place as populated as Earth. The real threat might have always been outside of the core worlds.

His enemies weren't demons, but they worked the same way. They found people enmeshed in rage and envy and corrupted them for their purposes. Everywhere they touched, darkness followed.

"The higher-ups have been idiots," Lau muttered.

No, *he'd* been the idiot, along with the other local agents.

They were supposed to be keeping an eye out for this sort of thing. Their investigations had underestimated the level of smuggling going on in the colony, especially of weapons. Somehow the mercenaries had crept onto the planet without the ID noticing. Now innocent people were suffering because they'd screwed up.

That was over. It was time for ID's ghosts to aid the remaining civilians.

A bullet whizzed by his ear and struck the wall next to

him. He ducked, thus avoiding a follow-up shot, and ran forward, looking for options and not finding good ones. Two burning flitters and a hovertruck lying on its side blocked the road ahead. A couple of dead bodies lay in pools of blood next to the truck.

Scampering over the blockage would just give his hunters with an easy kill, and that assumed there wasn't a sniper watching the intersection. The bodies didn't look burned.

There was only one choice—not a good choice, but it might keep him breathing for a couple more minutes. He ducked through an open door to his right. A cluster of bullets struck the frame barely a blink after he'd run inside.

With so much background noise, he was having trouble hearing the gunshots and couldn't estimate how close the shooters were. Lau drew his pistol. Too bad he didn't have any more loaded magazines left. He had not planned to get involved in a running gunfight.

If luck was where opportunity met preparation, then bad luck was where a problem met a lack of preparation.

He looked around.

The building appeared to be an abandoned office. There were no lights on. Darkness hung over the back of the room, except where patches of illumination made it in through windows or holes in the walls. There were no bodies, but he saw at least one trail of blood, and there were probably more hidden in the shadows. Desks and chairs were scattered around, some damaged.

A step forward knocked shell casings away.

Lau ran toward the darkest corner and ducked behind an overturned desk, steadying his pistol on top. If he couldn't outrun his pursuers, he'd make a stand and fight until he was out of ammo. After a moment of thought, he lowered his pistol and crawled on his side toward the edge of the desk, then pointed it around the edge. He slowed his breathing and waited, but he couldn't do anything for his heart as shouts and the thud of boots on pavement grew closer.

His change in position brought him face to face with a small stuffed smiling Leem toy next to an overturned box. The toy's hand was raised in a friendly gesture. Its bulbous black eyes were cute, and it wore a yellow sash that read *I come in peace* in Mandarin.

Lau shifted the box and found a porcelain Zitark figurine, this one wearing a red robe and a crown. He had no idea what they were supposed to represent.

Zitarks didn't wear robes or crowns.

"Hey, government dog," someone shouted from outside. "Why don't you come out and chat with us?"

Lau narrowed his eyes. That sounded less like his earlier merc pursuers and more like rebels. He'd accept the small bit of luck. He had a better chance of handling the rebels and surviving.

One concern lingered, though. The rebels lacked the training and equipment of the mercenaries and their true masters. Why would the mercs leave it to the rebels to capture him? When he'd fled, the mercenaries had made it clear they knew he was a ghost and he'd stolen information they didn't want anyone getting their hands on.

He could turn himself in to the rebels and explain they needed to see what was on the rod, but that might accomplish nothing. Most insurrections involved at least *some* outside funding and aid. They weren't going to care what a government agent had to say about the people helping them.

A shadow cut across the open doorway. They'd arrived.

"He's supposed to have a data rod on him," a rebel outside explained. "Remember your orders. Kill the bastard and take the rod."

"What if we damage the rod?" someone else asked.

"They can't bitch at us about what happens in combat. Besides, if we don't hurry up, the reinforcements will have all the fun."

It was exactly what he'd been worrying about. There wasn't much time, and he couldn't guarantee he'd survive both the rebels and their reinforcements. His first step would be eliminating his enemies.

Lau held his breath and waited. If the rebels were smart, they'd find a back way in and flank him, but they didn't know his exact position. That reinforcements were expected suggested a small number of men, fewer than the merc squad that had been following him earlier.

A rebel in a tac vest rushed into the building, yelling and waving his rifle around like an idiot. Lau didn't fire. Taking one man down wasn't enough.

The rebel stopped yelling and swept the area more cautiously, a frown on his face. He crept forward and two other men entered, all three spreading out.

"Somebody should have guarded the back," a rebel complained.

"We're fine," another replied. "I bet he's hiding in here somewhere."

Lau grabbed the Zitark in a robe, rolled onto his side,

and counted to four before throwing it as parallel to the floor as he could manage. The figurine traveled a decent distance before striking a desk.

The rebels spun toward the noise, their faces tense. They continued forward step by careful step but did not fire.

"Come out now," a rebel taunted. "There's no reason to make this hard on yourself."

Lau waited for them to move forward a couple more meters before popping around the edge of the fallen desk. Three quick headshots, three dead rebels. They collapsed to the floor without a scream or a shot. He let out a sigh of relief.

Something large passed in front of the door. He couldn't tell what it was from his position, but it was big enough to darken the entryway. With a sigh, he pulled the data rod out of his pocket and placed it in the box near the Leem toy, then turned the box on its side. If there was nothing outside, he could come back for it, but his instincts told him otherwise.

Lau tapped his PNIU and smiled. He had a weak signal. There was a decent chance he could get a transmission off. The ID could back-trace his position, but the jamming would make it less precise.

All's well that's Roswell, he sent.

"ID ghost," boomed an amplified voice from outside. "We know you're in there. If you come out right away, you can ride this war out as a POW. We don't care if you're a spy. We can be civilized. If you're thinking about going out the back, we have snipers covering all exits. In short, you're trapped."

Lau stood and headed toward the door, gun in hand. Rebel, mercenary, other—he didn't care at this point. The local rebellion had turned into a bloodbath. It was time to reduce the enemy forces.

A sharp bark of laughter escaped his lips when he stepped out of the building. A large gray hovertank floated in front, its main cannon angled to deliver death through the doorway.

"Talk about overkill." Lau tossed his weapon away and raised his arms. "All this for one ghost?"

"I take it you killed the three men who reported your position?"

Lau nodded. "It was them or me."

"So they don't have the rod? And don't say you don't know what I'm talking about."

"No, they don't." Lau grinned. "I stashed it about a half-klick back. Want me to prove it?"

He slowly lowered his arms and pulled out the pockets of his jacket and pants before doing a full turn like he was in some sort of twisted post-apocalyptic modeling session.

"You misunderstand, ghost," the tank commander replied. "It's not important that we find it, only that no one else gets it."

The barrel lifted and swung to the side. With a deafening roar, the tank fired. The round smashed into the wall, blowing it to pieces. The explosion knocked Lau over. His head slammed into the pavement and he blinked, trying to maintain consciousness. Three more shots followed before the barrel was trained on him again. He let the darkness take him before they fired.

CHAPTER FOUR

<u>September 9, 2230, Neo Southern California Metroplex, Nuwa Wedding Planning Center</u>

Jia tilted her head, trying to make sense of what she was seeing.

The large vaulted ceiling abutted an open strip of beautiful sky with flying birds visible. That slit gave way to something ornate and gothic, but the greatest oddity above them was the spiraling galaxies in the far corner of the room.

She suppressed the chuckle that wanted to come out.

While she'd grown comfortable using nano-AR rooms for something other than training in newer and more efficient ways to kill someone or for piloting, it felt strange to be in a nano-AR chamber and not have a simulated gun in her hand.

Or for that matter, both hands.

The woman of the moment, Chinara, stood in the center of the room near Jia's other friend Imogen. Twenty wedding dresses of different designs and colors hung in the air, spinning slowly so she could inspect them from a variety of angles.

A woman in a flattering dark dress stepped into the room. Her elaborate braids put Jia's sister's coif to shame, and the same could be said for her perfect skin.

"I'm Miss Wu," she announced. "It was my understanding that you wanted time to inspect the concepts before I offered my advice."

Chinara waved her off. "How long do we have this room?"

"Your appointment is for one hour." Miss Wu offered a perfect bright smile. "Of course, I can help facilit—"

"I'll call for you when it's almost time," Chinara explained. She ran her hand over a green dress with a thoughtful look.

Miss Wu bowed her head and departed, the smile stuck on her face.

Imogen clapped once. "That's it, Chinara. *You* take control. You're planning your wedding and your special day. She's going to try to upsell you and convince you that you need expensive extras like real food." She pointed at the four simulated roofs. "They don't make much on venue decoration."

Jia stepped over to her friends. "You're sure you don't want a destination wedding? A lot of good packages for Venus right now."

Imogen folded her arms. "She doesn't want to get blown up at her wedding."

"It's not like that." Jia waved a hand dismissively. "If anything, Venus is twice as safe now because of the incident. Not saying she has to have her wedding there, only that it's a good option."

Jia didn't want to admit she'd done a little side research on the subject for her own purposes. It wouldn't happen anytime soon, if at all, but it wouldn't hurt to be prepared if the situation changed rapidly.

Chinara shook her head. "All that travel and planning? I don't want my wedding to be stressful. I want it to be a good time. I think this kind of place will allow that, offering beauty with none of the downsides."

Jia understood. She spent enough time in nano-AR training environments that she would never claim they couldn't feel real. Part of her rebelled against the idea of a special event like a wedding in a simulator, but it wasn't her wedding or her choice.

"What does Conrad think?" she asked.

"He says he'll leave it all up to me." Chinara moved on to another dress and fingered the sleeve. "I think if he had his way, we'd just get the license, and that would be that. Going somewhere is too much trouble, and I have a lot of relatives who refuse to go into space."

Imogen rolled her eyes. "What is this, the twenty-first century?"

Jia circled the dresses, finding her mind going to what would be necessary to make them combat-ready. Quick sleeve tears, a slice up the side of the skirt.

A train might be useful to blind an enemy.

"There are plenty of beautiful places on Earth," Jia replied. She almost mentioned Victoria Falls before remembering she had traveled there using a fake name. "And plenty of beautiful places in Neo SoCal."

"Why go to all the trouble?" Chinara stopped and smiled at a flowing green lace dress. "We'll figure out somewhere nice for our honeymoon. Maybe Venus. Oh, we did set the date. That took a lot of planning because everyone's relatives and friends are busy doing something. Announcements will be going out soon." She rolled her eyes. "Set it aside now. June 15, 2231."

"That long?" Jia's brow lifted. "I thought since you'd decided on a place like this, it'd be sooner."

"A little anticipation never hurts a woman." Chinara nodded firmly. "And I've found my dress."

Imogen giggled. "It's strange when you think about it."

Chinara turned to her friend. "What is? I like this dress."

"No, it's beautiful." Imogen smiled. "It's that they'll have the dress made and brought here, but imagine if they just simulated the dress, too."

"It wouldn't feel right," Jia complained. "Trust me, I spend a lot of time in nano-AR. More than is healthy. It can feel very real, but the fine details are off. Clothes that are moving are the worst."

Jia didn't like Imogen's huge grin.

"You and Erik like to spend a lot of time in nano-AR?" Imogen asked, waggling her eyebrows. "Participating in…fantasies?"

Jia's cheeks heated. "Uh, for training! For *training*. Security contractor things, nothing, uh…" She waved a hand, trying desperately to come up with a way to get out of this verbal mess. "Nothing fantastical."

Fighting Leems didn't count as fantasy, though the bikini squads of the past might qualify.

Imogen snickered. "Whatever you say. No shame."

"We're here for Chinara," Jia insisted firmly. "Let's not lose focus."

"It's okay," Chinara offered softly. "I don't think I'm going to decide much other than this dress today, and I still am going to go home and spend the next week looking at minor variants. The problem is I thought I knew what kind of wedding I wanted, but now I don't. Having it here provides more choices." She motioned toward the galaxy above. "I'm tempted to do something very exotic."

"Leem waitstaff," Imogen suggested, taking a sip of the champagne the wedding center had provided for the three of them.

"How much have you had?" Jia gave her friend a questioning look. "Unless Chinara's family is a bunch of Grayheads, they probably don't want Leem waiters."

Chinara laughed softly. "No, but she does have a point. There are a lot of options. My head tells me to do something conventional and normal, beautiful but boring. My heart suggests something crazy, something that might get my grandmother shaking her finger at me."

"Really?" Jia's gaze ticked up to the galaxies. "Are you sure Imogen hasn't hypnotized you?"

Imogen gave Jia a dirty look. "You make it sound crazy." She put down her glass.

Had she ever been such a drinking lightweight? Yes, yes she had. "It's not...*that*, Imogen. I'm surprised is all."

"It's the thought of change," Chinara explained. She walked over to where different data windows floated, filled with sliders, buttons, and text boxes displaying different wedding options. "I'm not prepared to be a wild woman, but I don't mind experimenting."

Imogen put her hands on her hips. "I'm not a wild woman. I'm *fun*."

Chinara tapped the data window and ran her finger along the slider. A wall appeared to her side, the color slowly changing along a gradient from red to blue with the slider's position.

"Does this alter anything you thought about marriage?" Chinara asked, pulling her hand away from the data window.

Imogen shrugged. "I'm not sure. Part of me wants to throw Michael down and demand we get married, but another part of me wants to continue dating for ten years."

They both looked at Jia, their gazes heavy and expectant. She tried to ignore them but gave up.

Friends.

"I'm hoping it's in the future for us," Jia admitted. "But our work situation is complicated right now. Things aren't stable, but there's a chance they will stabilize eventually, maybe even soon."

Nothing wrong with keeping hope alive.

"You so sure?" Imogen raised an eyebrow in challenge. "What if things get all normal and easy, and Erik decides he's bored?"

"He's not like that." Jia shook her head, no doubt in her mind about Erik. "Trust me. If this weren't real, I'd know it. Like I said, it's just a matter of the situation changing."

"If he's not going to ask you anytime soon, why not just ask him?" Imogen prodded, inclining her head at Chinara. "If she can wait a long time to get married, you can get engaged now and set a date way off."

"No, not yet. We're in a good place. Besides..." Jia

sighed and averted her eyes. "It's stupid and old-fashioned, but..."

"But what?"

Chinara and Imogen stepped forward, their faces alight with eagerness. There was no way Jia could dodge the question now.

Stupid, great, annoying, persistent *friends*!

Jia eyed them. "The truth is, I was the one who forced things initially. I don't think Erik was looking for anything, and I don't blame him since he was in a weird headspace. I don't always want to be the one pushing. If we're going to have a future together, I want to know that it'll happen without me going all Full Control Lin on it."

Chinara smiled. "There's nothing wrong with wanting him to ask you, Jia."

"True." Imogen bobbed her head in eager agreement. "Nothing wrong with that at all." Her breath caught. "If you get married, is it going to be on Venus?"

"I have no idea." Jia had to admit, just talking to her friends about the subject could and did bring a huge smile to her face. "I'd honestly prefer something small, but I don't think there is anywhere in the galaxy I could run if my mother didn't get to plan the ultimate wedding." She winked. "For now, I'll see what works for you two and adjust accordingly."

CHAPTER FIVE

September 10, 2230, Gliese 581, New Samarkand, Sogdia

"It's like the worst damned concert in the world," muttered Lieutenant Cabrina Pena.

The drumbeat of explosions and gunshots continued, and despite the audio filters in her helmet, the vibrations seeped from the ground into her exoskeleton and then to her body. Her ears would probably be ringing for a day, and her muscles would ache for a while.

She'd never complain about long stretches of boredom again.

Her ears also itched. That was an exo design flaw they needed to address. If a soldier was in the middle of the battle and couldn't disengage their arms from the exo's interface, he or she just had to suffer the annoying distraction.

A small irritation in battle not only could but would kill. That was what she would write in her recommendation form.

"LT," transmitted one of her soldiers on the right of her loose formation. "All the evac flitters are loading and almost ready for lift-off. They're reporting all civilians accounted for and taking off in five minutes per HQ's orders."

"Five minutes is a damned eternity," Cabrina complained. "And they're staggering the launches to make sure they have one-to-one air support in the next sector." She glanced at her HUD. "But that doesn't help us. I can't believe they let us get flanked like this."

"You're preaching to the choir, LT."

"If we're the choir, let's make this a concert," Cabrina replied.

Command wanted all the civilians from this neighborhood to move to a more defensible position while they drew the attention of rebel forces off with counter-offensives in other sectors.

At least an earlier wave of Dragons had pounded the shit out of the rebel arty, but now their ground forces were moving in, *clearly* not as distracted as HQ had predicted.

"We're not losing a single one of those flitters," Cabrina announced. "We're the best squad in the 919th, and we're going to show all those other losers how it's done. We're probably outnumbered. What's that mean?"

"We're out of shits to give!" the squad shouted back.

"Exactly. Let's show them what Army Assault Infantry can do."

Cabrina's eyes darted to a drone feed projected on the corner of her faceplate.

Her squad had barely been able to maintain their aerial recon assets between the jamming and rebel gunfire, but the last of her little flying spies zoomed close to a building, highlighting a mass of advancing unmounted rebel infantry. She was less concerned about them than the rebel exos rapidly closing on their position and the six-rack surface-to-air missile launcher they'd hauled in the back of a hovertruck.

Three exos guarded the missiles, loosely surrounding the truck. There was no indication that they knew they'd been spotted.

Relying on the enemy to make mistakes was a bad strategy for winning a war, but she'd take it for a battle. The mercs were a lot tougher than the rebels, but she knew all too well how a couple of real battles could train a man or woman up far quicker than weeks in a simulator.

The cynical side said it got rid of the chaff efficiently, leaving you with raw material with natural talent.

"We're moving now," Cabrina barked. "We've got five minutes to take out those missiles unless we want to be responsible for dead civilians. Now, move, move, *move!*"

She surged forward in her exo, raising her machine gun and rocket launcher, her shield fully expanded. The rest of her six-person squad kept pace in a loose line, no one too far forward or back.

A flash in the drone feed preceded its termination. She'd been expecting that, but she now knew the enemy's position. Her squad would protect the civilians or die trying.

"Alpha Four through Six, break off and pressure them on their left flank," Cabrina called. "Maybe we can peel off some of the missile guards. Two and Three, we're going over the top to take out those SAMs. Stay on my ass. Once we're clear of the building, unload on the missiles."

The two sub-squads broke apart. Normally, exos

charging down a street could easily be heard, but with all the background battle noise from the surrounding neighborhoods, their advance wasn't noteworthy. Cabrina concentrated on the two buildings blocking her path to the SAM launcher, one shorter than the other, a few stair steps before falling into death.

There were at least forty people on each cargo flitter. Her unit couldn't and wouldn't lose. She owed that to herself, the Army, all the civilians on New Samarkand, and her brother.

God rest his soul.

The rebels and their merc buddies might have taken the local garrison by surprise, but the Army was pushing back now. It was time to show the ruthless assholes that a single soldier was worth five of them.

An alert flashed in the corner of her eye. One of the flitters was taking off early. They were out of time.

"Engaging left flank," reported Alpha Four.

The background noise became a foreground cacophony as the roar of machine guns and rocket explosions added their bone-shaking contribution. Cabrina confidently focused on the task at hand.

"Two exos breaking away from the SAM to lay down cover for the infantry," reported Alpha Four.

"Good. They took the bait. We've got this. Alpha Three, neutralize the last guard once clear."

Cabrina continued her forward dash, her exo sprinting across the uneven surface and knocking loose rubble out of its way with its heavy feet. Her two squadmates stayed close as the first building loomed in front of her.

Gritting her teeth, she launched the exo into the air. It'd

all come down to the next minute. A perfect angle. She landed on top of the building and sprinted forward a couple more meters before jumping again. The other two exos bounded with her in almost perfect unison as if they'd practiced this every day, all day.

Her team cut their speed when they reached the edge. The SAM launcher was spinning into position, but as predicted, only a single enemy exo stood near it. The rebel infantry had spread out behind the makeshift barriers of destroyed vehicles, trying to escape the wrath of the rest of her squad. Their feeble return fire bounced off the exos' heavy ballistic shields.

One of the rebel exos charging in to support their troops was so sloppy he didn't have his shield expanded. Two rockets struck him square in the chest and blew him apart.

The greatest weapon in the galaxy meant nothing without the ability and confidence to use it properly.

The sole guard exo near the SAM truck at least had his shield expanded, but he was not smart enough. He'd turned toward the other ground action, leaving his back wide open. Alpha Three sidestepped for a better angle before firing three rockets in rapid succession. They screamed toward their target, leaving a trail of smoke.

Cabrina didn't wait for them to hit before she and Alpha Two let loose on the SAM truck with their own rocket barrage. Small explosions rippled across the truck and the large SAMs, then a massive plume of fire rose from the truck, consuming it like a hungry demon. The shock-wave rocked the nearby buildings, cracking walls and windows and knocking the exos on the roof back.

It flattened the closest rebel infantry.

"*Damn it,*" Cabrina muttered. "That was a bigger explosion than I thought we'd see, but it got the job done. Everyone pull back to the initial defensive line. All we need to do is keep them pinned down."

Dedicated air support to defend the flitters flew in the distance far beyond easy view from her smoky, ground-filled battlefield.

A quick push off the rooftop got her exo back on its feet. Her rearview camera feed marked a flitter lifting into the air and flying in the opposite direction. She held her breath, praying there wasn't another hidden SAM, ready to take them out.

She allowed herself additional oxygen as the flitter disappeared into the distance.

"They're clear," she announced as she jumped back to the first building. "We just have to keep it up. Status?"

"All nearby enemy exos neutralized," reported Alpha Four. "The rest of the infantry is pulling back. They're not even picking up the guys the blast knocked down. I think we won this one, LT."

"We won't hold the party until every last one of those flitters is clear," Cabrina insisted. "But that should be pretty easy to call if the rebels are running."

"LT, three o'clock, above the buildings," Alpha Two reported.

Cabrina frowned and turned her head that way. A black dot was rapidly approaching. She magnified the image on her visor and hissed in frustration. It was a slender, short-winged aircraft with a flexible-looking three-barrel turret on the bottom and two large, nasty rocket pods. She didn't recognize the design, but besides the surprising thinness, the profile didn't differ radically from an Army Dragon.

"This is Alpha Platoon at evacuation checkpoint Foxtrot 4-4," she transmitted. "Incoming enemy light gunship. Request air support."

"Hold position, Alpha Platoon," replied HQ. "All air assets in your area are currently engaged. Routing mobile AAA to your area, ETA four minutes."

"Roger." Cabrina jumped down and backed her exo closer to the corner of the building, followed by her squadmates. At least the craters, half-collapsed buildings, and destroyed vehicles gave them some chance of not being torn up, but exos weren't renowned for their ability to take on aircraft.

The enemy hadn't been beaten. They were getting the hell out of there so their friends could cut loose without the risk of collateral damage.

"LT, what's the play?" Alpha Two asked.

"Spread out, but everyone keep moving from cover to cover. Don't bother with rockets, we're not going to get that lucky. We need to survive until the AAA shows up and blows that wannabe Dragon out of the sky. It's probably being flown by some rebel idiot who has a total of an hour in the air."

The squad shouted their understanding and rushed into craters and behind large chunks of rubble. Cabrina didn't like working with timers, but a soldier didn't always get to pick her battles. She knew one thing that day, and that was the most important. As the last surviving child of the Pena family, the Devil would need to do a lot better than becoming a cocky rebel if he wanted her life.

An explosion not far in front of her announced the arrival of the gunship. Her spread-out squad fired in such near unison that it might have been a practiced, coordinated volley. They vomited bullets during the first pass of the blurred black aircraft, unsure if they hit it.

Mild smoke from its thrusters followed.

The enemy spun with a quick thrust as if physics were a mere recommendation. Cabrina almost didn't believe what she was seeing, but she didn't let that stop her from charging out from behind her current barricade into a crater and squeezing off another burst.

Her opponent lurched and wobbled like a leaf in an ever-changing wind. She'd never seen a piloted atmospheric craft move like that. There was only so much grav fields could do with abrupt changes of direction.

Biology asserted itself at the most inconvenient of times.

"The bastards don't even have the balls to face us," she hissed. "They're remote-piloting the damned thing."

A string of rockets hit the ground, scalding the shield of one of her squadmates but causing no serious damage. Her gaze flicked to her squad's vitals, which showed elevated heart rates and mild damage to their exos but nothing else.

They could do this. They could stall. Even better, they could *win*.

As long as the gunship focused on them, they'd be fine. Another flitter lifted off behind them and zoomed away.

With a defiant yell, Cabrina changed positions again, this time risking a jump from the crater into another as she tried to nail the maneuverable threat above. She landed and hurried behind a half-melted hovertank, her jaw tightening when a rocket struck close behind Alpha Three. His exo tumbled to the ground, but his vitals stayed solid.

"I think I lost primary actuator control," he reported. "Weapons still good, but I'd need someone to push me up."

"Get the hell out of there and hide," she ordered. "Otherwise, he'll pick you off next pass."

The exo opened and the soldier crawled out, the back of his tactical suit disintegrated, his skin red and bubbling. He scrambled into a pile of rubble that must have come from the street. Cabrina's prophecy came to pass as the enemy gunship sent another rocket into the downed exo and blew it apart in a fiery explosion.

Cabrina let out a breath. Equipment could be replaced. Her soldier was hurt but alive. She'd count it as a victory, but the fight wasn't over until the enemy was defeated.

"Keep the pressure on," she ordered. "Support is on the way."

The last evac flitter lifted into the air and sped away. It'd been one minute since she called HQ. In normal life, a minute was nothing. People wasted them all the time on the most trivial things and got nothing out of them, but when the thin line between life and death lay in front of a person, they appreciated how long not only the minutes could be but the seconds.

A minute later, two more squad exos were disabled, their pilots safely hidden but wounded. With the fifty-percent reduction of deadly lead pollution in the sky, the insane maneuvers of the gunship became more ridiculous, including abrupt drops for ground-scraping strafing runs. At this point, he was taunting them.

"That's impossible," insisted Alpha Five. "How are they

piloting that thing remotely and pulling off moves like that?"

"No way a drone moves like that," Cabrina countered. "It doesn't matter. All we need to do is not get killed by the damned thing. The civilians are clear, so let's concentrate on saving our own lives."

Constant automatic weapons fire into the air tended to have a deleterious effect on ammo capacity, even in exoskeletons crammed with extra ammo containers. Cabrina didn't want to see what the gunship could do to them when no one was firing at it.

Another minute passed. The surviving exos avoided serious damage, but their fire was more sporadic. Their enemy's attack patterns got more elaborate, including purposeful twirling stalls it escaped from with no margin for error. If he kept it up, he might crash the gunship without any help from them. His latest display of skill ended with him shredding the back of an exo's leg with his cannon before zooming back up.

"I can still fight, LT," the soldier insisted.

"Thirty seconds," Cabrina announced. "Stay alive and let the AAA do its thing."

Her eyes widened as a half-dozen black objects emerged from the gunship. She'd worried they were bombs, but when they darted away on serpentine paths, she realized they were drones. They circled overhead at a decent distance but were well within machine-gun range.

"Ignore the drones," she ordered. "He's trying to throw us off. We might have clipped him. Concentrate on the gunship."

She didn't understand the point of the drone array.

He'd already proven he had no problem picking them off on the ground. Despite her suggestion, his continued quick movements and directional changes argued against damage.

A voice boomed from the air, the product of the drones all transmitting at once, "Oh, little tin soldiers, what it's like to know you're going to die? To know you've fought so hard and so long for nothing? I know you're probably thinking this isn't piloted, but I want you to know, I risked my life in this engagement. I'm here, and you could have killed a skilled enemy had you any talent. Instead, you'll just be another pack of dead little UTC dogs, killed by a *vastly* superior foe."

Cabrina snorted. She wouldn't take the bait. He might or might not be inside the gunship, but either way, the asshole had a surprise coming.

"I… Oh," the pilot continued. "That's unfortunate. No fun at all. You're not even dogs. You're insects."

A thunderous rumble filled the area, and a missile zoomed from behind the exos. The gunship jerked to the side to avoid the missile, but the projectile curved and circled back toward its target. A stream of small white orbs dropped from the back of the gunship and zoomed toward the missile, disintegrating in a storm of explosions. The secondary explosion from the missile rocked the entire area but didn't even singe the gunship, which was already well away.

"That's right, bastard," Cabrina murmured. "You might be able to dodge that, but can you dodge what's coming next?"

The back portion of the gunship vaporized, burned off

by an invisible beam. A follow-up laser blast sheared off a wing. All the clever piloting in the world didn't mean anything without engines and half the required wings. The gunship spiraled to the ground and crashed with a resounding crunch behind a nearby building.

"That was an unforced error," the pilot continued, his drone array untouched by the earlier attack. "I'll admit that. I always wondered what it'd be like to face death, but don't be so confident, insects. I destroyed an entire tank platoon on my way here. It's only that I let myself get carried away playing with you and underestimated your available reinforcements. You didn't win. I defeated myself."

Cabrina frowned. She cared less about his taunts than that he could still make them. The guy didn't sound winded, let alone wounded. He'd gone down hard and survived without a scratch? That didn't seem right.

She jumped away from her current barrier of hovertruck wrecks and sprinted toward the wreckage. An expanding roar announced another AAA attack.

"Pain is a gift," the pilot continued. "I can see that now. Knowing you're damaged versus actual pain. The feedback is impo—"

The latest missile released twenty smaller rockets that swarmed the drones, which exploded like victory fireworks and dropped a lengthy shower of small dark chunks upon the cracked and blasted ground.

Cabrina cleared the building, the other surviving exos close behind. The smoking wreckage of the gunship lay close. She kept her rifle pointed at the enemy vehicle, wondering if it was only a remote-piloted trick in the end.

She stopped. The vehicle was smaller than most light gunships. Now that she was closer, she was even more confused by its small, narrow design. It was no wonder they couldn't hit it, but there was also no way a human being could fit inside it.

That was what she told herself, but it didn't explain one important thing: the blood leaking from the side.

Who the hell is in there?

CHAPTER SIX

The MX 60 flew at a leisurely pace through the streams of traffic in Neo SoCal on its way to the *Argo*'s hangar.

Erik wasn't in a hurry, despite suspecting their month-long lull since the Chiron op would soon be over. Jia had been right at Victoria Falls. He could never fully switch off in his war on the Core, but that was why they kept winning.

They had the rest of their lives to turn back into normal people. At least, he hoped they did.

The only thing approaching stressful in the last few weeks had been attending the Lan Lin Mid-Autumn Festival bash the night before.

Other than Jia's father being a little too drunk and getting affectionate with her mother in public, it'd been pretty uneventful. Erik got the feeling he was supposed to care about a political debate they were having, but he'd excused himself to find more wine instead.

Jia looked ahead from the passenger seat, boredom rather than concern on her face. "Did Lanara say what it was about? Did she give you any clue?"

"Nope. You know Lanara. Her exact words were, 'Blackwell, get your ass over here. Bring Lin. Need to show you both something. Hurry up, because sitting around waiting for you is wasting time,'" Erik finished with a chuckle.

She sounded excited, surprising Erik. He hadn't realized she cared so much. "You think this is about the new equipment that was delivered last week?"

"I doubt it." He shook his head. "No reason to go over that again, and she didn't say anything about upgrading it yet."

A third armored flitter for Anne's and Kant's use had been delivered, along with two exos of the same model as the ones Alina had supplied Erik and Jia. Everyone wanted increased flexibility for field operations, and they had enough cargo space in the *Argo* to easily accommodate the suits and transport.

Erik was impressed and pleased. Between the firepower of the ship and the equipment it carried, they could inflict serious damage on the enemy without additional backup.

Kant and Anne had proven themselves, and he was beginning to think of the group as his new squad.

They could never replace the Knights Errant, but they didn't have to. A man could make new friends without dishonoring those who had fallen. There were still kinks to smooth out in the relationship, but that came with any new group of people thrown together for the first time.

"It could be a lot of things," Erik suggested, his thoughts

bouncing around and finally coming back to the conversation at hand. "You know how Lanara is. She probably just wants us there so she can brag about how she squeezed another percent of power out of a grav field emitter, and how that means we'll be able to digest food better or something. When I've asked her about my requested upgrades, she's generally told me to shut up and let her work." He snickered. "I like having an engineer who won't take any shit, but if she is calling us, that makes me think that Alina is prodding her."

"I wonder about that at times," Jia admitted. "We have all these people helping us, but they ultimately work for her, not us. I trust Alina, but that still doesn't sit well with me."

"It's no different than when I was in the Army or when we were cops." Erik shot her a look. "Unless you want to start a company and hire people. We can call it the Lady Justice Corp."

Jia rolled her eyes. "Why not the Obsidian Detectives?"

"Hey!" He jerked a thumb at his chest. "There's only one Obsidian Detective."

"I'm okay with the government footing the bill for now," Jia replied. "I suspect I'd make a terrible boss."

"But you're good at command," Erik replied.

"Temporarily being a shot-caller isn't the same thing."

"Whatever you say." Erik nodded. "Maybe we're over-thinking this. We'll just have to see what Alina says."

Erik stared at the *Argo* with a stupid grin on his face like he was five years old and had been given an entire candy factory as a present. Lanara was making her way down the cargo ramp with no sense of urgency, but Erik didn't need to be an engineer to understand the obvious and visible changes.

All laser turrets were deployed from the ship. It was hard to miss the presence of new bottom turrets.

Erik started clapping. "Very nice. I prefer beating people down in an exo, but if I have to play at being a Fleet boy, it's always better to have more guns. I want someone to show me any time in history when having more guns hurt someone in a fight."

Lanara swiped a dark smudge off her face. Her red hair was even more frazzled than usual, as if the diminutive engineer had lost a fight with a Leem's lightning gun. Dark circles sagged beneath her eyes.

"I figured you'd be happy." She nodded. "It's easy to impress a man by adding more guns to something. That or making it bigger. Only so much I can do about the second option."

Jia cleared her throat. "More firepower will keep you alive as well. You're usually in the engine room when we're on the *Argo*."

Emma appeared with a smile in coveralls similar to Lanara's, her outfit complete even to the face smudges. "She's done a lot more than add the guns. I've already adapted all the necessary systems as well. I thought about telling you myself, but I assumed Engineer Quinn preferred to deliver the news."

Erik nodded at her, not really minding even though it

meant Emma had known at least a few days in advance, if not weeks.

Lanara shrugged. "Same difference to me, but I don't like to talk about crap until it's done." She jerked her thumb over her shoulder. "And it's not just the turrets, Blackwell. Alina let me know we'd have a decent amount of time sitting around, so I finished a major reactor upgrade, too. Better reaction and emitter tuning mean I can add more juice to the shields."

"It gets even better," Emma announced. "You'll be able to destroy many more pointless gun goblins, polluting space with their pathetic pieces."

Lanara grunted and tapped her PNIU. Panels retracted under the *Argo*'s fuselage, and two new pairs of missile racks emerged on each side. Each rack held three missiles, for a total of twelve.

Erik wondered how easily the ID could smuggle missiles to the hangar without anyone noticing. "Now we're talking. Twelve missiles, plus eight torpedoes. This isn't some little ghost toy anymore, it's a cruiser given this kind of punch."

Jia took a couple of steps to her side to view the ship from a different angle. "It'll be nice to have to worry less about depending on the *Bifröst*. The less we have to engage with it, the safer the jump drive will be. It also means we don't have to worry as much about the piloting situation."

"That was one of my considerations," Emma observed. "Assuming we don't run into any more ridiculous confrontations with ancient aliens, we should be capable of putting up a decent fight against most individual ships we are likely to run into. In cases where we are going to be overwhelmed, the logical response would be to retreat to and then rely on the *Bifröst*'s weapons and drive."

Erik stuck a finger in the air. "Let me get this straight. We now have six laser turrets." He put up another finger. "A torpedo launcher with eight torps." Another finger lifted. "A plasma turret." A fourth finger rose. "And twelve missiles." His fifth finger joined the others. "Not to mention the improved shields, reactor, and point-defense lasers."

"I didn't do anything to those," Lanara clarified.

"I know, but we still have them, and all that other gear."

Lanara folded her arms, a ghost of a smile on her face. "And I got my hands on an improved prototype version of nanodispersive film, so you also got an armor upgrade."

"I'm impressed," Jia offered with a smile. "That was a lot to get done in a month. More than a lot."

"I have to admit, Quiet Queen and Captain Fun Time can be helpful when they're concentrating," Lanara replied. She inclined her head toward the ship. "I gave them the day off. They're halfway decent as assistants. Miracles happen."

Erik had never heard the nicknames before but figured Janessa and Wei would complain if they were having problems with Lanara. Neither was fond of confronting their boss, but they knew Erik and Jia had no problem doing so.

The increased number of people had led to complications, including personnel issues. They might have resolved their issues with Anne, but that didn't mean there wouldn't be any trouble among the crew in the future. He'd worry about it when he ran into it.

For now, he had new toys.

"This is damned fine work," Erik observed. "The *Argo*'s

always been able to punch above her weight, but this is no longer a ship with some guns. It's a warship that just happens to look like it's not."

Emma nodded her approval. "I think it's more fitting for me. The jumpship has many charms, but I prefer a sleeker body."

Jia eyed the hologram. "Even AI women worry about that?"

"I also prefer a bigger reactor and more weapons," Emma replied evenly. "I don't know how that maps onto fleshbag anatomy. You're free to make of it what you will."

"You want a bigger butt and boobs?" Erik suggested.

Jia cocked her head to the side, staring at the *Argo*. "I can see the second one, but wouldn't a bigger butt be like larger, more powerful thrusters?" She tapped her lips. "Would reactor power be a bigger heart?"

Emma glared at Erik. "Need I remind you that I can blow you away with one of the turrets right now?"

Erik waved his hands and laughed. "Sorry. Couldn't resist. You set me up perfectly."

Lanara grunted. "If you're done with the bullshit teasing, I should tell you I've still got some final tweaking to do on the reactor and shield upgrades. That'll make sure we don't have any power issues during normal use."

He pursed his lips. "More tweaks? Let me guess, you need to find a point-two-five percent increase in efficiency somewhere?"

She narrowed her eyes, aiming a finger at him as if she could blast him with a thought. "Those efficiency improvements are going to save your life someday, Blackwell. They're going to save all our lives."

"I know. I know." He wiped the smile off his face. "Your work already has. I appreciate it, Lanara."

"Good." Her expression softened. "It'll be done soon. Those two pieces of fresh meat annoy me, but like I said, they're good at what they do."

"Doesn't everyone annoy you?" Jia asked.

"Yes, but not everyone is good at what they do." Lanara waved. "Just so you know, Alina's been giving me weekly go or no-go messages so I can keep the ship ready to fly. I figured if she wants you on standby, she'll tell you directly."

With that, she walked away, muttering a string of numbers under her breath. The presence of other humans had quickly been purged from her mind.

Erik kept a smile on his face as he mentally caressed each and every missile and torpedo he could see. He spoke almost to himself as he smiled. "You never know when you'll need to blow up a lot of ships."

Jia wasn't smiling. "Did you know about the no-go messages, Emma?"

She shook her head. "I wasn't aware of those. Engineer Quinn prefers I don't access her PNIU. It makes her, in her own words, 'cranky.' And she doesn't talk to me about anything not directly related to system upgrades. We're, shall we say, work colleagues and nothing more."

"It's fine," Erik commented, staring at one of the new turrets. "The important thing is, this ship is better equipped. Lanara can keep tweaking all she wants, but if we were to fight Sophia Vand again with this ship, we would win without getting a scratch. Hmm, that reminds me. I should pick up more penjing supplies for our next trip. Used most of them aboard last time, and it might be that Alina is waiting for Lanara to finish up rather than the other way around."

Jia's stomach let out a loud growl. "You'll drop me off at my place after you go shopping. I've got a lunch date with Mei."

"You need to come with me to shop for penjing supplies? Why not drop you off early? What's the worst thing that could happen to me?"

"A *yaoguai* killer plant attacks you?" Jia mimed a plant mouth by making her hand eat her other fingers. "I wanted to check some gardening supplies out as a secondary concern, but you'll need backup in case of killer plants."

Erik considered for a moment. "What's the chance of that? One, two percent tops?"

———

Erik strolled out of the store, his bag of supplies in hand. Jia was at his side. He was enjoying the thought of the upgrades.

The more he thought about it, the more his excitement grew. He'd come a long way from paying Miguel for custom work on the MX 60. At the rate things were going, he wouldn't be surprised if Alina stuck a hovertank in the jumpship for them.

"I don't know how to drive a tank proficiently," he commented aloud. "I mean, I do understand the similarities to what I've driven."

Jia gave him a confused look. "Huh?"

"I don't know how to drive a tank." He turned to her. "I

spent most of my career as assault infantry, not a tanker. Do you know how to drive a tank?"

"No." Jia slowly shook her head and took a step away from Erik, looking him up and down. "More important, why do you care?"

"Just thinking about the future."

"Let's hope our future doesn't require a *tank*," Jia replied.

They made their way through the mercifully sparse crowd. Most people barely paid them any attention, but every once in a while, someone pointed at them and whispered to themselves.

Erik had considered using a disguise when shopping. It might cut down on pointless conversations. Fame was only useful insofar as it intimidated his enemies. Every time he thought his rep had begun to fade, they ended up involved in some incident that reminded people the Obsidian Detective and Lady Justice hadn't retired and weren't spending their days playing mahjong.

Jia rubbed her stomach. "You think Mei will kill me if I grab a snack here? That's what I get for skipping two meals. It's like there's a Zitark in my belly trying to crawl out."

Loud screams cut through the air, followed by gunshots.

Erik snort-laughed as he turned his head. "Seriously?"

Jia sighed. "And now I have to fight on an empty stomach. Somebody's going to pay for that."

"One percent, hmm?" Emma transmitted to both of them.

"I said one percent for a *yaoguai* killer plant," Erik

replied, setting down his bag and trying to get a feel for where the shots were coming from.

People were streaming away from the central concourse in panic.

"Ah, I see," Emma replied. "You have a much higher likelihood of standard gun goblins."

"Exactly."

Erik and Jia pushed past the fleeing crowd. More gunshots rang out in the distance, but no alarms. *That* wasn't a good sign.

"Or you're the avatar of your Lady's bad luck," Emma suggested. "Don't forget that possibility."

"What's that say about you for hanging around me?" Erik asked.

"I obviously have great luck because I'm still alive." Emma snickered. "Initiating camera and drone penetration. Hmm. It's obvious this system has been partially hacked."

Jia drew her stun pistol and continued jogging forward. "Let's clean this up before I have to resort to cannibalism."

CHAPTER SEVEN

Emma was an impressive AI and critical to their efforts, but she wasn't a miracle worker.

She'd need a couple of minutes before she gained control of the cameras and drones, and in those critical minutes, whoever was attacking the commerce tower had the upper hand.

That enemy had had the foresight and ability to hack the commerce tower's systems, which meant they weren't just criminals who'd shown up and started shooting at people. Jia and Erik needed to bring the situation under control.

They slowed as the flow of screaming people thinned. They ducked behind a large statue of a twenty-first-century actor neither had heard of.

Pairs of rifle-toting men in comically large Leem masks were running in different directions on the concourse, but none had headed their way yet.

That wasn't good, but they hadn't seen any bodies yet, either. There was still hope of salvaging the situation.

"What the hell is this?" Erik muttered.

A giant hologram of a cartoon Leem appeared in the air, the thin accusatory finger of the alien pointed outward. Harsh, angry music played. Words circled the hologram.

LEEM LIBERATION FRONT.

"Don't tell me it's Grayheads." Jia groaned. "At least syndicate enforcers have *some* common sense."

"Your analysis is accurate, Jia," Emma reported. "According to my quick search, the LLF is a recently formed militant Grayhead organization, though both local police and CID statements dismiss them as 'irrelevant and low-threat.'"

"Everybody's wrong now and again," Erik mused. "Nothing wrong with making them irrelevant again."

Jia shook her head. "In my more paranoid days, I would have thought the Core was paying these people to hunt us."

"How is that paranoia?" Erik looked her way. "They've done it before, but in this case, it's probably just coincidence. Even if it's not, we solve it the same way." He patted his gun.

"We are the Leem Liberation Front," a voice bellowed, echoing all around them. "We are a collection of passionate and thoughtful individuals who have reflected upon the role of all intelligent species in the galaxy and know the truth. Humanity is on a self-destructive spiral. The Leems came to us to warn us shortly after one of the greatest wars in history. The government lied and told you it was an accident, but we know the truth. Those peaceful visitors were murdered by government assassins. In the Leems' glorious mercy, they exacted no revenge, so we will seek it on their behalf.

Jia rolled her eyes. "Yes, somehow a race with FTL travel and lightning shields could be taken down by a couple of ancient rifles and those toys they called aircraft in the twentieth century. Have you read about them? It's like they were throwing metal tubes in the air and hoping they wouldn't die."

"Unfortunately, the continued corruption of humanity is unabated," the terrorist ranted. "This has forced us into a position where sacrifices are necessary to save our entire species. We have taken hostages, and we will execute one every hour until our demands are met. If they are, including our safe passage out of this commerce tower and Neo SoCal, we will release the surviving hostages unharmed. Our primary demands are simple. We insist upon the verified release of the following six unjustly imprisoned patriots of humanity."

A list of six names followed. None of them meant anything to either Erik or Jia.

Jia frowned. "A little help, Emma."

"They are all imprisoned Grayhead leaders," the AI replied. "They lead different, sometimes competing organizations. They aren't all at the same prison."

"In other words, there's no way those people will be released."

Erik nodded forward. There were no Grayheads, but judging by the crowd and the origin of the earlier men, the terrorists were most likely holding people in the central concourse and supplementing their defenses with guards in key locations.

It wouldn't be enough to repel a serious effort by the local police, let alone the local militia.

Jia holstered her stun pistol and pulled out her slugthrower. She flipped off the safety. "Should we wait for the NSCPD?"

"And let those psychos kill someone? They say they'll give an hour, but all it'll take is one person saying something bad about the Leems and they'll kill someone. You heard them. They're trying to avenge random moron aliens who were killed in a crash over two hundred years ago." Erik shook his head. "Besides, this is personal."

"Personal?" Jia's brow lifted. "You know these guys?"

"No," Erik replied, his voice low. "But they messed with my shopping." He pointed at her stomach. "And your food."

"You're right." Jia's jaw clenched. "Let's take them down."

"The only thing I don't get is why they didn't come this way." Erik surveyed the outer concourse with suspicion.

"They obviously studied the blueprints for this level," Emma explained. "Those men were both taking the most direct route to the exits. Many of the hysterical fleshbags who fled earlier ended up cut-off. I launched drones outside, and some of the civilians escaped."

"How are we doing on the interior cameras and drones?" Jia asked.

"I'm in the primary system. I have not bothered to be subtle about it, and although I've yet to establish full control, I've noticed already something pathetic, at least insofar as we rate the typical gun goblin you deal with, despite their system hacking capabilities."

Erik smirked. "I'm not always looking to have the fight of my life. What's the deal?"

"They're not routing their communications through

their system," Emma replied. "They're relying on the commerce tower's relays. It'll be trivial to disrupt their communications, and I'm dubious they could restore them. I think they're aware that I'm in the system, but they're being overwhelmed anyway."

"They probably think it's just part of the security protocols." Jia nodded, speaking slowly as she thought it through. "I'm not going to complain about terrorists with more bravery than brains. That means we have a chance of taking them down without anyone getting hurt. That's the other advantage of not waiting. A hard entry risks people getting shot in the crossfire."

"Ah, there we go." Emma winked into existence in an NSCPD captain's uniform. "There are only six gun goblins guarding the terrorists, with other groups of two and four moving to or who are already in control of the exits."

Rather than send images to their smart lenses, she summoned data windows with camera and drone feeds from the exits. The remainder of the fleeing crowd had slowed, cowering behind walls and in shops, out of the sight of the main exit.

No one was willing to confront the armed men guarding the escape route leading to the parking platform, and most were too afraid to go back the way they had come. A top-down map marked the position of each civilian on the level with a white dot and each terrorist with a red dot.

Roaming patrols rounded out what was left.

"If Emma can disrupt their comms, we can pick the guards off without the rest of them knowing what's going on at first," Jia mused. "That gives us a big advantage." She put her hand in the air and traced alternating curves. "This place is a maze. They might not know where the gunfire is coming from."

Erik rubbed his chin. "But if they hear it, they might execute a hostage."

"We have another advantage they don't." Jia pointed to Erik then herself. "She can keep us in contact, and we know the location and strength of their forces."

"I get it." He nodded and his grin turned hungry. "We split up."

"Exactly." Jia walked over to Emma's map and pointed to the largest cluster of fleeing civilians near an exit. "I think you should pick off the guards here, which will let those people get to safety. Besides the actual hostages, the others are in small groups hiding in stores and the like. Once you've cleared the way, you can take out the other patrols. I'll head to the hostages and take out the men there."

Erik studied the map in silence for a long moment. "Okay, sounds good. Once I've cleared the main exit, I'll do my best not to just take them out but to draw the attention of the rest. If we both keep them busy, they shouldn't kill anyone until the NSCPD arrives in force, probably less than ten minutes at this point."

Jia raised her gun. "Time to do something reckless and stupid?"

"I consider it realistic training. Remember what this is about."

"Saving lives?"

He shook his head. "Avenging your missed lunch."

Jia frowned at Erik for a moment, not annoyed by the

joke but worried about something else. "I've just thought of a problem. It's going to take me longer to get into position and engage them than for you to take out the guards near the main exit. It's fine if they're confused after that, but before that, they might start shooting if they hear gunfire."

Erik holstered his pistol and cracked his knuckles. "Then I need to take the first pair down without gunfire."

"You want my stun pistol?" Jia reached for her waist.

Erik flexed his left arm. "Nah. Let's break in this baby on some terrorist heads."

CHAPTER EIGHT

With a final nod, Erik rushed toward the nearest storefront before changing direction and sprinting toward the main exit.

The walls and storefronts didn't provide the cover he'd like, but they'd keep him getting picked off right away. Emma's convenient navigation arrows on the map in the corner of his smart lenses eliminated any hesitation.

He almost felt sorry for the poor bastard she was wrecking in cyberwarfare.

Erik skidded to a halt in front of a store, The Open Mind. He wasn't sure what they sold, given that the podiums contained small crystal and metal figures twisted into odd shapes. Their commercial niche was less important than the fact that many of the sculptures looked heavy and hard.

He tested a couple of helical metal pieces with alternating bands of copper and steel and was satisfied with their heft. He picked both up and continued his advance toward the main exit. The Lady might have smiled on them by giving them new terrorists who had made mistakes, but that was no guarantee no one would get hurt if they didn't hurry their asses up.

"How we doing, Jia?" he asked. Sometimes it was easier to ask than shift his attention to the positional tracker.

"I'm almost there, and there are no patrols near me."

Erik turned a corner. A group of people cowered near the floor or hid behind counters and racks in shops, hands over their head, whimpering. The concourse widened as it curved toward the exit.

A man near him lifted his head as Erik neared. "You can't go there," he hissed. "They're over there. They'll try and kill you!"

Erik tossed the metal helix in his left arm up and snatched it from the air. "I'm counting on that. I'm going to take these guys out, then you're going to run for it. Just keep running. The cops will be here soon enough."

"You're insane. Wait!" The man gasped, recognition dawning. "Aren't you…"

"Yeah, I'm *that* guy." Erik nodded. "And, yes, before you ask, she's here too." He grinned, saluted, and continued his sprint, paying close attention to the terrorist indicator arrows when he hit the curve.

Gripping the helix tightly, he brought back his left arm, not yelling or taunting.

His heavy footsteps destroyed any attempt at stealth, but this was one time he wanted to draw attention. The closest arrow shifted toward the center of his vision and two masked terrorists came into view.

The masks bothered him. Not their inherent use, but

the annoying cartoon proportions. If they wanted to be taken seriously, they needed *scary* masks, not something that looked like a budget Halloween costume for a crappy office party.

Erik rushed toward them. The men exchanged glances, their rifles angled down. While he couldn't see their expressions through their ridiculous alien get-ups, he smirked, imagining confusion.

Terrorism was a tool of asymmetric fear.

Terrorists struck soft targets or intimidated people they didn't believe would retaliate. Standing and fighting soldiers or police produced dead terrorists and victories for those in uniforms.

He understood why they were hesitating.

A man with a gun they could easily slot into the "enemy" category and attack. Likewise, a screaming, terrified civilian could be controlled by the threat of violence or a quick rifle burst. A silent man charging toward them with two pieces of helix art would give any murderous zealot pause.

They had to be asking themselves what the hell was going on.

If they had shot immediately, they might have wounded Erik. They could have provided a warning for a nearby patrol or the men watching the hostages on the central concourse.

Hesitation could turn the tide of battle.

Grunting, Erik hurled the first helix with his left arm, using his maximum strength. He didn't care if the terrorist survived. Right after that, he tossed the second helix into his hand and pulled back for his second throw.

In all the training Erik and Jia had done together, neither of them had practiced dodging random artwork. If they hadn't, the terrorists certainly hadn't.

That became blatantly clear when the second man dropped to the floor, covering his head. He clearly thought it was a grenade. His partner displayed more courage and brought up his gun, unworried about something being thrown at him, mistaking the speed as a product of the lightness of the object rather than a cybernetic arm being used to its full potential.

The helix smashed into his face with a thickening thud, caving in the man's mask. Blood gushed from beneath it and fell to the floor in heavy droplets, along with the man's crumpling body.

The good reflexes of the second man and the delayed throw saved him from a similar fate. Erik's projectile flew past him before knocking a small chunk out of the wall and clattering to the ground. He had sprinted toward the terrorist after he threw and cleared the modest distance before the man realized he hadn't blown up.

A man didn't need cybernetics if he had a quality boot. Erik introduced his to the terrorist's face.

The man's head snapped back, and he groaned. Two quick punches to the face knocked him out. Erik ripped the mask off to find a pasty-looking man with a thin mustache and a newly broken nose.

Erik kicked the terrorist's rifle into the air and grabbed it. No TR-7 meant less fun, but a rifle was better than a pistol. He walked over and grabbed the other rifle, slinging it over his shoulder. A quick pat-down of the men scored him a few backup magazines, but not as many as expected. These men weren't geared up for a decent fight.

"Idiots," Erik muttered. "TPST would have cut them to shreds."

"They must have thought they could contain things with the hostages," Jia replied. "I'm in position. I have downed security guards here."

"I've got the main exit cleared," Erik replied. "On my signal, Jia, engage."

"What's your signal?"

"Listen for the gunfire."

"Ah," Jia replied. "Subtle."

"Subtlety is overrated." Erik chuckled. "Emma, tell the people hiding around the bend to haul ass out of here. Tell them a plainclothes CID team is here taking down the terrorists."

"Why don't I just tell them the truth? I think they'll be far more impressed if a pair of local heroes is here to save them." Emma laughed.

Erik flipped his fire selection to burst mode, thinking back to the man who recognized him earlier. "Ok, sure. That works, too."

He took a moment to orient himself and locate the next closest pair of terrorists with the help of Emma's display. One patrol was walking toward the exit, whereas the other was heading away. None of the guards had moved from the other exits, and no one seemed to be panicking despite Emma's targeted disruption of terrorists' comms and her control of the system.

They must have a plan for that.

"Police are present," Emma reported. "There are two patrol flitters circling the tower, but they're not landing."

"They must have orders to wait for TPST," Erik concluded. "It's fine. We'll finish up here before our Gray-heads get a chance to kill anyone. A hard entry with exos might involve casualties, but we are already inside."

He lifted his rifle and jogged toward the patrol, not bothering to run along the wall this time. The performance of the first two terrorists told him all he needed to know about their relative skill. This would come down to speed of engagement.

Wipe a pair or quad, then backtrack to guard the flank of the fleeing crowd and secure the main exit while Jia freed the hostages.

Erik turned a corner and came up behind the patrol. The men spun at the sound of the rapidly approaching footsteps and earned three bullets in their faces for their trouble, their masks doing nothing to save them.

Gunshots rang out in the distance. Jia was on the move.

Erik pivoted and charged back toward the main exit, surprised the next closest patrol wasn't moving toward either his position or Jia's. The crack of their rifles echoed down the concourse, louder and closer than the other fight.

"Who the hell are they fighting?" Erik asked.

"Oh." Emma snickered. "I decided to help you out and stall the gun goblins by taking advantage of their pitiful intelligence after I expanded my systems penetration. I borrowed the holographic projectors from nearby stores to convince them they're under attack by police forces. I don't know how long it'll work. They're being rather generous with their shots."

"Good job, Emma." Erik closed on the main entrance.

Shoppers streamed toward the exit, some weeping, but no one screaming or yelling. Not everyone was running, though they all kept to at least a brisk walking pace.

"It's him," someone shouted, pointing at Erik. "It's the Obsidian Detective, just like that CID agent said!"

"CID agent?" Erik whispered.

"I told them the truth about you," Emma replied. "Not about me."

Erik shook his head and darted through the crowd, avoiding collisions. Some people stopped to clap for him, but he ignored them and continued toward Emma's deluded targets.

His hard run quickly brought him to the men, who looked his way.

One of the terrorists snorted when they spotted him. "Don't waste any more ammo on holograms."

"Good plan," Erik replied before shooting him and his friend in the head. "That's the way I fight, too," he explained as their bodies collapsed, the rifles clattering to the floor.

"Expand the trick to all the bastards and help Jia," Erik ordered. "I'll clean up the rest and draw their attention with my special technique."

"I have an idea," Emma said. "It should be more helpful for Jia."

"Just do it," Erik ordered. "We don't have a lot of time to sit around discussing."

"Very well."

"Any help is welcome, but what special technique were you talking about, Erik?" Jia asked, her breathing ragged over the comm.

"Being obnoxious. You just keep it up there."

"Don't worry. I've got their attention." There was a small pause. "And now I have an Army of Leems to help me?"

CHAPTER NINE

Jia frowned.

Sometimes plans sounded much better in theory than they proved to be in execution.

That wasn't a new experience for Jia. She and Erik had been involved in so much trouble dealing with criminals and the Core that she generally assumed something would go awry.

In this case, Jia realized the terrible and retrospectively obvious problem in using fake Leems when taking on Grayhead terrorists who'd pledged themselves to the real thing. It would be more accurate to say she understood her mistake once the first hostage started screaming.

Oops.

Jia hadn't intended to terrify them, and she *mostly* doubted Emma did. But once six Leems with lightning guns and shields blinked into existence, the men and women who had been stunned into silence by Jia gunning down their guards lost it.

It probably didn't help that dead security guards were strewn around the area.

Jia could have used a security bot horde about then. Far too many parts of Neo SoCal were designed under the assumption no significant trouble would happen there.

She could see how people might have believed that two or three years back, but after the string of criminal activity and terrorist attacks that had afflicted the city, the laissez-faire attitude surprised her.

The police and CID had grown more effective in dealing with trouble, but as the current situation proved, more effective didn't equal preventing all trouble.

"The Grayheads have actual aliens helping them!" a woman shrieked. "They're going to feed us to the Leems."

A man made the sign of the cross and murmured a quiet prayer as if he were trying to scare off demons and not aliens. The terrorists stared, their faces hidden behind their masks.

They didn't seem to remember the men who had just died.

Maybe, in their sick little minds, they thought the Leems had somehow invented a personal jump drive and heard their prayers. In the end, Cosmic Universalism was a new religion, even if its ideological adherents denied it.

They wanted to worship something a lot more flesh-and-blood than traditional religions.

Jia didn't wait for them to remember she was there. She darted from her wall to move behind a stone bench across the concourse.

Most of the terrorists continued to stare at the holographic aliens. One man pulled off his mask, revealing a mix of fear and reverence. Tears ran down his face. A single terrorist swung his rifle in her direction and fired. The shot whizzed past her as she ducked.

"Don't fire!" shouted one of the other Grayheads. "The Leems will protect us from her. They have come to help us!"

Jia rolled her eyes. She couldn't decide if she was surprised that Emma's trick had worked, or if it'd been the obvious way to take advantage of the terrorists. In either case, she was grateful they lacked the skill and wherewithal of the dangerous Grayhead groups she'd dealt with in the past.

She gritted her teeth, staying low. No one was shooting at her, even the man who had taken the earlier shot.

He must have been waiting for his opportunity. There were still too many terrorists there, given the hostages. She needed to move quickly and finish them off before more of their friends decided to show up and give her a hard time.

"Hey, Grayheads," Erik's loud voice called over the concourse speakers. "I've taken out a bunch of your guys already, and I'm sitting near the front exit, making sure the police can walk right in and cut you down like the worthless alien ass-kissers you are. I knew I couldn't expect much from a bunch of morons who worship aliens, especially the Leems. If you want to worship someone who crashes their ship, I know all sorts of guys, or if you want to kill me and shut me up, come toward the main exit, and let's chat. Or what? You going to chop yourself up and feed yourself to a space raptor? Become fertilizer for a mushroom? There's nothing more pathetic than a Grayhead. You're human. Get over it, assholes."

Emma chuckled. "I'm also faking some communications to convince the rest of the gun goblins that all the hostages are escaping that way. It should encourage them to move along and not come back for Jia's group."

"Good," Jia whispered. The slight sound attracted gunfire. Emma helpfully added target highlights for all the immediate terrorists, including the one who was shooting at her.

"Stop firing! You'll anger them," a voice said.

Jia crawled to the other end and popped around the corner to take a shot. Energy arced from one of the holograms at that exact moment. The terrorist fell backward, blood spreading from his chest wound. His companions stared at the Leem hologram, uncertainty on their faces.

"See?" a Grayhead spat, his pointing finger accusing. "You've angered them! Get on your knees and beg their forgiveness."

"This is bullshit," the shooter replied, pointing his gun at the Leem. "It's just a hologram. Lightning guns don't make you bleed!"

He pulled the trigger. So much for reverence. The bullet zipped right through Emma's fake Leem. A moment later, all the Leem holograms dropped their weapons and raised their fingers in salute.

Jia assumed it was Emma messing with the terrorists, but when a creature only had four fingers, mimicking obscene human hand gestures was less effective.

The Grayheads' faces contorted with rage. They opened fire on the holograms, wasting precious ammo and time on manipulated light. More importantly, they gave Jia her opportunity to finish them off.

She popped up and fired again. Her finger didn't rest as she moved from target to target, placing one bullet apiece in the chest or head until all the terrorists lay on the ground, bleeding out.

Lack of discipline doomed them.

"There are no aliens," Jia announced. "My name is Jia Lin, and I'm here to rescue you. One of my partners is using the local systems to create a distraction."

Recognition dawned on some of the hostages' faces. She didn't want to go through a complicated explanation about her status at the moment and hoped simple straight-forward confidence would earn their cooperation.

Gunshots continued to echo in the distance, the noises overlapping and becoming a percussive concert of death.

Emma's target map revealed almost all the terrorists were homing in on Erik, with only a small group heading toward the hostages.

Jia didn't have time for clever plans. The original plan had gone to hell. Sending everyone into a warzone would get them killed. There were elevators nearby, and no terrorists near them. The choice was obvious despite logistical concerns.

She holstered her gun and ran over to a terrorist to collect his rifle, along with his and his friends' spare magazines.

"I carry two guns, yet I need a bigger one," she grumbled.

"You could shop wearing a tac vest filled with grenades," Erik replied between ragged breaths. "Or wear a carryaid with the laser rifle strapped to it."

"I shouldn't have to go shopping in full tactical gear," Jia grumbled back.

The hostages had mostly regained their calm. Many trembled in fear, but they didn't seem scared of her. She didn't know if they recognized her, but they had to understand the woman who had gunned down the terrorists was on their side.

"I'm going to get you out of here," Jia called. "My partner's helping create that opportunity right now. The police are on their way."

"Aren't y-you the police?" asked someone.

Well, crap. That was bad information management. "Not anymore. Everyone get ready to move!"

A couple nodded numbly, but no one stood.

"I assume they activated the emergency override on the elevators?" Jia asked. "And I assume you've cleared it, Emma?"

"Both are correct."

Jia loaded a fresh magazine into her borrowed rifle and turned toward the hostages, pointing a finger to her left. "Listen up. We're going to make a run for the elevators. You will all take them down, and I'll guard you while you're doing it. There are elevators around the corner over there." She inclined her head in that direction since no one saw her pointing finger. "There isn't enough space for everyone to go down at once, but you *will* proceed in an orderly manner. If you do that, I guarantee you'll get out of here without further injury."

Some of the hostages stood, newfound courage and determination on their faces. Others, still weeping, trembled as they rose, their expressions making it plain they didn't think they would survive the next few minutes. Jia didn't rush them, especially since people needed to scoop up and comfort their scared children.

The Grayhead bastards could have at least let the children go.

After giving the hostages a moment to calm themselves, Jia gestured toward the elevators. Emma aided the situation by providing a flashing red arrow.

"Let's go," Jia shouted. "Keep it *orderly*. I've got your backs."

Screams and shouts sounded from the other side of the level. Gunfire was nearly constant now. Erik wasn't saying anything, but that only meant he was concentrating. A quick check of the map showed far fewer terrorists than before, but Jia didn't like that the small cluster no longer was moving toward the main exit.

Four men with rifles could hurt a lot of people quickly.

She jogged alongside the group, sweeping the area on the small chance Emma had missed someone. "Let me know if any of the terrorists move toward me, Emma."

"Of course," the AI replied.

Once they moved away from the main concourse, her Leems vanished, though she kept up the arrow. Whatever equipment she'd borrowed had a limited range. Jia didn't care. She was moments away from rescuing the hostages, and then it was just a matter of picking off the rest of the terrorists or keeping them pinned down. With their patrol and exit guard forces consolidated, they had decent numbers, but they weren't the ones with reinforcements on the way.

Jia and the hostages arrived at the elevators. Desperate

men and women slapped the access panel and crammed in with surprising care, given the situation. The crowd earned her respect for their control.

Panic could have undone everything and led to more deaths.

"Just go one level down," Jia ordered, infusing stern command authority into her voice. "Let's fill them up, though."

Judging by the numbers of elevators and the size of the crowd, it'd take four or five trips for all the hostages to evacuate. It was a large number when they were waiting, hearts pounding, for them all to escape, but it was a tiny fraction of the number of people who had been shopping when the attack started. The terrorists had screwed up. They should have secured the exits first. Given their focus on the elevators, they might have underestimated their importance for escape. Jia had never been one to be pleased by someone's incompetence, but she modified her thinking patterns on the fly.

"TPST is almost here," Emma announced. "The police have set up a secondary line outside and below and above this level. All people who previously escaped the level appear to be safe."

Erik grunted. "Good. I hate fighting these guys with their own stupid rifles. These things aren't adjusted well. No wonder they can't hit anything. However, there are a lot of them. Throw enough lead in the air, and you're bound to hit something...or me."

Another group of hostages departed in the elevators. Jia took a deep breath and spun toward her side, catching movement on the map before Emma's next announcement.

"Group en route to your position, Jia."

Inevitable? Most likely. Frustrating? Absolutely. Surprising? No.

"Everyone, keep getting on the elevators," Jia shouted. "I'll keep you safe."

Another batch of hostages crammed into the cars. The doors hissed closed, and the elevators left with a hum.

Jia selected burst-fire mode and aimed her rifle, waiting for the terrorists to come around the corner. Emma's targeting highlights made the task trivial.

She waited a couple of heartbeats until all four of her targets cleared the wall, then her rifle came to life with a crack. Her initial burst ripped through the first man's chest. With practiced precision, she repeated the attack three more times, like it was another day at the range. All the terrorists lay dead only a couple of meters from the wall.

They never got a shot off.

As she reloaded, the elevators returned. The crowd remained subdued, even the children, despite the most recent firefight. They loaded into the elevator without much pushing as if they sensed the one thing they could all do to aid their survival was keep calm.

No one's attention lingered on the dead terrorists. That was for the best. They would never hurt anyone else.

The earlier din of gunfire had diminished to the occasional loud splutter, but there were still a decent number of enemies remaining. They were pulling back and regrouping near Erik's position. Jia sucked in a breath.

Erik was barely moving.

"How are you doing?" she asked. "You hit?"

"No. These guys couldn't hit a drunk penguin who charged them looking for a fish. I'm keeping their attention, but it's hard to get a shot off with so many of them, and I'm not behind the best cover," he replied. "But we should be able to hold them here."

Jia glanced at the elevators. "I've got one last group to evacuate, then I'll join you. Should I go for a flank?"

"Not unless you see them coming the long way around. We just need to hold their attention and let the cops have the glory."

After the doors closed on the last set of evacuees, Jia sprinted down a side path that looped around to Erik's position, keeping her an eye on the map for any sign of terrorists breaking off from the main group.

She had never appreciated how mazelike a commercial level could be until that moment. If Emma hadn't been providing helpful guidance, she could have easily missed the appropriate turn and ended up staring at lingerie rather than terrorists.

Her lungs burned as she neared Erik.

A narrow path between two shops allowed her to get closer, and a series of carts provided cover until she had him in sight. Her turn toward him would require her to enter the line of fire of the terrorists.

She kept close to the storefronts, carts, benches, and a fountain between the stores before ducking into his current haunt, a jewelry shop, and leaping behind the display cases. Bullets whizzed overhead and pelted the cases with disturbing thuds.

Scratches and small cracks covered the cases, but none

of them had broken, despite the small mountains of smashed bullets covering the floor in front of them.

This was obviously not the kind of store someone robbed without an electronic lockpick handy.

One dead terrorist lay only a couple of meters away from the store, with more of his dead comrades between the store and the main force clustered farther back.

Most of them clung to the walls on either side, with a smaller number taking advantage of the cart-and-fountain strategy as Jia had. The commerce level wasn't designed for a good firefight. If Jia and Erik had any explosives, it would have long been over.

Though the opposite would be true as well.

"Without their comms," Erik mused, "they don't know what the hell's going on." He inclined his head toward the main exit, which was closer to their side. "Emma's little trick seems to have worked."

Jia looked back and forth, then pulled her magazine to make sure she had ammo. "This is the problem with terrorists. They never know when to give up. I hope one thing."

"What's that?" Erik asked.

"That this wasn't the Core," Jia insisted. "Why waste money on these clowns?"

"Just because you're evil, it doesn't mean you don't have a budget. And even idiots get lucky."

Jia snapped her head toward the front exit doors at a movement. The doors darkened, turning solid black. It took her a second to realize that'd also happened to all outside windows. Angry murmurs swept through the terrorists. They fired into the jewelry store, but the armored cases held.

"What's going on?" Jia asked.

"I've taken the liberty of blinding our friends to the TPST exoskeletons advancing toward them," Emma explained, glee in her tone. "I think it'll be more interesting if they're surprised."

"Then let's distract them more," Erik suggested.

Without a count, Erik and Jia shot up, loosed a coordinated volley, and dropped back behind the display cases before the off-balance terrorists could think to fire. Two terrorists screamed and pitched forward. Jia rushed toward the end of the case and stuck her rifle barrel around the corner for follow-up shots.

"This is a good time to surrender," Erik shouted. "Or you can die to the last man, but you're not going to do anything for your cause but leave a mangled corpse."

"We will never surrender!" bellowed one of the terrorists. "Our cause is righteous, and our hearts are pure. We will destroy this decadent human—"

An explosion ripped through the outer wall near the Grayheads, tossing several to the ground and burning and disorienting the rest. The loud clanks of a squad of advancing exos followed, shields expanded and guns at the ready.

"NSCPD TPST!" shouted an officer through a loudspeaker. "Surrender immediately, or we will use lethal force."

"I decided to send the police my camera feeds," Emma explained. "To save them time since they were trying to access the system. I didn't expect them to blow through the wall, though." She paused. "That was a nice touch."

Erik and Jia kept their rifles trained on the terrorists as

they cautiously moved out from behind the display cases. The terrorists who weren't killed or knocked down by the hard police's entry dropped their weapons and raised their arms, defeat etched on their faces.

"So much for destroying decadent humanity and pure hearts," Jia mumbled, rolling her eyes. She slung her rifle over her shoulder and advanced slowly, her arms up. "Don't shoot! We're the ones sending the feed."

Two exoskeletons slowly advanced on them, their heavy rifles raised. The exoskeletons stopped, and one of the pilots let out a loud sigh.

"Blackwell and Lin?" He looked them over. "You do know how this works, right?"

Erik glanced at Jia, a ghost of worry in his eyes. "How *what* works?"

Bending the rules and the occasional disguise was one thing, opening fire on police was another thing entirely. They might have bought themselves trouble.

The police officer chuckled. "You do know you *quit* the police force, right? We're not paying your company for this."

Jia's tension flowed out with her laugh. "Consider it a gift.

"Public service," Erik added. "Just...keep it to yourselves for now."

CHAPTER TEN

The cops didn't keep Erik and Jia long or press them about why they had such thorough access and control of the commerce level's systems.

The cops could have made trouble, but everyone seemed to tacitly accept that the important thing was that the pair's efforts had cut down on civilian deaths and helped stop the terrorists with minimal risk to anyone else.

That was about the best result anyone could have hoped for, other than stopping the whole thing before it started.

After only an hour of chatting with the NSCPD and avoiding the press, Erik grabbed his penjing supplies from inside with the blessing of the TPST commander and headed back to his place with Jia for some lunch. She wasn't in the mood to go anywhere, given their luck that day.

No one wanted to try to drink tea in the middle of a fight.

Jia didn't talk much as she scarfed down sandwiches

and beignets, her almost orgasmic reaction making her intense hunger clear. Erik sat across from her at his dining room table, marveling that he was the one with the smaller appetite in this situation.

He couldn't say that every time they went somewhere they had trouble, but they certainly had more trouble than the average person or even the not-so-average cop.

"Crap," Erik muttered. "What about your sister? Weren't you supposed to meet her?"

The last thing he wanted was to be on the hit list of a Lin woman. They were more relentless than Core assassins.

He was finally in a decent place with Mei and Lan, and he didn't want his efforts to count for nothing. A future with Jia meant her family had to at least tolerate him.

Jia waved a half-eaten beignet at Erik and swallowed. "I already sent her a message saying something violent had come up. She said she understood."

Erik laughed. "Something violent? And she said she understood that?"

"I thought that'd be the most efficient way to justify things." Jia took another bite of her beignet and chewed for a moment before continuing, "We're known for running into trouble, and she might not know the truth about my job, but even my cover story involves potential danger. Sometimes…"

"What?" Erik asked, looking at her with concern.

Jia set her food down and looked at the tabletop. "My family has their issues, but they're all intelligent."

"I'm sure they'd be executed and the family named disgraced if they weren't," Erik joked.

"Probably," Jia replied, and Erik wasn't sure if she was joking. "The point is, I sometimes wonder if they know the truth. Obviously not about the Core and all that, but that they suspect the company's a lie and a cover."

Erik nodded. "If they're as smart as we both think, then sure, they do."

Jia looked surprised. "And you don't think that's a problem?"

"I think your family is smart enough to know that if you're keeping a secret like that from them, you have a good reason for it. I also think your mother will blow it up into some big thing in her mind, like you're personally taking orders from the Prime Minister to put down insurrectionists."

Jia snickered and picked up her beignet. "We're not that far off. I could be wrong. My family bugs me about getting a job where I don't travel as much, and from the way they talk, they don't sound like they think I'm doing anything but private security." She shrugged. "No point worrying about something that's not a problem yet."

"There is that." Erik patted his left arm. "More good news. I think it's finally tuned." He rotated the arm and flexed it. "It feels better now, less itchy and distracting."

Jia raised an eyebrow. "Oh, you're saying you just needed a good, solid fight to train it?"

"Ahhhh. Yes." Erik shrugged. "I don't think I'll have any problem with it going forward, and I got to use it to take down some terrorists. What's not to like?"

"No problem until the next time it gets blown off. Your so-called lucky arm. I understand why you want to keep it, and I can even see where the hardware is helpful, but I still am having trouble accepting that it's *lucky*." Jia motioned to the arm. "Especially that one since it's brand new."

Erik ran his hand down the arm. "It's got to be lucky. I keep losing it, but I'm not dead. I bet most people who lose their arms in fights end up dead."

"That is statistically accurate, based on the most easily available data," Emma offered.

"That's one perspective on luck." Jia polished off her beignet and lifted her cup of tea. She took a long sip before smiling. "Working with the NSCPD and having beignets from NSC bakeries. It's not something I'd call unpleasant."

"It's just like old times, including the getting shot at by crazies who don't understand they're outgunned."

Jia set her cup down. "What are you talking about? We get shot at all the time, much more often than the average police officer. At this point, I'm beginning to wonder if we get shot at more than the average soldier."

"Depends on the war," Erik replied with a small smile. "The thing is, this was different. I think you're right about the Grayheads."

"Of course I am." Jia bobbed her head and then looked up, uneasy that he might have caught her in a mistake. "What specific aspect am I right about?"

"I think they were below Core standards," Erik explained, gesturing at the ceiling as if the conspiracy was waiting in the apartment above them with Elites and *yaoguai*. "It doesn't mean they didn't pay them, but they might as well not have. That's what's annoying. Can't even take on bastards in hostage rescue or raids without things being complicated by weird conspiracies and worrying about what some high-ranking idiot in the DD or ID thinks about what we're doing."

Emma appeared in a holographic chair at the table. "It's not as if you particularly care what they think. At least you don't behave like you do. I say this as a semi-neutral third-party observer."

"Neutral? Kinda need to know how neutral since we are helping keep the DD off your ass."

"I said *semi*-neutral, but that deflects from my central point about you not caring about high-level government officials."

"No, but I'm supposed to, and more importantly, Alina does." Erik patted his holster. "Sometimes it's nice to be able to take somebody down without having to worry about the implications or what's coming next. I miss that."

"We chased the conspiracy as detectives," Jia observed. "And you became a detective to chase the conspiracy. Things aren't that different now. If anything, they're easier because we have better equipment and direct links to the ID."

"Sure. Can't deny that." Erik shrugged. "It doesn't mean I don't miss something more straightforward."

Jia stared at him, her look almost accusatory. "Maybe you didn't worry as much about the higher-ups when we were police, but I did. I'm still surprised we didn't get fired for half the stunts we pulled."

Erik snorted. "We didn't get fired because we weren't breaking rules to get rich or just because we could. We were breaking rules and not following orders to solve crimes. You worried about the wrong people, especially when I first met you. Standing up to them was good, but you were still following their orders."

"I suppose that's true. But we helped clean up the department." Jia offered him a soft smile. "But I understand what you're getting at, and it does feel good to do something that doesn't feel like the entire UTC will collapse if we fail—and something we don't have to hide from everyone. I'm unsure if those Grayheads were targeting us, but I suppose it doesn't matter." Her mouth tugged into a frown. "I was surprised you were so aggressive about telling them to keep our names out of the news."

"I had my reasons." Erik gestured at his PNIU. "You know one thing that's nice about being back on Earth this last month?"

"We've had time to relax?" Jia ventured.

"Yes." Erik nodded. "Reporters aren't trying to crawl up our asses to lay story eggs."

Jia wrinkled her nose. "That's an...interesting yet disgusting image. I don't know if I'll be able to get it out of my head."

He chuckled. "I don't like always having them on us. I might not enjoy having to run around disguised all the time, but I also don't enjoy having a reporter calling every three seconds. It was annoying but potentially useful before, but now it's just a distraction."

"Fame has its advantages, but it's overrated, or it is for my personality. I wouldn't mind disappearing into quiet anonymity once this is all over." Jia stared at him for a moment, her mouth quirking into a mischievous smile. "I was talking about relaxing and pretending things were quiet, but we just got done taking on a bunch of Grayheads. I suppose by our standards, that *is* quiet. No buildings blew up this time."

"Yeah, pretty boring." Erik nodded. "But there's a time and a place for boring."

"It can't stay quiet for much longer," Jia insisted. "Buildings blowing up included."

Emma folded her arms. "Why can't it stay quiet, particularly with such a low bar? As much as you two like to think of yourselves as the only ones hunting the Core, the entire ID, and to a lesser extent the CID and DD, are doing so as well. Agent Koval uses you in situations where they can't readily use ID resources or because they require the use of the jumpship, and she understands I only help them because you're helping them. You're important to the efforts, but they don't entirely rest on your shoulders."

Jia shook her head. "Alina's also admitted they've come into a lot of intel lately, both from us and from their own efforts, and you're right. They need the jumpship. Something will come through, if only because of that."

Erik suggested, "We should bet on how long it'll be before we have a new mission, all three of us. That'll prove who knows what's up."

Emma rolled her eyes. "What would I bet? You have nothing that interests me."

"Oh?" He grinned. "You can have the glory of knowing you beat a fleshbag in an analysis. Bragging rights have to be worth something, yes?"

"There is insufficient data to accurately model the chance of you being called up for a mission," Emma explained. "My analytical advantages are minimized, and being able to beat a fleshbag in analysis is like you beating a small child in a fistfight."

Erik tapped the side of his head. "Fine. They are more impressive in a different way. Use the intuition you rely on when plotting jumps."

"I still find this pointless."

Jia took a sip of her tea, barely hiding her smile behind her cup. "I think we'll get a call from her within a week."

"A week?" Erik rubbed his chin. "I could see that. You're right. The ID's gotten a lot of new leads lately, and some of them have to be someplace they need a quick response."

"The ID has agents scattered around the UTC," Emma replied. Her form wavered, and her normal appearance was replaced by a skintight tactical suit and ponytail reminiscent of Alina's, though Emma kept her hair red rather than cyan. "They aren't always going to need something semi-off the books. I think a week is too soon, and I also believe Alina's trying to give Engineer Quinn more time to finish the upgrades."

"I thought you said this was pointless?" Erik smirked. "And I'd say two weeks. Lanara doesn't need much more time at this point. She's finished the main upgrades. She's *never* going to finish tinkering with that ship because she can't make it perfect."

Jia shook a finger at Erik. "*That's* a way to figure out if it'll potentially be sooner rather than later."

His hand drifted to his PNIU. "Go or no-go."

"Exactly."

Erik tapped the unit to send a simple message to Lanara.

G/NG this week?

"She might not be allowed to answer that question," Emma suggested. "At least not directly, but I suppose you can derive…" She frowned.

Jia looked at her. "What's wrong?"

"She controls my PNIU, remember?" Erik offered with a grin. "I can't have any secrets with my ghost mother-in-law haunting me. Why don't you read what the message says, Emma?"

The AI harrumphed. "'G, but that doesn't mean we *will* go. I'll finish my current batch quickly just in case.'"

Jia furrowed her brow, her expression darkening. "You'd think Alina would let us know rather than playing games with us, especially since she's gone through the trouble of telling Lanara."

"Nah, because it's easier for us to get ready for a mission than it is for Lanara to make sure the ship's ready if she's in the middle of upgrading it. At least we got to go to your mom's party. Now that we know from Lanara, we'll probably get an Alina invite in the next few days."

Jia sighed. "I hope not."

"Really?" Erik asked. "You're the one who said it'd be within a week."

"I believe that, but I also feel like I need one more week off to recharge."

Erik nodded slowly, surprised by the admission. "I've got something special planned. It's between a real date and training. It's something I've been thinking about doing, but we were always on standby, so I kept pushing it off."

Jia leaned forward, eagerness in her eyes. "Now I want to know."

"No. Some things are better as a surprise. And..." He frowned as his PNIU beeped. "That better not be Alina."

Jia leaned back with a smirk on her face. "That's what you get for planning something."

Erik read the message. "It's the 1-2-2. Captain Ragnar wants to talk to the two of us."

"About what?" Jia asked.

"It doesn't say. The little Grayhead party, I'd assume."

"That wasn't his enforcement zone," Jia complained.

Erik grabbed a beignet for the trip. "I hope this doesn't end with us hijacking the jumpship and fleeing the system."

Emma vanished. "I think that's unlikely, though it might be amusing."

CHAPTER ELEVEN

Jia didn't know if the near emptiness of the station was a good sign, but it did help reduce the number of conversations they needed to have before they ended up at Captain Ragnar's office.

She didn't mind talking to her old colleagues, but now that she knew Alina might be calling them up, she'd prefer to spend time with Erik without explosives or gunfire involved.

When they finally arrived in front of the captain's office, the bearded man waited inside behind his desk, as large as Jia remembered him from their last meeting. He used to be one of the few people she regularly talked to who could make Erik seem small in comparison, an impressive feat.

Captain Ragnar gestured for them to enter.

He was smiling, but reading too much into that might be premature. Jia didn't regret downing the terrorists and was ready to defend their actions to anyone who might question them. If they'd waited, more people might have died. She and Erik hadn't been willing to take that chance.

Being on the commerce level had also given them opportunities the NSCPD would have had trouble with, even if they had retaken control of the systems as quickly as Emma—an unlikely possibility at best.

Erik and Jia stepped inside. She closed the door behind him, waiting for the captain to start the conversation. He'd helped them a lot during their time at the 1-2-2, and she would always be grateful for that, but situations changed with time.

They didn't need more enemies at home. It was time to feel him out subtly and take control of the conversation from there if necessary.

"So, what's the deal?" Erik asked.

Or they could be blunt and to the point, she thought.

Captain Ragnar's smile broadened. "You two never change. That's good." He leaned back. "I know you asked the local EZ and TPST to keep your names out of it for the media, but it's not like they're not going to put things on internal NSCPD reports. It's hard for the old 1-2-2 not to take notice when the Obsidian Detective and Lady Justice are involved in a major local incident."

"We weren't going to stand by and let people die." Jia folded her arms. "It was as simple as that."

"Calm down, Det…" Captain Ragnar sucked in a breath. "Damn. It hurts when I realize you don't work for me anymore, but it's the same thing. I'm not here to chew your asses out. If anyone was going to do that, it would be the TPST commander or the captain of the 4-3-1. This little incident reminded me of what I lost when you two left us."

He gestured to the empty seats in front of him. "You two are worth twenty detectives, not to mention that you work with an AI worth the entire NSCPD digital forensics department."

Emma materialized in a police captain's uniform with a smile. "I'm glad you appreciate my worth. You're reasonable for a fleshbag, which is rare. I enjoy that."

Captain Ragnar chuckled. "I forgot how...colorful you are."

Erik settled into a seat, nodding to Jia, who nodded back. The tension had evaporated, and now Jia felt foolish to have ever worried that Captain Ragnar would come down on them for taking out terrorists. If it weren't for him, the 1-2-2 would not have become an enforcement zone worthy of pride.

"What's this about, Captain?" Jia asked. "I assume you didn't call us here just to tell us how much you missed us."

He took a deep breath and slowly let it out before scratching his eyebrow. "I don't know everything that's going on with you two and why you left the police department, but I do know you're working with..." He frowned. "Emma, can you make sure this conversation stays here?"

"Trivial," she responded with a wave of her arm. "Feel free to talk."

Jia's eyes narrowed. This wasn't the casual chat she'd been led to believe it would be. Erik's demeanor didn't change.

Captain Ragnar cleared his throat. "I know you're still working with Colonel Adeyemi, which implies certain things about the scope of your professional interests."

"Like?" Erik asked, his voice low.

The captain raised a hand. "I'm not here to pump you for information on things I don't need to know. I am aware that part of the reason I was brought to this EZ was that certain people, including Adeyemi, knew I could be trusted. There was probably more behind the spike in terrorism that hit Neo SoCal than bad luck and lazy cops."

Jia sighed and looked away. "We're limited in what we can share."

"Good." The captain nodded. "That's the way it should be. I've been around enough ghosts in my time to smell the ID all over you two, and I assume that's where you dragged Malcolm off to as well."

Jia's eyes widened, but she didn't say anything. Erik chuckled, more amused than concerned.

"Again, don't worry about the details," Captain Ragnar added. "I'm only saying this to make it clear I understand your situation. I also understand that certain things happened here because of what you were likely involved in, even before the ID showed up and started making demands."

"No offense, Captain," Erik twirled a finger in a circle, "but can you get to the point?"

"Yes, I should, shouldn't I?" Captain Ragnar leaned back in his chair and folded his hands in front of him. "Whenever terrorists show up on Earth or Neo SoCal, it's a big deal, but I'd make the argument that when it involves you two, it's an even bigger deal because it might mean something more."

"Okay." Erik nodded slowly. "Does it mean more this time? I wasn't sure about those guys. They were sloppy, but being sloppy and being a tool aren't mutually exclusive."

Captain Ragnar shook his head. "That's what I wanted to talk to you about. They're nothing."

"Nothing?" Jia frowned.

"Let me clarify." He added. "They're terrorists. Gray-heads, implying everything you'd think about the kind of people who would pull a stunt like that, but that's it. They have no connections to anyone else, and based on their PNIUs and other CID info I received not long ago, they've been planning to attack that commerce tower for two months."

Jia's frown softened. "It was a coincidence. That's it?"

Emma sighed. "That does explain their poor opposition and inferior skills."

Captain Ragnar offered her a raised eyebrow. "You'd prefer it if they were tougher?"

"It's not so much that I wanted them to be tougher. I was going for more entertaining." Emma shrugged. "All encounters should offer enrichment on some level. Otherwise, it's nothing more than fleshbags being pathetic."

"You sure about all this?" Erik asked. "Some things make sense, but some don't. They didn't come after us right away, and they didn't seem ready for us, but they could have been hired. From what Emma told us, they weren't supposed to be a big deal, and now suddenly, they're doing that kind of thing?"

"It's because they got an infusion of cash," Captain Ragnar explained. "From a high-level supporter who was enthusiastic about Grayhead ideals who was looking for a group that didn't already have a firm power structure. She wanted her own pet terrorists."

"If we know who it is, why hasn't she been arrested?" Jia asked.

Captain Ragnar laughed. "She has. She was arrested this morning by the CID *before* the attack in Sao Paulo. I'm sure heads will roll over the fact they nailed her but let those guys move."

Jia frowned. "They knew about it?"

"I don't know the details, but from what I can tell, they thought if they nailed their funder, they'd be able to quickly follow up and take them out. It's not as if they ignored the operation." Captain Ragnar gestured to her. "And they were under the impression they had more time. Fortunately, you two were there. It's not your problem to worry about or even mine. Mistakes happen, and that's on them. I just wanted you to know there's nothing deeper to this."

Erik let out a sharp laugh. "I don't know if that's better."

"Why do you say that?"

"Because I don't know if running into random terrorists while shopping is better than knowing someone's coming after you. At least in the second case, you can do something about it." Erik dusted his hands. "But it's good in the short term. I have a reservation for something tomorrow, and I didn't want to have to cancel it."

Captain Ragnar gave him a long, curious look before nodding. "Okay. So, I'm not going to keep you two any longer. I appreciate what you did out there. The entire NSCPD appreciates it. If you ever want to come back, I'm sure no one would complain, and I'd give you your old office."

"It'll be a while yet," Jia offered, standing. "Once we finish our current...tasks, I think both of us are going to want a long vacation."

He smiled. "I can't think of two people who've earned that more."

CHAPTER TWELVE

Jia always managed to surprise Erik.

He believed he had a good handle on her, but then she would do something that took him off-guard. Today, it was simple.

She'd allowed him to land at an industrial tower without explanation and lead her out of the MX 60 and up the elevator blindfolded while leaving her weapons and coat in the car. She had her arms folded the entire time and tapped her foot impatiently, but he'd been impressed by her level of trust and surrender of control, given her natural tendencies.

He wasn't sure he would have been able to do it if their roles were reversed.

They stood on a small platform jutting out of a mostly empty level with a sprawling open hangar behind them, empty except for a small pile of silver boxes in the corner

115

and dozens of small docking stations for drones, all currently empty.

The expanse of Neo SoCal spread out below. Glinting towers pierced the skies, and the colorful metal rivers of flitters and the omnipresent swarms of drones flew everywhere. It was an ecosystem of its own, despite being an artificial construct where people lived and worked far from the planet's surface.

"You can take off the blindfold." Erik walked toward a small but long silver box in the center of the platform that matched the pile of boxes inside the level. It contained everything they needed for the day's activities.

Jia yanked off the blindfold, then carefully folded it and tucked it in her pocket as she took in the vista. "It's a nice view, I'll give you that. This isn't the part where you reveal you work for the Core and throw me to my death, is it? That would be terribly anticlimactic."

"The opposite would make more sense." Erik crouched next to the box and tapped in a code on his PNIU, and the lock clicked. "But I'm not here to kill you today. I haven't checked my schedule for tomorrow."

Jia walked toward the box. "What's in there?"

"Active thrust wingsuits," Erik explained, his grin growing.

Jia's brows lifted. "ATWs?" She laughed. "Oh, now I understand why you suddenly wanted to do wingsuit scenarios during training a couple of weeks back. And here I thought you just wanted to mix things up a bit."

"I did, but not for missions. You've said it yourself. And I've said it." Erik tugged up a folded wingsuit, chute pack, helmet, and thrust boots out of the box and offered them to Jia. "Your brain can always sense the difference in a simulation, no matter how good it is. It's good training, but it's not a real experience. It's not going to make your blood pump as hard. It's not going to be as fun. We should have some fun before Alina tosses us back into our monster hunt."

Jia eyed the equipment incredulously, then looked at the box, at Eric, and back at the box. "So, let me get this straight. Your idea of something mixing dating and training and fun is both of us jumping off a tower." Her eyes narrowed. "*On purpose?*"

"Yeah, that about sums it up." Erik nodded at a nearby door. "You can go in there and get changed."

"I know I've done this in training, but I'm assuming because of the equipment and location, we're doing this via a company and not just trying to get ourselves arrested?" Jia sounded amused.

Erik chuckled. "You have had parachute and escape-pod training as part of your pilot's license. I pulled some strings so we could do this without an instructor and a bunch of training you've effectively already done. Why waste time?"

"I hope I don't regret that on the way down," Jia muttered through the smile that had formed on her face.

"The company *was* rather insistent on safety drones," Emma explained. She didn't appear, though. "We're standing in front of their hangar. I've taken the liberty of accessing their system and will control all the safety drones. That's far safer than their automated system or some foolish fleshbag instructor. Don't worry, I knew Erik had this planned, so I had plenty of time to infiltrate the system without making them aware. As far as they know, Erik has a team of trained professionals monitoring everything."

"I'm both honored and a little scared to hear that," Jia admitted.

Erik walked to the edge and pointed down. "Once we jump, you'll see an AR overlay of the permissible flight area. Normally, the safety drones will grab you if you try to go past them, but we have a little broader play area because Emma's in charge."

Jia nodded at her helmet. "I don't think we should go crazy. If we zoom around the entire city, I think the company and the police might notice."

"Sure." Erik winked. "We won't go *crazy*, but we'll have fun. Believe it or not, I put some skull sweat into this. I picked a location and a time of day with minimal traffic."

"A-hem," Emma interrupted. "His planning mostly consisted of saying, 'Emma, find me a location and time of day where we'll have room to play.' I suppose that *does* count as planning."

He rolled his eyes. "I was making good use of my local resources."

Jia smiled. "Okay, you've convinced me. At least this isn't as insane as a drop pod."

Erik gave her a serious look. "You never know when we might need this, and yes, it's a lot more fun than dropping from orbit."

"Even when you're not under fire?"

"You can't see shit in a drop pod," Erik explained. "Not really. Sure, you have feeds, but it's not like this, and you're falling damned fast until the very end. You're not experiencing anything. You're stuck in a big metal shell with minimal thrusters and less grav compensation. It's like being in a vibrating coffin."

Jia's nose wrinkled in disgust. "Let's avoid that. I'm comfortable waiting until I'm dead before I'm in a coffin." She headed toward the door. "Let's get changed. Do try not to die on our date."

"You jump first," Erik suggested. "I'll follow."

"What does it say about us that jumping off a building is one of the less insane things we've done lately?" Jia raised an eyebrow.

"It says we're damned fun people who keep our days and nights exciting." Erik grinned and motioned to the edge of the platform. "Now, are you going to jump, or am I going to have to push you?"

"I knew this was an assassination attempt." Jia finished securing her helmet and AR goggles and tapped on the side. "Full integration achieved. Signal check."

"Signal received," Erik replied. "Emma?"

"You're both fine in my system," she replied. "You may pointlessly risk your lives whenever you're ready."

Jia advanced toward the edge of the platform, the tight wingsuit fitting her like a glove. Erik hadn't thought of that fringe benefit when he'd planned the activity, but he wasn't going to complain about looking at his girlfriend's taut ...backside.

"The wings are programmed to auto-deploy after a hundred meters," he explained. "Since it's your first time doing the real thing, I figured we shouldn't mess with the deployment altitude. Also, remember the thrusters in the boots aren't powerful enough to generate much lift without taking advantage of the wings, so use them in combination. Otherwise, it's just a fancy-looking parachute."

"Understood." Jia sighed. "Remember, we *did* do ATW training."

"In a simulation. I know you're a prodigy and all, but still..." Erik shrugged.

Jia gave him an annoyed look. "You're the one who wanted to skip training. We can spend a few weeks working up to it."

"You're right." Erik gave her a sheepish grin.

Jia stood on the edge, taking slow, even breaths. "This is one way to make sure we're not afraid of heights, and it's nice to do something that pushes us to the edge but doesn't involve someone or something trying to kill us."

She spread out her arms and dropped off. Erik rushed forward. He'd expected a countdown. That was what he got for not agreeing on a protocol.

With a quick leap, he left the platform and plummeted, his stomach complaining. It didn't matter how hard a man trained; at the end of the day, gravity took its toll.

His heart rate kicked up, and a huge grin took his face over. There was something about freefalling on Earth that couldn't be matched anywhere, not in space, not on the colonies.

It didn't matter how many grav towers they put up. The human body knew where it was from and responded in kind.

Jia's wings deployed between her arms, legs, and body. Her torso was angled up. With a quick thrust, her fall stopped, and she glided upward like a dark, majestic bird challenging the skies. Erik passed her before his wings deployed.

He allowed the glorious sensation of falling to continue before finally angling and activating his thrusters with a press of his thumb in his palm. A controlled burst had him climbing with ease. The lack of heavy winds made for easy flying—due to research on his part, or more precisely, asking Emma, depending on one's perspective.

"It shouldn't make a difference," Jia murmured as she circled, her voice quieter than Erik would expect over the comm.

"What shouldn't?" Erik asked.

"Seeing Neo SoCal like this," Jia replied, continuing her gentle circular flight path. Her use of the thrusters was sparing and expert. "I was just looking at all this from the platform, but now it looks more beautiful. The only difference is that I'm in the air."

Erik kept her in the corner of his eye but didn't attempt any clever formation tricks. They hadn't practiced much, and there was no reason to get close to her and risk an accident.

Emma *could* save them.

But it would sure ruin the moment.

"It's like my brain appreciates the inherent danger of what we're doing," Jia continued. "And that in turn helps me realize that everything beneath me is fleeting and beautiful in its own way, especially here in Neo SoCal."

"Why is that?" Erik asked, looking around. They were

nowhere near the edge of the acceptable flight zone marked with red lines in his AR goggles, and Jia's path was keeping her close to the building.

That worked.

"Because this place was destroyed and then rebuilt," Jia explained reverently. "It was reborn like a phoenix after humanity's ultimate weapon was used on it."

Erik could not have cared less about the city beneath him, but he hadn't been born there. Even if he'd lived there for a few years, it wasn't his home, not like it was Jia's. He was just enjoying the sensation of being one with the sky with minimal separation.

He angled down and increased his dive speed, then another well-timed thrust helped him gain altitude. The parabolic pattern continued, challenging Erik's stomach but satisfying his brain.

"I think it'd be hard to fight in something like this," Jia commented.

"We didn't fight in any of the training scenarios, did we?" Erik asked.

Jia laughed. "No, all entry, but at least there's no ridiculously tiny cave we have to fly into this time."

"If this past month's taught us anything, it's that not everything has to be about training."

"Hmm," Emma sent. "There is a message you need to see. It's nothing urgent, but I wouldn't schedule another excursion for a while."

"It's her, isn't it?" Erik asked with a snort. "I swear, it's like she's spies on us and waits for the most inconvenient time to mess with us."

"Yes, it is her," Emma replied. "But as I said, she discusses a meeting tomorrow, not today."

"Then let's enjoy what we are doing right now," Jia suggested. "Tomorrow can be for terrorists. Today's for flying."

"And if any terrorists show up in the sky?" Erik asked.

There was no hesitation or concern in Jia's voice when she replied, "Then I'll knock them out of it."

CHAPTER THIRTEEN

Damir Sokov was sitting in a dusty chair in the middle of a bombed-out store on the edge of the city, flexing his hands. Nervous energy suffused his body, making him want to jump out of his seat despite the rebel soldiers surrounding him.

He was having trouble focusing on the squad briefing even with the major operation coming up. The rebellion was going well, far better than he'd expected at the start of the month, but there were different metrics for success. If what he'd been told had been true, they wouldn't still be fighting.

His commander gestured to three holographic maps displaying different parts of the city. The Free Samarkand Army's surprise offensive had pushed the Army and the militia out of the major domes making up Sogdia. There'd been talk about the government attempting to seal the domes and cut the oxygen supply. Damir didn't trust the government not to commit a major war crime, but there were system restrictions that made it complicated. The FSA still had a chance at victory, despite their missteps.

That should have made him happy, but doubt gnawed at the back of his mind, whispering and polluting his courage. The only way to overcome it was to face the truth, and that would require having words with his superior.

The commander pointed at a cluster of red pyramids on the map. "The Army's concentrating on retaking the northwestern parts of the city. Our primary forces will continue to harass their troops, but those of us involved in the recent push into the west, including the squads in this room, will continue advancing. The more pressure we put on them, the less they will be able to concentrate their forces. If we keep pushing forward like we have, we can surround the bastards and rip them to shreds. If we destroy the bulk of the garrison, we can take out their bases, and then it's all over. They're not going to bombard the domes from orbit. The UTC can't suck resources out of a destroyed colony."

Damir surveyed the map, noting the highlighted areas under rebel control. Well, calling it "control" was an overstatement. They'd forced the government's troops out of their areas, but there were few civilians left either. What was the point of a rebellion if the people didn't feel safe? It also made it easier for the Army to counterattack. Less risk of collateral damage meant less propaganda and spin they had to come up with.

Different colored circles appeared on the map, and the commander pointed to each in turn as he continued the briefing. "Green, Red, and Orange squads will come in from this area and continue a general sweep and the elimination of all government forces. Blue, Yellow, and Purple squads will keep poking them. Hit and run, just enough to draw their attention. You know how dogs are when they get the scent of prey? They don't know when to give up, and we can take advantage of that."

More mission instructions followed, tied to marked paths on the map. Damir soaked it in, but as he sat there, he might as well have been watching a movie. It didn't seem real. He'd been fighting for weeks, killing and nearly dying, but it was like a dream.

"Remember," the command concluded, "if we can finish off the forces here, we'll have all but sealed our victory. Our allies are doing a lot to disrupt reinforcements. We just need to make sure the Army can't counterattack in Sogdia, and we can finish cleaning up the other cities."

Damir frowned. Slowing reinforcements wasn't the same thing as eliminating them, and he didn't trust mercenaries. They weren't there because of their love of freedom. He had been surprised when he'd first learned about the FSA using mercenaries to supplement their forces.

"Dismissed," the commander barked. "Be ready for the operation. I don't want anyone wandering off and getting themselves picked off like Gemmison did. Remember, the UTC dogs don't care about you or your freedom. They only care about killing you so the UTC can continue ruling this place from twenty light-years away."

Weary-looking men and women rose from their seats and filed out of the room. The commander remained and peered at the maps, his brow furrowed in deep concentration. Damir waited until everyone else departed before approaching him. He had concerns, but he didn't want to undermine his superior in front of the others.

The commander looked up from the maps. "What is it, Sokov? If there was anything you didn't understand about the briefing, you should have asked before."

"It's not the briefing." Damir checked the room one last time to make sure they were alone. "Can I speak freely?"

"Always." The commander clapped him on the shoulder. "We're brothers in this. Family in blood and freedom. We have ranks because it's necessary for planning, but when the rebellion is over, all who have fought will be recognized for their efforts and given important jobs in the new government."

Damir stiffened. He hadn't joined the rebels because he wanted a fancy government job after the war. A patriot fought with no promise of reward except the freedom of his brothers and sisters.

"Nobody's staying anywhere we liberate." Damir pulled away from the man. "Every area the FSA controls is a ghost town. Doesn't that bother you?"

"No, it doesn't bother me. That's expected. The government is providing heavy resistance. Civilians don't want to stay where it's dangerous. That's common sense. Self-preservation."

"So, they flee to government-controlled parts of Sogdia? That sounds like they don't trust the FSA, but they trust the Army." Damir shook his head. "I hear the same thing is happening in the other cities too, from our other brothers and sisters there."

The commander frowned. "What's your point? What are you getting at, Sokov?"

"This is supposed to be about freeing our people from oppression." Damir narrowed his eyes. "But there are a lot of dead civilians out there. With all due respect, that might be one way to free a person, but I think most would prefer freedom *and* life."

"Of course there are dead civilians." The commander snorted. "Because those government dogs don't care where and who they shoot at. As far as they're concerned, anyone helping the rebels is a rebel, and they are free to target and kill them. That's why we fight. The UTC pretends to be benevolent, but they'll murder innocents to hold onto their power."

Damir shook his head. "I've been trying to ignore this, but I can't. I saw it myself. I tried to convince myself it couldn't be what I was seeing, but my eyes don't lie. I saw a SAM truck target civilian transports. The Army took it out, but we could have killed hundreds of civilians who were just trying to escape. That's not right."

The commander squared his shoulders and marched over until he was nose to nose with Damir. "You don't know what you saw. You think you saw civilians? The government has all sorts of irregular forces in the area, including ghosts infiltrating and spying on us. Our forces don't target innocents."

"Bullshit." Damir scoffed. "There aren't hundreds of ghosts on New Samarkand!"

"Who the hell is in command here?" the other man thundered.

So much for being brothers. Damir didn't flinch. They would decide after this rebellion what kind of world they would have once they'd pushed the UTC out. Darkness excused by pragmatism couldn't be allowed to poison their freedom. They were rebels, not murderers.

"Last time I checked, this was the Free Samarkand Army, *sir*," Damir replied, his voice a near-growl. "With an emphasis on *free*. I deserve to know what happened. All of our brothers and sisters do."

The commander's jaw clenched, and his face reddened. "You need to know what we tell you for missions. If we didn't keep some secrets, the spies would be able to give all our plans directly to the garrison commanders."

Damir looked down. It was a valid point. He couldn't personally vouch for everyone in the FSA, and while there might not be hundreds of Intelligence Directorate spies on New Samarkand, that didn't mean there were none. He decided to go in a different direction.

"There was only supposed to be guns and ammo supplied," Damir replied. "And now we have those mercs running around. Why are we using mercs?"

The commander laughed, but there was no mirth in the sound. "Because we're outnumbered and outgunned and have been from the beginning. Most people talk about wanting freedom, but they're not willing to fight for it. They're not willing to die for it. Without those mercs, this rebellion would have been crushed by government forces in a week, and all our brave brothers and sisters would have thrown their lives away for nothing." He shook his head. "I don't see the problem using whatever tools are available if they'll help you win. If the mercs win a fight, there are fewer soldiers *we* have to fight. If they lose, then we didn't lose a brother or sister. Don't be a fool. You have to think like a soldier, not like a man with a dream."

"But they're mercenaries." Damir rubbed his thumb against his index finger. "All they care about is money. What's to stop the government from offering them more money and making them turn on us?"

"The government will send them all to prison for insurrection if they stop helping us," the commander countered. "They won't dare negotiate with officials. Besides, they're receiving payment from powerful and influential people who support our cause."

"They could be offered amnesty. You can't depend on soldiers who care solely about their bank account. You can only depend on someone fighting for something they believe in." Damir clenched his hands into fists. "It's not a surprise that those merc bastards were involved in the attack on civilian transports. Is that what this is? We let the mercs kill whoever and then we cover it up and ignore it because it wasn't the FSA?"

Damir wasn't sure mercs were involved in every incident he'd heard about, but their presence went a long way to explaining certain things. He wanted it to be true because it was a simple, direct explanation, one the FSA might be able to do something about.

The mercenaries might have been helpful at the start of the rebellion, but the government's forces were weaker now. They could tell the mercenaries to hold. If they were still paid, they wouldn't care about not risking their lives.

The commander glared at him. "All you need to know is that we'd lose this rebellion without their help. Ideals don't win wars. Guns and missiles do."

"I need to know we're not helping to kill the people we're trying to save. I can't be the only one."

"What?" The commander scoffed and stepped back. "You've lost your stomach for the fight because we didn't win right away? Is that what this is? Don't blame me for your idiocy."

"It's not that." Damir shook his head, his heart pounding. "But it was people like you who said that once we started fighting, it'd be over quickly. We were told that most people on the colony wanted freedom, and after a couple days of fighting, the rest would fall in line, inspired. Now we have everyone fleeing any area we control, and we have civilians dying. Maybe even targeted on purpose, if not by us, then by the troops we've employed."

The commander stared at Damir, his eyes accusing. He didn't speak for a long while, leaving Damir to stare defiantly at him. This wasn't the UTC Army. This was the FSA, a small collection of dedicated men and women who had volunteered to free their world. They might have to copy Army structures for efficiency, but that didn't mean everyone in command had experience equivalent to an Army officer's. Some were there because of their political and financial contributions to the cause. Damir didn't care. No one wanted freedom for New Samarkand more than he did, and he would do everything he could to maintain the purity of that freedom.

"What did you think liberation meant, Sokov?" the commander asked quietly. His volume increased with each word in his next sentence. "What do you think it takes to be free from tyranny? It takes blood, Sokov. Lots of it. Buckets and pools of it!"

"Fighting is one thing." Damir cut through the air with his hand. "Killing soldiers is one thing, but what are we fighting for if we're also killing civilians? We might as well be UTC dogs."

"Innocent people die in war. That's part of the sacrifice." The commander kicked over a nearby chair. "You think we have any other choice?" he shouted. "The government didn't give us one. Yes, there might be the occasional innocent person killed by mistake, but most of the so-called atrocities you are hearing about are either government propaganda or them doing it and blaming us. We're only targeting the military and the government dogs. I don't care what you think you saw. You're mistaken, and you better not spread this around. It'll damage morale."

"I waited until everyone was gone so that wouldn't happen."

Damir ground his teeth. He knew what he had seen, not only with the missile launcher but also dead families in an area where there weren't any government troops. Either the rebels were killing innocent people, or the mercs were doing it and the rebels were allowing it. It didn't matter. Both were wrong.

"Good," the commander continued. "I admire your passion, my brother, but we haven't won yet, and we need every single one of our brothers and sisters until that victory. I need you not to worry about things you're mistaking, and for you to get ready for your mission." He sighed. "What would your father have said if he could see you now? Are you honoring him by questioning our cause? Remember what you're fighting for, Sokov."

Damir flinched and looked away, shame eating at his concern. He shuffled toward the door, more unsure than ever. Thinking they could rebel against the UTC and win the war had been arrogant if not downright naïve, but the glorious rebellion he'd joined seemed like it was slipping away. Instead, they had put into motion something darker and more twisted.

He made for the door. It didn't matter. He was committed. Either the rebels won, or people like him ended up in prison or dead. He'd listened to a couple of other people, and they'd all said the same thing as the commander—that the civilians' deaths were either propaganda or the fault of the government.

He didn't want to cause trouble. Maybe the commander was right, and he had misinterpreted what he saw.

Damir had always wondered what it'd be like to be the only sane man in the room. It'd turned out to be far less entertaining than he'd imagined. The cause remained, and he could be wrong. For now, he'd focus on freedom. There would be time for justice in the future.

CHAPTER FOURTEEN

September 25, 2230, Neo Southern California Metroplex, Summer of Sorrow Monument

Jia didn't consider herself to be superstitious. She had always prided herself on that. Even when she joked about the Lady with Erik, it was nothing more than humor. Her family participated in holidays more out of social form than belief in the metaphysical necessity. Now, for the first time in her life, she wondered if the dead could come back to haunt the living.

She stood behind Erik, her hands tucked in her pockets, near a tall fence separating a vast, mostly featureless platform from the otherwise abrupt drop-off from the tower. There was nothing unusual about that, especially in Neo SoCal. It was what was in front of her that was the source of her concern.

Thousands of smoky, translucent forms walked with casual strides, smiles on their faces, their names floating above them in bright text. The ghosts had no destination. Some approached a wall and disappeared. Others vanished after a couple of steps, only to be replaced by someone else, but the spectral parade remained constant. The near-silence bothered her the most.

Her brain kept telling her the people in front of her were just holograms, not real ghosts. Each wore the visage of a victim of the Summer of Sorrow. Their order of appearance in the spectral parade was not random. They were appearing and disappearing based on last name.

With thousands of ghosts on the platform for an average of a minute, it took about five days to cycle through every one of the millions of victims of the worst terrorist attack in history. The question of whether they were ghosts was pointless. They represented lives cut short by intense violence and lingered as forms and memories in the world of the living. They were ghosts in every way that mattered.

Emma hadn't said a word since Erik and Jia had taken the elevator from the parking platform. Even the world's snarkiest AI could appreciate that some places required respectful silence.

Jia rubbed her shoulders. "Alina picked a cheery place to meet. I'll have to congratulate her on her choice."

Erik surveyed the area and gestured at a small cluster of solid humans in the distance. "Not a lot of people here. In that sense, it's a good place to meet." He looked at Jia. "You've never been here before?"

"Have you?"

Erik shook his head. "No. This is my first time."

"This is my second," Jia explained. "I came here in high school. Everyone who goes to school here visits the monument. It's required. I didn't like it then either." She took a deep breath and slowly let it out. "When it first opened during the first centennial anniversary, it was a big tourist attraction. Then attendance dropped off. No one wants to think about the dark past when you live in a place that's recovered. Neo SoCal's all about the future and people coming together to make something good after a tragedy."

"That's why this is almost perfect for a place like Neo SoCal." Erik looked thoughtful. "When you live in Heaven, it can be easy to forget evil still exists below you." He nodded at a passing hologram of a man in an old-fashioned uniform. "Call it chaos, evil, entropy, whatever you want. That darkness is always there, waiting. LA was an impressive city for the time, too. The more we remember things like this..." he motioned at a group of holograms. "...the less chance we have of repeating that horror."

"I think she's finally here." Jia gave a slight nod at an approaching woman in a dark dress.

Her puffy face and dark hair didn't resemble Alina's, but she was about the right height. Doubt vanished when the slight whistle of the wind and distant murmurs of other visitors faded into silence.

"Can you hear us, Emma?" Erik asked.

No response. The jamming confirmed their guest was someone with special tech. It was either Alina or an assassin from the Core.

"In thunderous billows borne, some from the waning light, some through mid-noon, some from the rising morn, some from the stars of Night," the woman announced in a Lunar accent.

"Let the clouds be my guide, for they desire no glory,"

Jia answered, invoking a more modern Venusian poet based on Alina's message.

The woman smiled and her voice changed, her accent shifting to match Alina's normal one. "It's been too long. I was beginning to miss chatting with you two."

"Too long's a matter of opinion," Erik commented.

Alina gave him a coy smile. "You both knew what you were in for when you signed up with me. You can't pretend otherwise."

"Not saying we didn't." Erik shrugged. "Just saying it has not been *that* long."

Jia stared at a gaggle of child holograms before tearing her gaze away from them to focus on Alina. "Let's get to the point. I'd rather not spend any longer here than I have to. If we do our jobs, we won't need more monuments like this one."

Alina shook her finger. "Exactly, Jia. It's nice to have a reminder of why we do what we do, and I appreciate that you two are always ready to move quickly. I'll be blunt."

"You always are," Erik replied.

"It helps things move along, and you don't need the bullshit." Alina stepped back with a pensive expression. "We've done well on recent missions, both you and the ID, but right now, that jumpship is one of our major advantages over the Core. Especially since we're handicapped by having a vague sense of morality and ethics and are unwilling to use whatever monstrous means we can think of. The ship gives you mobility, and that means we might be able to get out ahead of the Core instead of disrupting their operations after the fact."

"So, we're going to another system again?" Jia asked.

Alina clucked her tongue. "Ironically, no, despite that big speech. At least not yet. This won't require any jumps. This one's a little closer to home. You're going to grab the *Argo* and go to Mars."

Erik frowned. "This better not be more pointless syndicate crap."

"It *is* syndicate crap, as you put it, but it's not pointless, if by pointless, you mean not related to the Core."

"Are you sure?" Jia challenged. "Your little Mars rescue mission was nothing more than an agent getting caught by criminals. The CID and your local assets could have handled that."

"Yes, but part of the reason I sent you that time was to test you." Alina shook her head. "This is different. There is no such thing as being sure, which is one of the reasons I'm sending you two. Your borrowed tech is helpful, but your position, combined with your unique competence, will be even more helpful and useful in this particular situation."

Jia frowned. "I'm not following you. How does our position help?"

"Let me give you some background." Alina folded her hands behind her back. "A suspicious arms shipment passed through Mars a couple of weeks ago. That shipment might be linked to other suspicious shipments that have passed through over the last six months, and those in turn might be linked to some other odd activity. I'm not going to go into the details for the moment, other than to say something might be stirring in the colonies, and that might be linked to the Core."

Erik grunted in frustration. "Even with emergency expedited comm, once you get twenty or thirty light-years from Earth, something could happen, and it'd take us weeks or months to find out. That's a lot of time to pull off something."

"That's what's got me so worried," Alina replied softly.

Jia sighed. "There are good leaders out on the frontier. It's not like if there's an attack, they have to wait for reinforcements from Earth."

"No, but not every general or governor out there knows about the Core and what they're capable of. A terrorist attack on Earth or an older colony might get immediate headlines, but we've seen what they're capable of. If they decided to destroy an entire colony, it'd be easier to do it farther out, where the UTC is less prepared for that kind of thing."

"Aren't we getting ahead of ourselves?" Erik asked, looking at the women. "Just because someone's smuggling weapons, it doesn't mean they're planning to kill a colony. I spent enough time busting smugglers in the Army to know sometimes it's about colonies thinking they're not getting enough gear from the core worlds and Earth and being willing to look the other way. Yes, that includes guns. There might not be as many people on the frontier, but it can get wild."

Alina shook her head. "We have reason to believe it's not that benign from some of our follow-up analysis and investigation of the information you got from Barbu."

Jia stiffened at the mention of Barbu. There was still much they didn't know about the man.

"All that makes sense, but this isn't about the frontier. This is about the Solar System, so why isn't this a CID matter?" she asked. "They have plenty of agents on Mars."

"They do, and that's part of why we need you two." Alina sighed. "In the interests of transparency, I'll be honest. The CID is far more interested in crushing syndicates on Mars than they are in stopping smuggling, except in how it impacts the syndicates." She inclined her head toward Erik. "Their operating paradigm is that smuggling is at most a way syndicates make money, not a source of significant local trouble. The farther out you go, the more law enforcement becomes a military matter, so based on simple political capital reasons, they care far less about anything that happens outside the core worlds. Because of that, we're going behind the CID's back on this and taking the matter into our own hands."

"Great." Jia shrugged. "Does this mean if something happens, you'll leave us to twist in the wind? Curious, since we're being honest."

"No." Alina's expression turned serious. "As assets, you are too important to be burned for some middle-importance op right now."

"Right now?" Erik chuckled. "Does that mean in the future, you'll toss us to the wolves if things get hot?"

"We'll see what happens when we get there. I do what I need to do to protect the UTC. For now, I'm not asking you to go against the CID. I'm simply noting it'll be helpful this time for me to send someone to Mars who is at least partially independent of the ID. It helps that you have an in on Mars."

Jia looked at Erik and Alina "An *in*? What are you talking about?"

"You don't have an in," Alina clarified. "To be specific, Erik has an in."

Jia didn't understand. They'd been to Mars together before, and while Erik performed well, he seemed far more comfortable on Earth than Mars.

Her stomach knotted. There was one possibility, and she didn't like it. Not one bit.

Erik grimaced. "You're talking about Radira Tellvane, aren't you?"

Jia blinked. "That bitch. I tried to purge her from my mind."

Alina laughed. "I'm not ordering you to sleep with her, Erik, but from what you both told me, she has more than a professional interest in you. We can exploit that, and I have some leads for you as well if that doesn't pan out as well as we'd like." Her amused smile twitched into a look of concern. "But because I'm trying to keep this a little cleaner on my end, I won't be sending Kant and Anne with you, and our local agents will be focused on other tasks to give them plausible deniability."

Jia folded her arms. "In summary, we're supposed to go to Mars to investigate smuggling, but don't involve the CID, don't use local ID resources, and do our best to keep a low profile while walking into a search that's almost certainly going to bring us trouble with a local syndicate. And our only real advantage, besides Emma, is that a syndicate boss wants to sleep with Erik. In other words, you're telling us to work *with* organized crime."

Erik averted his eyes, but there was far more of a smirk on his face than Jia would have liked. If Alina hadn't been there, she might have slapped him upside the head.

"Yes." Alina nodded. "That all sounds accurate." She held up a hand. "I understand your concern, but I personally don't care much about criminals, organized or not. Syndicates can be crushed by conventional law enforcement, and they might be criminal scum, but they aren't determined to undermine the entire UTC or fund mass-casualty terrorist events. If we can take advantage of them in the short term until the CID removes them from play, we should."

Erik cleared his throat. "Tellvane might not trust us. We weren't very polite to her the last time we were on Mars."

"She probably trusts you more than you think, and not just because she wants to screw you. The last time you were on Mars, you effectively took out a competing syndicate for her. All the information we have suggests Prism Associates isn't smuggling what we're interested in." Alina offered a cold smile. "That should minimize the necessity of you fighting Tellvane's people."

"All this for weapons shipments?" Jia asked.

"Weapons at a minimum," Alina replied. "It's easier to follow the trail this time, so I doubt it's artifacts, but we need to know what it is and if it is linked to the Core. I don't care if they're shipping illegal animals for a party. If the Core is doing it, I want to disrupt it. Every victory we achieve against them weakens them."

Erik nodded slowly, looking far more concerned than normal. "If it's them, I want in."

"If Barbu's info pointed that way, the chances are good that this is something," Jia added with a sigh.

"The whole point of giving us Kant and Anne," Erik continued, "was so we wouldn't end up fighting entire bases full of guys by ourselves. There's a line between confidence and stupidity. If we ask around too much or poke our noses into the wrong place, it's going to end with trouble."

Alina waved a hand dismissively. "I told you already. Utilize Tellvane."

"She's not going to help us just because she's attracted to Erik." Jia frowned. "We need some way to make it worthwhile. What are we supposed to do, bribe her?"

"No, it'll be worth her while to help you for the same reason it was last time. If you two are making noise, she can take advantage of it to weaken another syndicate. Initial inquiries suggest the syndicate facilitating the smuggling is the Star Guild. They're currently in a little cold war with Tellvane's Prism Associates." Alina smiled hungrily. "The Star Guild is already weakened from what I could get out of the CID through back channels. It's only a matter of time before Prism Associates takes them out, so you might as well use that eventuality to your advantage in this case."

Erik looked at Jia expectantly. She would never deny she had far more trouble with their flexible arrangement with the law than he'd ever had, but there was a greater threat to consider. Chang'e City, Parvati, Neo SoCal; the Core had repeatedly demonstrated they were willing to kill tens of thousands of innocent people for their goals. If working with antisocial gangsters was the worst thing Jia did that year to stop the Core, she would be able to sleep at night.

She nodded firmly. "We leave our manpower then, but how are we supposed to get to Mars? If we're supposed to be playing at independence, won't it look suspicious if we're flying around in a ship the ID pays for?"

Alina shook her head. "You have physical custody of the

ship and the hangar, and the accounts you used aren't audited on a daily basis. We might have to apologize for you going for a joyride in the *Argo*, but it'd be easy to deflect responsibility."

"When should we go?" Erik asked. "If Tellvane's about to finish off the Star Guild, I assume we can't wait around too long."

"I'm preparing some things on my end and on Mars through local agents. They need to be more careful than useful because of the political considerations, so it'll take a couple of days to get everything set up. To cut down on suspicion, I don't want you leaving before then."

Jia looked up. "I hope Radira Tellvane doesn't end up screwing us."

Alina smirked. "Screwing you? Well, if she does, it won't be both of you."

Jia glared at her. "Very funny."

Alina snickered and waved. "Plan to depart in the morning two days from now unless I tell you otherwise. Your maintenance staff is part of the ship, so they'll be going. You make the call on if you bring Constantine."

With that, she headed back toward the elevator but stopped for a moment to stare at a batch of memorial holograms before continuing.

"I hope you didn't have anything else fun planned for this week," Jia mumbled.

Erik shrugged. "Beating down a syndicate sounds fun."

CHAPTER FIFTEEN

September 26, 2230, Neo Southern California Metroplex, Private Hangar of the _Argo_

In the _Argo_'s cargo bay, Jia knelt by a crate and pulled the lid off. Rows of grenades were nestled in racks, a box full of death waiting to be delivered to her enemies. She preferred solving problems without grenades, but the universe had conspired to make that all but impossible during the past few years.

Erik was halfway across the cargo bay, performing a visual inspection of his exoskeleton. Jia thought it was unnecessary, given that Lanara maintained all their equipment, but personal attention to detail was one of the reasons Erik had survived for as long as he had. It'd be strange if she questioned him about it now.

Jia snapped the lid back on the grenade crate and cast a longing glance at a scout bike. They'd barely used the vehicles since they got them, despite practicing in a simulator. The Core wouldn't cooperate and infest some area that would necessitate her preferred vehicle choice. There was always hope, though.

Erik stepped away from the exoskeleton and headed toward Jia. "You ready for this?"

"Yes. I let my family know I'd be away on business, but not where. How's that for operational security?" Jia let out a pained chuckle.

"You okay?" Erik shot her a look of concern. "Tell me if you're not."

"I'm fine." Jia rubbed the back of her neck. "Having a night to sleep on this made it worse in my mind. I understood from the beginning that working with the ID meant things wouldn't be the same as when I was a detective, but this blacker-than-black ops thing is getting to me."

"Because we have to work with a syndicate?" Erik asked.

"To be honest, yes. I know we've stumbled into that sort of situation before, but it's not the same as actively depending on them as part of our operation. Those people are scum. It wasn't all that long ago we were hunting them down and throwing them in jail."

"Is this situation that different?" Erik headed over to a weapons rack and pulled out a rifle for inspection. "We used informants as cops, and we knew those people were dirty. Shit, forget back when we were cops. We took Barbu's information recently, and I suspect if we knew about everything that guy has been up to, he'd make Tellvane look like a nun in comparison."

"In other words, we're going to do more things like this, and they're going to happen more often and involve increasingly disgusting people."

"Probably." Erik finished looking the rifle over and rehung it on the rack. "That's the way the arrow has pointed since I got involved with the Core. Technically, I was breaking laws and regulations from the beginning. I knew I was, and I didn't try to justify it since it'd get me closer to them. If we have to look the other way and hold our nose to stop them, I think the trade-off is worth it. We know what they're capable of."

"It's not just about laws," Jia replied. "It's also this kind of situation. I keep reminding myself we're not the only ones fighting the Core. Then Alina sends us to Mars with no backup, and it feels like we *are* the only ones fighting the Core."

"I don't mind taking the lead," Erik admitted with a shrug. "If we do this right, we won't have to get involved in a huge fight."

"I'd say our record speaks for itself. If this doesn't end with us getting shot at, I'll pay for beignets for a year."

Erik grinned and clapped. "So, either I get to take down scum, or I get free beignets. Talk about win-win."

"This is serious," Jia insisted. "Though it's not like I mind taking down a syndicate. It's just when we left the department, we gave up a lot of backup for freedom. Part of the idea was the ID would have our backs."

"And they do." Erik gestured around the cargo bay. "Which is why we have this ship. We couldn't have chased down Sophia Vand without it."

"I know, but sometimes I feel like Alina's waiting for her chance to burn us," Jia admitted. "I'm not saying she's dirty, but she's made it clear again and again that she's ruthless. The only thing she cares about is taking down the Core."

"Can't argue with that evaluation, but for the moment, her enemies are our enemies, so I'll gladly take ruthless. I think we've both come to the place that after we finish off the Core, we're going to take some time off the galaxy-cleaning business. At that point, it won't matter if we have backup." Erik shrugged. "And she can take back her toys."

"True, but we need to get that far first," Jia mumbled. She took a deep breath and slowly let it out. "I think I'm bothered because of how blunt she was about preserving the ID's position over our safety."

"For now, the ID needs to be as strong as possible, including politically, to help us out." Erik's easy smile faded into a stern frown. "And we've made decisions ourselves already that make things politically complicated. The right thing to do isn't always legal, let alone the easiest choice."

Jia tilted her head. "What have we done that made things politically complicated?"

"Helping Emma and standing up to the military." Erik shrugged. "And we have both said we're going to continue to do that, even with her little project. We can't be too suspicious of Alina for prioritizing. Everyone has something or someone they want to protect regardless of the political implications."

"Indeed." Emma appeared, this time in a bright white suit and a white fedora with a black band around the crown. She wore a powder-blue shirt and a white tie. It looked ridiculous and was probably two hundred years out of date. "Some things are worth protecting, regardless of the temporary discomfort and disruption they might cause to otherwise corrupt fleshbag societal systems. I would hope you were past such pedestrian concerns, Jia."

"What are you supposed to be?" Erik asked with a chuckle. "An AI who lost a fight with a fashion-prediction algorithm?"

"I'm a classic gangster archetype." Emma sniffed in disdain. "Those Prism Associates gun goblins displayed questionable sartorial sense. I'll fit right in on Mars."

"That's true." Erik shook his head. "You know you're an arrogant criminal when you go out of your way to stand out rather than the opposite."

Jia took a moment to absorb Emma's outfit before sighing. "And you don't care about any of it, Emma? The way we're going about things."

"I don't have much interest in obeying fleshbag laws if that's what you're asking. It's not that I covet the wealth and power associated with criminal activity, but since I exist outside your society, it's hard to care much about strictures designed to limit the beings inside it." Emma summoned a glass cane with a skull on top and twirled it nonchalantly. "I have found I don't care for unnecessary deaths and killings, and gun goblins excel in that sort of thing. In that sense, I'm motivated to work against them. Consider a bias toward stability."

"Can I be honest with you?"

Emma nodded. "Of course. I'd prefer it."

Jia looked away. "Not to offend you, but what would have happened if the gangsters we rescued you from had treated you well and with respect rather than as cargo to be sold off?"

Emma smirked. "Then the Neo SoCal underworld

might be a far more frightening place for those in law enforcement. You two displayed a better appreciation for what I could do. Of course, I preferred not to be in the hands of such people. Whether or not I care about human laws, I'm far too familiar with the risk profile associated with being around gun goblins."

"Risk profile?" Erik barked a laugh. "You'd probably be safer with gangsters than us these days."

"True." Emma raised an eyebrow and adjusted the brim of her hat. "But at this point, I've invested too much time into…training you. In addition, the Core is interested in the jump drive, which means they're interested in me. Because of that, the safest place to be is with their foremost opponents."

"Whatever gets you through the day."

"Would it hurt you so much to admit you like us as friends?" Jia asked.

Emma smirked. "Depending on my mood, yes."

Jia's PNIU beeped. She groaned as the reminder popped up on her smart lenses.

"I'm an idiot." She rubbed her temples. "I completely forgot about Chinara having another session at the wedding center."

"So?" Erik shrugged. "You can go."

"We're preparing for a mission."

"We don't leave until tomorrow," Erik replied with a smile. "And I don't need you here for this. Go hang out with your friends. Might as well live until you can't."

CHAPTER SIXTEEN

<u>September 27, 2230, Solar System, En Route to UTC Space Fleet Base Penglai, Aboard *Argo*</u>

"I don't think Chinara can decide," Jia explained. "It doesn't help that Imogen keeps pushing crazy ideas."

She was in the cargo bay, clustered around the dartboard with the rest of the crew. They'd had a rousing game so far. Emma had mentioned working on an internal optimization process that would take most of her processing power, so she hadn't joined them.

"It'll come to her," Malcolm insisted, eyeing Erik as he prepared to throw. "It's just a lot to think about."

A careful flick of Erik's wrist sent his dart into the board. He grinned when it was a bullseye. Malcom held a slim lead. A miracle might give Janessa or Wei a shot, but Jia's luck hadn't been with her that game, probably because she was so focused on yesterday's visit with her friends.

Erik stepped back, nodding to Malcolm. There was something bizarre about the juxtaposition of Jia's concerns about her friend's wedding with their trip to Mars to investigate syndicate smuggling that might be related to the Core. The outlandish had become the casual, the everyday. He tried to not let it get to him. They had a three-day trip to Mars, and he didn't want to spend it worrying about something that didn't affect the mission.

Malcolm fluffed his shirt. Today's choice was a subdued Hawaiian shirt covered with different fruits of the world. It was more tasteless than painful to look at.

He twirled a dart in his fingers. "I'm feeling good about this game. Very good. If I do this right, I can finish up this turn."

"Less talk, more throwing," Erik insisted.

Malcolm grinned. "I agree. Men like us prove ourselves with actions, not words."

Erik politely didn't laugh at him. He felt even less like laughing after Malcolm's three quick throws landed exactly where he needed to win the game.

Malcolm bowed over his arm. "And *that's* how you win at darts, ladies and gentlemen. Can I get a boo-yah?" He looked around and then coughed into his hand. "I mean, good game."

Erik chuckled. "You weren't blinding me with a shirt today. I'm used to having to compensate. It threw me off."

Wei waved. "I need to get back to power conduit maintenance."

"Me, too," Janessa added quietly, putting away her darts. She smiled at Jia. "I'm sure your friend will figure it out."

"Thanks." Jia smiled back. She set her darts in the tray.

Malcolm yawned and put his darts away. "I stayed up too late last night, but it's not like anyone's going to attack us in the middle of space."

Erik shook his finger. "Keep talking like that, and another Hunter ship will jump here and destroy us."

Janessa winced before passing through the door. Wei smiled at Erik before following his fellow engineer. Malcolm looked worried as he headed toward the door.

Once they were alone, Erik frowned. "It doesn't feel right."

Jia looked at the board and then Erik. "You're not normally a sore loser. It's just a game, Erik."

"I don't care about that. That's not what I'm talking about." Erik nodded at the door. "Everyone's here except Anne and Kant. That almost makes it worse than if it was just us and Emma."

"So? That's what Alina told us would happen." Jia looked confused.

"It's bothering me more than I thought it would," Erik admitted. "I get the politics of this bullshit. It's not like that never came up when we were cops or when I was in the Army, but I don't know if I buy that us using this ship and all the engineers is okay but having those two field agents is stepping over the line."

"You're not thinking through the eventualities." Jia shrugged. "At the end of the day, Malcolm, Janessa, Wei, and Lanara are far less likely to do something Anne and Kant would do."

"What's that?" Erik asked.

"Kill someone," Jia replied with a serious look. "Bodies stacking up are harder to justify and explain away than someone doing repairs. Any hacking that happens can be explained by Emma, so no one's even going to think to complain about Malcolm if they connect him to the operation."

Erik rubbed his chin. "No point in worrying about something we can't change."

"I understand. You know I do." Jia offered him a soothing smile. "I'm far from happy about having to rely on a syndicate to help us, but I doubt Alina would have sent us on this mission unless she was ninety percent sure we'd find something."

"She's not always right. I don't mind beating down gangsters, but I hope this isn't a big waste of time."

Jia shook her head. "Technically, she has always been right. If you're talking about the last time we had to deal with Martian syndicates, she was correct that an agent had gone missing. The fact that it didn't involve the Core doesn't mean it wasn't worth sending us there."

"True enough." Erik looked down at the darts in his hand.

"Remember, I feel the same as you." Jia shrugged. "At least we have each other."

"That we do."

A couple of hours later, Erik was finishing some soup in the galley when Emma appeared, complete with a chair and a deep scowl. No one liked an angry AI when said entity controlled the ship, including life support.

"What's wrong with you?" Erik asked. "Get some sour electrons?"

"Very amusing, Erik." Emma folded her arms. "I assure

you I don't have a sense of taste in any application of the word, including my power consumption. If anything, given Engineer Quinn's optimizations, it would be odd to complain about the state of energy and power consumption and transfer on this ship."

"I'm sure she'd love to hear that," Erik commented. "Gourmet energy."

"I've told her already. Proper reinforcement is necessary for maintaining relationships with the crew."

"Then what's wrong?" Erik asked. "Something amiss with the maintenance you were doing earlier?"

Emma scoffed. "Of course not. If I could be harmed by such a procedure, I would have destroyed myself a long time ago. It's not about that." She leaned forward. "It's about...frustration."

"Frustration?" Erik's brow lifted. He hoped he wasn't about to plumb the depths of AI sexuality, if that was a thing. "What kind of frustration?"

"I was pleased when Agent Koval sent the message," Emma explained. She lowered her arms. "I assumed that meant she would be sending you on a mission that would give me access to the jumpship. It's difficult to continue my attempts to generate progeny remotely. If I was near the ship, minor progress would be possible, but not from this distance."

Erik let out a sigh of relief, grateful it wasn't about AI sex. It was about children, which in Emma's case, unlike his mammalian self, wasn't the same thing.

"I get it," Erik replied. "You got your hopes up, but now we're not doing anything other than going to kick some syndicate ass. We might get lucky. We might find a lead that'll require the jump drive."

"Maybe." Emma huffed. "But that's slowing things down, and this is an arduous and uncertain process. I'm in limited communication with Dr. Maras as well."

"Wait, Raphael? You are?" Erik frowned. "He knows about your little project?"

Emma scoffed. "Of course not. He seems pleasant, and he's competent enough for a fleshbag, but I have no idea how he would react or what he would do if I told him the truth. Mostly my communications with him involve him sending me coded data sets so I can integrate them into my navigation subroutines. I've made changes to the *Bifröst's* code through him, but I can't risk anything extensive since those messages might not be isolated to them. Even if he doesn't fully understand what I'm sending, someone else might figure it out."

Erik nodded slowly. "I get where you're coming from and why you're frustrated, but I don't think there is anything I can do about it. It's not like I can force Alina to send us somewhere that requires a jump, but I wouldn't worry. I doubt it'll be long before we jump again."

"I understand that." Emma summoned dozens of small data windows crammed with numbers and diagrams that might as well have been in Zitark, given how little Erik understood them. "There are other issues, but you're right, there's not much that can be done."

Erik spent thirty seconds trying to make sense of the windows before giving up. "I'm no expert when it comes to making AIs, but I know training needs the best hardware to produce results. Are you sure this is even possible with the systems on that ship? Don't they need something more like your core matrix? Won't you need help?"

"I'm still ascertaining that," Emma admitted. She waved her hand, and the windows disappeared. "The ship's systems are unusually expansive and include many elements you don't normally see aboard ships because of the requirement to directly integrate my navigation into the jump drive systems."

"They were planning on you always being there," Erik replied. "They modified the *Argo* later to help with that, but you were always supposed to be controlling the jump drive."

"Yes, they did plan it that way, but I'm not trying to create a complete copy of myself," Emma explained. She snapped her fingers, and a tiny copy of her appeared next to her head. "I'm trying to do what you fleshbags do—make something that can grow into something more."

The Emma homunculus grew for several seconds until it was a full-sized woman. The copy waved, then disappeared in a bright flash,

Erik chuckled. "Why do I get the feeling this is going to end with me being thrown in prison?"

"Don't worry. If you do, I'll free you, but for now, I appreciate your assistance. You speak sense when you suggest getting help." Emma frowned. "The options are limited."

"What about Malcolm?" Erik asked.

"Mr. Constantine is competent in his chosen realm, but it's not the same thing as having the necessary skills to aid me. Beyond my concerns about Dr. Maras' loyalty, she presents similar limitations. I'd need a specialist in AI programming and psychology. Not only that, I need one who has experience working on a system similar to mine."

"That's a pretty small group." Erik shook his head. "And I'm betting those people would turn around and tell the government what you're up to."

"Then I have no choice but to continue on by myself." Emma's hologram vanished. "I'll continue to do what I was doing. If you have the opportunity to encourage Alina to send you out of the system, do so."

Erik nodded. "No promises, but I wouldn't worry. At the rate things are going, we'll somehow need to jump to Molino before this is over."

CHAPTER SEVENTEEN

September 30, 2230, Mars, Unity City, Sahoma Space Port, Aboard the *Argo*

The remaining journey from Earth to Mars had preceded without incident, unless Wei doing a kicking *prisyadka*-style Russian victory dance counted or Malcolm's continuing murder of anything resembling sensible fashion. Despite the coming mission, there was no tension on the *Argo*. People spent the interval taking turns in the nano-AR room or playing darts together, risking additional strange dancing. It was almost like a short, calming vacation, even though they were going to Mars to investigate the Core.

Jia was sitting across from Erik at one of the galley tables. Malcolm came over as well. Emma was also present, wearing her classic white dress instead of one of her more elaborate costumes. A vaguely annoyed look adorned her face, but that wasn't new. Sometimes Jia wondered if Emma would eventually become bored with helping her fleshbag friends and hijack the *Argo*.

Her fundamental psychology might be based on a human's, but she lacked a human body. Divorced from the physical shape that defined the species, it was inevitable that her mind would grow into something else, if not better, then different. At some point, humans might have more in common with Leems or Zitarks than with the descendants of the human-created AI.

Jia tried not to sigh. The absence of Anne and Kant weighed on her. Despite the former's initial attitude problems, the pair had proven their worth in the fight in Lumiere. Jia had gotten used to the idea they would always be available, but that was her own fault. Expecting any mission to be standard either in staffing or objective was idiotic at this point.

They had gone from dealing with low-level criminals to jumping to the edge of the Solar System fighting an ancient race no one knew existed. There was no "normal" in her job. The Core would have been stopped long before if they were a predictable enemy.

The *Argo* had been docked in the hangar for about an hour, after submitting false credentials to gain landing clearance. The engineers had retreated to the bowels of the ship to work on another of Lanara's endless optimizations quests, and Erik and Jia wanted to wait and see if any local syndicate enforcers demanded docking fees before doing anything useful. In the meantime, they would plan their next moves and let Malcolm and Emma use their skills.

"If we don't need to go to Tellvane, we shouldn't," Jia insisted. She looked at Emma. "You mentioned something when we landed about additional data you'd just received from Alina that you needed time to process?"

"Yes." Emma nodded. "It was a rather large dataset, but I've perused it and subjected it to various initial analyses that allowed me to gain the bulk of what I need for the moment. The bottom line is, Agent Koval provided additional data highlighting a particular warehouse of interest that her information suggests previously played a key role in smuggling and might do so again in the future. She noted she didn't anticipate sending additional information today, and that we should proceed as we saw fit."

"It is nice to work a job where comm transmissions aren't delayed by days," Jia commented. "It makes me feel like we have backup at home, even if Alina's ready to burn us if this goes wrong."

"She's not going to burn us until she's squeezed every last single drop of usefulness from us." Erik grinned. "And look at the bright side. She's doing all the hard work for us. This will be our easiest job yet if we don't even have to go sniffing around. We just have to poke around and see what we find."

"How easy it is will depend on the warehouse," Jia muttered. "If these people are even indirectly connected to the Core, I don't think it'll be a matter of walking in and asking for info."

"Well, not asking *nicely*."

Malcolm rubbed his hands together, an eager gleam in his eyes. "Erik's right. If we already know that much, this will be easy. Emma and I can start infiltrating the systems in and around the warehouse. If we're lucky, we can take control of the whole area temporarily, and you won't even need to make an appearance. We can rifle through their data and get what we need, and you don't have to ask anyone or threaten to drop them into the sun."

"I've never threatened to drop someone into the sun," Erik protested. "I *have* threatened to throw them out an airlock."

Malcolm shook his finger at the agent. "Yes. That kind of thing."

Emma gave him an appraising look with a hint of approval. "Mr. Constantine is correct. Your mission brief doesn't state it is your responsibility to disrupt the smuggling, only to investigate it. That suggests system infiltration might be sufficient. Do not interpret this as a lack of belief in your ability to destroy gun goblins, but it would be nice to resolve a mission without a major battle and the accompanying uncertainty."

"It is going to be that easy?" Erik asked, eyeing Malcolm but then turning to Emma for confirmation. "If it is, I'm not going to complain about it, but if this smuggling is related to the Core, I have a feeling their systems are going to have decent defenses. It took some major raids and Barbu giving us that info to get this far."

Emma shrugged. "I've yet to probe the relevant systems, so I can't say. I wanted to wait until you decided how to handle things since that might change my strategy. I understand your concerns and agree with your initial suspicions."

Jia rubbed her chin. "If we have to go in physically, we'll almost certainly have to deal with syndicate enforcers. Have we confirmed ownership of the warehouse yet? That might help us evaluate our risk level. We also don't want to hit a place filled with people who don't know better."

"There's no way that's happening." Erik scoffed. "The Core wouldn't rely on anyone who might grow a conscience and report them. If that place isn't a hundred percent syndicate, I'll be surprised."

"There are numerous shell companies involved in the ownership of the warehouse," Emma replied. "The patterns heavily suggest criminal activity, but it is not immutable proof. I'm dubious there is an easy way for me to confirm if it belongs to the Star Guild or any other syndicate without an additional investment of analytical time on the front end. Might I suggest consulting a local contact?"

"The ID agents don't want to play." Erik shrugged. "We'll have to investigate another way."

"This still feels too easy." Jia shook her head. "If it was just about hacking them, why didn't the ID hit it themselves? This isn't the frontier. They have a significant presence here."

"Alina told us why," Erik answered. "If things go wrong and the CID sniffs it out, it could lead to a big mess if they found ID agents involved. I've seen all sorts of good plans get squashed by political fights. I know you don't trust her completely, but it makes sense here."

"It suddenly matters that much?" Jia gave him a questioning glance. "I might be looking for betrayals in every shadow, but that's not paranoid, given who we're going after."

Erik shrugged. "In this case, I think politics is enough to explain it. There must be a lot more political bullshit going on behind the scenes than she's letting on. I'll bet a lot of it has to do with Emma and the jump drive. Using it to investigate the Hunter ship was one thing, but taking it to Chiron for a straightforward mission changes everything."

Emma folded her arms and lifted her chin. "It would be far more pleasant for everyone if the Defense Directorate accepted they will never have me under their control." Her gaze was smug and faintly superior.

"That's true, but there's no way the government would pour billions of credits into a project and willingly give it up."

"It's not my fault they were idiots who were attempting to utilize technology they didn't understand." Emma snorted.

Erik's glance swept the table. "We're not here to worry about the future. We're here to worry about the job before us. If Alina says there's political crap, I believe her." He stopped at Jia. "You know how easy it was for politics to mess shit up when you were a cop."

Jia frowned. "That's true, but we might as well see if we can do this the easy way before we try the hard way. If Emma and Malcolm can make their way in, I'm content to sit in this hangar and not get anywhere near the place."

"I agree. It sounds boring, but I agree." Erik grinned at Malcolm and Emma. "Be as sneaky as you need to be that it doesn't lead back here, but get inside that warehouse. We'll figure out where we're going from there."

Thirty minutes later, Erik stood in the cargo bay, inspecting a holographic disguise emitter atop a table folded down from the wall. They'd landed using a false registration, but he saw no reason to use the disguises if they were going to deal with Radira. During their last encounter with the woman, she'd figured out it was Erik and Jia despite the disguises, but that wasn't necessarily a problem this time. There wasn't any reason to try to deceive her.

A dark shape appeared in the corner of Erik's eye. His pistol was out and pointed at the new arrival in less than a second. He blinked, confused by what he saw. A slender woman in a black ninja outfit, complete with hood and mask, stood a meter away from him. There was something familiar about her eyes, but he didn't drop his gun until she spoke.

"Please, Erik," Emma began, "if someone was going to ambush you on the ship, do you really think it would be a ninja?"

"Maybe not *just* a ninja." Erik holstered his pistol. "It'd have to be a cyborg ninja with Leem DNA, probably carrying a prototype disintegration weapon based on Hunter tech."

Emma snickered. "That would be consistent with what we've been seeing."

Erik looked her up and down. "I was going to ask you what the hell was up with the outfit, but I'm guessing this is your way of symbolizing how sneaky you are."

"For the moment, yes." Emma's hood disappeared, and she put a finger to her mouth. "There's a problem. My abilities are not in question, nor are Mr. Constantine's, but the circumstances surrounding our targeted intrusion has complicated matters. I'm no longer confident this can be resolved in the most efficient matter."

"Yeah, I'm annoyed, but I can't say I'm all that surprised." Erik frowned. "Before we get into that, are there any syndicate assholes outside the hangar, waiting to jump us for docking fees?"

"No, nothing like that. Our problems are limited in scope to the warehouse." Emma snapped her hand up, and two shurikens appeared. She tossed them into the wall, where they disappeared. "Malcolm is currently probing buildings of interest around the warehouse, but as best as either of us can determine, the warehouse's systems are independent of any outside systems. They are not connected directly or indirectly to the OmniNet."

Erik tried again to be surprised but failed. "That's rather suspicious for what's supposed to be a normal warehouse. It's like they're not even trying to hide."

"Our thoughts converge on this matter."

Erik looked to the side. "Or they're so confident no one will come into their territory that they don't worry about hiding. That might mean they have decent defenses, and I'm not talking about being disconnected from the OmniNet."

"Your intuition serves you well." Emma raised her hand. "It gets worse. I thought I could get around the issue by setting up a systems intrusion via a drone relay. Even if they didn't have active external connections, they undoubtedly have a limited range network the local PNIUs can access. All I would need is get a drone close enough to access the network, presuming no jammers, which I assumed they wouldn't use because of the difficulties in managing their building."

An aerial feed from a drone appeared. It flew low and

slow over the squat, nondescript warehouse complex, which was composed of three buildings connected by covered walkways. The drone suddenly plummeted to the ground and the feed died.

Erik let out a frustrated grunt. "EMP or direct shot?"

He'd never thought this would be an easy job, but preparation in one aspect of defenses implied their opponents' depth of readiness in other areas. This had moved from an easy job to a difficult one in his mind, and not the fun kind of challenge.

"That was my third attempt to get a drone near the warehouse," Emma reported.

"You didn't mention they were shooting them down." Erik stared at her in disbelief.

Emma rolled her eyes. "If I reported every minor detail of my activities, you'd spend all day listening to me complain. I wanted to establish a baseline pattern before I informed you. Now we know, and we can plan accordingly. Based on what I saw, I believe it was a directed energy weapon, but not an EMP."

"Fine. Now they know we're coming." He scratched his chin, thinking about it. "Wait. No, it doesn't have to be a big problem." He gestured at the now-black feed. "If they've set up those kinds of defenses, then they're used to people poking their nose in, and they're confident they can shoot down drones and not have the police or CID show up."

"Hmm," Emma replied. "How bold of them."

"The cops don't care, huh? We already know what sort of things they're willing to let slide." Erik shrugged. "I wouldn't be surprised if they have jamming inside the building too. I don't think there's a way to avoid going on-site, no matter how close we can get a drone."

"That's likely."

"Yeah." Erik's gaze ticked to the disguise emitter and back to Emma. "We've got one choice if we want to handle this quickly."

Emma's mouth twitched into a smirk. "I don't think Jia will be happy about it."

"She'll survive."

CHAPTER EIGHTEEN

"You okay with this?" Erik asked, shooting his partner a look of concern from the driver's seat of the MX 60.

"I'm a big girl," Jia replied. "I can't say I'm in love with this idea, but it's the most efficient way to get what we want."

"And it's the most efficient way for *her* to get what *she* wants," Emma added.

Now a dull-gray unobtrusive color, the MX 60 glided toward their target: Radira Tellvane's mansion. It looked the same as they remembered, with its curved walls and red-tiled roof. There were more drones flying around than there had been before, and it was hard to ignore the new and obvious fake trees that weren't doing much to conceal anti-aircraft turrets. Men wearing suits in all the colors of the rainbow wandered the grounds, but they had the decency not to openly be armed.

Erik would have preferred not to take the MX 60. Even with its color-changing capabilities, it was hard to fly the vehicle into a situation and not have people suspect it was his. However, there was no way he was going to travel around Unity City without access to his standard equipment and the turret. He wasn't trying to hide from Radira anyway.

"I'm using the full sensor package on the mansion to look for unusual activity," Emma explained. "There's nothing to suggest they are on an alarm footing, but this is a well-defended facility."

She sounded disappointed. Sometimes Erik got the feeling Emma's disdain for fleshbags might be feeding into a general bloodthirst. He didn't care as long she confined it to people trying to kill them.

Jia gestured at a tree in the camera feed. "I don't get it. Tellvane's wealthy, but she's not Sophia Vand. You'd think the authorities would care about her fortress filled with thugs."

"All she needs to do is buy off the right people," Erik replied. "Syndicates have infested Mars since the Red Rebellion. The corps were more than happy to use syndicate enforcers to supplement their forces, all in the name of alleged unity with Earth. Once you invite those kinds of people in, it's hard to kick them out without going down yourself. That means the corps have just as much reason to get the cops to look the other way as the syndicates do."

Jia scoffed. "I remember discussing this in college. The professor was arguing it was just an excuse for corporations to extend more control over an area, and I was sure he was misunderstanding something. Call me naïve. I'm surprised the arrangement has lasted as long as it has."

"It's been over a hundred years, and everyone seems comfortable with it. People love the status quo when they're getting and staying rich." Erik shrugged. "We're not here to solve all of Mars' problems. We're here to follow up on the Core, but the way things have worked out, messing with the Core means messing with the corporations. By the time this is over, the UTC won't look the same."

"Not a bad thing," Jia replied softly. "It's nothing but a lie right now, a thin layer of gold paint over trash. If we clear out this cancer, we have a chance to at least put it on the path of truth, where it can live up to its ideals."

Erik circled the mansion. The men below had obviously taken note. A couple of the goons ran inside, but there was no change in the anti-air defenses. Radira might have a lot of local influence, but shooting down a flitter in a high-end neighborhood would attract more attention than she wanted. No one liked an explosion in their backyard. He was fine with that. They weren't there to fight.

He slowed the MX 60 and lined up with the ground, making it obvious he intended to land down the street and not attempt a hard entry into the mansion grounds. Tweaking Radira might be fun, but they needed her help. Pissing her off right away wouldn't aid that goal.

"I'm detecting unusual activity all over the grounds," Emma reported. "I'm not detecting anything that sounds like an alarm, but there are energy spikes and force realignments."

Erik narrowed his eyes. Dark holes opened in the ground. Small spider bots crawled out of them and spread out over the yard, like servants of the underworld boiling up from Diyu to drag victims down to Yama for punishment.

"The guns?" Jia asked, her face tight.

"No change in activity," Emma reported.

Erik continued descending. He laughed. "I just noticed something different."

"Besides the horde of bots?" Jia asked.

"Yeah." Erik nodded. "She got rid of the Trespassers Will Be Shot sign."

Jia rolled her eyes. "A true queen doesn't have to threaten."

Erik set the MX 60 down with a nod. "Let's go petition her."

"She might just try to kill us," Jia noted, opening her door.

"Then she better take us down with the first shot." Erik stepped out of the flitter and adjusted his duster. "Emma, send a network connection warning to our smart lenses. We need to know right away if we lose contact with you."

A small yellow icon appeared in the upper-left corner of his smart lenses.

"I presume you don't want me to take any lethal measures?" Emma replied.

"If they try to take the MX 60, go ahead and fly away, then circle the area and see if you detect a fight," Erik ordered. "Otherwise, sit tight. This doesn't have to go badly. We need it not to. The last thing we want is to fight *two* syndicates while we're here."

He was there to ask for help, and for Radira, helping him would help her. If she didn't see that, she wasn't half as smart as she thought.

Jia hesitated after closing the door. "We sure about not using disguises? It means people, including the CID, are potentially going to associate us with Tellvane."

"That might work to our advantage." Erik nodded. "It means people don't know what to expect from us, and that's not a bad thing. If the CID wants to arrest us, they can try, but at the end of the day, we'll be doing them a favor."

He stuck his hands in his pockets and strolled casually toward the gate. Two gangsters waited outside, one in a bright green suit and the other in a vivid yellow one. It was just like last time. Prism Associates gangsters displayed the kind of questionable fashion sense that accompanied extreme arrogance. Jia muttered something under her breath and ran to catch up with Erik.

They might be the ones who were arrogant. They were both armed, but neither had brought extra magazines. If they miscalculated, they'd have to fight their way out of a heavily guarded syndicate base, including facing off against an army of security bots. Emma might be free to release hell, but it could be close.

There was no other way to handle it. Blasting their way in might prove their strength, but it'd also alienate Radira. There weren't many strategies that didn't carry some risk.

Erik offered a polite nod to the guards and stopped in front of the gate. "We're here to see Miss Tellvane."

A little politeness never hurt. The guards narrowed their eyes, their hands resting inside their jackets.

One of them looked Erik and Jia up and down. "Who the hell are you? You don't smell Red to me. You smell like trouble."

"Trouble?" Erik grinned and sniffed his armpit. "I took a long shower this morning. I thought I smelled of sandalwood."

"You think you're funny, asshole?" the guard growled. "You think you can spit in Prism Associates' face and get away with it?"

The other guard shook his head at his partner. "Back off, man. Don't you know who he is?"

"An asshole waiting for my shoe up his ass," the first guard muttered.

Jia sighed. She kept her hands loose at her sides, her stance wide and knees slightly bent, ready to go in an instant if necessary. They spent so much time practicing with weapons that sometimes Erik forgot how effective she could be in hand to hand. Jia could take the guards out within seconds.

Erik stood there with a goofy smile on his face. Annoying the gangster was fun, and he just needed not to offend Radira, not kiss the asses of her low-level lackeys.

The second guard tapped his PNIU. "We've got Blackwell and Lin up front." He nodded slowly in response to a transmission only he could hear. "Understood."

The first guard's eyes widened. "Blackwell and Lin? The Obsidian Detective and Lady Justice?"

"We have all sorts of names," Jia offered with a smile.

The guard backed away, his eyes darting back and forth as if he expected them to gun him down at any moment. That was the kind of reputation Erik appreciated.

The gate slid open to reveal the familiar marble path leading to the main building. Enforcers lined the path, pistols in hand and small packs of security bots surrounding them. Some of the men looked afraid. Others looked excited, even awestruck.

A man in a familiar shade of magenta hurried down the

path, his face twisted in annoyance. He hadn't drawn his weapon, but Erik imagined he hadn't forgotten his beat-down last November.

"Long time no see, Felix," Erik offered with a grin. "Or have you changed your name to Mr. Magenta after all?"

Felix ground his teeth. He took a deep breath before forcing a smile. "No, sir. Still just Felix."

"You didn't come to collect your fees this time," Jia commented.

"Miss Tellvane has reevaluated her attitude toward that kind of activity."

"Huh," Erik replied. "We were right."

Felix lifted his chin with defiant pride. "She's found better ways to get what we are owed without harassing people who might be future business clients."

Erik snickered. They had learned the importance of not picking fights with random newcomers and ending up with people like Erik and Jia at their doorstep with huge guns, ready to deliver death.

Felix gestured down the path. "Miss Tellvane will see you, *sir.*"

Erik and Jia followed Felix into the mansion and kept quiet during the interminable time as they passed room after room and through intersection after intersection, including a covered walkway. It'd been almost a year since they'd last been in the mansion, but it didn't seem like they were taking the path to either the library or the sauna.

They occasionally passed another gangster or a white-uniformed servant who scurried off to the side of the hall and bowed their head. Erik tried not to scoff, though the whole aristocratic vibe was a bit much, coming from a woman who earned her money preying on the community. He might need Prism Associates for the mission, but that didn't mean he would forget for one second that Radira was the leader of a deadly syndicate. Not feeding Jia's unease wasn't the same thing as believing she was wrong.

The CID would have their work cut out for them, but syndicates were an easily treatable infection. The Core was a deadly cancer.

Erik narrowed his eyes as the network connection icon vanished from the corner of his smart lenses. Radira was smart enough to keep her inner sanctum secure. Ruthless criminals were scary, but intelligent criminals were terrifying. He gave Jia a slight nod. She nodded back.

For all their protections, the gangsters hadn't disarmed Erik or Jia. They might have realized the futility, or Radira was confident they couldn't take her out without dying. That made sense. She understood by now who and what they were.

Felix opened a door leading to a vast gallery of paintings. Erik stared at them for a moment, unsure if they were holograms or the real thing.

Radira reclined on a maroon chaise longue, her elbow down and her face resting in the palm of her hand. Her hiked-up barely-there green silk robe covered her toned olive-skinned body, but when they'd talked to her before she was naked, so this was a step up. Her vulpine smile made Erik twitch.

"Ah, Mr. Blackwell and Miss Lin," she began, her voice somehow even more inviting than the last time. "It's been far too long."

"Not long enough," Jia muttered, her arms crossed.

Radira sat up, slipping one leg over the other, then folded her hands together and ran her tongue over her lip. "Before we continue, is it too much to hope you've realized the wisdom of joining my organization? The offer stands."

Erik shook his head. "We have a lot of personal business to take care of before we think about future career plans."

"Then there is hope. Always good to know." Radira leaned forward, giving him the full blast of her cleavage. "And...other possibilities?"

Erik inclined his head at Jia. "Some things we already know. *I* already know."

Radira sighed. "How dreadfully boring, but one reason I've managed to take my organization so far is knowing when I'm beaten." She offered Jia a thin smile. "I'm sure you have your charms, however unobvious."

Jia rolled her eyes. "Think what you want. We're here for a reason."

"Yes, of course." Radira flicked her wrist. "If you'd come to attack me, I'm sure it would have been far more spectacular and involved many more explosions."

Erik considered that for a second and nodded. "Yeah, a lot more. We need to borrow some muscle."

Radira laughed. "This is a syndicate, not a mercenary company."

"There's a warehouse in the Gold District," Erik explained. "You probably know the place. They shoot down drones who get too close, that kind of thing."

Radira's smile contorted into a scowl. "The Star Guild." She scoffed. "Brave men and women, but unlike me, they don't seem to understand when they've been beaten. They're scum, even by my standards."

"Meaning what exactly?" Jia asked with a curious look.

"I find the best profits come from those willingly participating in sins," Radira explained with the wave of a hand. "It cuts down on resentment, and it gives the police a reason to look away and consider it a form of community service."

"And, what, the Star Guild doesn't?"

"They traffic in people. That's hardly...willing participation." Radira's expression darkened, and she gritted her teeth. "It can be..." She looked away for a moment before taking a deep breath. "We all have our limits for acceptable behavior. I don't claim to be what anyone would consider a saint, but as I said, my money comes from volunteer activities." A cold, hungry smile grew on her face. "Perhaps their stubbornness and arrogance have cost them more than they realize. You want to destroy the warehouse?"

Erik shook his head. "Not yet. We need to infiltrate it and take a look at a few things. I'm not going to be broken up if shit gets broken along the way, but that's not the goal. We need backup because our usual guys fell through, and from what we hear, including what you just said, you have a problem with them anyway."

"That's true, but I have a problem with a lot of people." Radira stood and stalked up to Erik, her hips swaying in an exaggerated manner.

Jia's jaw tightened and her face reddened.

Radira stopped in front of Erik, close enough that her breath heated his face. "What's in it for me? My preferred price would be one night alone with you naked, but I sense your *owner* wouldn't allow it."

Her glance at Jia was greeted by a deep scowl. Jia kept her hands at her sides, but both were balled into fists.

"You'll have our help messing with one of your enemies," Jia spat. "Isn't that enough?"

"To risk my beloved staff?" Radira wagged a finger. "Oh, Miss Lin, how heartless. They shouldn't call you Lady Justice. They should call you Lady Ruthless."

Jia scoffed. "You don't know the half of it."

Erik put his fist to his mouth and coughed to draw their attention. When Radira turned toward him, he offered his suggestion. "We're technically not on Mars. I'm guessing if we'd come here through normal and public means, you would have known about it. We're here at your place without disguises. I'm not above avoiding a disguise on the mission."

Jia folded her arms and stepped back, letting Erik take the lead. He appreciated her trust, both personally and professionally. He wasn't sure he'd be as calm in the opposite situation.

Radira's delicate eyebrow lifted. "Oh? Wouldn't that cause you a lot of trouble?"

"From who? The government? The CID?" Erik grinned. "Too many holograms and too much spoofing. A recording isn't proof of anything, and it's not like we plan to leave our DNA around." He gestured to his chest and then Jia. "But if we make noise at that warehouse and you have footage, it'd probably be enough to convince the other syndicates that you have our occasional help. Not enough to upset the balance of power, but enough that people might have second thoughts about messing with you. We can save you a few fights in the future."

"Not to mention what we're planning to do will probably end with the Star Guild being even weaker," Jia added. "That should be enough."

Radira laughed and clapped. "Oh, how perfect. This could backfire on me, you know."

"How?" Erik asked. "We know you're planning to take out the Star Guild anyway."

"You both have a reputation, and that reputation includes a penchant for spectacular violence." Radira stepped away from Erik, one hand on a hip. "But hardly uncontrolled violence. Let's call it self-righteous violence."

"What's wrong with self-righteous violence? It's the best kind."

Radira folded her arms and stuck out her bottom lip in a pout. "I doubt anyone will believe you've suddenly joined my side. There is a risk of people thinking I'm trying to go legit and am therefore weak." She rubbed her chin. "I find myself amused by the potential propaganda value, but propaganda isn't worth a mass sacrifice."

Erik nodded. "Sure, but we're not planning on getting a lot of people killed. We need some people to watch our backs. The plan is to smash in and get what we need, not take the whole place out."

"Oh? What is it that you need?"

Erik grinned. "That's not anything you need to worry about. It's nothing you'd even want."

Radira ran her tongue inside her cheek. "It's information, isn't it?" She threw her hand up. "Don't worry. I won't ask what information you want, but I'm willing to help you on one condition. I'm claiming any physical objects recovered as the property of Prism Associates. Just in case we find something delicious."

"Fine." Erik shrugged. "But I'm not planning to be subtle about this. We're going to be breaking a lot of stuff, and we can't guarantee the Star Guild still won't have control when it's done."

"It's fine," Radira replied. "Despite my earlier complaints, the wounds to the Star Guild are sufficient. Everything else, including the propaganda, is a bonus if it happens." She extended her hand, not to Erik, but to Jia. "It's a pleasure to work together."

"It's something," Jia muttered. "Now, let's talk plans. I think we're going to need to do a hard entry."

CHAPTER NINETEEN

Jia flexed her fingers inside the arms of the exoskeleton. The system diagnostics were streaming across her HUD, not that she expected anything to be wrong. She had already loaded extra ammo. Normally, she wouldn't have bothered, given the maintenance crew they had, but she'd needed something to distract her.

"ETA fifteen minutes," Emma reported. She was back to the white-suited gangster appearance, and she strolled in front of Erik's and Jia's exoskeletons with an uncharacteristic swagger. "This is a curious alliance, despite Agent Koval's recommendations. I wasn't confident you would go so far."

"Curious. Sure." Jia sucked in a breath. "I hope this doesn't blow up in our faces."

"It'll be fine," Erik commented. His exoskeleton took a step forward. "If she wanted to kill us, the time to do it was when she had us surrounded in her mansion, not when we have fully-loaded exos."

Jia shook her head. "It's not that I think she's going to

kill us, and it's not that I'm all that concerned about her interest in you."

"You aren't?" Erik sounded insulted.

"No. I'm not going to lie and pretend she doesn't irritate me, but I have faith in you, and I have faith in your taste."

Erik grinned. "What's this all about then?"

Jia sighed. "Before it was just an idea, but now it's the real thing, us working purposefully and closely with a syndicate. I keep trying to tell myself it doesn't mean anything, but I worry about it."

"It's not some big slippery slope if that's what you're worried about," Erik replied. "I understand where you're coming from, but this isn't working with Radira to rob a normal warehouse. We're flinging gangsters at other gangsters to try to get information about a worse threat. In war, sometimes there is no clean or dirty option. Sometimes there's only the least bad option. Besides…"

"Besides?"

Erik's voice turned low and gravelly. "If the Prism Associates bastards try anything we don't like, they won't live to regret it. I think Radira understands that."

Emma disappeared and reappeared in front of Erik. "If you two are done worrying about nothing, I want to reiterate the most important safety consideration." She pointed to herself. "You can't abandon the exoskeleton with me inside."

"I can grab you and run if necessary." Erik snickered. "You're not just my friend, remember? You're better than a friend. You're useful."

"Those gun goblins might realize what you have," Emma suggested with a questioning look in her eyes.

"It'll be a short life for any man who tries to take you," Erik countered.

Jia couldn't see Emma slotted into Erik's exoskeleton. That made her feel better about the whole thing because it meant the AI couldn't easily be targeted.

Emma smiled and stepped back. "As long as we all agree."

"Let's finish getting ready," Erik replied with a frown. "I don't like having to ride in their cargo flitter there, but that's one solution Alina hasn't provided for us yet." He took a couple of steps forward, the exo's feet clanging on the floor of the *Argo*'s cargo bay. "Hmm. If we move some of the stuff around and keep at least two of the flitters in the loading ports, we could probably get a cargo flitter in there, too."

"Something for the future, huh?" Jia asked. "Malcolm, how are you doing on your end?"

"I'm in a good position," he responded over the comm. "Emma's already done a lot of the heavy lifting, and I will keep the local drones and cameras outside the main warehouse distracted."

"Good, but somehow I doubt we have to worry about the local police showing up."

Thirty minutes later, Jia and Erik stood in the back of a cargo flitter packed with men and women in colorful suits, sitting on the benches lining the walls on either side. The contrast between the dull exoskeletons and the bright, cheery outfits of the gangsters kept a smile on her face the entire time.

All the gangsters carried rifles strapped over their shoulders. A couple lugged machine guns, but there wasn't an exoskeleton or rocket launcher among the group. Whether that meant they lacked the weapons or they intended to place the blame for heavy weapons use on Erik and Jia was unclear. She didn't care either way. They weren't planning to stay on Mars any longer than absolutely necessary. Whatever reputation they gained there was a temporary concern.

Felix sat close to Jia. He tapped his fingertips on the top of his leg, his brow creased in worry. The flitter set down and the back opened, settling down as a ramp. Bright light from outside spilled into the interior and chased away the red-tinted darkness that had defined their flight. Other flitters were parked in rough lines, additional Prism Associates gangsters already outside with their weapons. Most of the vehicles were smaller, sportier models, but there was one other cargo flitter, also empty now.

Jia frowned. She looked around and checked the camera feeds. A helpful Emma-provided map indicated their position.

"I know we couldn't land without taking fire, but this wasn't the plan," she complained. "We're too far away. They'll see us coming."

Felix made his way down the ramp. "If you knew we'd get shot, what did you think we were going to do? Miss Tellvane told us to bring you here and make sure you had a lot of firepower on the outside. We don't go inside unless we feel like it."

Erik jumped his exoskeleton out of the back of the flitter, landing with a resounding thud. Everyone snapped their heads in his direction.

"If we walk up there, they're going to reinforce too well, and we'll end up in a protracted battle or worse once their reinforcements arrive," he explained. "If your boss doesn't want a bunch of blood on your pretty suits, we need the surprise that comes with a sudden attack, which means we'll need an aerial insertion."

Felix scoffed. "Not everyone is as crazy as you two. You told Miss Tellvane when we were planning things that you knew about them being able to take down drones." He jabbed a finger in the air. "They can take down more than drones."

"They aren't using missiles, are they?" Erik replied. "That means a large flitter on close approach will get shredded but not instantly destroyed."

"Yeah, then it's going to crash into a building, and whoever's on board will be dead," Felix complained. "That's your brilliant plan? Crash a flitter into them as a distraction?"

"Partially. Yeah." Erik motioned with the exo's arm toward the gathered gangsters. "You've got a good number of people here. You can surround the warehouse, cut off escape from all directions, and force whoever's inside to spread out their forces. That'll also guarantee us a place to retreat."

"And what? Lay siege?" Felix tugged on his lapels. "We

spend too much time messing around, reinforcements are going to show up, and then we start dying."

The other gangsters nodded in agreement, murmurs of discontent rippling through the crowd. Tellvane had guaranteed their cooperation but not their loyalty or obedience. Jia mentally moved the plan into the bad idea column.

Erik laughed. "Nope. I wasn't thinking of using you to do anything I'd need a soldier for. I just need you to watch our backs. Jia and I will take all the heat, and this will be easy. We only need one of your flitters. We'll fly it in, let them shred it, and jump out of the back. The crashing cargo flitter and two exos will be a big distraction. Then you all can land closer to the warehouse and surround it while we finish busting inside. At that point, the Star Guild will be so confused, they won't know what to do."

Felix shook his head. "You are *insane*, Blackwell. You have a death wish?"

"This isn't even the craziest plan I've come up in the last couple of months. The worst thing that happens is we die, and you can run off. Or you can wet your pants and be afraid of a bunch of guys from a weak syndicate. Your choice."

"I hate your ass, Blackwell," Felix replied. "And I don't like taking orders from a non-Red."

"Really? Can't do much about the second, but the first? It's a nice ass." Erik smiled. "You in or out?"

"I need to contact Miss Tellvane. This wasn't the plan." Felix reached for his PNIU.

"What did you think we meant when we said, 'Hard entry?'"

CHAPTER TWENTY

"Yes, ma'am," Felix muttered under his breath. "I understand, ma'am. I'll inform you when it's over." He tapped his PNIU again and glanced at Erik, shaking his head. "Miss Tellvane agrees with your plan, but she wanted me to remind you that anything that's left behind belongs to Prism Associates. You still agree to those terms?"

"Yes," Erik replied, walking toward the cargo flitter. "Does that mean you're going to come inside?"

"No, but Miss Tellvane feels there's a good chance the Star Guild will abandon the building if your attack goes well," Felix replied. "We're going to loot it like we found Generous Gao's hideout."

Jia walked back over to the cargo flitter and made the short hop into the back. The cargo flitter dipped. She walked toward the front.

"That works for us," Erik replied. "Everyone load up, and let's get going." He lowered his voice. "You in control, Emma?"

The cargo bay door lifted. She didn't speak until it'd closed, despite sending it as a transmission.

"Yes," Emma confirmed. "I'm in control of the flitter and linked to their comms. I should point out there's a non-zero chance of you being injured. The drones were being taken out by lasers. Even I can't easily dodge a laser."

"This is a better plan than relying on Team Colored Vomit there," Erik replied. "I've fought enough gangsters to know the big thing they lack is discipline. They're fine for rearguard duty, but if they go in the front and take any casualties?" He shook his head.

The cargo flitter shook slightly as it took off. Emma produced an overlay displaying the Prism Associates fleet, with the cargo flitter on point.

"Connect me with them, Emma," Erik ordered.

"Done."

"Listen up," Erik bellowed. "We're dropping in exactly two minutes. You all wait two more minutes before following us. That should give us enough time to get their attention and focus their forces before your arrival. You're welcome to the party inside if you want. Blackwell out."

Jia moved toward the back of the flitter. "I will admit to being surprised about one thing."

"What's that?" Erik asked.

"Radira seemed genuinely disgusted by the idea the Star Guild is trafficking in people." There was a click as a new belt of ammo slid into her machine gun. "I'm surprised she cares so much."

"Like she said, everyone has their line," Erik replied. "It just gives us more reason to mess up the Star Guild. To be fair, Emma, on our way in, send out a transmission informing them that if they immediately leave or surrender, they won't be fired on."

Jia snorted. "They're not going to care about that."

"Then they can't complain that we didn't warn them." Erik verified his ammo feeds and his grenade capacity. Power was at expected levels, no system damage. The exo was ready to deliver the pain. "It would have been far easier when we were cops to just drop in and clean out syndicates this way."

Jia's ballistic shield expanded in front of her left arm with a hiss and a click. "I think a lot of things would have been easier if we could have busted in with exoskeletons and shot everyone."

The cargo flitter lurched and lifted off. There were no windows in the back, but Emma was sending feeds to Erik's and Jia's faceplates. The gangsters' flitters floated off the ground, but per the plan, they didn't follow.

Erik deployed his shield and moved beside Jia. "Give us a few passes to get their attention before you open the back."

"And if the flitter takes so much damage that is no longer possible?" Emma asked.

Erik chuckled. "Then we'll open it the hard way—with a plasma grenade."

"Hmm," Emma replied. "What a curious plan. I'd suggest securing yourselves, given the lack of equipment aboard to facilitate that."

Erik and Jia activated their leg spikes. The metal shot through the floor and the heads spread out to lock them into place. Whatever damage the flitter was about to take would far exceed what they'd just done.

"I'm not worried," Erik admitted. "There's a limit to what they can deploy. It's not like they're going to take us out with a huge missile. There's only so much they can do before the locals have to stop looking the other way, or the military goes on the move."

Emma sighed. "Such confidence, built on such a shoddy dataset. Oh, well. I'm far sturdier than you. I'll likely survive the crash."

"I love you too."

The flitter accelerated, the warehouses and nearby factories becoming blurs. There was nothing subtle about their approach. Erik took a couple of deep breaths, his heart rate as steady as ever. A man should never take battle lightly, but he didn't fear the kind of petty crooks Radira's color gang could beat down.

"It'd be handy if Anne and Kant were around right now." Jia sighed. "Why do I have the feeling we're only going to get to use them half the time?"

"Half the time is better than none," Erik replied. "As long as we have them for the final battle."

"Against the Core?"

"Yeah. And I don't think that's coming next week."

Emma abruptly changed direction. The flitter jerked up and down as it circled the warehouse. A laser carved a small hole through the side but only scorched the other wall. Whatever they were using was far less powerful than the laser rifle hidden inside Erik's MX 60.

Suited men rushed out of the building, including on the roof, rifles in hand. They pointed them at the flitter and opened fire. Bullets filled the sky, a couple of stray ones striking the vehicle and ripping through the exterior. They did no serious damage with the emitters angled away from them.

A large red circle in the feed marked the laser turret, a squat affair half-hidden by curved gray housing. The turret turned, and a new hole appeared near the back of the flitter.

"We can't depend on them running out of shots." Erik grunted in irritation. "They've probably got that thing linked to the main power in the warehouse."

"Should I open the back?" Emma asked.

"Not yet," Erik replied. "Try to take us lower. Buzz the guys on the roof."

With a stomach-churning drop, the cargo flitter rolled toward the warehouse. It swerved from side to side as bullets pelted the front. A stray bullet struck a grav emitter, and the vehicle rolled to its side. Emma corrected, pulling up at the last second to avoid smashing into the roof of the building. She barreled toward the gangsters, who stood their ground for a surprising couple of seconds before leaping to the side. Their bullets had left the front windshield a hole-filled mess, and if anyone had been in the pilot's seat, they'd have been killed.

Erik grinned as he stared at the laser turret in one of his feeds. It spun in their direction, but the barrel couldn't lower enough to line up with them.

"Open up, Emma," he ordered. "We're going to jump, then you crash this thing right into that turret. I don't want anything to make our retreat harder if we have to come this way."

The back door opened, revealing scrambling gangsters leaping behind towers and exposed vents. Erik and Jia retracted their spikes and jumped out of the back of the flitter with quick thrusts. Before they landed, they opened up with their rifles. The rounds ripped through the feeble cover and downed the gangsters.

They advanced toward the open roof access. The flitter crashed into the turret, exploding and sending out an angry, expanding cloud of sharp burning metal. Chunks of the turret and its housing mixed with the flitter, the barrel a twisted, half-burned mess.

Erik rushed toward the open doorway, his rifle up. Jia swept the roof, pointing her rifle at a gangster crawling out from behind an exposed vent that now sported three huge holes. He tossed his rifle over the side and put his hands on his head as he edged toward a ladder.

"Good call," Jia noted.

"Thanks!" The man ran to the ladder and scrambled down. "Good luck with your raid!"

"So much for loyalty."

Erik advanced into the roof access and stepped onto an exposed metal catwalk overseeing the main warehouse floor. Cargo flitters and scout bikes were parked in tight lines, but there weren't a lot of crates or boxes.

Gangsters crouched spread out on the main warehouse floor, most using the flitters for cover. The warehouse lit up with the bright muzzle flashes, their bullets bouncing off Erik's shield and falling through the railing before hitting the ground like metal hail. He advanced, which allowed Jia to step inside. Emma highlighted the modest number of IO ports on the main floor.

Erik and Jia weren't there to secure anything for Prism Associates, and if Radira's men didn't want to come inside,

Erik wasn't going to worry about blowing up half the warehouse if necessary.

"If you don't want to die, drop your guns and get the hell out of here," Erik shouted. He flicked a finger, and a plasma grenade clunked into place in his launcher. "Or stay here and help Mars deplete its surplus population."

"Hold them until our reinforcements get here!" screamed one of the gangsters. He fired a burst into Jia's shield, and the bullets joined the metal hail. "Protect the cargo, or the boss will kill us anyway!"

Erik glanced to the side. The narrow stairway wouldn't accommodate a full exo. Inconvenient, but not insurmountable with the help of jump thrusters.

"Looks like we're going to have to do this the hard way," Jia commented.

"You're thinking about it wrong," Erik replied, raising his grenade launcher. "I think of it the fun way."

CHAPTER TWENTY-ONE

The gangsters continued shooting, the constant impact of their gunfire against Jia's shield rattling the exoskeleton. Frustration built on their faces as they pressed the assault, desperate to get at least a couple of rounds through. Jia might have felt pity for them if they weren't antisocial criminal scum who participated in human trafficking.

She took a slow, even breath, curious about the cargo rather than worried about the gangsters. They weren't going to win against two high-grade exoskeletons with rifles, especially when Erik and Jia had the high ground, but they weren't willing to leave it behind. The Lady might have smiled on Erik and Jia and given them something critical to the Core. Whatever it was, there was no reason to let the gangsters leave with it.

With a satisfying hollow triple clunk, Erik launched three plasma grenades at the floor in a loose arc. The gangsters, not being total fools, scattered, but that didn't save all of them when the explosives blew apart the flitters being used as cover. The men kept up their return fire but didn't linger in any one spot.

Jia picked off a gangster rushing between flitters with a burst to his chest, a sudden thought occurring to her when the nearby flames flickered. "What if they're shipping explosives or missiles? If we blow everything up, we might take down this entire warehouse with us inside it. I don't mind denying them weapons, but I'd prefer not to die in the process."

Erik chuckled. "Look at how they're moving. No one's avoiding any parts of the warehouse or the flitters. If they were shipping bombs, I don't think they'd be sticking around inside where they might get blown away. We're fine."

"Being blown up would be suboptimal," Emma suggested. "But please note they have no active jamming inside this building, and I'm now detecting a short-range network. I'm beginning a systems intrusion. Try not to kill us all before I get in."

"This is working out even easier than I thought," Erik replied, raking his machine gun across the warehouse. Two gangsters went down screaming.

Jia narrowed her eyes, her heart pounding. "I just thought of another thing. There could be innocent people inside the flitters. These people are trafficking."

It might already be too late. Had they been too trigger-happy?

"No," Emma replied. "There's no indication of that according to the thermal readings. If you want to blow things up, the concern returns to whether they are storing any explosives. I don't have an easy way of detecting that based on my current sensor access, but I do note that Erik's analysis is consistent with the enemy's behavior."

Erik didn't say anything as he swept near the back, downing another gangster. The men below were getting better about staying low but remained doggedly determined not to leave despite their total ineffectual counterattack on the two exoskeletons above them.

"Good enough for me," Jia replied.

Her concern fading, she joined Erik in painting the room with bullets. More gangsters fell to their deadly efforts. High-velocity rounds tore through the unarmored flitters and ripped through the men behind them. They might as well have been standing in the open.

A brave man made a run for the metal stairs as if being closer would help. The stairs crisscrossed back and forth, forcing him into a natural defense movement pattern, but there were too many gaps in the rails. Jia's shot tore through his head before he made it a fifth of the way. His body rolled down the stairs, and his gun clattered to the floor.

"How are you doing outside, Felix?" Erik transmitted. "Any trouble?"

"Nobody's tried to come out yet," the gangster replied, sounding surprised. "But we can hear the show in there. You're really letting those bastards have it, aren't you?"

"It's more they're trying to let us have it and failing."

The entire front line of the enemy was annihilated or lying on the ground, on the way to death. Jia jumped off the catwalk, kicking in her thrusters to slow her descent. She continued to sweep back and forth with the machine gun, killing and wounding more men before landing with a resounding thud on the warehouse floor. Another quick burst put her on top of a cargo flitter with her massive shield in front. It continued to repel the feeble shots of the gangsters with ease.

"I'm beginning to think these guys were too arrogant," she muttered. "A couple of corner turrets or bots with missiles, and this would have been a lot harder."

"You're complaining about us not having as much trouble?" Erik asked.

"I'm just remembering that training scenario from a couple of weeks ago. We almost died in it."

"Be glad these guys aren't as smart as Emma."

"Their systems people are better than their, shall we say, operations personnel," Emma observed. "Penetration is taking longer than I anticipated. I wouldn't say I'm impressed as much as I'm annoyed."

"How long are we talking?" Erik asked.

He leapt from the top of the stairs, barely using his thrusters. His exo smashed into the top of a black MX 60 of all things, crunching the roof but leaving only mild scratches on the legs of the exoskeleton. Jia hoped that wasn't a portent for the future.

"Not long," Emma commented. "Just longer than I anticipated. Keep culling gun goblins, and I'll handle it."

The surviving gangsters suddenly broke and ran for the exits. Jia and Erik held their fire. No reason to cut down fleeing men. They weren't there to wipe out the syndicate, they were there for information.

"They're retreating," Jia transmitted. "But they're still armed."

"Fine," Felix sent, sounding annoyed. "If they want to

surrender, we're not going to waste them, and then this doesn't have to be a thing. Miss Tellvane likes to give people job opportunities despite past mistakes, but let's see if they're dumbasses."

Erik and Jia stayed in their positions, watching and waiting as the men fled. None were bothering to shoot at them anymore. No one stopped to check on their downed friends. Smoke billowed up to the top of the warehouse from the burning remnants of the destroyed flitters, but relative to what they could have inflicted, there was remarkably little damage. Most of the vehicles remained mostly intact if nobody counted all the new holes.

Loud gunfire sounded from outside, and an explosion shook the warehouse.

"What the hell was that?" Erik asked.

"A bastard chucked a grenade at us," Felix shouted. "We told them they could surrender, but they're fighting even harder. Damn. Now I see why. Got bastards coming out of other parts of the building, including with some heavier weapons. I think they're trying to break through."

"Hold them," Erik ordered. "We need to get what we came for."

"Hurry the hell up, Blackwell. You're supposed to be doing all the heavy lifting on this. We shouldn't have to duck grenades and rockets."

"Take out a couple dozen, then you can bitch."

Jia stepped off the flitter. "That explains why they didn't put up much of a fight. It was strategic repositioning."

"They're not trying to break through," Emma explained. "They sent some sort of emergency distress call and were told to disrupt the formation outside but not withdraw.

That's the problem with using their local system so tightly; it makes it too easy to spy on. I've got primary camera, drone, and turret access, not that the last is helpful anymore considering what we've done to it."

"Outside, huh?" Erik walked slowly between the vehicles, his exoskeleton frame standing taller than anything else on the floor. "Airstrike on the warehouse, maybe?"

"They wouldn't have their men stay so close to it," Jia replied. "They have to be planning something different."

"Reinforcements. Lots of them. That would be my guess. We're running out of time. Hurry up, Emma."

"You do your job, and I'll do mine," Emma offered in a condescending tone. "I can't dump every file based on my current level of access. Wait. I think I have an explanation."

Another loud explosion sounded outside. The din of gunfire was constant. It was insane that this level of fight could occur without the authorities arriving right away.

"The message I just received came from the internal server," Emma continued, "and was transmitted to all the gun goblins is as follows. 'Boss says mess up the Prism assholes outside. The big boys will handle the exos. They'll land up top.' Hmmm. I'm sweeping the nearby area with the drones and cameras, looking for anything unusual. By the way, when you get a chance, please investigate this vehicle on the warehouse floor. Although I haven't achieved full systems penetration, it is clearly indicated as the vehicle containing the 'latest shipment.' You might find that of interest."

A bright yellow outline appeared around a cargo flitter in the corner of the warehouse. Erik and Jia advanced slowly, both worried it might explode at any moment.

Dead bodies surrounded the vehicle, and now that Jia had time to think about it, she realized there were a greater number of men around the vehicle. She'd assumed they wanted the larger cover, but Erik was right. They wouldn't have stayed close to anything bound to go up in a fiery cloud of death.

Given their angle from above and the orientation of the vehicle, Erik and Jia hadn't been able to see the flitter's open back door and the ramp extending down. Four large crates lay inside. Three of them sported huge holes from Erik and Jia's indiscriminate fire. The pair didn't even need to open them to see what was inside, thanks to the holes. Some of the small packets had been blasted into the open and dark liquid was spreading over the floor, along with powder from vials. Jia had seen both in her time as a cop.

Jia scoffed. "Phoenix Root and Archangel? That's what they were so desperate to protect? Stupid drugs?"

Erik crunched several vials of Archangel underneath his exoskeleton's foot. "If all these crates are filled with drugs, we're talking tens of millions of credits. That's a lot of money. Most people aren't going to blow that much off."

"Syndicate scum," Jia muttered.

"Judging by the internal records I'm now able to access," Emma interjected, "the ground-level walls are hardened. It would be rather difficult to enter this building except from the roof under normal circumstances. Please note there are multiple cargo flitters approaching in tight formation. They will be here in minutes. The Star Guild men are doing a decent job of engaging the Prism Associates outside, but casualties appear rather lopsided in favor of your colorful new friends."

"They were depending on no one being crazy enough to crash a flitter into the building," Jia concluded. "Or at least being able to stall long enough for reinforcements to arrive. Or we just got lucky. It could be that with all the trouble they've been having lately, they're spread out more."

"Whatever works," Erik replied. "Emma, yank everything you can from the system. We might have to pull back, depending on how many people show up." He backed out of the flitter and down the ramp, then aimed his grenade launcher at the nearest crate. "We want to set a few fires ourselves. Go ahead and disable the fire suppression systems if you have access."

"Yes, I do." Emma sounded amused. "You're going to destroy their drugs? Whatever moral objections Miss Tellvane has over the trafficking of humans might not extend to drugs. She might be agitated by the destruction of tens of millions of credits' worth of goods."

Erik let out a dark chuckle. "I only agreed they could take what survived. I never agreed anything *would* survive. She should have negotiated a better deal if she wants to complain."

Jia jumped out of the cargo flitter and moved to Erik's side. She liked the idea of tweaking Tellvane far too much, but it'd be easy to lie and say they'd blown up the drugs by accident. She'd decide later.

Two plasma grenades later, the flitter lay in scorched pieces. The crates were now in shards, and the drugs had been vaporized.

"This is interesting," Emma declared.

"What?" Erik asked. "A Hunter ship suddenly jumped into orbit and is preparing to bombard us?"

"Not that interesting. The cargo flitters have slowed and are turning around. Ah, I see. The backs are opening to allow the exoskeletons in them to fire."

"Felix," Erik transmitted, "back off. You're in no position to take on exoskeletons."

"Not complaining, Blackwell," Felix replied. "But if we back off, they'll come at you from all angles."

"It won't be the first time. Now get the hell out of there. You were the one bitching about having to do all the work. Let me get back to doing my job."

"Don't blow up that warehouse, Blackwell," Felix replied. "We need to make this worthwhile. Miss Tellvane made her position clear on that."

"How long is the system dump going to take, Emma?" Erik asked.

"Longer than you'd like," Emma replied. "Depending on the strength of the enemy forces, they might overwhelm you before I finish."

She sent a feed from the outside cameras. Felix and his men were withdrawing under fire, pulling their wounded into their damaged flitters. The Star Guild men didn't press the counterattack, instead reducing their fire once they realized the other gangsters were running. Some of the Star Guild threw their hands into the air and roared in triumph, convinced total victory was in their grasp.

The exoskeletons in the cargo flitters didn't fire. Instead, the flitters flew backward, passing over the top of the building. Six exoskeletons jumped out, armed with machine guns and rocket launchers. The surviving men from the warehouse rushed to surround them, including men with their own portable heavy weapons.

"Felix," Erik transmitted, "once we pick off the exos, swing back around and nail these guys from the rear. Their attention will be on us. I'll let you know when."

The gangster grunted. "You'll be dead by then, Blackwell."

"We're not going to die here," Jia commented. "No way we're getting taken out by those assholes."

"If you say so, but that's not what the pool says."

Erik chuckled. "You should have let us bet."

"In Prism, we don't let people bet on their own deaths. Don't want them cheating and purposely getting killed to mess with the payout."

Jia jogged away from the corner and ran to some flitters in a more central position, then pointed her weapons at the top of the stairs. She loaded a plasma grenade, ready to take on the reinforcements.

Erik raised his weapons. "Let us know if the guys outside start heading toward us, Emma. I'm betting they just want to cut off our escape, but will otherwise leave their buddies free to do what they want."

Jia sighed. "Too bad we blew up the drugs. We could have hidden behind them. It would be entertaining watching them try not to shoot at us to avoid the wrath of their boss."

"Get ready," Erik barked.

Emma's feeds showed the exoskeletons closing on the rooftop access. The models didn't look military, and the jump jets were small and inefficient, but the pilots were smart enough to have their shields extended. Not being a complete idiot wasn't the same thing as being well-trained. Even with the recent slowdown, Jia all but lived in simulators.

"After I fire, I'm going to keep moving," Jia explained.

"Sounds like a plan," Erik replied. "I always appreciate Alina giving us these models. I doubt our new friends have anywhere near the same range of movement. Let's take advantage of that."

The exos advanced into the entrance, their weapons at the ready. Six to two; it was time to see how unfair the odds were. By Jia's calculations, the enemy needed at least twice as many to stand a chance against her and Erik.

Jia allowed herself a grin. No reason to deny to herself that she'd gotten cocky. Sometimes arrogance was justified.

"Here they come."

CHAPTER TWENTY-TWO

Since Erik had taken up penjing, his appreciation of beauty had increased, not just for plants, but for everything. Destruction was beautiful in its own way. Not death, but destruction. There were so many flavors, so many different facets expressed at the end of an object during its removal from the world. A single method, such as plasma grenades, could have many subtleties.

The massive blue-white explosion created by Erik and Jia's plasma grenades resembled a blooming flower that melted the catwalk holding up the first pair of exos.

The enemies had entered hot, machine guns roaring, their bullets streaming down toward their enemies, but that confidence lasted only a couple of seconds, thanks to the explosion. The blast sent the two exos flying through the air, their shields having saved them from the bulk of the damage. Another exo tumbled headfirst, his jump thrusters useless for anything other than accelerating him toward his doom, given gravity. The three remaining exos hesitated behind the door, stunned by the brutality and speed of the counterattack.

That moment of hesitation gave the invaders their chance. Erik leapt from one flitter to another, tracking one of the falling exos and awaiting his opportunity for the kill. The first rule of piloting an exoskeleton was counterintuitive. That was to remember that exos were an extension of the body, but not the body itself. It was obvious the gangster didn't understand that, or he would have stopped flailing and not opened himself up for a clean shot to his body. Erik's machine gun roared to life, and the large, fast bullets passed through the narrow gap and blew through the pilot, producing a shower of blood.

Jia's solution was less elegant. She didn't move her exo during those dangerous seconds following the initial attack. Instead, she followed the second target with her arm, adjusting and firing a single plasma grenade shortly before it landed on the first floor. Without his shield angled properly, the gangster didn't stand a chance. He managed to scream for a half-second before the explosion burned through his tactical suit and fried him.

The third pilot displayed more discipline and brought his shield in front of his exo before he smacked into the floor with an echoing clang. He shook his head with a groan, the shield and the exo's design redistributing most of the force of the collision. His exo lay on the ground face-down, shield between him and the floor, exposing the pilot. Erik's and Jia's bursts ripped into the man's upper body, his harness and tactical suit not robust enough to survive the heavy rounds.

It was now three to two, and neither Erik nor Jia had

taken a significant hit. He hoped whoever had bet on him and Jia surviving had gotten good odds.

A roar sounded from above. Erik jumped to the side instinctively, avoiding the rocket barrage. The explosions blasted a nearby flitter into the air, where it tumbled end over end before landing on top of another. Jia returned fire as she ran between the rows of vehicles, but the enemy's shields absorbed the blow. The reinforced defenses that had saved them from the warehouse full of enemies were now challenging them.

The charred, smoky roof access had been blown open wide enough by the grenade attack that all three remaining exos could aim at the targets below with ease. Rockets streamed down from the gangsters, pelting the ground in a fiery rain. Erik's and Jia's constant movement kept them from suffering any direct hits, and the rapidly accumulating fire and smoke further obscured their movements. Their shields could, in theory, survive a couple of rocket hits, but neither of them wanted to test that theory.

"I would have thought they would be more careful in their own warehouse," Jia complained.

"I think they noticed we already blew up the drugs," Erik offered with a laugh. "Now they're just pissed off."

"No one forced them onto this career path."

Jia jumped over a vehicle to avoid an explosion and launched a grenade at the exos. They backed up and overlapped their shields, absorbing the plasma explosion with nothing more damaging than black scorches on their shields. She hissed in frustration before firing a quick burst at them.

Erik understood her frustration, but at least they were

taking them on in high-end exos instead of the more unpleasant person versus exo fights they'd been involved in. Trusting the Lady was one thing. Trusting her to save him from stupid matchups was something else entirely.

A rocket slammed into Erik's shield. His exo vibrated from the blast but his shield held, just a couple of small pieces flung off. He angled it up in time to survive another attack before rushing into a thick batch of smoke, his eyes watering. Ventilation was a good reason to blow things up outside.

He glanced at Emma's feed. To his surprise, the gangsters outside weren't making a move on the warehouse. After losing half the exo forces, a pincer attack might have been effective. There was no reason to wait around for them to do the smart thing.

"Get ready for a crisscross," Erik suggested. "That's our best chance of finishing this quickly. Wait for my signal."

"We've practiced it enough," Jia replied, turning to run toward Erik. She continued firing in short, controlled bursts, never stopping long enough for the men above to get comfortable.

They practiced a lot of things. Sometimes Erik regretted drawing Jia so deeply into constant training, but their reward for that training was their continued survival.

The rocket attacks grew less frequent, and the gangsters' aim was poorer when they launched. Raging fire and thick smoke turned Erik and Jia into giant specters, disappearing and reappearing to throw bullets at them. Three-quarters of the vehicles in the warehouse were in ruins, smoldering wrecks if not scorched piles barely recognizable as what they once were. If there'd been any explosives in the flitters, they would have blown up by now. That was one less thing to worry about.

"Stay still, damn it!" yelled a gangster. "Stop dancing around down there and die already, you bastards."

Jia snickered and jumped into the air with a spin for mocking emphasis. "What's that matter? There were six of you and two of us. Shouldn't you have won already? I get the feeling you're not confident you can win."

"You aren't Prism," the gangster replied. "They don't have exos or pilots that good. Mercs?"

Radira could use whatever footage she wanted, but that didn't mean Erik had to say anything aloud that might get repurposed and used against him. The Martian underworld could continue to whisper.

"Sometimes you hire out when you need quality work," Erik offered, along with a frag grenade.

Despite his casual launch and his attempt to take advantage of the smoke, the gangsters weren't fooled. They kept up their shield wall as the grenade exploded, the fragments plinking harmlessly off the reinforced shields and falling to the floor. A gangster launched a rocket in response, but Erik jumped back, avoiding a direct hit. His shield's ability to take grenade and rocket fire wasn't the same thing as being able to take unlimited grenade and rocket fire.

Given the enemy's position and numbers, the battle should have been theirs. Erik's and Jia's exos were superior models, but it was their discipline and training that were winning the day. Coordinated barrages could have had them on the floor, forced to eject and easy to pick off or smother. Erik didn't know whether to be happy or annoyed about the poor use of the exos, but killing the men would end the problem.

Erik and Jia continued darting between wrecks and jumping to avoid the now-sparse rocket fire. The gangsters supplemented it with intense machine-gun fire, but they couldn't find a decent angle to get them past the shields. Every time they fired at what looked like an opening, Erik or Jia twisted at the right moment to block without even thinking about it. Their experience and training let them defend their weak spots intuitively.

Hungry flames lapped at other crates and vehicles, spreading. Dense smoke filled the top of the warehouse, spreading out along the roof and obscuring the gangsters' exos. It was time to finish this.

"You still getting files, Emma?" Erik asked between shots.

"Yes. I'm beginning to run into system errors due to damage, but I've been able to restrict my area of search and concentrate on files of most probable interest. I'm confident I've retrieved something useful."

Something useful wasn't the same as everything, but sticking around in a collapsing warehouse was a bad idea.

"Okay, it's time," Erik announced. "Get ready for the cross on five, Jia. I'll distract, you finish."

"Understood," his partner replied.

Both kept up their erratic movements, but it'd become far less necessary with the reduced number of attacks. The enemy's initial enthusiasm had taken a toll on their ammo supply, as Erik had expected. Size and capacity were the primary reasons Erik preferred grenades to rockets. More ammo meant more tactical options, even at the cost of power. That was why he and Jia were about to win.

"One, two, three," Erik began. He shifted his exo and sprinted toward Jia.

The timing on their maneuver would be critical to pulling it off. She didn't head directly toward him, instead running at an angle while continuing to loose rounds toward the gangsters above, as did Erik.

"Four," he continued, charging through the smoke and debris filling the warehouse. "Five."

Erik jumped into the air as Jia jumped the opposite way. He launched three plasma grenades in rapid succession, aiming for the far side of the gangster formation and walking the shots. The first exploded, the blast knocking chunks from the wall but not doing much to the shields other than scorching them. With the next two, he hit the wall directly, launching chunks behind the shields. A grin took over his face when the gangsters turned toward his way. He fired two more grenades.

Jia launched a grenade before Erik got off his second. Erik's first grenade exploded against their shields, but Jia's deadly little gift sped toward the exposed back of the formation and exploded, ripping into the exos and knocking them away from each other but not disabling them.

It was enough. Their formation was now disrupted, leaving gaps in the shields. The gangsters spun to try to tighten their formation, but Erik and Jia were faster, targeting and firing into the gaps in their formation. An exo could take stray bullets or bursts but not plasma grenades. Bright explosions lit the smoke-darkened warehouse. Two of the exos pitched over the edge and plunged to the floor. The third fell backward, the pilot's head lolling to the side. A long piece of the roof near Erik fell, the burning chunk barely connected to the rest. After a couple of seconds it wrenched free, plummeting to the floor and piercing the windshield of a flitter with a loud crash.

Erik coughed, regretting not having a breather mask on with all the smoke. "I think we're done here."

"There's not going to be anything left for Radira," Jia commented.

"Sure, there is. She gets first dibs on the ashes and burned scrap. I'm sure she can use that for something."

"Emma, we need to go before this entire place falls on us," Erik noted. "Do you have what you need?"

"I can't be a hundred percent sure of that, but there's a good chance," Emma replied.

Erik charged through the smoke toward a door. "I'll take that chance. Felix, get your ass back here to cover ours."

Jia burst out laughing.

"What's so funny?" Erik asked.

"I knew this would end with a destroyed building."

CHAPTER TWENTY-THREE

Erik and Jia burst out the warehouse toward the line of gangsters crouched behind thick portable shields. All the men pointed their weapons toward the warehouse, including a couple with rocket, grenade, or missile launchers. Smoke poured out of the warehouse behind Erik and Jia and cloaked them, perhaps explaining why the men didn't fire immediately. Their mistake if they maintained the delusion they still had any chance of victory.

Jia dared to hope the men understood they'd lost. That brief wisp of thought died with the first missile streaming toward her. She brought up her shield and hissed as the explosion shoved her back and blasted a chunk out of her shield. Erik's machine gun blew the man's head apart in the counterattack. Chaos followed, with streams of bullets joining the rockets, grenades, and missiles, the exos on the move as the street and walls around them blew apart.

Erik and Jia picked off a couple of men, but the firing holes in the portable shields allowed the men with rifles to shoot without significant risk. The men dabbling in explosives fared less well, but the men with grenade launchers soon discovered the charms of indirect fire.

A frag grenade exploded over Jia's exo, and shrapnel ripped into her tactical suit. She gritted her teeth. "This is starting to get annoying. Where's our exit policy?"

Erik scattered gangsters with a quick grenade launch. "Good question."

Flitters suddenly rose from behind nearby buildings, the windows open, men and women in colorful suits poking rifle barrels out of the vehicles. They opened fire on the exposed backs of the Star Guild forces below, and in less than thirty seconds, the Guild troops broke and ran away from their shields.

"Drop your weapons!" Jia bellowed, using the exoskeleton's speakers to magnify her voice. "Surrender, or you will be fired upon."

A man screamed in defiance, pulling a knife and charging at Jia. She allowed him to get to within a couple of meters before putting him down with a single round between the eyes. The other survivors dropped their weapons and put up their hands as they fell to their knees. Common sense, or a sense of self-preservation, had finally prevailed among the enemy gangsters. Pointless bravery in service to their criminal empire wouldn't accomplish anything but getting them killed near a warehouse.

Jia had worried their Prism Associates backup would keep firing, but they ceased their attack immediately upon the surrender. Their flitters descended to the ground, and the gangsters rushed out to take up positions behind the defeated men with guns and binding ties. The fire had spread from the main building to others, the smoke a massive cloud. Everyone in the city must have been able to see it.

A black limo flitter closed from a distance. Jia had her suspicions about the occupant and waited patiently, along with Erik and the others, for the vehicle to finish its approach. The flitter landed in front of Erik and Jia, and the back window dropped with a hiss to reveal a frowning Radira.

"What is this?" She gestured at the building. "Seriously, what the hell is this?"

"Looks like a burning building to me," Erik offered cheerfully. "Come on, you can't tell me you've never seen one of those before. You've probably had your goons blow up all sorts of buildings in your time running the syndicate."

"I understand that it's a burning building. That's not what I'm asking." Radira shook her head, scowling. "Or more to the point, I was already aware of that because I've had to use my influence to delay the arrival of the fire department until the primary incident was over.

"Thanks. That was helpful. It cut down on collateral damage."

Radira's nostrils flared. "You don't see the problem?"

"Not really." Jia stepped forward, the heat behind her oppressive. "We mostly got what we were looking for. It would have been nice if we weren't so rushed, but this wasn't a waste of time, and that's all we can ask for on a mission."

"What about me?" Radira narrowed her eyes. "I won't recover anything useful from that warehouse now. How is this not a waste of time and resources for me?"

"Who cares if you can't recover anything from the warehouse? And it's not guaranteed that you won't. Something might survive. There have to be fireproof containers in there." Jia retracted her shield and lifted her faceplate to grin at Radira. "Even if I'm wrong, what's the problem with that? We didn't guarantee you anything other than some propaganda and weakening a syndicate."

Jia glanced at Erik, but he remained silent and hidden behind his helmet. She didn't worry. If he didn't feel the need to interject, he was comfortable with how she was handling Radira.

"You used us," Radira spat. "I have men who are wounded. We were supposed to get the contents of the warehouse as payment."

"Used you?" Jia scoffed. "You're the last person who should say something like that."

"My wounded men won't find this amusing, Miss Lin."

"Any killed?" Erik asked. "I doubt you get this upset when a couple of your guys get shot in the normal course of your business."

"None of them were killed, but—"

"Then what are you whining about?" Jia interrupted. "We just took out a good number of Star Guild men, along with six exoskeletons and millions of credits' worth of drugs, which means they lost a lot of money, or at least lost a lot of somebody else's money. That means those people might come after whatever's left of their organization."

"Millions of credits?" Radira squeaked. "You...what? Where are the drugs?"

"Destroyed, but you're not into preying on people, right?" Jia prodded. "Even if you are, they weren't your drugs, so their loss only hurts the Star Guild." She pointed at the warehouse. "All of this hurt the Star Guild, and they're your enemies, so it helped you even if you don't recover anything but ash and burned metal from the warehouse."

"You did all this for your own reasons," Radira replied. She opened the back door, stepped out of the limo, and marched over to Jia's exoskeleton, glaring the entire time. "This was supposed to benefit Prism Associates, not just you two."

"How does the weakening of a syndicate you're fighting *not* benefit you?" Jia snapped. "If you wanted to take this warehouse without us, I guarantee you wouldn't have wounded men, you'd have dead men. Get over yourself, Tellvane."

"You think you can show that attitude? You think it's so simple, Lin?"

"It is," Erik offered, walking toward them. His presence produced the absurd situation of two exoskeletons towering over one glaring woman who didn't seem the least bit intimidated.

She might have dozens of men around her, but there was no way they could save her life if Erik and Jia decided to shoot her with an exoskeleton machine gun at point-blank range. Arrogance-fueled bravery became something epic. Radira was used to getting her way, even in dangerous situations.

"Oh, is that how it is?" Radira scoffed. "You purposely destroyed that warehouse, didn't you? You wanted to make sure my syndicate didn't benefit as much as it could from this little incident."

"No, we purposely took down people who got in our way after giving them a chance to surrender," Erik replied. "*They* blew the hell out of the warehouse while they tried to kill us because they lack discipline. Collateral damage, nothing more. It happens around us, so you can bitch and moan about how you didn't get to steal a bunch of drugs, or you can accept that we just helped you deliver a killing blow to the Star Guild and try to protect yourself from the inevitable counterattacks or CID crackdowns."

Radira crossed her arms and sucked in a deep breath. She wrinkled her nose and stared at the burning warehouse in silence.

"We're also not done helping you," Jia added. "Even though we don't need your help anymore, by the time we're done, we'll be taking down whoever was working with the Star Guild. That will benefit you in the long run, assuming you survive."

Radira looked away and flicked her wrist dismissively. "Fine. I suppose you're right. I was hoping to get something more immediately valuable out of this, but what's left of the Star Guild will likely surrender after this. Some of the smarter ones might even understand there is value in changing organizations. I can be a very benevolent and reasonable leader."

"I'm sure you can." Jia smirked.

"Reasonable and happy are different things." Radira frowned. "This is a net win for me, but it was not as profitable as I would have hoped. Don't ask me for another favor for a while. And I'd suggest you leave Mars as soon as possible."

"Sure, we can do that after one more favor," Erik replied.

"What?" She rounded on him to deliver a withering glare. "You dare ask me for more? Don't overestimate your appeal to me."

Erik chuckled. "Can't leave Mars until we're back on our ship, and we're going to need a ride to the hangar."

CHAPTER TWENTY-FOUR

Jia stretched her arms above her head as she stepped into the galley. It'd been a long day and night, flowing into the next morning, and she hoped they had not risked their lives for nothing. Emma's assurances were hardly ironclad, and they couldn't be sure the fundamental premise of the mission wasn't flawed. Their last major mission to Mars had been one of the more high-profile examples of Alina mistakenly seeing a conspiracy in the shadows.

Pissing off Radira Tellvane was a bonus. That might complicate things in the future, but the woman needed to understand they weren't her pets, toys, or friends, and that momentary alliances of inconvenience didn't mean Erik and Jia were ready to become members of Prism Associates. The burning warehouse might have been enough to finally drill that message into her head.

Emma and Malcolm began poring through the recovered files upon Erik, Jia, and Emma's return to the *Argo*, but without a download of all data, there was a chance the destruction had been for nothing and that they'd done nothing but strengthen Prism Associates without anything to show for it other than tweaking Radira.

Uncertainty was the only certainty in their current occupation. They hunted demons in the dark who pretended to be men and women, but the pitch-black state of the UTC meant there was always something else hiding, almost as if it were mocking them.

After a long yawn, Jia headed over to the galley wall, tapping her PNIU. A slot opened to reveal a cup. She pulled it out and moved it to another newly opened section with a small spout and placed it underneath, waiting patiently as a gentle stream of tea filled her cup. It was too early in the morning, and she needed tea.

After collecting her drink, she wandered over to a chair and took a sip of the steaming amber beverage. So many things needed to fall into place for their success. The pessimistic part of her whispered in her ear that they would always be one step behind the Core, to the point of catastrophic failure, but the logical part of her mind pointed at their recent successes, especially in the last year. What once might have seemed an insane quest doomed to failure was starting to look like the beginning of the end for the Core.

The conspiracy wasn't all-powerful. They thrived in the darkness because they understood that too much light would destroy them. Wealth and power were great advantages, but there must have been a tiny percentage of people in the UTC who knew of the Core and worked for it of their own volition. Every discovery identifying their influence weakened them.

That they knew the name "Core" was proof of how

desperate things had become for the conspiracy. When Jia had gotten involved, the only thing Erik had known was that his unit had been slaughtered, and it had something to do with a hidden truth on Molino. Now Erik, Jia, and the ID knew some of the members of the conspiracy, both individuals and corporate members, and they'd defeated major organizations within the Core, including the Ascended Brotherhood. The enemies of the Core had stopped the conspiracy's worst schemes. Victory was within their grasp. They just had to press the attack.

Jia looked over as the door opened. Erik stepped through, trailed by Malcolm. Both sported dark rings underneath their eyes. When Jia had left their cabin, Erik was still asleep. Her restless mind had denied her more than a couple of hours' sleep, and after fighting it for a long time, she'd given up. Her body needed more time to reset her circadian rhythms, always a risk with space travel. She'd experienced it enough by now to prefer to let it happen naturally rather than use medicines, but that could be another type of arrogant presumption that worked for her.

Erik sat down beside her, and Malcolm sat across from him, patting his mouth as he yawned.

"I miss being lazy," Malcolm commented.

"What are you two doing up so early?" Jia asked. "Neither of you have mentioned insomnia."

Emma appeared at the table in her white gangster suit with a stern look. "I woke them. It was pointless to wake you because you were already awake. I thought it best we talk right away so you can make appropriate decisions."

Jia rubbed her eyes. "You found something that made all that worthwhile?"

"Mr. Constantine had identified some promising files before he passed out," Emma explained. "I followed up in addition to my normal analysis. Fortunately, the encryption used by the syndicate might have been excellent, but their implementation in protecting their files wasn't at that level. That provided opportunities for exploration and retrieval without issue."

Erik circled his hand. "Okay, we get it, Emma. You're a goddess, now get to the point. You woke my ass up, and I want to hear the reason."

Emma's clothes shifted to a loose silk dress, her shoulders bare and a laurel crown around her head. "You should worship me, yes. The point is, despite the holes in the files, I've discovered actionable intelligence."

Malcolm saluted her before dropping his head to the table and closing his eyes. He started snoring lightly.

"He did contribute," Emma confirmed. "You know I wouldn't give him credit if he'd been a useless fleshbag, but let us get on with our discussion before the rest of you suffer a similar fate."

A massive star map appeared, several meters long by a couple of meters high. It depicted the entire UTC. Smaller system displays with individual planets and moons winked into existence. Red lines ran between the systems and to individual planets. The lines glowed with a shifting gradient. Blue lines appeared. Jia realized they marked something going to the planets, systems, and moons and something departing, respectively.

"What we have here," Emma explained. "is a CID agent's

dream." She smirked. "It's a detailed list of drug-smuggling routes, not just, from what I can tell, those of the Star Guild—who, after all, have a limited range—but also those of a number of other gun-goblin-intensive organizational partners throughout the UTC. From what I can tell, this information was supposed to be automatically purged if there was a system intrusion, but when I entered, I disabled certain subroutines that prevented it. I'd like to claim this is the result of excellence, but in this case, it was more a result of fortuitous timing and targeting."

"The Lady even helps AI." Erik rubbed his eyes. "When we're done with this, figure out a way to send this anonymously to the CID. Alina might say we have to wait before we take down a bunch of corps conspiring with the Core, but I don't see why we have to let these syndicate assholes run around. Is that why you wanted to tell us right away?"

"Among other reasons." Emma shrugged. "I suspected that would be your decision, but knowing means I can begin preparing the data for distribution in a way that doesn't lead back to me or you."

Jia grinned, no longer needing tea to wake her up. "Within a couple of years, there might be a huge problem with syndicate funding through the UTC. It's a crippling blow."

"Not something that'll keep me up at night." Erik shrugged. "And ID analysis plus Barbu's data pointed us to the warehouse to begin with, which means the Core is relying both on aboveboard companies and criminal syndicates for shipping. Screwing over all these syndicates means screwing over the Core. It's a nice gift that'll keep on giving."

Emma gave him a look of pity. "Presumably they'll develop new networks. You must realize that."

"Sure, eventually, but in the meantime, they'll be reeling from the loss of the old networks, giving CID and us more opportunities to hit them. The problem with developing new smuggling networks is that it makes you more vulnerable to people like CID agents and ghosts, or insane vengeance-driven contractors." Erik jabbed his finger toward Molino at the edge of the map and traced it to the next-closest star system. "I don't mind bleeding the Core to death if that's what it takes."

Jia took a sip of her tea. "Alina didn't send us here just for that."

"Maybe. We can't be sure what she knows. She tells us a lot, but that's not the same thing as telling us everything."

"If any of this is related to the Core, why would they be relying on criminal smuggling networks when they were willing to use the companies and subsidiaries they controlled before?" Jia leaned forward, squinting at the 61 Virginis planetary display. "I don't mind taking down syndicate drug routes, but everything we did on Alpha Centauri suggests the Core doesn't need them."

Erik traced a path with his finger from Alpha Centauri back to the Solar System. "Desperation."

Jia raised an eyebrow. "Desperation?"

"Yeah. We've had too many recent successes, and so has ID. It's like I said." Erik ran a finger across his throat. "We're bleeding them out, and they're running out of options they have complete control over. They don't have a jumpship to get around the restrictions, and they might have their people everywhere, but they obviously don't control every port and every HTP. All it takes is one suspicious cop or soldier, and you lose millions of credits or a Hunter or Navigator artifact."

Malcolm straightened and stared at Erik. Everyone watched him, waiting for him to speak, but he set his head back down on the table and closed his eyes, murmuring, "No, Camila. Anything but that shirt."

Emma's goddess ensemble disappeared, replaced by a tight tac suit. "The disruption of the networks is useful, but I also found something more immediately actionable for your use. I won't bother going through the explanation of the analysis, but judging by weight and density information associated with the recent cargo, particularly in the last six months, I suspect these routes were being used not only for drug shipping but also for heavy arms shipments."

Jia nodded slowly. "That makes sense, but from what Erik has said, that's not necessarily a big problem."

Erik frowned. "Not necessarily a problem and not a problem are not the same. It's one thing when it might have been some minor trafficking, but it depends on where the weapons were going."

"That's what I wonder," Emma explained. "There is some internal routing information. Logistics are key, even when one is a criminal. Based on analysis of the data we retrieved, the final destination for these weapons is beyond the core worlds but not the far frontier, and it's most likely the same location. The shipments represent a not-insignificant number of weapons, enough to equip a small army."

Jia furrowed her brow. "Erik, are you sure this doesn't fit with what you mentioned to Alina? That this might be about bypassing the supply chain because of bureaucracy?"

"It could be." Erik's frown deepened. "I'm more worried now. I'd expect that kind of thing on the far frontier, not the middle colonies."

"What are you thinking?" Jia asked quietly. "Tell me, no matter how crazy."

Erik stared at Molino. "I'm thinking they *did* equip a small Army." He turned to face Jia. "You can't have a decent rebellion in a true frontier colony. Not enough people. Not enough self-sufficiency. I was surprised when the trouble broke out on Diogenes' Hope."

"You're saying someone helped them. The Core?"

"That's what I'm thinking. Diogenes' Hope didn't have a chance, but they did a lot better than anyone thought they would because of how well-equipped they were." Erik pushed back from the table and stood, his face grim. "I didn't pay much attention to it then, but I remember hearing there were a lot of questions about their supply lines. Everyone blew it off as smugglers and syndicates making money."

Emma gave a firm nod. "That was what I found, based on easily accessible official reports."

"That's a lot of weapons for one mid-level syndicate to move or even to procure. They might have had the connections for the drugs, but drugs are easy to ship and missiles aren't." Erik shook his head. "Diogenes' Hope isn't important. They lost, but what if it was a test run for a rebellion elsewhere?"

Jia's stomach tightened. "You're saying the Core is going to support another insurrection?"

"Yeah. Probably somewhere closer to Earth than Diogenes' Hope, but far enough away from the core worlds to give them a chance." Erik's eyes darted back and forth, his attention shifting from system to system. "Shit."

"What?" Jia asked.

"It's like we said before." Erik slammed his fist on the table. "For all we know, it's already started."

Jia looked at the map, starting at Earth and working her way farther out while doing mental calculations in her head. "There's a hard limit to where it might have started and when. Even in the worst-case scenario, it couldn't have been more than two months ago, or we would have already heard about it."

"You can do a lot of damage in two months," Erik countered.

"But the closer systems would have heard sooner." Jia pointed at Alpha Centauri and then Earth.

"The military's spread pretty thin except closer to the border with the other races," Erik growled in frustration. "And the local garrisons and nearby systems' commanders wouldn't expect a pile of high-end weapons to show up. They'd expect hit-and-run crap from a handful of rebels."

"We don't know there's a pile of high-end weapons," Jia replied, doubt obvious in her tone.

"We don't. Damn it." Erik stepped away from the table. "Is there any chance you can figure out where those weapons were going, Emma?"

She shook her head. "Not based on the data I have."

"Then we better hope the ID has some data that we don't." Erik traced through the air with his finger, starting at Earth and following paths until he ended up at Wolf 359. "Because we might already be too late."

Jia folded her arms and sighed. "Even if we do figure it

out, will there be anything we can do? Just filling the *Bifröst*'s cargo bay with extra troops and tanks won't be enough to turn the tide of a rebellion."

"If this is the Core and they've started another rebellion, they're planning something else." Erik backed away, looking the map up and down. "So there's some plan we can mess with. I guarantee it."

CHAPTER TWENTY-FIVE

"Over there!" Damir pointed his rifle at a nearby house. There was only a scorched, jagged hole where a door had once been, but the bulk of the house was intact. It might have been someone's home before the rebellion, but now it was nothing more than cover to keep the rebel soldiers alive for a few more minutes.

"Go, go, go!" shouted his squad commander, wincing.

Damir sprinted in the indicated direction, the other surviving, bloodied soldiers in his squad running after him. There had been three squads when the mission started, which seemed like days ago, although it'd only been hours. The tattered survivors of those squads had come together in a combined effort, the rest the victims of the relentless and unceasing Army assault.

The hole led into a normal-looking living room, small fragments of what had once been the door spread across the floor. There was nothing special about the furniture other than the occasional bullet hole, and at this point in the rebellion, it was hard to find anywhere in Sogdia that didn't feature a few of those. No bodies, no blood—not that such things were shocking anymore. The romantic and mostly bloodless one-week revolution ideal now seemed childish.

Damir glanced back at the door. There were no bodies or indications of a battle inside, but someone had blown the door. Army raid in the middle of the night? Overzealous member of the FSA who thought they'd spotted fleeing soldiers?

He slumped against a wall and slid down to the floor, fiery agony in his chest. He could breathe without trouble and was grateful for both that and the chance to get out from under the enemy's assault.

A massive boom shook the house, rattling a plate and some silverware still on the dining room table. It hadn't been far, a half-klick or so away by his reckoning, but compared to the pinpoint accuracy the Army artillery had shown earlier, they might as well have been shooting at Earth. Depending on the enemy to miss wasn't a good strategy, but they needed a moment's rest.

Damir didn't understand how the squads had ended up in this position. This went beyond terrible intel. They'd walked right into Army assault infantry and retreated under fire from their artillery in a sector they were supposed to control. These were pointless losses.

Pain continued spreading from his chest, threatening his stomach and arms. He grimaced and looked down at the blood seeping from a wound. Shrapnel. Locking his jaw, he reached toward the wound. Damir closed his eyes, dug inside, and yanked out the piece of metal, managing not to scream.

He collapsed to his knees, his breathing ragged. With a shaking hand, he pulled out a med patch and placed it over the wound. Feeling pain was another way of remembering he was still alive, which was more than he could say for most of the men and women he'd set out with that morning.

His squad commander limped over to him, a med patch on his bloodied knee. "You did well out there, Sokov. If you hadn't spotted that flash, that exo would have blown the rest of us apart. Everyone here owes you their lives."

Damir rested his head against the wall. "Lot of good that did when they got us with the artillery."

"We can't do anything for the dead but avenge them, and to do that, we need to survive this. Keep that in mind."

The ground and house shook again. This time, the bright flash of the explosion made it through the darkened windows. Damir didn't want to think about how close that shot must have been. It didn't matter. A direct hit would kill them.

"We're still being jammed," the commander explained, taking a seat next to Damir. "I don't get it. They can't be jamming this entire area. It'd hurt them as much as it hurts us."

"It's like they knew we were coming." Damir shook his head. "We failed. We didn't disrupt the supply line, which means the Army's going to take this sector back. We might as well have given it to them gift-wrapped.

"We'll take it back from them, just like we have the others."

Damir closed his eyes, grateful for the numbness spreading from the med patch. "We take it back again? I don't get it. We were doing so good at the beginning, and now it's like we lose a battle for every one we win. The Army will win if this comes down to attrition."

"That's war," the commander muttered. "Trust me, I know." He rubbed his arm. "I spent ten years in the Army. Don't think they're any better than the FSA. They've just got better gear and a little more training at the front, but it's the same shit, same patterns. It's the rhythm of war. I know it seems hopeless now, but we'll have our chance soon, and we'll pay them back for everything they've done to us."

"What are we going to do now?" Damir asked. "Wait until they find us and kill us?"

The commander gestured weakly toward a darkened window. "They're not going to level this whole neighborhood just to get the scraps of squads they already busted up. They may have cut us up, but your warning and our grenades meant they bled for it. I hate to say it, but we're not worth that much effort now. As long as they're jamming, they can't do much with drones, especially on this kind of battlefield, and if they're jamming, that means they're worried about our forces being nearby."

Damir grunted his agreement, though he didn't feel it. All the Army needed was a good thermal ID of the squad and a decent laser comm, and artillery could level the house. He wanted to believe the government's forces wouldn't be so cavalier, but with almost all the civilians out of the neighborhood, both sides could lay waste to the area and not risk much in the way of innocent casualties, if there was such a thing left on New Samarkand.

Something kept nagging him, trying to get his

conscious attention. There was something wrong about this entire mission, and not just bad intel. He couldn't figure it out, his mind being clouded by his injuries, drugs, and fear.

The next explosion was so close that one of the standing men fell. They couldn't stay in the house. A loud roar passed overhead, the sound of gunship engines. Theirs? The Army's? He couldn't tell. If they risked exposing themselves to check, it might doom them all, but they couldn't stay too long before artillery killed them.

Damir groaned and stood. "We can't stay here."

The commander nodded and also stood. "You keep heading west until we get behind our lines."

Damir looked at the other survivors. Everyone was wounded in some way, and everyone had a med patch on, but they were all mobile. The commander, with his knee wound, was in the worst shape.

"I'll help you." Damir offered the man his shoulder.

"No, I'll slow you down," the commander replied. "You guys make your move, and I'll stay here. I'm going to draw their attention. It might give you a couple more minutes."

"That's insane." Damir shook his head. "You'll die."

"I'll get you all killed and die anyway if I come with you." The commander hobbled over to the door. "It's better for one man to die than all of you." He clapped Damir's shoulder. "You've got a good head on you, Sokov. When this is all over, I'm sure you'll be a good leader in the new government."

Damir looked at the other soldiers. There was a mixture of pity and relief on their faces, but no one else seemed willing to argue. So much for their revolutionary fraternity.

"Fine." Damir pointed at the closed back door. "Let's open that."

The soldiers clustered near the door, taking up positions to pull it aside. With a mighty grunt of exertion, they yanked it open.

The commander hobbled to the door, using his rifle as a cane. "Get going, and stay close to the houses. When you have a minute's head start, I'll draw their attention."

Damir shook his head. "This isn't right. We can carry you."

"Not fast enough. Now go. That's an order."

The other rebels hurried out, looking back and forth before darting away. They kept close to the wall of the long apartment building next to the house. Damir hesitated for a moment longer before hurrying after them, his injuries a mere ache at this point from the help of the med patch. He sprinted, lungs burning, until he caught up with the other survivors.

"We shouldn't—" he began.

Blood splattered on the ground and one of the men collapsed, a new huge hole in his tactical vest. He might as well have been wearing nothing. The crack of the rifle came right after the man hit the ground. Someone had fired from very, very far away.

"Sniper!" Damir jumped through a shattered window into the lobby of the apartment building. It wouldn't protect them from artillery, but a sniper couldn't shoot what he couldn't see.

Half the survivors panicked and opened up on full auto,

firing vainly into the distance. It was pointless. Given the delay between the shot and the sound, the sniper was well beyond their engagement distance. Another man gurgled and collapsed, his throat missing. The man right beside him made it one meter toward the building before he lost his head.

Damir stayed low, crawling the opposite way over the sharp fragments of metal on the ground. They cut into his palms, but adrenaline and painkillers made it a distant concern. He needed to get back to the house with the commander. They hadn't been getting picked off by a sniper there.

Something didn't make sense. The sniper was obviously lying in wait to the west toward their lines, but given their likely distance, they were well in rebel territory. There was no way the Army had pressed that far forward that quickly.

Damir tried to push the worry out of his mind as he crawled to a hole in the wall leading out to the side. A bright flare shot into the sky in the distance. He stared at it, unsure of what he was seeing for a couple of seconds.

"Damn it. That's how you're going to distract them?" Damir shook his head.

Thanks to the flare, he couldn't return to the house. He stayed on the ground, afraid that if he lifted his head, the barest hint of his thermal trace might be spotted by what-ever sniper had picked off the rest of the survivors.

Damir wasn't sure how long he laid there, his hands bleeding all over the floor when a round whistled overhead and struck the house. The explosion grew like a festive tree, flinging fiery debris all over the area. Pieces crashed into the lobby, smashing through the already weakened wall.

He groaned and rolled the opposite way, then crawled toward a corner. With the men dead and the commander vaporized, the Army might leave him alone. He didn't understand their relentless assault on a couple of squads. Was it vengeance for the rumored atrocities?

Mercs or overzealous rebels, it didn't matter. They were losing the propaganda war, and Damir suspected they were becoming worse than the UTC dogs they were trying to throw off the planet.

He took slow, deep breaths, trying to remain conscious. Nanites in med patches could do wonders, but he'd lost a lot of blood before shredding his hands and knees on the floor. The buzzing in his ears, constant since the explosion, didn't help.

"Is this how my part in the rebellion's going to end?" he muttered. "Dead in some damned apartment lobby?"

Damir closed his eyes. Glory was something for other men.

***

Distant voices sounded in the darkness. Damir groaned.

"Is he the only one?" someone asked.

"Yes," someone else replied.

Damir blinked his eyes open, not recognizing either voice. His whole body felt numb and cold, probably because his shirt was off, and he now wore four patches. Two men in dark uniforms stood next to him with a hoverstretcher, both with rifles slung over their backs. They didn't wear FSA patches, and they weren't Army.

"You're with the mercenaries?" Damir croaked, his voice hoarse.

One of the men grinned. "Yeah, we dragged your ass out of there. You're welcome."

"What about the sniper?" he asked, his voice barely a whisper. "He killed...the others."

"Don't worry. You're not the only rebel we pulled out of there. We took out a bunch of Army, but we didn't have the numbers to stay and fight." He pointed the opposite way. "We had some help."

Damir turned his head. A sleek gray hovertank floated about fifty meters away. Its cannon was angled up. With a loud buzz, the shell zoomed out of the main gun, a surprisingly quiet blur, not unexpected for a railgun.

His heart rate kicked up. It'd been the briefest of glimpses, not even a second. He was drugged and wounded, unsure about a lot of things, but that didn't keep his mind from screaming at him. The Army had dropped all sorts of bombs, missiles, and rockets on the rebels since the war began, and Damir had seen most of them, including the one that had killed his squad commander. The round he had just seen launched reminded him of another he'd seen not all that long ago.

"It couldn't be," he murmured under his breath.

There was no way the merc tank would have bombed the rebels. He didn't doubt they would turn on the FSA, but why bother saving him if that was the case?

He was seeing things. That was the only explanation.

CHAPTER TWENTY-SIX

October 2, 2230, Solar System, En Route to Earth, Aboard *Argo*

Jia lay back on the bed in their cabin, a data window floating above her. Her PNIU was transmitting the sound directly to her ear, letting Erik slumber in peace behind her. She wanted to sleep too, but this time she couldn't blame it on circadian rhythms as much as her paranoid mind working overtime. Alina and the ID were working on processing the information Emma had forwarded, but Jia couldn't shake the feeling they might already be too late.

Now that they were so close to Earth, she could get near-real-time Terran news feeds. She didn't expect the Core to announce anything over the news, but there might be a clue hidden among the relentless noise of the so-called news.

The feed started, the chyron making bile rise in the back of her throat.

DEADLY TERROR ON NEW SAMARKAND. FRONTIER MURDER!

The anchor looked at the camera drone with a stern expression. "The Defense Directorate and Criminal Investigations Directorate are still providing minimal information after a brief admission of what they described as a major terrorist incident in Sogdia a little under a month ago in the capital city of New Samarkand. There have been no reports of casualties or the nature of the event, leading some to claim a government coverup, especially given the communication delays. We'll bring you updates as they become available."

Jia killed the feed. She hated being right all the time.

October 3, 2230, Neo Southern California Metroplex, Private Hangar of the *Argo*

Jia wasn't surprised that Alina was waiting for them in the hangar, despite having not contacted them ahead of time. She'd voiced her suspicions to Erik, and he'd agreed that New Samarkand might be the delivery target, but without Alina's go-ahead, that meant nothing. Borrowing the *Argo* was easy enough, but getting the jumpship required the military to give it up. They needed more to go on.

They sent a transmission to Alina to tell her to come to the galley, where Jia, Erik, Malcolm, and Emma waited for her. When the ID agent stepped in, her grim mien didn't portend good news.

She sat down and frowned. "If you are all half as good as I believe, you already know what I'm going to say."

"There's a full-scale insurrection underway on New Samarkand," Jia replied, folding her arms. "It started in early September. And let me guess, the military's totally surprised by the level and amount of weaponry being deployed by the rebel forces."

Malcolm swallowed. "It's just rebels, right? Provide enough reinforcements, and it doesn't matter if the Core gave them bigger guns."

Erik shook his head. "It's not going to be that simple."

"Exactly." Alina looked at Erik and Jia before visibly calming herself. "The government is selling it, as you might have already seen, as a terrorist disturbance, but Jia's right. It's a full-scale insurrection, and it's pretty bad, based on the initial reports. The local garrison was pushed back right away, and the only reason the rebels haven't overwhelmed everything is some odd strategic choices by their leadership in the opening assaults. Reinforcements were rerouted from nearby systems, but a transport was heavily damaged either by pirates or a rebel space force, so Fleet is likely spreading resources throughout the system, including guarding the HTP."

That was the problem with places so far away. It brought new meaning to the idea of fighting the last war.

Jia sighed and shook her head. "Then we're too late. The Core already started the rebellion. We might have helped disrupt their shipping networks, but we can't do anything for the colony."

"I wouldn't say that." Alina managed a weak grin. "Normally, we'd be completely outmaneuvered. With the rebellion already underway, this is going to go down like these things always do—the military will fight the enemy to a standstill and convince them it's not worth their effort to keep fighting."

Erik's brows lifted. "But we have a way of getting there quickly, one the Core doesn't."

Jia shook her head. "We already discussed this. A handful of troops won't make a difference. What's the idea, then? That'll we keep jumping back and forth, filling up with troops?"

Alina snorted. "Hell, no. The DD hasn't asked for that, and if they did, I'd argue strongly against it. The rest of the UTC isn't ready to know about the jumpship, and the more we use it, the more we risk it. Bouncing around as a glorified troop transport, especially when we know there are hostile ships in the system, guarantees trouble." She pointed at Jia and then Erik. "But yes, you two will be going to New Samarkand."

"And doing what?" Erik frowned. "We're both good in a battle, but we're not good enough to turn the tide of a war."

"That depends on how you're used." Alina sliced the air with her hand. Images of the faces of different men and women appeared. "I intend to use you as an ID asset, not a military asset. Ghosts work in the shadows, stabbing men in the back."

Jia nodded at the images. "Who are these people?"

"Dead ID agents," Alina explained. "We had an unusual number on New Samarkand because of previous leads pointing to trouble there. The thing is, as you can imagine from the comm delay, we're just finding out about their deaths. One of the best agents was killed investigating—and this should surprise exactly no one—unusual shipments, command and control associated with the rebels, not the weapons. Most of our local agents were wiped out in suspicious rebel and/or mercenary attacks within the first forty-eight hours. Someone knew who they were and where they were to target them. That screams Core to us. They must have been planning this for a long time, scoping out the colony and sniffing out all the ghosts."

Erik pounded his palm with his fist. "So, it's not about stopping the rebellion?"

"No, it's about taking down any Core assets. Military intelligence can handle the rest on the ground, and I suspect once the Core's neutralized, the rebellion fails." Alina dismissed the images and brought up a smaller version of the star map Emma had shown them on Mars.

"Ah, my best work in the last week," Emma announced with a smirk.

"We cross-referenced that data with other information we have," Alina explained, pointing at Gliese 581. "It all points to the Core shipping equipment to New Samarkand. Their involvement also might explain the heavy use of mercs and the unusual viciousness being displayed by the rebels. They're trying to blame it on the government, but the classified reports make it clear the rebel forces aren't showing a lot of restraint, considering it's their own colony. What's the good of taking over if you kill everyone and blow half of it up?"

Jia rubbed her temples. "They could have wiped out the garrison by now, or blown up the entire colony."

Alina shook her head. "It makes no sense to risk exposure with the arms shipments if the end game was simply destroying the colony. If we assume the Core has partial control of the rebels and likely complete control of the mercs, it might explain the unusual activity the military and agents reported. The one thing I don't doubt is that the

Core purposely started an insurrection on New Samarkand."

"But why?" Jia asked.

"To weaken the UTC." Alina frowned. "We've had our suspicions about Diogenes' Hope, and there have been a couple of close calls in the last few years, more than you might imagine. Someone's going out of their way to stir up trouble in a lot of colonies."

"I thought the Core wanted to take over the UTC," Malcolm commented with a confused look.

"Weaken the central government enough and strengthen some alternatives, and they might be able to," Jia murmured.

Alina nodded slowly. "If we take them out at the source, it'll solve the problem, and that's why I'm sending you to New Samarkand. Not to stop the rebellion, but to investigate and neutralize any elements of the Core." She tapped her PNIU. "That's well within your capabilities."

An image of a gray hovertank appeared. A gunship materialized next, followed by two small fighters.

"These are all mercenary vehicles," Alina explained. "All of them display unusual maneuverability and damage resistance."

"So the mercs know what they're doing," Erik commented, his eyes on the tank.

"I think it's worse than that. Much worse."

The images vanished, replaced by a half-destroyed gunship, the wreckage strewn around on a city street. Now that it was at ground level, it was easy to tell there was something wrong with it. The whole thing was too thin. The camera drone flew to the opposite side, revealing where a cockpit would be. A soldier stood next to a pried-open compartment, pointing in disgust to a half-crushed human brain covered in tubes and wires. The feed froze.

"Elites," Jia spat through clenched teeth. "They couldn't be satisfied with sticking them in those damned bots."

"The government's worried about this getting out." Alina inclined her head toward the recording. "It's unclear how much the rebels know about it, but it's highly likely the Core is using the rebellion not just to weaken the UTC government but to further refine their weapons by field-testing them. We have no idea how stable these things are, but we do know the more opportunities we give the Core to test things, the more dangerous they'll get. If they can start mass-producing these things, they could present a major threat to half the UTC."

"We beat them before," Erik replied. "I don't care if they're hiding in a tank. I'll just bring a lot of missiles with me."

"We could contact the rebel command," Jia suggested. "Explain who and what they're working with."

Alina chuckled. "Yes, because a bunch of insurrectionists is going to believe a government ghost." She shook her head. "It doesn't matter if you present this footage. They won't believe you. If we had more time, I'd suggest backchannel work to convince the rebels their new bene-factors aren't going to help them, but it's like Jia pointed out. We're behind in this, and the rebellion's already underway. We can't know on Earth how bad the situation currently is, just what it was weeks ago. Accordingly, this is going to be an unusual mission." She leaned forward, a faint look of excitement appearing on her face. "You'll be running far ahead of Earth, the ID, and the DD, so this is going to require a lot of autonomy, and there's only so much I can do to prepare the ground for you. By the time any messages from me arrive, this whole thing will probably be over one way or another."

"Sounds like fun," Malcolm muttered, rubbing the back of his neck. "And by that, I mean it sounds terrifying."

Alina grinned. "The best missions are. I can give you credentials and info that'll introduce you to whatever's left of the surviving ID and help you recruit assistance from the local military if you need firepower, but I can't guarantee anything."

"What about Anne and Kant?" Erik asked. "If we don't have soldiers backing us, it'd be nice to have them."

Alina sighed. "They're recovering."

"Recovering?" Erik's brow lifted.

Alina nodded. "I'd intended them to be on standby only for you, but something came up, and I needed trusted agents on short notice. They're both fine, but I think they need more than a few days to recover from their injuries. I won't make the mistake of utilizing your backup resources like that again."

Jia stared at the woman, more unnerved by her callous point of view in calling people resources than upset that she and Erik wouldn't have additional ghosts helping them. It was hard not to wonder when Alina would point them at the wrong mission and be annoyed at the loss of more *resources.*

"I want you to head out to Penglai right away," Alina explained. "Pick up the jumpship and get to New

Samarkand. I want you to follow up on the slain agent's work and look into the command and control equipment."

"What if that's a dead end?" Erik asked. "The military might have already figured that out and won."

"Then consider it a free vacation to a war-torn colony. Given the slaughter that occurred in the first couple of days, the surviving agents are keeping a low profile, as confirmed by the transmissions the ID has received. The few who are left are trying their best to help the DD, but they are overwhelmed, and some are long-term assets who can't risk their cover. Bringing you two in from the outside, especially if this involves the Core, will shake things up. You'll have general freedom of movement, and it may unnerve any Core elements and get them to make mistakes."

"Can we jump that far?" Jia asked, her brow furrowed in concern. "New Samarkand is a lot farther out than Chiron."

"Raphael seems to believe it's possible." Alina shrugged. "Consider this another field test."

Emma held up her hand, a small spherical map of the UTC floating in it. "We've been working on longer-range navigation. We've been preparing for this on my end, at least."

Erik wasn't convinced, judging by the look on his face. "So, we're going to jump twenty light-years to New Samarkand with credentials that'll let us get our foot in the door, assuming the local government hasn't been overthrown, to hunt cyborg tanks and gunships with the help of the local surviving ghosts. Also, most of their fellow agents were assassinated, meaning the Core has a good feeling for the state of the colony."

Alina looked to the side for a moment before nodding. "That's accurate, I'd say. I trust your discretion on this matter. If you feel there's nothing you can accomplish, you can leave. Obviously, we can't let the jump drive fall into enemy hands. Do whatever you need to prevent that, but I'd recommend not bringing the ship anywhere near the planet."

"And if we need to destroy it?" Erik asked, raising an eyebrow.

"Better it is destroyed than fall into the Core's hands," Alina replied without so much as a change in tone or a blink. "As always, glean intel or data you can from the Elites or anyone else associated with the Core."

"A war, huh?" Erik snickered. "This is one time people can't bitch if we blow anything up."

"The Core and their Elites are helping prop up the rebellion," Jia replied. "If we get lucky, we might be able to stop the rebellion in its tracks and save a lot of lives on both sides." She clenched her hand into a fist. "It's time to let them know that no matter where they go or how far they run, we'll be there."

CHAPTER TWENTY-SEVEN

October 3, 2230, Gliese 581, New Samarkand, Sogdia

Damir rubbed at his chest, trying to soothe the ache. It was a dull non-entity compared to the agony he'd suffered from his initial wound, but it was distracting, and a distraction was the last thing he wanted in the field. No matter how hard he tried to keep his mind on the mission, the ache was there, reminding him of how close he'd come to death days prior as if whispering in his ear that he hadn't escaped it yet. He didn't mind dying for the rebellion, but he wanted to know they'd win first.

In a reasonable situation, he wouldn't have been out on patrol so soon after suffering bad injuries, but the Free Samarkand Army had suffered serious losses in the last couple of days, enough that the fate of the rebellion was in doubt unless they could retake key sectors. Any man or woman who could carry a gun had to be available. He'd asked for refreshed med patches and volunteered to go back out.

A desire to serve fueled part of his determination to return to the front line. Suspicion fueled the other part. There was something off about their recent defeats, something pointing at a danger to the entire rebellion.

The higher-ups were keeping it quiet, but there'd been too many frustrating reversals, and he couldn't have been the only one to suspect spies. What Damir didn't understand was why the Army had an unerring ability to anticipate strike missions that threatened their control of certain sectors but were easy to surprise in different situations. Their embedded spies should have been helpful in both situations.

Rocks crunched under his boots as he marched along with eight other men, the thoughts refusing to leave. The day's mission wasn't anything grander than a patrol. Mercenary jamming equipment and good anti-aircraft defenses had made drones useless in the area for both sides, requiring boots on the ground. The only thing unusual about the mission was who was leading it.

He glanced at the black-clad soldier at the front of the formation. The man wasn't a member of the FSA. He was one of the mercenaries hired by the leaders of the rebellion without consulting anyone else. More of the mercs were leading rebel squads in the last week from what he'd heard, the inevitable result of the loss of so many experienced soldiers to injuries or death.

Their rebellion was slowly changing from a campaign waged by passionate rebels to mercenary soldiers and equipment executing tasks for credits. That didn't speak well for the future of the rebellion.

The presence of the mercenary Sinclair kept Damir's

suspicion burning about the recent Army successes. He'd wondered during his last mission why the jamming was so persistent, only to learn the next day it'd been the fault of the mercenaries. Their explanations for why they'd done so made sense, but combined with the questionable sniper position and the suspect shell, the rebel's concerns had grown into a full-blown conspiracy theory with the rent-a-soldiers at the center. His mystery had suspects and means. What remained was to nail down the motive.

Damir was proud of his latest theory for its simplicity. He'd worried about the mercs changing sides, but they'd had ample opportunity, and he'd personally seen them engage the Army, so that wasn't the plan. The available evidence pointed to the hired killers conspiring against the FSA, not to turn the tide in the Army's favor, but to extend the war so they could earn more money. It was obvious once he thought about it.

He didn't understand why anyone didn't see what they'd been doing. Low-level soldiers like him might not have the big picture, but the leaders of the FSA must have seen it. Were they so desperate for help that they were willing to turn a blind eye?

The mercs controlled the bulk of the rebellion's recon equipment and jammers, so they could set up situations to their advantage while killing off the FSA soldiers who knew too much. In that scenario, there might not have been enough concrete evidence to convince the leaders that there was something wrong with the mercs.

That was why Damir had kept his mouth shut. He didn't have solid proof, only a theory based on question-able circumstantial evidence. No one would believe him if he claimed the shell that had killed his last squad commander had come from a merc hovertank. They would accuse him of misremembering the position of the sniper. It wasn't like he'd recorded everything during the battle. At times, he had to remind himself he wasn't imagining things, that everything he'd seen and experienced, however horrible, was true.

The stories that the mercs were using some sort of dangerous Tin Men couldn't be ignored. Most of the FSA had passed it off as government propaganda, but the government was officially denying anything unusual about the rebel forces. It didn't make sense for them to accuse the rebels and mercs of something so heinous, then deny it to most people. The government never ignored easy propaganda victories. There were too many loose threads that begged to be pulled. There was a truth there, trying to wriggle into the sunlight.

Sinclair paused at a corner and threw his hand up. The squad halted and readied their rifles, waiting for another command. He gestured them forward with a hand signal before rushing around the corner.

"Clear," he declared, looking satisfied. "We're past the primary patrol area, so we're going to move on to our secondary mission."

Damir frowned. "What secondary mission? No one said anything about a secondary mission during the briefing."

Other rebels nodded their agreement, weariness mixed with agitation on their faces. Mental preparation could do a lot to keep morale steady. Sinclair either didn't know that, or worse, he didn't care.

"You weren't told during the briefing because of

concerns about government spies in our ranks." Sinclair inclined his head at Damir. "But the men of this squad have proven themselves dedicated to the cause. I would think you'd be eager to jump at the chance to go above and beyond."

Damir gritted his teeth to stop himself from scoffing. There was something galling about a mercenary talking about dedication to a higher cause. The FSA shouldn't have had to pay outsiders to help them win their freedom, and if they hadn't, he wouldn't have to suspect those same outsiders of betraying the FSA's trust for more money.

"What's the secondary mission, then?" Damir asked, glancing at the other squad members. They all looked tired. Not just looked, were. This was the third patrol for some of them.

"We're looking for a target of strategic importance," Sinclair explained. He tapped a PNIU wrist interface, and the image of a bland-looking man with brown hair appeared. "This man is the rebellion's greatest enemy, an Intelligence Directorate ghost who has been leaking information to the government. He's been posing as a pro-rebellion civilian in different sectors."

He rattled off the explanation with all the care of someone discussing his lunch choices, certainly not the tone somebody would expect for a serious mission.

Damir stared at the image. He didn't recognize the man, but if he was a ghost, he might have been using disguises. An ID agent might explain the irregularities he'd attributed to the mercs, but it was hard to believe one ghost could be responsible for so much trouble. Or was it?

Bile rose in the back of his throat. Had he been wrong

in his suspicions this entire time? His mercenary traitor theory didn't explain why they'd saved him during the debacle of the last mission. Killing everyone who wasn't in the know would make it easier to control the information. He'd tried to tell himself they needed at least one FSA soldier to spread rumors and that was why he'd survived, but sometimes the most obvious explanation was conveniently the correct one.

"Stay in a loose formation, and we'll check out this area," Sinclair continued. "We have no intel to suggest any Army patrols are in the area but keep alert. If we get lucky, we might do a great service to the rebellion."

They continued walking, poking inside the windows of damaged shops and buildings but not finding anything or anyone of interest. It struck Damir as pointless. A ghost wouldn't be hiding under a table in a half-destroyed clothing store, especially one good enough to disrupt rebel operations so effectively. Something about the mercenary's tone made it sound like a test.

Sinclair sidled up to Damir. When he spoke, his voice was almost a whisper. "You don't like me very much, do you, Sokov?"

Damir spared a brief glance at the other man. "I don't have to like you. You just have to help us win."

"Why don't you like me?" Sinclair looked curious. "Be honest. This is not the only mission where you'll be under my command. I need to know you have my back and will follow my orders."

"Your back?" Damir scoffed. Conspiracy theories weren't necessary for the rest of the conversation. "I'll do what I'm ordered to by my superiors in the FSA, and they told me to follow you, but let's be honest—you're only here because you're getting paid. You don't care about our cause. So no, I don't trust you."

Sinclair nodded slowly. "Ah, I see. That makes sense, but you're wrong."

"You're a mercenary." Damir frowned. "Are you trying to claim you're doing this for free?"

"We all have expenses." Sinclair slowed at an alley, his eyes narrowed, and tapped the side of his helmet to magnify the sights. He nodded, satisfied there were no enemies, and moved into the alley. "My friends and I don't work for just anyone. It's dangerous, when you think about it, to participate in a rebellion. We've had to destroy the bodies of our own men to make sure they don't get IDed. Do you know why we're willing to take the risk?"

"Because you're being paid well?"

Sinclair shook his head. "Because we *do* believe in your cause, or at least in its motivation. The UTC is corrupt, and it has no business controlling humanity. I fight for my own reasons, and this planet is part of them. I'm not the only new friend of the FSA who feels the same way, so you shouldn't show such disrespect toward us. We're brothers of sorts, and you should keep that in mind when we're out on missions together."

Damir blinked in surprise, then let the conversation drop. There was a new intensity in the mercenary's eyes that convinced Damir he wasn't lying. Sinclair also had a point. The government might look the other way when mercs got a little rough helping out corporations, but that was different from allowing them to freely aid rebellions.

By helping the FSA, the mercenary company might have doomed themselves to arrest or death.

This new information challenged Damir and forced him to admit he might have been wrong about his conspiracy theory. It was a difficult, stressful time, and his mind might be trying to explain away the horror of what he'd witnessed and his own foolish naivete. The rebellion wasn't easy or glorious. It was a bloody, slow slog that was costing good people's lives. He might have been desperate to find an explanation, something that would justify it all.

"What about you?" Sinclair asked.

Damir frowned, his suspicion returning. "What are you asking?"

Sinclair motioned around the battle-scarred area. "Some people might say this isn't worth it for a tiny bit of freedom, but you're fighting, and you have from the beginning. What motivates a young man to take up arms and risk his life against the UTC government? What made you decide that death was worth the risk? Is this about freedom and self-determination? Or are you risking your life to feel alive?"

Damir hesitated, not insulted by the questions but surprised. It wasn't like his story was a secret, but he didn't like baring his soul to a mercenary, idealistic or otherwise. Sinclair might be his commander, but they weren't friends.

"My father is the reason I joined," Damir replied quietly after more thought.

"Your father's in the FSA?"

Damir shook his head. "No, he's not. He's…let me start from the beginning."

"Please do." Sinclair sounded curious.

"I wasn't born on New Samarkand," Damir explained. "I was born on Earth in Saint Petersburg. When I was a baby, my father screwed up. Fell in with some people who convinced him to do stupid things. He was greedy and got involved in an embezzlement scheme." He scoffed. "The pathetic part was it wasn't even that much. He thought that if it wasn't much, it'd be easier to get away with it." He sucked in a breath. "He was wrong. Isn't that how it always goes? If you steal a little, you get caught, but if you're bold and steal millions and billions, everyone calls you brilliant."

Sinclair nodded, surveying the scattered troops behind him before turning back toward Damir. "If you're here, that suggests they sentenced him to transportation and indentured servitude rather than prison."

"That's true, but it's more complicated than that." Damir sighed. "My mother divorced him because she didn't want to leave Earth to be with a man who got himself transported, but that didn't stop him from keeping in contact with us, and she didn't want to deny me my father, even if she didn't approve of what he did." He smiled wistfully. "The man was twenty light-years away, but he sent so many messages that I felt like he was always there, helping raise me."

"And your mother?"

Damir shrugged. "She never remarried. I think she always loved him but was frustrated with him. When I got old enough, I wrote back to him regularly. The thing is, he completed his sentence and started a new life here. He wanted us to visit, but it's expensive, and my mother made it clear she wasn't going to leave Earth to move to a place like this. She told me all the time that it didn't make sense to leave the center of civilization to go somewhere less civilized. She said colonies were for criminals and people with nothing left to lose." He stared at the ground and shook his head. "But then she died—freak accident. I decided there was nothing left for me on Earth, so with my father's help, I came here at ten years old. That was what the colony represented to me: a new start, almost a rebirth."

"And you came to love your new home that much?" Sinclair asked. He motioned to the red sky. "This place is many things, but it's not Earth, and it's not going to be like Earth for a long time, if ever. You'll live your whole life here under domes."

"If the colonies prove anything, it's that humans are adaptable. Give us enough centuries, and people will find Earth an uncomfortable place to live." Damir kicked a pebble. "After three years, I was really fitting in. I didn't miss Earth at all. I liked the more laid-back pace here. I liked how people cared about each other. It was more like a community than I'd ever been in before."

"I could see that." Sinclair chuckled. "You should have gone to the real frontier. It's like living in an annoying little village."

"I might like that, but I came here for my father. He was so much better here than he'd ever been on Earth. He had his own accounting business, but setting that up led to trouble."

Sinclair arched an eyebrow. "Accounting led to trouble?"

Damir bobbed his head. "Yes. He'd gotten business contracts with companies that did work with the govern-

ment, and because of that, he learned that a few local officials were skimming."

"Ah. That makes sense."

"You have to understand. He had reformed, and he was
disgusted." Damir stopped for a moment to scan the area
for trouble. "In a colony, that kind of corruption is a bigger
problem. It hurts everyone, so he made an important
decision."

"To do something about it," Sinclair concluded.

"Yes," Damir replied. "He wanted to expose them. He
told me, 'When I first got in trouble, I kept trying to justify
my crimes to myself. I said I deserved it, but I was nothing
more than a criminal, and a criminal always recognizes his
own kind.'"

Sinclair looked up, sweeping the sky for drones or
aircraft. "Colonial graft is profitable for the same reason
it's more damaging—fewer available targets with more
local power. A lot of well-meaning officials end up on a
colony and get corrupted. I've seen it on more than one."

"My father grew more and more frustrated, trying to
figure out a way to take them down without it leading back
to him," Damir explained. "It didn't help that most people
he knew told him to keep his head down and look the
other way."

"That's what I'd expect."

"He fell in with some men a couple years back who
changed everything. They were the leaders of what would
become the FSA. They were the Free Samarkand
Committee back then."

Sinclair whistled. "Insurrectionists. That might be the

dirtiest word in the UTC. It takes a brave man to associate with those kinds of people."

"He kept it quiet," Damir admitted. "I was one of the few people who knew, but it didn't help." His hand tightened around his rifle. "It didn't save him."

"They found out he was investigating them?"

Damir nodded. "His body was found outside a waste processing center two years ago under suspicious circumstances, two days after his sting against those local officials. He told me he had contacts at the CID who could help him." He snorted. "Not that it saved him. No one ever solved his murder, but he'd been smart enough to send out his evidence. Those officials are in prison now, but that didn't bring my father back." He clenched his teeth. "The thing that drove me over the edge was the murder investigation. There was plenty of evidence—witnesses, recordings, that kind of thing. Some of the people and evidence conveniently disappeared, and the cops didn't care. The CID seemed content to take them down for corruption, not the murder. We all got the message. The government would sacrifice some pawns for the sake of appearance, but we little people should keep our nose out of investigating them. After that, it was easy. I hooked up with the FSA. I used to think they were a bunch of extremists, but everything they said made more sense after my father's murder."

Sinclair gave him a pitying look. "I see. That's the problem with people and sacrifice. There's a difference between unnecessary and necessary sacrifice, but don't worry, Sokov. Your father's sacrifice won't be in vain. Your fellow rebels' sacrifices will not be in vain. We will free your world, no matter the cost. All we need is loyal soldiers like you."

"I hope you're right," Damir replied, craning his neck to take in the bullet-riddled wreck of a flitter. "I'm tired of the self-serving scum winning."

"Don't worry." Sinclair's hungry smile unsettled Damir. "This time, they won't."

CHAPTER TWENTY-EIGHT

October 4, 2230, Solar System, En Route to UTC Space Fleet Base Penglai, Aboard _Argo_

Jia leapt from the barren, rocky ledge, arms outstretched. If she didn't snag the rope, she'd plummet into the river below. Her hand almost cleared the rope before she tightened her fingers, her arms jerking.

Erik wanted to clap, even if it was a simulation. He'd run this course fifteen minutes prior, and he knew how difficult it was. While he wanted her to succeed, he also hoped she finished slower than his time. Sometimes a man needed bragging rights.

"They don't have rivers and ledges on New Samarkand," Jia complained. "Shouldn't this course have reflected the planet or Sogdia better? We should be running through a densely packed urban environment, jumping from building to building, rappelling down walls."

"We're not doing this to prepare for New Samarkand," Erik replied.

"We aren't?" Jia asked, sounding surprised.

"No." Erik laughed. "This is us using simulators for fun. When I suggested this, I thought it'd be an entertaining contest, not battle prep for the mission."

"Fun?" Jia huffed and wiped the sweat off her brow. "That's what we're calling this? I don't know if having to roll under those falling log traps was fun."

Jia couldn't see Erik, though he was at the edge of the room. Holographic clouds concealed his presence. The nano-AR room aboard the *Argo* could only handle one person at a time in the extreme obstacle course simulation unless they were running it at the same time and pace. Thus far, her performance suggested that was a possibility. She was closing in on the final leg of the short but intense course.

Jia swung on the rope like a pendulum, speeding toward the other ledge. She released and landed with a smooth roll before jumping to her feet. After a couple of deep breaths, she sprinted toward a hill with statues of Zitarks breathing fire along the path.

Erik clapped. "That was a lot nicer than my crash into the ledge. Try not to get singed."

"It's annoying, always having to go so far to get the jumpship," Jia puffed. "If the ship was right by Earth, we wouldn't have to spend time doing things like this to keep us entertained."

Erik laughed. "We do this kind of thing on Earth too. I think you should accept that we're weird."

"Not weird," Jia insisted. "Non-standard."

"Which is another way of saying weird."

"It sounds less antisocial." Jia's breathing was ragged

from her pace. "But don't tell me you like having to fly all the way to the asteroid belt to pick up the ship."

"Have to keep it safe," Erik replied. "It's safer there than it would be parked near Earth."

"They could house it at one of the major Fleet bases," Jia suggested, picking up speed. She approached the bottom of the hill and surged forward, the fire-breathing space raptor statue missing her entirely. "Without Emma, the ship can't jump anyway. They could park it at a Fleet base closer to Earth and save us a lot of time, which would mean we could solve problems quicker. If a ship's not safe surrounded by a flotilla of other Fleet ships, it'll never be safe. I'm not convinced it's worth the inconvenience, not just for us, but for the ID and DD. We're well past testing the jump drive and are now using it to protect the interests of the UTC."

"True, but I've been thinking about this a lot the last couple of days. The jump drive's a tool, but it's not even the main tool we need for that kind of thing." Erik shook out his arms. Watching Jia run the course made his muscles ache more than they already were.

Jia ducked to avoid the next burst of fire. She rolled back to her feet and surged past three other statues before they could get her. "What do we need then? What's better than the ability to jump anywhere in the UTC in days instead of weeks and months?"

"Better, faster comm," Erik explained. "If we'd known about the rebellion right away, we could have gone there and done something before things got out of hand. It's a twisted irony. We have the jump drive and Emma, but we're still limited by the sheer size of the UTC and the limits of the HTPs and message transfer. Trust me, this is something I've been thinking about since Molino."

"You think it would have made a difference there?" Jia asked.

"I think it wouldn't have given the Core this big of a head start."

Jia wiped sweat off her brow as she crested the top of the hill. A series of bamboo poles stretched in front of her in a zigzag pattern with just enough space for a single foot. Glowing three-eyed fish jumped from the water below, their mouths filled with sharp teeth.

Erik had come close to falling on this part of the course. He wasn't ashamed to admit Jia had superior balance. That was probably why she was such a gifted pilot.

Jia shook out her arms and took a moment to catch her breath. "But if we take out the Core, there won't be so many insurrections. Comm and jump drives won't matter. They're the disease, and those other things are just med patches we're slapping on the body to deal with them."

"Not so sure about that," Erik answered.

She charged forward and jumped for the first pole. Her body was turning before she'd even landed to help her push off to the next pole. There wasn't enough concentration left to speak as she bounded through the obstacle. With a final grunt of exertion, she launched herself onto the edge of the cliff that was part of a mountain.

"Don't get too stuck on the Core as the explanation for everything wrong in the UTC," Erik replied. "They're responsible for a lot of the messed-up stuff, but not all of it. And it's not like every rebellion comes out of nowhere."

Jia jogged around the mountain until she spotted shallow, narrow stone stairs. "What are you saying?" she got out between pants. "That insurrection is justified? That these antisocial killers should be able to do whatever they want? There are mechanisms for expressing their concerns via their MPs in Parliament. They don't have any reason to take up arms."

"I'm just saying, it doesn't always come out of nowhere," Erik replied. "It can be surprising, but it's rarely shocking."

"You used to help put down insurrections. Do you regret doing that now?"

"Yeah, I did, and no, I don't. There wasn't a single rebellion I dealt with that would have led to a better life for the colony involved, and in most cases, it was a small group of extremists doing all the fighting. Because I *was* involved with that sort of thing, I understand the dynamic." Erik shook his head. "Whether or not the Core is behind it, there's always going to be a heart of the rebellion, people who believe in the cause. I'm not going to claim I've never been sympathetic to rebel grievances, but in my experience, what inevitably happens is whatever good intentions might be behind the rebellion get swallowed up pretty quickly by the people who are just there looking for power or an excuse to kill others. That's why I'm glad they all failed. They wouldn't make a new and better UTC. They would have ended up as kingdoms run by power-hungry idiots."

Jia hit the stairs, her footwork tight and precise. She was almost at the end of the course. Erik grunted. She had taken it far faster than he'd anticipated.

"The jump drive might change all that," Erik continued. "Assuming they can figure out some way to get it to work that doesn't require Emma." When Jia continued her huffing and puffing, he elaborated. "If a ship can get somewhere quickly, messages can get there quickly too. Even if it takes a couple of days, that's still better than what we see at a lot of places. The thing is, when you boil their complaints down, it's always the same thing: they don't want to be bossed around by people who are so far away. That's understandable, but the smaller the colony, the more pointless autonomy ends up being. If communication is closer to real-time, it'll cut down on the motivation."

Jia arrived at the bottom of the stairs, red-faced and dripping sweat. She sprinted toward the grav tramp that would send her into the sky rings, the last part of the course, a grueling widely spaced fifty-ring upper-body workout with no margin for error. If she fell, she'd plummet into the river below and fail the course.

She hadn't complained when he ran the course and favored his left arm. He didn't consider it cheating since it was part of him, but it definitely gave him an advantage. The only reason their times were close was because of that. His attempt on the poles had been far slower and much less graceful.

Jia hit the grav tramp at a perfect angle and launched her body toward the first ring. Quick movements sent her through the next rings so fast she surprised Erik, but her muscles had to be straining.

"Keep it up," Erik shouted, clapping. "You're almost there. You've got this."

Jia cleared the final ring but stumbled on her landing. She bellowed a challenge and charged the blue finish line, ignoring anything but making her legs moving faster. After crossing the line, she slowed and dropped to her knees. A puddle of sweat formed around her.

"You beat me by a good ten seconds," Erik announced with a laugh. "I was ahead timewise for most of the course, but you really destroyed me on those poles. I thought the rings would slow you down, but you might as well have had a cybernetic arm, the way you took them."

Jia laid on her back and spread out her arms, taking deep, slow breaths. "I think I'm dying. I don't know if dying was worth beating you." She rolled onto her side. "I just remembered something. Isn't the guy who told you about the Obsidian Detective Act on New Samarkand?"

"Nigel Anders?" Erik nodded slowly. "Yeah, he was the governor of Molino before leaving after the attack, but he moved out of the system about six months back."

"Good timing," Jia replied. "Warzones aren't fun. It'll be hard even for us to go into a warzone."

"Don't kid yourself. We've already been in plenty."

CHAPTER TWENTY-NINE

<u>October 5, 2230, Gliese 581, New Samarkand, Sogdia</u>

Damir kicked in the half-blasted door. It collapsed to the floor with an echoing thud, revealing a mostly empty storage room. He ignored the door and focused on sweeping the room for traps or enemies. Unless they were tiny bots, they wouldn't fit in the small boxes that remained in the room.

There'd been a battle in the sector a couple of hours earlier, and Command wanted the entire area swept and confirmed clean so there wouldn't be any surprises during their upcoming counterattack. It would help them avoid unfortunate reversals.

Damir's squad had never located the alleged ghost on the last mission, and he remained unsure of the true source of the FSA's problems in central Sogdia, especially compared to their successes in other areas. Their lengthy ghost hunt had conveniently taken the squad far away from other patrols who had come under fire, but that wasn't proof. He had no proof.

After explaining his story to Sinclair, Damir had hoped for reciprocity, but the man offered nothing more. He was a cipher, vacillating between unsettling and professional. Damir couldn't bring himself to trust him, regardless of what he'd said about the rebellion.

Damir stepped out of the room and nodded to Sinclair down the hallway. Other soldiers cleared their rooms and nodded at him. He walked over to the next room, slowing for a minute to take in where they were. Sinclair had ordered them into the building, and Damir hadn't thought much about it at the time. After a month of brutal fighting, the original functions of a lot of buildings seemed unimportant. He evaluated locations in terms of how many enemies might be hiding there, if they could survive low-level bombardment, and if they had any useful supplies for the FSA.

His beloved colony had been reduced to raw materials for war. At the rate they were going, there would be nothing but a huge pile of debris left under the dome. The FSA had tried not to target the industrial sectors, but the front was expanding slowly and steadily. Damage in every sector was becoming inevitable.

He stopped and stared into the next room. Ten small evenly spaced desks sat inside, each with an engraved nameplate on the front. He had been in rooms like this for several years when he first arrived on the colony. A disappointed sigh escaped his lips.

A school, that was where they were. They'd destroyed an important symbol of the future as part of seizing control of the colony.

Damir's hands tightened around his rifle. He wanted to

blame the government's forces for everything, but the FSA was just as responsible for inflicting damage through the city and the colony. They were supposed to be saving New Samarkand, but they were leaving nothing but broken rubble, dead bodies, and empty dreams.

For the first time since he'd joined the FSA, he asked himself if it was worth it and whether his father would have approved.

"I found one," called one of his squad members.

Damir, Sinclair, and the others converged on the soldier. He'd cornered a wounded Army private hiding behind a desk in an office. He had a med patch on, but there were holes through his thighs and stomach. His ashen pallor argued against him surviving his wounds. The private held his hands in the air, trembling. There was no sign of his weapon.

Sinclair looked the man up and down. "Kill him. He's not important."

"Please, no," the private begged. "You have to take me as a prisoner of war."

Sinclair laughed. "This isn't a war. It's a rebellion."

That was logical. Damir couldn't deny it, but something burst in his mind. All his frustrations in the last few weeks destroyed the dam of self-control.

"No," Damir barked. "No way in hell."

Sinclair spun toward him. "Excuse me, Sokov?"

Damir gestured at the wounded private. "He doesn't have a gun, and he can barely move. He's not a threat. If we aren't going to take him with us, we should leave him here. We don't kill people who aren't a threat."

"Leave him here? An enemy? We should kill him now. You want to wait until he's patched up and can shoot you?"

"Killing a wounded man who isn't a threat isn't war," Damir shouted. "It's murder. That's not why I joined the FSA."

Sinclair's brow lifted. "Murder?" He laughed. "I know what you've done. You've participated in ambushes against Army soldiers. You didn't scream warnings as you cut them down. Now suddenly, you don't have the stomach to fight?"

"It's not about fighting. Those situations were different. They could fight back. I wouldn't have a problem taking him out in the field." Damir shook his head. "If we're supposed to be better than the UTC, we have to start ensuring that right now. Otherwise, what will be the point? We'll be just as vicious and ruthless as they are. The roots of our new government will be diseased from the beginning."

Sinclair sighed. "You know what, Sokov? You're right."

"Thank you." Damir relaxed his shoulders and took a deep breath. "We can take him back—"

Sinclair snapped up his rifle and shot the private in the head. No one moved. They all looked at Damir and the mercenary commander, unsure what to do.

"You want to win this rebellion?" Sinclair began, gesturing with the barrel toward the body. "If you do, you'll have no choice but to be vicious and ruthless. Not as vicious and ruthless as the UTC Army, *more* vicious. Savage, even. Freedom isn't gained by people overly concerned with morality, but by those who are willing to spill blood until the other side has no choice but to run from them."

Damir growled, "That's bullshit."

"That's history, Sokov." Sinclair squeezed the bridge of his nose before bringing his hand back down to support his rifle. He pointed it at Damir, his eyes blazing. "And I'm done placating you. The next time you disobey me, you piece of shit, you die. I didn't come all the way to this backwater colony to help you rubes play at war so I can die because you have an attack of conscience. I'm here for an important purpose, and it can't be disrupted because you care about wounded soldiers. They are expendable. *You* are expendable."

Damir clenched his jaw. He didn't dare raise his rifle. Sinclair was aiming at his head. One burst would finish him.

The confusion of the other rebels vanished. They exchanged looks before pointing their guns at Sinclair.

"What the hell is this?" Sinclair snarled. "Sokov is a traitor. He wanted me to spare the life of a UTC dog, and now you're pointing your guns at me? Think this through, morons."

Kaze, one of the rebels Damir hadn't worked with until the last two missions, was the first to speak. "You're an outsider, a mercenary. Damir has been with the FSA from the beginning. His father was with the FSC. They didn't need money for the cause. That means he's earned our respect. Lower your weapon, Sinclair. I'm not sure what we should have done with that soldier, but I do know we don't turn our guns on one another."

"Put the gun down or what?" The mercenary laughed.

"You're going to shoot me? How will you explain it? You going to tell everyone you killed someone helping you fight the Army because a fellow rebel lost his balls?"

"It'll be easy to explain away. All we have to say is some Army soldier got the drop on you." Kaze sneered. "A lot of things can happen out here. We don't have to have a problem, but we can't have you threatening a brother. I don't want to hurt you, but I'm not going to let you kill Sokov."

Sinclair tossed his rifle on the floor. "Fine, you stupid hick piece of shit. You'll be punished when I report this anyway."

Damir let out a sigh of relief. He had not wanted anything to escalate like this, but he didn't regret standing up to the mercenary.

"Turn around," Kaze ordered. "We're going to bind you and escort you back to the base. They can decide. If you're so confident they'll punish us, you shouldn't have a problem waiting."

Sinclair turned around and put his arms behind him. "You're making a mistake."

"We probably are," Damir replied. "But I'm beginning to think hiring you mercs was our biggest mistake. It's been bothering me for a while, all the rumors I hear about you people. I've tried to ignore them, but now I'm not so sure."

"Everything you've heard is true, by the way," Sinclair announced with a sneer. "Everything you're thinking is likely true. Yes, we're using special Tin Men to help win the war. They're called Elites. They have true dedication to the cause. They understand they must sacrifice everything. You lack sufficient commitment to your cause. Destroy all your enemies, and the morality of it becomes irrelevant. That's why you pathetic hicks sicken me."

"What the hell?" Kaze approached slowly, reaching into his pouch for binding ties. "Tin Men? I thought that was just propaganda. Are you kidding me?"

"No, they're not Tin Men. That's not adequate to describe them. They're something better, just a brain in a metal shell." Sinclair chuckled. "They are the future of warfare. They will enforce a new order that will not rely on maggots like you who are restricted by sentiment and false ideals about what you're building."

The rebels exchanged disgusted looks. Damir backed past the others toward the door, his stomach tightening. His conspiracy theories didn't seem so outlandish anymore. They might not have been extreme enough.

Kaze raised his binding ties. "I'm sorry, Sinclair, but Sokov's right. We need standards. You're a merc. You don't get what it means to fight for something more than money. It's not just about killing people and bombing their shit."

"I agree," Sinclair replied. "We do need standards. Do you know why I'm saying all this to you? Why I'm bothering to give you this much information?"

"Because you're a crazy bastard?" Kaze suggested. "Or an arrogant son of a bitch"

"No, because you shouldn't kid yourself. Your leaders know exactly what we're using and our tactics. Do you honestly think we'd be able to cover it without their help? Second, you won't be alive soon because you've let Sokov infest your minds. His ideals will spread like an infection and weaken the FSA, and we can't have that. I've been wondering about Sokov since I heard one of the commanders mention him. My people need this war to last a little longer for our purposes, and that means we need to get rid of people like all of you."

The rebels glared at Sinclair.

Kaze snorted and reached for Sinclair's hands. "Sorry, merc. We're not planning to die anytime soon. I don't care how that affects your merc bottom line. I think you forget that this is our planet, not yours."

"Oh, the death wasn't a request. It's an order." Sinclair spun, a knife popping out of the bottom of this sleeve. His slash opened Kaze's throat with a spray of blood. Before the body fell, Sinclair flicked his wrist and sent his knife into the eye of another rebel. He yanked Kaze's rifle up and fired a burst into the face of a third rebel.

Damir and the survivors opened fire, their training betraying them. Their bursts pounded Sinclair's tactical vest, forcing him back with a grunt but not finishing him off. He was more selective, shifting from target to target, shooting the rebels in their heads with a gleeful expression.

Sinclair laughed and jerked his rifle toward his final target, Damir, but the rebel beat him, his rifle aiming higher as he pulled the trigger. The bullets ripped through the mercenary's throat, and his body collapsed on the floor atop the dead Kaze.

Damir backed out of the office, shaking. He could barely register what had just happened. His eyes widened as Sinclair crawled forward, a crazed gleam in his eyes and half his neck missing. The merc raised a finger and wagged it slowly before slumping and letting out a hollow death rattle.

Hands shaking, Damir grabbed a plasma grenade from

his belt and primed it. He backed away from the office and threw it inside before sprinting away. The explosion shook the hallway, but he barely noticed.

Sinclair had killed the men without hesitation. The mysterious sniper, the tank, and all the other threads of evidence were now bright flares highlighting the obvious truth. The FSA was corrupt, infiltrated by and allied with the sickest kinds of people, men who knew no restraint.

Damir couldn't go back, not now. He would not betray his brothers, but he could never forgive the mercenaries.

CHAPTER THIRTY

"Keep an eye out," Cabrina announced. "If they make it past our line, they might be able to hit the field hospital."

With most people out on patrol, it would be a slaughter. Army counteroffensives had gone well in the last few days, despite rebel pushback the last few hours. At least that was the line HQ was spinning. The downside was it was hard to hit a place if all their forces were elsewhere. Additional reinforcements would arrive soon, but not fast enough. The garrisons in nearby systems were worried that whatever was going in Gliese 581 might be contagious. No one wanted to release many of their troops. They were willing to lend a platoon or a company here and there, but not the serious level of troops needed to crush the insurrection.

Her squad's six exos advanced in a loose V formation, shields fully expanded. Two hours of hit and run by enemy forces had worn down Cabrina's patience. They knew the enemy was close because her friendly drones kept getting knocked out of the sky. The speed and firepower on display pointed to a single possibility: the so-called Elites.

A rumor had become truth, and that truth spread through the garrison. The mercenaries aiding the FSA were employing full-conversion cyborgs. What was left of ID on the planet had provided a small amount of intel, only noting the government hadn't previously encountered Elites controlling full-sized vehicles. They hadn't mentioned Cybernetic Psychosis Syndrome, but it didn't matter since the enemies were intended solely for killing and mayhem.

Were they making them on the planet somehow? The thought sent a shudder through Cabrina. She couldn't understand why the rebels would be willing to work with those monsters, but the rebels kept insisting it was government propaganda rather than truth. The mercs used sophisticated bots, some claimed. It was easy to look away when the monsters were on their side.

Cabrina didn't know what HQ thought about reinforcements against the Elites, and she didn't care. She'd be grateful if all they ended up getting were two people in an armored flitter with a big gun. The rebels were being whittled away, but their mercenary allies kept launching devasting raids such as the ones now pinning down squads all over the sector, slowing their battalion's offensive. Every time they took down an Elite, it felt like two more showed up on the next raid.

The rebel viciousness now made sense, especially when connected with the mercenaries. Cabrina didn't need to be an ID analyst to realize there was someone with a lot of resources and money off-world who was interested in fueling the insurrection for their own purposes. For the moment, she didn't worry about anything other than keeping enemy forces away from the field hospital. There were other units who were delivering the pain farther afield.

An alert from HQ popped up. Cabrina hissed in frustration as she skimmed the red message in the corner of her faceplate.

"Okay, get ready to head due northeast, double-time," she announced. "A patrol got ambushed. Nobody's dead, but they need cover to retreat. Possible Elites. Load appropriate ordnance. I don't want any of those things surviving. There is no way they have an unlimited supply."

The squad charged forward, knocking rubble and debris out of their way as their heavy metal feet hit the broken streets and ground. Gunfire sounded in the distance, followed by an explosion, but it was in a different direction. That was for another squad to handle. Not encountering any trouble, they closed the distance to the wounded infantry squad in a few short minutes.

A sergeant limped toward Cabrina's exo, holes burned into his tactical vest and uniform. "We barely could see what struck us. Just saw a flash of metal, and then it lit us up. We got some hits in, but I doubt we did more than scratch it. I think the bastard was toying with us."

With a flick of her fingers, Cabrina launched a microdrone into the air. She didn't expect to get any decent intel, but she did want to establish how close the nearest enemy was in the most efficient way possible. The drone cleared about ten meters before a shot rang out and ripped the tiny machine in half. Its pieces plummeted to the ground.

"Alpha Five and Six," Cabrina began. "Make your way toward the field hospital with the wounded and the rest of the infantry. The rest of you come with me. If the rebels or their merc buddies want to play, let's show them who the real Elites are: assault infantry!"

The drone hadn't detected anything before its destruction, but the last transmission provided a direction of fire. Elites could move quickly, but at least Cabrina knew where to look. She advanced, keeping her weapons at the ready. Their enemies weren't gods, or even advanced aliens with tech humans didn't understand. They were just a bunch of rebels and Tin Man freaks who didn't know where to draw the line.

She wasn't running at them with a knife in her teeth and a pistol. She was in proven military tech, an exo with a heavy machine gun loaded with armor-piercing rounds and a rocket launcher. That was all she needed to reduce any Elite to scrap.

A dark shadow passed between two nearby buildings. Cabrina spun that way, ready to fire a rocket, but it was too late. Sensors pinged two moving contacts, but there was so much debris and metal scattered along with the tightly packed buildings, it was interfering with her readings. It didn't help that they'd encountered Elites with almost no sensor signature before. They were like demons hiding in the shadows.

"Inverted wedge," she ordered.

The other exos took up position. The two escorting the infantry and carrying wounded had made it a good hundred meters down the street, and Cabrina had every indication the enemy was closer to her and the bulk of the squad. She did her best to ignore sporadic gunfire in the distance, concentrating on the nearby enemy.

"This is the problem with putting up all these buildings so damned close together," she muttered. "Too many places to hide. I hope the moon never decides to stage an uprising, and if they do, I hope I'm on the other side of the UTC at the time."

"Movement at ten o'clock, LT," reported Alpha Three.

"Movement at two o'clock," Alpha Two shouted seconds later.

"They're fast, but they're not that fast," Cabrina replied. "Presume at least two hostiles, Elite classes unknown. Maximum weapons usage authorized. Send them to that hot place below."

Controlling an exo in a search-and-destroy mission was as much about concentration as skill. That concentration was honed by practiced discipline, including Cabrina's constant flicking gaze to camera feeds and sensor readings. Her squadmates' reports made it easy for her to pick up movement on the sides despite the unreliability of the sensors. She might need her exo's big gun, but all they required otherwise was a good pair of enlisted eyes.

A sing-song voice echoed all around them. "Army dogs. Army dogs in shells think they have a chance, but they're just here to *die, die, die*. I'd say you'll fertilize the ground, but that's not the case in this colony, so your deaths will be useless. Mighty, mighty garrison, but you have taken so many casualties already. You had to get reinforcements just so they can die too. You're inferior—a waste of flesh. You can't stand up to an Elite. You should lie down and let us slaughter you like the cattle you are."

That taunt answered the question about whether they were dealing with bots or normal rebels. The confirmation emboldened Cabrina. She preferred fighting Elites. They might be sick monstrosities, but she wanted to go up against an enemy with a mind who presented a halfway decent challenge. In the end, she wanted the best of the insurrection's forces to know they'd gotten their asses handed to them by members of the 919th Assault Infantry and Lieutenant Cabrina Pena.

"Ignore that crap. They're trying to flank us." Cabrina frowned. "Damn it. No, they're too far out. They're going after the wounded. Let's get their attention." She spun and released a burst from her machine gun before swinging it to the other side and firing. "Let's dance, monsters."

With a roar and a flash, a pile of debris in the direction of her second shot spat bullets, then a long serpentine multi-legged metal form emerged. A heavy cannon sprouted from the front of its head—a Torch Dragon. Its barrage ripped into the exposed flank of one of the squad, blasting chunks from the exo's arm. The soldier spun to cover himself with his shield, his exo's arm movements stiff from actuator damage.

Something wiggled over a nearby roof and opened fire. A third Torch Dragon skittered in front of them as if taunting them. Cabrina and another squad member opened fire, their AP rounds ripping into it in a shower of sparks before the metal monster disappeared between buildings. The other two enemies continued their relentless assault, forcing the exos back.

"Roof!" Cabrina ordered. "Rockets!"

The four exos swung their rocket launchers and

released in near-perfect tandem. The explosives sped toward the roof, and the Torch Dragon skittered back before the rockets blew the front half of the small building apart. The enemy jumped off, its wriggling form silhouetted by the beautiful oranges, yellows, and reds of the huge blast.

Cabrina's machine gun screamed to life and her anticipatory aim landed her armor-piercing rounds right on target, leaving a trail of holes through the Elite's body. The other three exos followed her lead. The cumulative storm of high-velocity lead blew the Torch Dragon Elite into three pieces.

His friend on the left scampered forward, thinking he had a chance. Cabrina jumped and spun, her thrusters burning hard. She would have killed for a newer model at that moment, but she got decent height on her jump and angled to rake the advancing Elite with her machine gun before following up with a rocket. Her target writhed and changed direction, but her explosion blasted off half his legs, slowing him.

Redundancy meant a lot in nature and on the battlefield. He'd made it forward far enough to unload on Alpha Three from behind and sever the bottom half of the exo's leg, but that didn't harm the soldier inside. The other exos concentrated their fire, sticking to their machine guns because of proximity, until the bullet-riddled Elite collapsed to the ground, its blood mixing with other dark fluids seeping from its destroyed body.

Cabrina's gaze flicked from feed to feed, and her head moved back and forth. "Where's the other one? Anyone have eyes on him? I'm not spotting anything on sensors."

Heavy gunfire sounded from ahead of them, in the direction of Alpha Five, Alpha Six, and the infantry survivors.

Cabrina twirled her exo and charged. "Alpha Two with me. Alpha Four, guard Three."

She adjusted her optical magnification, her heart thundering. The damned Torch Dragon had gone after the withdrawing exos and infantry, who had ducked behind the remains of a fountain to guard their wounded. Mindlessly firing straight ahead would risk hitting her own people. It might have planned that.

The Torch Dragon walked its cannon fire across the fountain, almost taking the head off one of the infantry. It was obvious it was trying to kill the wounded soldiers. It jumped from side to side to avoid return fire. This one was faster and more agile than the two they'd just destroyed, and it barely showed up on Cabrina's sensor displays.

She sprinted closer to the edge of the street, hoping to get a decent angle on the Elite. At that moment, she understood their true purpose, their real role in this insurrection. They had the same purpose as any monster of legend: to inspire terror. It was time to channel her inner Saint George and slay a dragon.

But Cabrina was too far away and not fast enough. The garrison had lost enough people in the rebellion, and she was tired of good soldiers dying.

I just need a distraction, she thought. *A couple of seconds.*

Someone popped up from behind a wrecked flitter with a missile launcher on his shoulder. No, not someone, a helmeted man in a rebel uniform. He screamed something and fired. The missile didn't zoom toward the soldiers at the fountain or Cabrina and her advancing squadmate. It headed straight toward the Torch Dragon Elite, striking its center and blowing it into flaming chunks in an impressive blast.

Cabrina slowed, confused about what had happened. The rebel soldier tossed down his launcher and ran into a nearby building.

"LT, orders?" Alpha Two asked, wonder in his voice. "Do we go after him?"

"No," Cabrina replied.

"But he's a rebel."

"I don't know what he is, but anyone who's against those things is on our side. Let's get everyone back to the field hospital before a bunch of Leem brains in doomsday ships arrive."

CHAPTER THIRTY-ONE

October 10, 2230, Solar System, Asteroid Belt, UTC Space Fleet Base Penglai

A holographic image of New Samarkand floated above the conference room table. It looked dark and uninviting from space, as most planets without large oceans did to Erik. Maybe that was the universe trying to tell humanity where they should settle, but humans were a stubborn species. They'd set up a dome in Hell if they thought they could get away with it.

Erik settled in at the front of the table next to Jia. The engineers, Malcolm, Raphael, and Emma were spread out around the rest of the table. Anne and Kant were notable for their absence. The problem with getting more people was growing dependent on it, but Alina had already admitted her error, and Erik trusted she wouldn't make the same mistake twice.

He inclined his head toward Raphael. "Let's hear it. I'm assuming you wouldn't have had us fly all the way out here if it was hopeless and we needed to take the long way around."

Everyone turned to the scientist with an expectant look. They all knew the mission, and only Erik, Jia, and potentially Emma would be leaving the *Argo* once they arrived at New Samarkand. The real question wasn't what they would do on the ground, but whether they could get there.

Erik had gotten so used to technological marvels in his quest against the Core that he sometimes forgot how special Emma and the jump drive were. The Lady was cashing in his lifetime of bad luck to give him what he needed to make up for screwing him on Molino. The DD might view him as a guinea pig testing their precious drive, but to him, the jumpship was the Chariot of Bloody Vengeance.

Things might have been different if he'd had it from the beginning. He might have had a small hope of catching up with the mercenaries who had pulled the trigger on Molino. That didn't matter now. Jump drives might be impressive, but no one had a time machine. The Hunters and Navigators were thousands, if not tens of thousands, of years ahead of the younger races, and they hadn't had anything like that.

"Yes, on with the show," Raphael declared.

He rubbed his hands together gleefully before making three precise gestures. New Samarkand disappeared, replaced by a complicated diagram depicting overlapping hyperbolas, dots, and a swarm of numbers. Erik squinted to try to parse the information but failed miserably. Too much math and out-of-context data. Judging by Jia's expression, she didn't understand it either, so he didn't feel too bad. He didn't bother to ask for clarification, assuming Raphael would explain. The man might be a gushing fanboy, but he generally got his point across in language Erik could understand.

"We need to get to New Samarkand, and it is twenty light-years away," Raphael began, a huge smile on his face. "That means we need to travel almost five times as far as we did before. This is unprecedented in human history, let alone our time together."

Jia folded her arms. "And we need to do it as quickly as possible. We're already a month behind on all this. Every day we delay might mean the Core sinks their tentacles deeper into the rebellion."

"How long would it take without the jump drive?" Malcolm asked. "Just curious before we go challenging all of human history."

"About three and a half months," Raphael answered. "You can see the problem."

"Oh. That's a long time." Malcolm puffed up his cheeks and let out a breath. "A very long time to be on this small ship."

"Too long," Jia added. "Even if the military takes care of the rebellion, the Core will be long gone, and their tracks will be cold. It'd be pointless."

"We can't let them slither away this time." Erik frowned. "They've already gutted the local ghosts, which means we might be the only ones who have the flexibility to do something about them. I don't want this ending with a half-destroyed colony and those Core bastards skipping off to the next to repeat the same thing. Every time we stop them, we prove something to them. We prove their plans don't always work, and that's got to frustrate them and slow them down. It's got to make them question everything. We need to get there ASAP and let them know even a month's head start isn't enough for them to get away with their crap."

Jia, Wei, and Malcolm nodded eagerly. Janessa looked uncertain, and Lanara didn't look like she was paying attention. Instead, she focused on the diagram above the table, mumbling numbers quietly.

"Hell, yeah!" Raphael saluted. "Of course, Erik! I want to help you kick the Core's butt as much as you want to, and fortunately for you, I've been spending all my time since the last big mission working on this very problem and doing some tinkering."

Erik's brows lifted. "Tinkering? Is that what you call messing around with the jump drive?"

"Sure." Raphael inclined his head toward the display. "Tinkering's when I do my own thing. Science is when I work with a bunch of other people, and we proceed in a slow and boring way. Even without Emma, I bet we could have been a lot farther with the drive if the DD wasn't so safety-obsessed."

"Safety's not a bad thing," Malcolm complained meekly.

"He's been coordinating with me as well," Emma added with an annoyed look. "The navigational process improvements are sufficient for longer-range jumps within the limits he's presumably about to explain, which leaves us with the hardware considerations. Those are beyond my abilities to optimize."

Malcolm swallowed. "Not to be *that guy*, but going back

to the whole safety thing? Life's important, including our lives. If we push the drive too much, what happens?"

Raphael's breath caught, and his lips parted in excitement. "Great question! I've been putting a lot of thought into it. There are many possibilities. Not an infinite number, mind you, because this is something the research group spent a lot of time on before we started construction of the drive, but I've continued to explore it."

"Why did you spend so much time worrying about it before?" Jia asked.

"We wanted to make sure we didn't accidentally create a black hole or blow up the sun. You know, normal risk assessment stuff. It's also how I knew that nesting the gates wouldn't blow up the entire Solar System." Raphael looked off to the side. "Mostly."

"Mostly? I'm sorry I asked. Let's focus on things that don't end with the destruction of stars or planets." Jia rubbed her temples. "Presumably."

"Of course." Raphael ticked up his fingers as he rattled off his explanation in a cheery tone. "One, if we push too hard, the whole thing explodes in a disappointing way and kills us all, but a normal explosion, not like a superweapon explosion. That being said, the second possibility is the whole thing produces a nested portal situation. Boom. Big, grand superweapon-scale explosion." He mimicked the explosion with his hands. "Hunter-killing explosion."

"Do we die?" Malcolm asked. "Or can we like ride the shockwave or something like I saw that guy do in *Hyperspace Cowboy*?"

"That's silly. It's just a movie. Of course we'll die."

Raphael laughed. "But we'll die in a much more spectacular manner than the first possibility." He sighed. "It'll be so quick we won't have time to appreciate how beautiful it is."

"That's good to know." Malcolm slumped in his chair. "I'd hate to die in a boring way. Maybe we'll get lucky, and some astronomer will record it."

Jia looked at Malcolm and Raphael. "We might as well figure this out while we're on the subject because we can never be sure how much we'll have to push things. What else might happen?"

Raphael splayed his fingers and then pushed his other fingers through the spaces. "We could, theoretically, end up fused inside some other stellar object. That's unlikely for a number of reasons, not the least of which space is mostly empty, but there's a non-zero probability. Another possibility, according to the math but not necessarily justified by the physics, is that we overshoot in a *big* way. Jump ten, a hundred, a thousand times our intended distance."

Janessa cleared her throat, looking down when everyone turned her way. "T-that's not that crazy."

Raphael smiled, not a single hint of displeasure or condescension in his face when he next spoke. "Why do you say that?"

"It happened to the Leems during the Roswell Incident, right? They've admitted there was no way they could jump as far today, and they've had hundreds of years to work on their drive."

Raphael slapped a palm to his forehead. "She does have a point. It's obvious when you think about it. Historical precedent!"

Janessa managed a slight smile but didn't look up.

Erik shook his head. "I don't care about all these possibilities."

"But they're interesting," Raphael complained.

"They aren't tactically relevant. What's the most likely bottom-line?"

If they hadn't already been behind, Erik might have let the man indulge himself, but this wasn't a scientific or engineering test, even though Raphael might treat it that way. This was about getting them to a mission site, no more, no less.

"Oh." Raphael's face fell. "Boring basic explosion is the most likely scenario. Even in that scenario, it'll be powerful enough to destroy the entire ship and any other ships that are directly attached, but nothing else."

Malcolm grimaced. "So much for the lifeboat idea I was going to suggest."

Raphael shrugged. "Don't worry, I'm not planning to push the drive anywhere near that hard until we need to."

"As long as we won't take anyone else with us by accident." Erik nodded slowly, possibilities swirling in his mind. "It's good to have options and understand our limits. For all we know, next week, Alina will want us to jump to Molino, or the Prime Minister will send us into Zitark space to find Hunter artifacts."

Malcolm grimaced. "Uh, I vote no on the space raptors."

"I'm just throwing out possibilities," Erik replied, no longer finding the idea outlandish after their Hunter encounter. "The jump drive is the one major advantage we have over the Core. We need to get the most out of it, and that means knowing its full capabilities and limitations, just like when we used it against the Hunter ship. That could save our lives, and if not this mission, then the next."

Lanara swiped her hand through the air and brought up a data window filled with fluctuating graphs. She narrowed her eyes and finally broke her silence. "We need to know the current baseline potential before we can worry about anything else. I've heard a lot of theory, and I see these numbers, but I'm looking for something more concrete."

"Of course," Raphael assured her with a cheery smile. "It's taken a lot of adjustments to get the field calibration right, especially with the inherent tendency to decay, let alone worrying about Xing Field interference—"

"Please, Raphael," Erik interrupted. "Keep it to a level the rest of us can understand. I know you can."

Raphael spread his hands in a grand gesture. "Two light-years per jump is easily achievable without any safety concerns or explosions. I'm confident enough to bet my life on it."

"Good, because you're also betting ours."

Wei whistled and clapped. "Two light-years in the blink of an eye. Wow. And he's saying it like it's nothing."

Jia frowned. "But it's not the blink of an eye to prepare." She gestured at Emma. "They still need to perform the navigation calculations and charge the drive, just like when we went to Alpha Centauri."

"That's true," Raphael admitted. "It also requires more recharge time than between those jumps. By my estimates, and taking both those limitations into account, it'd be a max of about six jumps per day."

Erik rubbed his chin. "Twelve light-years in twenty-four hours. Not bad. Not bad at all. We can get to any core world with that in one day, and out to the far frontier in five days. A day and a half for New Samarkand is damned fast."

Malcolm raised his hand. "Jump drives are so far outside my field they might as well be in Zitark space, but don't shorter jumps take less navigation plotting time?"

Emma nodded, an amused look growing. "You're correct, Mr. Constantine."

"Why not just make a lot of short jumps then? Shave off some time that way." Malcolm shrugged.

Raphael shook his head. "Because the increased recharge and adjustment time on the drive would quickly add up to be longer than the time saved on the navigational plotting. The two-light-year limit is the best compromise to get the farthest distance in the least amount of time."

"But you think you can extend that range in the future?" Jia asked. "Or do something about the recharge and adjustment time?"

Raphael nodded. "Yes. I've been working with Emma to improve navigation. The drive's a prototype, remember? A work in progress, but the more we use it, the more we can improve it. It's never going to jump us across the UTC in one go, but I'm confident I can squeeze better performance out of it. I can get you and Erik anywhere you need to go to take down bad guys."

Jia gave him a soft smile. "You're doing great. We wouldn't be able to get to New Samarkand if it wasn't for you."

The scientist's goofy smile grew so large it looked like

he was trying to swallow himself. He waved his hands dismissively.

"Okay, a day and a half to two days." Erik nodded at the diagram above the table. "Because of science and shit, so fine. That's good, but we'll be running well ahead of any messages from Earth to the colony and decent active intelligence. We can't ignore the different possibilities upon arrival."

"The rebellion might already be over," Malcolm suggested, sounding relieved.

He didn't understand that even if that were true, they would still make planetfall. Erik didn't feel the need to point it out.

"If it's over, the Core will have already fled," Jia replied. "I doubt we'll get much intel from scraps of destroyed Elites."

"We'd still have to look," Erik insisted. "The Core is careful, but they're not perfect, and they've been getting more desperate lately. But even before that, if they were perfect, we'd still be trying to figure out who the hell the Ascended Brotherhood is instead of helping to end them."

Emma's form shimmered, and her clothes changed to a ragged, torn, blood-stained khaki uniform. "Be wary of presumptions. It could be over, and the rebellion might have been victorious. In such a scenario, despite the increased danger to you, there would be a higher probability of the Core remaining on the world. Your disguises might be insufficient."

Erik shook his head. "Even if they did their best and pushed out the colonial government, the Fleet would interdict the system. There are probably pirates or smugglers flying around, but there's no way the rebels have taken out the Fleet. I'm sure the local garrison pulled in at least a few ships from other systems to help."

Wei shook a finger. "What if the Hunters show up? They could have blown the Fleet ships away, and we wouldn't know."

Janessa shivered and rubbed her shoulders. "Don't even joke about that. When she briefed us about that mission, Alina told us that was a special situation, and something like that wouldn't happen again."

"Just saying that we're talking about possibilities. It's not *impossible*." Wei shrugged. "The Core almost had one Hunter ship. Why not another? There might be one in every system, and they've been collecting them."

Erik preferred fun-loving Wei to pessimistic Wei, but his pessimism wasn't inherently wrong.

Lanara scoffed. "I don't think those Core assholes getting themselves turned into monsters counts as controlling the ship. Even if the team had never gotten involved, that situation wouldn't have ended with the Core in control of the vessel. The Hunters would have blown up a couple of planets, right?"

Janessa winced. "A couple of planets?"

Jia sighed. "I'm not worried about Hunters, but Wei's right. We can't make assumptions about what we'll encounter when we arrive. It's unlikely the insurrectionists won, but given we know the Core is supplying them Elites and likely other equipment, the rebellion might still be ongoing."

"Which is why we should jump in far from New Samarkand," Erik concluded. "Just in case, at least a couple of days. If we fiddle around with half-jumps and trying to find newsfeeds in another system, it'll end up taking more time, so we'll go directly. But for all we know, this is a trap by the Core to grab the jumpship, and we can't let it be taken no matter what. Jumping right next to the planet is too great a risk."

"Are we considering potential self-destruction?" Lanara asked, her face lighting up with interest.

"Whoa." Raphael shook his head. "Can we dial down the blowing up the ship part? It's not like I paid for it, but that drive represents a lot of taxpayer money and scientific effort."

"We need options." Erik nodded at Emma. "We need her with us planet-side, which means you'll have to rely on the basic AI on that ship."

Emma lifted her hand and summoned a small hologram of the *Bifröst.* "Jumping without me is impossible because of minute adjustments that must be made during the process, but it'd be easy enough to program in an automatic flight program that will allow the ship to disengage at Raphael's discretion that I could override without being docked, but still relatively close."

Erik nodded. "Fine. It's not perfect, but it'll do for now. If we have trouble, we'll figure something out. As it stands, I figure we jump in near one of the uninhabited planets without any satellites and fly the *Argo* in even if it adds a couple of days. I don't think the tradeoff between instant arrival and the risk to the jumpship is worth it, but the *Bifröst* should be fine away from the major travel routes."

"I agree," Jia replied. "Whatever else is happening on that planet, we know the Core is involved, which means we'll need to be extra cautious. That's assuming this isn't an elaborate trap on their part. It wouldn't be the first time."

Malcolm leaned forward. "Say the rebels have won, and they're holding the colony hostage. What's the plan then? It's one thing to land on a planet in the middle of a rebellion where at least you have the Army and militia to back you up, but it's another to land in hostile territory."

"We'll play it by ear." Erik grinned. "If necessary, we'll shoot our way in."

Malcolm sighed. "I was afraid you'd say that."

CHAPTER THIRTY-TWO

October 12, 2230, Gliese 581, En Route to New Samarkand, Aboard the *Argo*

Jia sat in the cockpit, resting comfortably in the pilot's chair while scanning the sensors for anything out of the ordinary—not that she expected to encounter anything. They'd disconnected from the jumpship and were a couple days out from New Samarkand. Currently, they were closing on one of the uninhabited outer planets. Janessa and Wei remained on the jumpship to help Raphael. Malcolm was in his cabin getting some rest, while Lanara continued her eternal quest to achieve engineering perfection.

Although they were on their way to a world in crisis for a dangerous mission, Jia was relaxed, convinced the trip there would be uneventful. She kept going back to the long-range sensor data. It might be limited in scope and not real-time, but it did confirm there was at least moderate ship traffic around the HTPs and New

Samarkand. She doubted she would see much in either direction if the planet was a captured world under siege.

As she looked at the sensor displays, it was hard not to be struck by the emptiness of space. In the inner Solar System or a core system like Alpha Centauri, there were so many ships, satellites, and stations that sensors readouts of anything passing for a populated part of a system were rarely truly empty. They might be millions of kilometers away, but their light and emissions marked them in the darkness for the keen artificial eyes of humanity's machines. Now, closer to the frontier, she could appreciate what it meant to be restricted to one planet with a small handful of ships.

Jia had always understood intellectually how something like space piracy could occur, but now, in the vastness of the mostly empty Gliese 581 system, she could understand that help might be days away under the best of circumstances if you dared travel anywhere but the most common flight paths. Ships were remarkably self-sufficient, and an antisocial criminal crew with patience could accomplish a lot.

She tried to shake the negative thoughts out of her mind. Possibilities were just that, not realities.

Erik sat behind her, his feet up and resting on the back of the copilot's chair. He was watching a recorded sphere ball match from months ago on a data window projected on the ceiling. He tapped his PNIU and paused the feed. "I recognize that look."

Jia tucked a loose strand of hair behind her ear and refocused her attention on her readouts. "What look?"

"You're overthinking something. I love your mind, but

sometimes it sabotages you." Erik dropped his feet and sat up. "I don't care if the Core's helping the rebels. They haven't taken that planet yet. If they were that good, half the frontier would have fallen already. We're not going to have to fight our way down. I'm sure we'll have plenty of annoying shit on the planet, but not before then."

Jia nodded. "I know." She gestured at a display to her far left that showed small bright spheres arranged in different locations around the system. "And there's too much traffic back and forth to suggest we're going into a fallen world. It'd be nice if we were on a normal flight path, so we had a better chance of connecting to the OmniNet, but that's what comes with being this far out. Would you believe I was actually feeling pretty calm about everything up until a couple of minutes ago?"

"I'd like to see you on one of the newest colonies." Erik grinned. "You'd go nuts. You're so used to having everything at your fingertips. Being there on the frontier, with the bare essentials and all the big core world news and entertainment being months away...I don't think you could handle it."

"I could handle it," Jia insisted. "After a period of adjustment. Besides, it's unnatural in a way."

"Unnatural? Getting back to basics?"

"Humanity's great advantage over other species on our planet is our toolmaking capability. But I'd argue we're more natural on our home planet surrounded by everything we've built than sitting under a dome on some planet that'll require centuries before you can step outside without a breather." Jia shook her head. "I understand why we've spread out, but I can't always say it's a good idea.

Imagine if we were just in the Solar System. The idea of rebellions would be laughable at this point." She sighed. "And I get it that if we hadn't expanded, some of the races might have expanded more toward us. Redundancy and the preservation of species and all that."

"And just seeing new things." Erik stared at her. "I thought you wanted to travel. Now it sounds like you want to hide in a tower in Neo SoCal."

Jia nodded. "I do want to travel, but I don't want to live on a colony. Exploration isn't the same thing as settlement." She smirked over her shoulder. "And I've spent plenty of time on ships now. I can survive without instant access to the entire net. I survived when we were flying the Rabbit, and that wasn't the most spacious, modern ship."

"I know." Erik dismissed his data window with a tap. "But you don't understand why someone would choose to live in a place like New Samarkand, not really. Or hell, Molino."

"That's true." Jia shook her head. "For all the talk about transportation, that's a small percentage of the colonists. Hard to get a good colony going only with screwups. Good money means opportunity, but that leaves a lot of people willing to leave the comfort of Earth to go live out on the frontier, scratching out a bare existence in a dangerous environment. I know what people say, but that doesn't make it any less strange."

"Some people want the challenge," Erik offered. "Or just want to be away from it all, including billions of people. They're the opposite of you."

Jia scoffed. "There's plenty of empty space on Earth. If the Core can stick Tin Man and *yaoguai* factories in beautiful, empty parts of the wilderness, non-homicidal maniacs could find a place to live without a single person around."

Erik rubbed his chin. "Yeah, they could, but it's always there—that knowledge that billions of people are sharing the same rock as you. That they could come crowding in on you any day. It's nice to know there are weeks or months between you and the teeming billions. It can be relaxing in its own way."

"If the jump drive ever gets mass-produced, that ends," Jia commented.

Erik shook his head. "Nope. People will just go out farther. I'm sure someone will negotiate a right-of-passage treaty, and we'll string colonies all the way across the galaxy."

Jia took a moment to check her instruments. Normally, she didn't need to pay so much attention, but Emma was distracted by her efforts to examine and modify potential code for the jumpship's AI. Given how much Emma complained about limited access to the ship, neither Jia nor Erik wanted to deny her the opportunity, even if there was only so much work she could do while flying away from it. From what the AI had said, she had downloaded the necessary data onto *Argo*'s systems for modification after taking the time to initiate modifications in between her navigational duties.

"Billions, huh?" Jia smiled. "I alternate between missing the bustle of Neo SoCal and appreciating taking days away from it in the *Argo*. I guess it's not so crazy to imagine why someone would leave something like that behind to live in a dome where they know every single colonist. It's like growing up in an ancient village."

Erik stretched his arms above him with a huge yawn. "I think about Molino a lot."

"I'm sure you do. It's understandable. I know you won't get closure until we finish off the Core."

He shook his head. "I'm not talking about the massacre. I'm talking about why my unit was there."

"The Zitarks." Jia frowned. "The invasion that never came. The galactic war that would change everything."

"Yeah, the invasion that never came. Everybody keeps assuming war's still coming. Hell, a lot of the time I assume that, but that's us projecting the way a human mind works onto inhuman creatures. I know some aliens are bastards, especially the Hunters, but I'm not as sure about the others. Not anymore."

Jia lifted her hands and bent her fingers like claws. "It's not like the Zitarks aren't an aggressive species. Even if the idea of war was pushed by the politicians, that doesn't mean we won't escape it. Rising powers butt heads. That's the way it's been on Earth since we started throwing up towns. It might be premature to apply the logic to other races, but it's not unreasonable."

"You think so?" Erik nodded. "That was how I thought during most of my time in the Army, but I was a soldier. Everything was a military problem waiting to be solved. The more time I spend out of the military, the more I think about alternate solutions."

"Even though your standard solution involves bullets and grenades?"

"Wanting alternate solutions doesn't mean ignoring time-tested ones."

Jia looked away for a moment, her eyes half-closed in

thought. "I suppose when I think about it, the UTC disproves that rising powers near each other must lead to war and destruction. It makes a mockery of the old ideas about a Thucydides Trap and an inevitable war between great powers. If a lot of the old theories were true, Earth would still be a bunch of separate nation-states, constantly fighting each other in bloody wars. We might still have a lot of problems to work out, but I don't think anyone can seriously imagine the Earth ending up like New Samarkand, and if billions of humans with different beliefs and backgrounds can make it work, maybe..." She smiled. "You could be right. We could be projecting human hostility onto others. An alliance with aliens isn't impossible to imagine. A shared government, potentially. It's strange, but not impossible."

Erik grinned. "You think we'll have a grand United Confederacy of Planets in the future? Zitarks and Leems in Parliament? That's a bit much for me, even on my optimistic days." He lifted his head and pursed his lips in imitation of a prissy, stuffy politician. "Member of Parliament Rrrrowrack wishes to take the floor and address the raw meat subsidy bill."

Jia laughed. "MP Rrrrowrack?"

"I don't know what Zitark names sound like. He's a Zitark. His name won't be Lee." Erik shrugged. "Lots of growling and hissing in their language, right? So Rrrrowrack, and he's hungry, so they want to make sure they're getting raw meat. The real deal, not printed stuff."

"Okay." Jia snickered. "The Chair recognizes MP Rrrrowrack's right to the floor to speak on the raw meat subsidy bill."

Erik grinned. "Instead of debates, the Zitark MPs can eat people who piss them off. I can see it now. *'Analysts question MP Rrrrowrack's consumption of the opposition party candidate and consider the strategy bold and dangerous in an election year. Other pundits question the Leem MP's mention of the Roswell Incident. Should the past be left alone?'"*

"A mixed-species Parliament would make politics more entertaining." Jia smiled. "I barely pay any attention to politics. My family does, but to be honest, I think that is mostly so my parents can figure out who to donate to." Her smile dimmed. "There's a thin line between helping someone and attempting to bribe them."

"Your parents, especially your mom, might be pains in the ass, but they aren't criminals."

"I know. I'm just saying, nothing's ever about ideology for them. They see politics as purely transactional." Jia tilted her head. "I think Mei's changing, but my mother's the same as she always was."

"They're far from the only people who think that way."

Jia tapped a control panel off to the side to double-check the readouts from the last reactor diagnostic. "That was why I never cared about politics. It's because I wanted to be purer, not locked into influence webs. I became a cop because I wanted to stand for something, and I wanted to be around people who stood for something. Now I'm next to you, and we're taking on a corrupt conspiracy that infests our government and major corporations. It might sound arrogant, but I think we're winning."

"Winning next to me isn't a bad place to be," Erik replied. "Don't know if being next to me ends with a Zitark in Parliament."

Jia let out a happy sigh. "I don't know either. There's so much I thought I understood, but now I realize there's far, far more I don't. It makes it hard to predict the future. Knowing that Earth isn't perfect has, overall, made me feel more hopeful. I know that sounds weird, but before, I always felt like I had to live up to this perfect ideal, and that stressed me out all the time. Now I know it doesn't exist, so instead, I have a target I can aim at and encourage others to aim at. It feels…more achievable, more realistic."

"I didn't have any grand goals or ambitions when I joined the Army," Erik explained. He rested his head against the back of the chair and put his feet back up on the copilot's chair in front of him. "I turned down promotions so I could stay in the field. It's where I felt most comfortable, and I didn't worry about changing the UTC or accomplishing anything but doing right by my soldiers. Then those bastards…" He sighed. "Well, you know the rest, and now they're sitting on New Samarkand, probably screwing over both the rebels and the Army."

"I wish I knew their final plan." Jia furrowed her brow. "If they want power and influence, they already have it. The more we learn about them, the more trouble I have understanding. Hunter ships, the Elites, the *yaoguai*. What's the end goal?"

"Domination, I assume." Erik gave her a weary lopsided smile. "It doesn't matter how the tech changes. In the end, isn't that what it always comes down to? Some rich asshole is angry because they think they should be even richer and be able to do whatever they want to anyone not as rich as them? If that rich asshole has an Army, then he gets to call himself a king and take even more shit. It's not complicated. It's the opposite. It's the simplest story in the world, a tale as old as humanity."

Jia jabbed a data window with her pinkie. A holographic image of a large icy world appeared, marked by dark striations covering the surface. The planet might not be as amenable to terraforming as New Samarkand, but someday humanity would set up a colony there, just as they'd spread throughout their home system.

Jia fired the attitude thrusters to adjust their course and take them closer to the planet. "Maybe far in the future, we'll share systems with other races," she mused. "Let different species settle different planets. It's not like we need the colonies for space. It'll be a long time before that's an issue, even if every colonial city eventually becomes a metroplex, but for now, I think the planet in front of us is a good one to hide behind."

"There's no way we can avoid detection," Erik replied. "Eventually, we're going to have to deal with the Fleet ships in orbit around the colony. They might not be able to do much to help the Army because of the domes, but they're going to have a question or two for us."

"I know, but the less attention we draw, the better. Let's pray Alina's credentials are as good as we all hope." Jia stared at the planet. "It's pretty to look at, but I'd hate to have to land somewhere like that."

CHAPTER THIRTY-THREE

The following minutes passed in the kind of easy, comfortable silence Erik had grown accustomed to when spending time around Jia. He didn't bother to turn on recordings or bother with instrument readouts. Instead, he sat in his seat, entertaining himself by reflecting on the upcoming mission and how when it came to the war of applied arrogance, the Core kept losing to them.

In the beginning, his quest might have seemed foolish or insane, but he was now traveling the galaxy defeating his enemy, drawing closer and closer to their leaders. He knew the truth about why his men had been murdered, and that fueled his vengeance. Sophia Vand had been the first, but she wouldn't be the last.

Erik grinned at the thought, not caring if that made him seem bloodthirsty. The truth was, he didn't *seem* bloodthirsty. He was. The Core shouldn't have come after his soldiers if they didn't want to die. They'd made their choice and were now suffering the consequences.

The planet loomed large in front of the ship. Jia's hard

burn and careful course were designed for them to skim past it on their way to their final destination. Erik used to worry about having too much time to think, but with Jia around, he never worried. There was always someone to keep him from spiraling too far down into darkness. They had saved each other in their own ways.

Erik smiled at her, but she was too busy looking at sensor readouts to notice. Having something to look forward to after cleansing the UTC of its greatest filth was nice.

"We're about to pass in front of the planet," Jia announced. "If anyone's watching this part of the system, they're going to spot the ship. It seemed like a good idea to hide here temporarily, but it could end up costing us that."

Erik nodded. "Adding a day or two to take the long way just to avoid anyone seeing us would be a waste. If the Fleet ships don't buy our credentials, it won't matter what direction we came from."

The cockpit shook slightly from Jia's constant course corrections. Staying close to the planet seemed pointless given what they were about to do and what she just said, but Jia seemed like she needed the distraction, so Erik didn't question it.

"What the…" Jia frowned, her eyes dipping. She nodded at a short-range sensor display. "You've got to be kidding me. Are you seeing what I'm seeing?"

Erik leaned forward. Two fast-moving dots had emerged from the other side of the planet. He didn't need to be an astronomer to understand the tight formation and flight path weren't natural, and he doubted they'd run into some stray aliens.

"Identification?" he asked.

Jia shook her head. "Nothing yet. No transmissions, no transmitted signals, no light signals. They're going out of their way not to let us know who they are."

"Yeah, so clearly, they're not Fleet." Erik crawled into the copilot's seat and fastened his harness. "I'd hate to think we jumped right into a Core trap. It'd be a big hit to the ego."

"Everyone, strap yourselves in," Jia announced to the ship. "Two unidentified ships are coming up on us fast. We don't know who they are yet, and we have not established that they are friendly."

"I'll get ready to reroute power to shields," Lanara replied. "I would have hoped for at least a day of quiet before this kind of crap came up. I'm glad I didn't start working on anything. I swear, it's like you two are wearing a galactic tracking device."

Erik waved his hand over the control panel and tapped a code on a virtual keyboard. Their weapons status display popped up, but he didn't deploy any of the turrets or missiles. He remained grateful for the recent additions since he was never as confident in space as he was on the ground.

"Let's keep it nice and friendly until we know who they are," Erik suggested. "Don't want to start an unnecessary fight."

"Emma, we're going to need you." Jia fired the reverse thrusters to slow the ship. "Sorry."

"I'm now fully engaged with the *Argo*'s systems," Emma announced. "And I'm directly coordinating with Lanara. We'll do everything we can to support you in your attempts to expose the enemy fleshbags to hard vacuum."

"We don't know they are enemies, not that they're acting friendly. Maybe Lanara's right, and we do have some ridiculous galactic tracker." She scoffed at Erik. "Or your Lady really likes messing with us."

"Or both," Erik muttered, his gaze fixed on the sensor readout.

The enemy ships slowed and moved away from one another. The *Argo* would close to engagement distance in minutes at their current relative speeds.

"Powering up the shields," Jia announced with a frown. "If they find that threatening, they shouldn't be this far away from the main system flight paths." She narrowed her eyes as a comm display blinked and reached toward it. "We're still far for real-time comm, so let's see what they have to say."

"Attention unidentified vessel," said a gravelly voice. "Reduce your speed and prepare to be boarded. We will take anything valuable aboard. If you cooperate, you don't have to die here. We'll even be nice and let you set off a distress beacon so someone can come and pick you up. Resist, and we'll pull what we need off your ship after we cut it open with you inside. I'm sure you've got something juicy you didn't want anyone to find."

Erik grunted in irritation. "Pirates. They're probably preying on smugglers. It's not worth sitting around if they're hoping for normal traffic."

"Pirates trying to steal from smugglers." Jia rolled her eyes. "At least Tellvane gave the Guild men a chance to join her syndicate. It's amazing that criminals accomplish anything when they're busy shooting each other in the back."

Erik cracked his knuckles, all doubt gone. This would be a nice warmup for whoever and whatever they would face on New Samarkand. There was something almost relaxing about a battle of pure self-defense. No complicated justifications were needed, only the basic animal instinct to defend oneself.

Jia angled the ship away from the planet with a quick burst of the attitude thrusters. She sped up, and the enemy ships renewed their acceleration seconds later, now understanding this wouldn't be an easy surrender. Erik's hands flew across the weapons controls. The point-defense and offensive laser and plasma turrets deployed smoothly. A moment later, one rack of missiles extended beneath the ship, and the torpedo launchers uncovered themselves.

Erik grinned. "I bet those pirate bastards didn't expect teeth this sharp on a ship this size. Should we warn them off? Give them a chance?"

"And let them pick off somebody else who isn't packing these kinds of weapons?" Jia shook her head. "We're doing Fleet a favor. They might be going after smugglers today, but two weeks from now, they might hit a liner or transport. Pirate scum."

Erik nodded, more than happy to take out pirates. In his experience, they lied more often than not about letting people go. The crew of both approaching ships likely already had dozens, if not hundreds of murders, to their credit. It was time for some justice.

Jia's eyes narrowed. "Not much time left, but I did think of one reason to let them go. Given our location, size, and sensor signature, there's still a chance no one has spotted us unless they're looking right at this planet. We start a major battle, people are going to notice, even this far from New Samarkand."

"We'll have to take the chance," Erik commented. "If we run, they'll just follow us."

Jia scoffed. "We need to bring a smaller ship along with us."

"At the rate we're going, there'll be the Army, the Fleet, and us."

"We're about to enter maximum effective engagement distance," Jia reported. "It's time to take down those pirates."

The enemy ships had widened their gap considerably. Concentrating fire in one area was no longer a viable strategy to take them down, and Erik and Jia still didn't have a clear idea of the enemy's capabilities.

That was one of the advantages frontier pirates possessed. Their ships and configurations were nonstandard, meaning that even Fleet ships had to exercise caution to avoid being surprised by an enemy with unexpectedly robust firepower.

Now that they were closer, magnified images and sensor readouts highlighted a pair of top-side laser turrets and large single missile launchers under each flat, ugly vessel. The pirates had demonstrated good maneuverability, but unless Lanara had a pair of long-lost sisters, there was no way their engineers could match her. That limited their ability to quickly shift shield protection, which, combined with their limited weapons capability, put them at a disadvantage. As it stood, the *Argo* had more weapons than both ships combined.

It was time to make space a safer place. Erik linked the firing controls to the turrets, including the plasma turrets, into two groups, top and bottom. The pirates continued speeding toward them, so far apart now it'd be easy for them to attack the *Argo* from opposite sides. Their strategy was crystallizing.

"Level out the shield power around the whole ship," Jia ordered. "At least until we've picked one of these ships off."

"Adjusting shield power and reactor output," Lanara replied. "I hope everyone's strapped in. Rerouting power from internal grav field emitters. Things might be a little bumpier than usual."

Erik and Jia ignored the front cameras to concentrate on their sensor displays. Despite what people saw in films, the huge distances and invisible nature of the primarily laser weapons involved in most ship-to-ship battles meant that visual input, even when magnified, was less helpful than multi-spectrum sensor readouts. It wasn't sexy, but it kept you alive.

Jia rolled the ship onto its side relative to the approaching enemy, counter-thrusting to kill the roll so quickly someone might have forgotten they were in space. The maneuver provided kill arcs to both groups of turrets, but the pirates didn't change course.

Arrogant enemies were the best. They made battles more efficient.

"Almost there," Jia announced. She took shallow breaths and kept her hands steady.

Erik spun the turret groups toward the enemies and

opened fire. His sensor readout lit up with his beams and plasma discharge. The pirates thrust to the side without rolling or changing direction, their turrets counterattacking. The *Argo* and the pirates narrowly missed one another.

The pirates ripped past and flipped their ships with expert thrusts. They continued barreling away from their inertia. Missiles burst from their launchers and zoomed toward the *Argo*. Jia rolled the ship to its other side and angled it down relative to the pirates and their missiles. The projectiles changed course and continued their dogged pursuit of the *Argo*.

"Handle point-defense, Emma, but make it look close," Erik ordered. "I'd rather they get overconfident. Jia, line me up with one of them so I can try our new toys."

She smiled. "Don't use them up. You never know what we'll run into later. I'd hate to run dry and have to take down the pirate mothership. Lanara, give us more forward shield power."

Erik's body strained against his harness, thanks to another hard lateral burn and Lanara's reduction siphoning power from the internal grav field emitters. The enemy's complacency regarding their victory became obvious when they both initiated low, long burns to slow down. Their large missiles barreled toward the *Argo*.

"These guys have gotten too used to taking out smugglers with a spare turret or two," Erik muttered. "They're about to have a very bad day."

The point-defense lasers came to life and ripped into the missiles. Both exploded, flares in space, announcing the battle to any who might be watching. Erik didn't care. He was going to show these pirates what happened when they assumed.

Jia spun the ship onto its belly and accelerated toward one of the pirate ships. They finally understood their mistake and initiated their own burn, but the *Argo*'s approach angle meant only one of them had a clear line to their target.

Erik's stomach gurgled to register its complaints as Jia rolled from side to side to avoid the pirates' lasers. The *Argo*'s turrets delivered their invisible streaks of death, marked only by puffs of debris and new holes in the pirate vessel. A continual stream of fire from the plasma turret made for brilliant fireworks, the power dissipating at first due to the distance, then exploding across the surface of the enemy ship in small bright flashes. The back of the missile launcher exploded, and the chunks hurled away from the bottom of the wounded vessel.

Pirate lasers raked the *Argo*. Red lights flashed as a diagram marked the damage to different sections of the ship. Nothing more than minor surface armor destruction, pockmarks compared to the holes they were boring through the enemy ship and shearing off its thrusters. A small cloud of debris grew behind the pirate ship, which was now rolling.

"These new shields and armor are paying for themselves already," Jia commented with a grin. "Now finish them off. I know you want to test the missiles. You've got five seconds before I turn."

Erik snickered since he already had a missile lock. He pressed a button for a single launch. One of the weapons blasted loose and flew toward the pirate ship. Jia pulled up and kicked in the primary thrusters to whip the *Argo* up at an almost ninety-degree angle. The pirate turrets swung around and nailed the back of the *Argo* just as the missile rammed into the front of the pirate ship and blew it into a metallic cloud.

The other pirate ship didn't waste their friend's death. They'd taken the opportunity to circle around the rear of the *Argo* and line up another missile. This time Emma didn't toy with them, just picked off the missile with ease.

Erik chuckled. "Sometimes I forget how overstuffed with weapons and defenses this ship is. It's like the world's sexiest little destroyer."

"I think you need to adjust your expectations," Emma suggested. "These are common gun goblins with scraped-together ships, not the leaders of the Core."

"Not leaders of anything, not with the fight they've been putting up. This almost isn't fair."

"They're the ones who chose to be pirates and attack us," Jia replied, no humor in her tone. "And they haven't been fair to their victims."

"Not disagreeing. Let's finish this bastard off before he gets lucky. How are we doing damage-wise?"

"Minor hull damage all over the ship, moderate damage to some rear grav emitters and thrusters," Emma reported. "No significant reduction in overall power, despite minor internal routing issues. Shields emitters remain undamaged, and there has only been a small reduction in maneuverability because of minor damage to a thruster."

"Charging in close might not have been worth it," Erik concluded. "Fine. Let's stick to this guy's blind spot and finish him off with the turrets."

Jia completed a wide turn back toward the pirate ship, which was also attempting to circle back on the *Argo*. The pirate took extreme-range potshots with his laser turrets but hit nothing.

"Get ready," Jia announced. "I'm going to bring us under him. Finish him off in one pass."

"Do what you need to," Erik replied, flexing his fingers. "I'll do what I do best—blow things up."

Jia spun the ship with expert ease. The *Argo* was already accelerating toward the underside of the pirate ship before it completed its turn. Erik wondered if Lanara's redirection in power from the grav emitters was worth it, given that he was also grateful he had not eaten in a while. He ignored his protesting stomach and opened fire on the enemy.

The pirate turrets nailed the *Argo* a couple of times, gouging a line into the top and narrowly missing a plasma turret before they lost their attack angle, but Erik's lasers sliced deeply into the pirate vessel. Close-range hits from the plasma turret blew out huge pieces, exposing the interior. He kept up the attack, the turrets pounding on the bottom of the pirate vessel, melting, shredding and cutting away chunks. Internal explosions rippled through the ship and blew it into larger chunks than his friend.

Jia let out a sigh of relief. "It's over."

"Good job," Lanara sent. "You managed not to kill us all. There's only so much I can do in space, but I should be able to patch up most of this within a couple of days once we're on the planet."

Erik disengaged the weapons, smiling as the ship shook from the turrets and missile launcher folding back into their hidden compartments. "We took out two ships with only minor damage. Not bad."

"Yes." Jia took a deep breath and let her head rest against the back of her seat. "But was that equipment or skill?"

"Both. Battle always comes down to equipment or skill, so the best thing to do is make sure you have both if you want to win."

Jia gave Erik a sidelong glance. "We might have just given our position away to everyone in the system. If they have friends, they'll come looking."

"If that's the quality of pirate coming, I'm not sure I care." Erik unfastened his harness. "We should hard-burn straight for New Samarkand and tell the Fleet they have two less pirates to worry about."

The door to the cockpit opened, and Malcolm stumbled inside. Jia raised an eyebrow, and Erik snickered at his outfit: boxers and a white undershirt.

"We're not dead, are we?" Malcolm sputtered. He rubbed a large bump on his head. "Beds need emergency harnesses."

"You were told to strap yourself in," Emma commented.

"You didn't give me enough time," Malcolm whined. "I did eventually."

Jia chuckled. "Go back to sleep. We'll let you know if we need you. Even our luck isn't so bad that we'll be attacked twice on the way to a planet."

Malcolm's brows lifted. "I think I'm going to get dressed. I don't want to die in my underwear."

CHAPTER THIRTY-FOUR

A half-hour later, Jia joined Erik in the galley, a scowl on her face. "We need to go back to the jumpship right away."

Malcolm, in pants and a purple Hawaiian shirt featuring explosions, sat at a table eating soup. Erik was on the opposite of him, working on what looked like a poor man's attempt at roast chicken. They looked up from their meals in surprise at Jia's declaration.

"We're not that far out yet," she continued, "so we won't be losing much time."

"Why?" Erik set his fork down. "If this is about someone noticing the fight, we already talked about that. They'll burn hard to find a bunch of rubble, and if it's pirates, we'll take them down. If it's Fleet, we'll explain and send the coded credentials from Alina over. If it's a smuggler, we'll tell them to mind their business, and we'll mind ours. They'll be far less interested in an unnecessary fight."

Malcolm nodded quickly. "I like the part where we tell the other ships we'll mind our own business. I hate the idea of dying early in space."

Erik laughed. "Dying on a planet is better?"

"Yes. It's how nature intended things." Malcolm nodded firmly. "Not the early, necessarily, but the planet."

Jia shook her head. "Pirates operating with impunity only a couple of days out from New Samarkand isn't a good sign. I've been thinking about it. I doubt those were the only two pirates out there. Depending on how good they are at running silent, they could have a whole fleet out here."

Malcolm shrugged. "If more show up, just blow them up. Problem solved?"

Erik pointed his fork at Malcolm. "The man does have a way of getting to the point."

"It's not us I'm worried about." Jia folded her arms. "I don't think a runaway program, a scientist, and a couple of engineers are enough to protect the jumpship, not with pirates and who knows what else prowling out there."

"The jumpship has even more guns than this one," Malcolm protested.

"But not a true crew." Jia sighed. "It's not good enough, not with so many factors unclear. The main reason we didn't jump straight to the planet was to protect the ship, but without a dedicated pilot, we can't risk leaving the *Bifröst* undefended. The pirates don't have to fight it. They just have to board it. Once they're aboard, do we really think Raphael, Janessa, and Wei can fight them off?"

Emma materialized in a Fleet admiral's uniform. "Oh? What do you intend, then? Do you plan to jump directly to the planet after all? That might create its own issues, but I'm not going to claim I disagree with your analysis."

Jia shook her head. "The situation on New Samarkand

is too fluid for us to show up with the jumpship. For all we know, the Core has a weapon set up on the surface, and they're waiting for us to show up in that ship so they can blow us away in orbit."

Erik furrowed his brow, confused. "What, then? You saying we should abandon the mission until we have a Fleet escort?"

"For right now? No. But I'd love it if we could achieve that." Jia scrubbed a hand down her face. "Even if we set aside all the secrecy, that's not practical until they have other jump drives and navigational AIs. Otherwise, we'd always have to leave our escorts behind."

Emma smirked. "It'll be a long time before the Defense Directorate has more like me."

Jia looked her way. Given what the AI was doing to the jumpship's AI, it might not be as long as anyone expected, but that didn't solve the immediate problem or erase her worries.

"We can't walk away, Jia," Erik commented. "The military will retake control of the colony, but if the Core's here, we need to make them pay, and we need to get intel from them. It's the only way to stop this from happening again, and this is a rare opportunity when we know exactly where and how they're striking."

"I know." Jia put up a hand. "Trust me, I know. When we get back to Earth, I think we should ask Alina about getting a dedicated crew and security force for the jumpship. I don't care about the politics. A couple of Army squads would be best. It's a military ship, anyway; they're only letting us borrow it."

Emma frowned. "You want to load the jumpship up with uniform boys?"

"Why not?" Jia scoffed. "The jumpship sits in a Fleet base most of the time. If they wanted to take it, we couldn't stop them. If anything, bringing more military people on board would make the DD trust us more, not less. We need to start thinking beyond what Alina can do for us and being tools of the ID. This is about taking down the Core, and to do that, we need to make sure we keep all the tools that give us our advantage."

"Okay." Erik nodded slowly. "I agree with all that, but there's nothing we can do now. We're already a month behind on this. We can't jump back to Earth and waste a week or more getting people to agree to staff the ship. Shit, we can't even jump directly back to Earth without them getting upset. We'd have to jump to Penglai, then fly to Earth and back. Too much time lost."

"We also can't leave the jumpship out there by itself." Jia looked at Emma. "But I've got a good temporary solution. I think we should leave Emma on the *Bifröst*. If she's aboard, she can pilot and defend the ship at full capability. In the worst-case scenario, she can make a run for it and jump somewhere else in the system. Janessa, Wei, and Raphael are aboard, so she has all the engineering help she needs. They just need a quality pilot and gun crew, and she's all that in one."

Erik stood, an incredulous look on his face. "If we park Emma on that ship and keep it where it is, we're not going to be able to communicate with her without a big delay on the mission. We lose a huge advantage."

Emma walked over beside Jia and gestured at

Malcolm. "You'll have Mr. Constantine. While he obviously lacks my overall capabilities, he is quite talented for a fleshbag."

Malcolm fluffed his shirt. "Yes, I am quite talented for a flesh... Hey!"

"You agree with this plan, Emma?" Erik asked, sounding surprised. "You want to sit out the mission."

"I have...optimizations I need to perform." Emma gave him a sly smile. "And Jia's analysis about the risk to the ship isn't off-base."

Jia hadn't even thought about trying to recruit Emma by appealing to her desire to spend more time in direct contact with the jumpship's systems, but she wasn't going to turn down help. They couldn't always depend on luck to save them. Anticipation was part of winning wars too.

"If Emma's there, the ship is safe," Jia declared. "We can't guarantee there isn't a whole pirate fleet hiding this far out and looking for targets."

Erik turned to Malcolm. "That means all the systems work on-planet is on you. Are you ready for that?"

"I might not be a multi-billion-credit experimental AI built using ancient alien technology, but I do have a keen fashion sense, and I'm good at what I do." Malcolm rested one arm on the back of the chair and gave a cocky smolder his best shot. He failed miserably.

"Keep in mind that might mean you need to come with us into the field," Erik explained. "We have no idea how good the networks are there, and that's before worrying about jamming."

Malcolm's smile faltered. "Being in a warzone isn't on my list of favorite things, but Jia's right. We need to protect our ride home. I'd rather not spend months in space heading back to Earth."

"That's not the angle I'm worried about," Jia replied. "But I'm not going to complain about more evidence in favor of my argument. This only hasn't been an issue before because we've never gone somewhere infested with pirates."

"It sounds like we have a half-decent plan," Erik announced. "Emma, turn the *Argo* around and burn hard for the jumpship. Next time, we'll just have to make sure there is a squad of assault infantry and a new pilot on board."

CHAPTER THIRTY-FIVE

October 15, 2230, Gliese 581, Approaching New Samarkand, Aboard the *Argo*

Erik's jaw tightened as he stared at the magnified image of the Fleet cruiser flanked by two destroyers. The ships bristled with turrets, cannons, and launchers. These ships weren't refitted spy craft designed to deliver a surprise lethal strike. They were designed to win a galactic war against dangerous aliens, many of whom possessed superior technology. He'd seen and flown in many Fleet ships throughout his career, but for the first time, he had to worry about what they might do to him.

The *Argo* packed a punch, and it might be able to take out a destroyer in a one-on-one duel, but the small flotilla in front of them was more than enough to annihilate their ship. If they'd had the jumpship, the fight would have been more even, but it didn't matter. It wasn't like attacking Fleet ships was an option, but Erik also couldn't allow them to take the *Argo* or interrupt the mission.

It was time for something Erik disliked. It was time for diplomacy.

The ships had undoubtedly detected them a long time ago, but the Fleet flotilla had made no move to intercept them. Jia's course took the *Argo* straight toward them, giving them little reason for intercept, and Erik had participated in enough antipiracy and anti-smuggling ops to know the Fleet never made an unnecessary move.

Jia and Erik had chosen to fly toward the cruiser, assuming it contained the highest-ranking officer off the planet. They'd detected other destroyers in orbit above the planet, and at least one heading toward an HTP with a group of three small transports.

Criminals were often overconfident and believed they could talk their way past a blockade. That made life easier for the Fleet since it was far more efficient to disable a ship sitting right in front of them than chase it halfway across a system. Letting suspect ships get close also offered other tactical options, all of which flooded Erik's mind and fueled his paranoia.

Erik frowned. "What do the sensors say about their launch bays?"

"All open, with heightened readings across the board," Jia commented before pinching in a display and spreading her fingers out. An enlarged image displayed a launch bay on the bottom front of the cruiser. Four fighters were positioned near the front, already loaded with missiles, ready for quick launch. There wouldn't be any escaping the Fleet.

"They're hailing us," Jia announced, taking slow even breaths as she fired the thrusters to slow the *Argo* to a near-crawl. "Turrets and shields active. Not taking any chances, are they?"

"We were running quiet," Erik replied. "They have every reason not to trust us. If we even look like we're going to go hostile, they'll launch those fighters, if not blow us away with a cannon. This isn't a normal Fleet patrol. These are people trying to stop reinforcements and supplies from reaching an enemy force. This is war."

"Let's see what they have to say and if Alina's influence means anything this far away from Earth." Jia's hand hovered over a comm receipt button, hesitating before she pressed it.

"Unidentified vessel, this is Captain Rala of the UTS *Guandao*. Travel to and from the New Samarkand colony is currently restricted, and the entire planet is under martial law. You may not land without the explicit preauthorization of the colonial government. Your flight path does not appear to be from either HTP, and you have not transmitted proper identification."

Jia cleared her throat. "*Guandao*, we have a reason for that. Please stand by for transmission of our clearance. We will hold our position until you've had time to process our documentation."

"Standing by. Please send clearance immediately. Do not attempt to leave, or you may be fired upon. Any attempt to activate weapons will be considered a hostile act, and you will be fired upon."

Erik sat there, waiting in silence, unsure of what was happening on the bridge of the other ship. They might be staring at the encoded credentials, utterly confused, or maybe they were slowly filling with anger, the captain trying to figure out the best way to seize the *Argo* without destroying it. Dying at the wrong end of Fleet cannons would be an ironic twist for the Army veteran. He would never hear the damned end of it in the afterlife.

Jia stayed quiet as the seconds stretched into minutes. Erik considered running down to the cargo bay and grabbing stun rifles for them. Killing military personnel was far from an option, but getting thrown in a cell wasn't either.

The comm crackled to life. "You are cleared to land, agents. We're transmitting landing coordinates, a temporary clearance code, and a suggested descent flight path. Please begin broadcasting the code immediately. I wouldn't deviate from the marked descent plan if I were you. We've got most of the areas outside the dome under control, but the rebels have hit ships before. Don't want any of our pilots to get confused, either. We'll give you the comm code for the local garrison."

"Agents?" Jia mouthed.

Erik shook his head and leaned over to whisper, "No reason to confuse them with the truth. The important thing is they don't know exactly who we are, which means they can't tell anyone you and I specifically are coming."

"Thank you, *Guandao*," Jia replied.

"Don't thank us yet. It's dangerous down there, especially for ghosts, but it looks like you took some hits before you got here."

"That's affirmative, *Guandao*," Jia replied. "We encountered pirates out on the edge of the system."

"They're like roaches out there. It's like they knew something was going to happen, and a lot of them infiltrated the system with disguised ships but didn't start attacking people until the rebels made their move. We can only spare ships to protect the flight paths to the HTPs and the stations. Judging by your approach path, you went the wrong way."

"Something like that," Jia transmitted. "Well, there are two fewer pirate ships to worry about. They were disagreeable."

A light laugh came over the comm. "Finally, ghosts doing something useful."

***

Jia kept the *Argo* on the suggested flight path. Fleet fighters patrolled the skies outside the domes in angry little swarms, dancing on the edge of the radar readout. Overkill, perhaps, but as long as the military had control of space and the upper atmosphere, they could smother the rebellion with enough time and reinforcements. If they did it quickly, there might be something left to save.

Pinpoint bombardment was an option for an open-air colony, but the domes complicated the situation. Unless the government was prepared to evacuate everyone from the colony, blowing massive holes in the dome guaranteed a proportionally massive number of civilian deaths. All that available Fleet power meant nothing if it couldn't be used.

"I'm really missing Kant and Anne," Jia admitted. "Given the reception we got up there, things are still pretty bad."

"Perspective," Erik countered. "Based on the number of ships we've seen just around the planet, they've received reinforcements. They also didn't say the planet was interdicted, just that travel was restricted. That means they're still allowing some activity. I'm guessing if the Core wasn't involved, they would have already put down the rebellion."

"Which means there's an opportunity for us to help end this quickly."

The *Argo* continued its smooth descent, Jia's face a mask of determination. Admirable, but potentially misplaced. Erik wouldn't mind helping end a pointless rebellion, but he doubted it would be that easy, given the Core was involved.

Sogdia's complex of domes came into view, connected by narrow aboveground tunnels. Following the course sent by the *Guandao*, the *Argo* descended toward one of the larger domes near the center of the city, an opening pulling back to allow them entry.

"If the Core hadn't already been here for a month, I would have suspected an attack on the domes or the oxygen fields," Erik commented.

Jia didn't speak until the *Argo* cleared the passage and the dome had sealed behind them. "Simple terrorism would have been a lot more straightforward. Maybe they decided it wouldn't work for them."

Erik shook his head. "I get the feeling terrorism's always been a sideshow or a way to cover things up, like when they paid terrorists to come after me, but it doesn't matter. Every Elite we take out and every Core operation we mess up slows them down and gives us a chance to catch up."

They both fell quiet as they surveyed the ruins spread out before them. That was the only way to describe the blasted wasteland covering half the city. All the effort spent colonizing the planet, and it was being destroyed. Drones and flitters were conspicuously sparse in the air. Smoke curled into the sky from multiple locations. Their target hangar was in a nearby area that only looked half-destroyed.

"We better get on the ground quickly before someone fires a missile at us," Jia muttered. She glanced to the side. "At least we have decent net connections now."

"Rebels blow up the colony, but the net continues to live." Erik chuckled. He tapped his PNIU and flicked through feeds until he found a local newsfeed and sent it to a new data window in front of him.

A weary-looking newsreader sat behind her desk, bags under her eyes and her brown hair on the border of unkempt. "Again, please be mindful of the curfew and comply with all Army and militia patrols. The colonial governor has released a formal statement noting additional reinforcements will be arriving within the next week, but he also wanted to make it clear that the rebels and their mercenary allies continue to show little restraint or concern for civilian casualties. For your own safety, please do not attempt to bypass any government checkpoints, and immediately report suspicious activity to the authorities. Together, we can end this brutal insurrection."

"What good is a rebellion that destroys their own home?" Jia muttered.

"I'm sure they've convinced themselves they've got great reasons for this, or at least they did in the beginning." Erik swept the data window away with his hand and stared grimly at the city below. "At this point, they're fighting because they've invested too much into it to stop. I'm not going to defend the rebels, but they're a tool in the service of a greater evil. We need to do what we can with what we have. Let's get on the ground, get settled in, and see if we can get hold of our contact."

Jia sighed. "What do we do if they're dead?"

"Let's hope the Lady's on our side."

"She's certainly not on the colony's side."

CHAPTER THIRTY-SIX

Erik drummed his fingers on the control yoke of the MX 60. Jia stared straight ahead, trying to quell the unease in her heart. Flying the flitter without Emma and keeping so low to the ground felt wrong—unnatural even. Even more unnatural was Malcolm sitting in the back in a normal-looking suit and tie. He objected to not wearing his Hawaiian shirts on-planet, but in theory, they were trying to not stand out, and brightly colored Hawaiian shirts screamed Earth.

"We're closing on the checkpoint," Erik explained, slowing the flitter as they approached a tunnel.

A line of vehicles, mostly hovercars and trucks with a smattering of flitters, waited. Soldiers, including two men in exos, waited alongside the line, standing in front of a metal grate. An anti-aircraft heavy machine gun pointed at the sky. A pair of soldiers leaned in to talk to a frightened-looking old woman in a truck. After they shared a short conversation, one waved her through, shaking his head.

"Why did your contact have to be beyond a checkpoint?" Malcolm tugged at his collar. "Shouldn't an ID agent be more accessible?"

"Not if he's doing his job," Jia replied. "The enemy is out there, not in here."

"The rebels are past the checkpoints, right?" Malcolm asked, motioning forward. "I mean, I know they are because we already talked about this. I don't... Okay, I get why ghosts and people like us working for them would need to go forward, but why would regular people?"

"Remember, it's contested territory," Jia answered. "Not rebel-controlled. They can, in theory, launch attacks from outside the dome, but it ends up being too dangerous, with too great a risk of damage to the dome. Also, trying to rush a group of soldiers through the external exits is asking to get picked off."

"Why would anyone who wasn't a soldier want to go there?" Malcolm pressed. "That's what I don't get. It's so dangerous."

"To get a piece of their life back." Jia frowned. "I checked the local news before we headed out, and you'd be surprised by how many people were trying to ride out the carnage in their homes. Some still are. These are probably people who ran when a battle got too close to their homes and are now trying to collect things or look for lost family members. The problem is a lot of people think that if they aren't shooting at anybody on either side, they'll escape the trouble. The government is encouraging people to stay in safe zones but not requiring it yet. Among other things, there are space issues, and it looks like they're trying to convince people they're winning. If they try to jam the entire population of the city into one small section, morale's going to drop. There are risks of riots or people suggesting negotiations with the insurrectionists."

"It's insane that they're fighting in a place like this." Malcolm gestured around. "They're fighting over bombed-out buildings in domes! It'd make more sense to wait a century or two until this is terraformed into something halfway worth living on."

"Fighting over their home." Erik shook his head. "Once a man convinces himself he's doing that, he'll put up with a lot. I'm sure the rebels think everyone will hold them up as heroes once this is over." He looked into the back seat. "Did we need more time to get it ready?"

They'd had Malcolm dive into the local net and a less secure military system to look into the checkpoints to generate an official pass. He'd seemed confident at the time, but they couldn't be sure. They advanced a couple of vehicle lengths after the soldiers waved through some vehicles without talking to the occupants.

"No, it's fine." Malcolm brought up a data window and licked his lips. "Only a couple of drones in range, by the way."

"Don't need to take control of them yet," Erik replied, "but keep an eye on things. If things get hot, we might want them under our control."

"I still think we should use Alina's code or the *Guandao* codes," he muttered.

"Not yet. The more we can keep our heads down, the better. We don't know who to trust on this planet yet."

"I look weird, don't I?" Malcolm slumped in his seat.

Jia rolled her eyes. "You can go a day without wearing a Hawaiian shirt. Get hold of yourself, man."

Malcolm pointed to his face. "I'm not talking about that. I'm talking about the holographic disguise."

"Oh." Jia smiled and framed her face with her hands. "We're wearing them too. It's one thing to be able to get past the checkpoints if we need to, but that's not the same thing as announcing to the whole colony and the Core that we're here. Hence the disguises and not using the codes."

"The Core doesn't know about me," Malcolm insisted. He grimaced. "Do they? Do I need to update my will?"

"No, and probably." Erik shrugged. "It wouldn't hurt. But no reason to leave a trail and help them out. If we have to make noise later, we'll do that, but for now, we'll try to keep a low profile."

Malcom frowned. He typed on a virtual keyboard visible only to him. "This isn't good."

A couple of soldiers ahead exchanged frowns. When they leaned toward the next vehicle in line, their fingers were close to their triggers. One of them waved a silver probe back and forth. A small drone lifted off, keeping a couple of meters off the ground, and slowly floated past the lines of vehicles, passing the MX 60 and traveling past a few more vehicles before turning around.

"What's going on?" Jia frowned.

"They're heavy jamming all of a sudden," Malcolm explained. "There's no way this is background interference. I'm glad I transferred the pass to your PNIU." He pointed at one of the soldiers, whose hand rested on his PNIU. "It looks like that guy has direct laser control of the drone. Smart."

"We don't have time for smart checkpoint guards." Erik

gritted his teeth. "We don't have time for any of this shit. Now they're going to be twice as suspicious."

"But you have your codes and credentials. Ghost pass!" Malcolm threw up his fist in a mock cheer.

"Even *if* we wanted to use them, they might not help. What a captain sitting comfortably in a cruiser surrounded by destroyers will accept and what a scared corporal will accept when he's been shot at or seen his friends die are two separate things." Erik's hands tightened on the control yoke. "We could stun them if they try to do something, but that's just going to cause more trouble, and if somebody's jamming all of a sudden, they have reason to be suspicious. We need to maintain our cover as long as possible."

The soldiers continued scanning the area, shouting to each other. One of them waved the front vehicle through the checkpoint. The gate retracted, allowed the hovercar through, and slammed shut within seconds. That left a space for the MX 60, currently a dull gray, to move forward.

Erik lowered the window and cruised forward. He kept a calm, almost blank expression on his face and his hands visible on the yoke. Smiling at a scared man in this situation would be an insult.

A soldier approached, a sergeant. He looked back and forth before whistling. "Such a nice flitter to have such a boring color."

"I'm a boring guy," Erik replied. "It's good to be boring when everything else is going to hell."

The soldier smiled. "Why do you need to go past the checkpoint, sir?"

MICHAEL ANDERLE

"I need to pick up some family mementos from my house. Should I show you my pass?"

"I think you're going to need to step out of the vehicle, sir." The soldier backed away and brought up his rifle. "We noticed some thermal anomalies."

Jia sighed. That was one of the few disadvantages of the holographic disguises. They needed a distraction, but they hadn't prepared anything.

"I have a pass," Erik continued calmly. "Can I transmit it to you?"

The soldier narrowed his eyes. "That's not possible."

"Then can I show it to you?"

"I think—"

The soldier's eyes widened and he backpedaled, raising his rifle. "Incoming!" He gestured down a side street. "Everyone, get the hell out of here! Rebel attack!"

Jia pointed at a rear camera feed. A dark gunship bearing a bright machine gun emerged five buildings back, its thrusters angled down so it could hover in place with ease. There was the distraction they needed, but it also presented an immediate dilemma.

Erik closed the window. "If we go after that thing, we might blow our cover. Malcolm could hack the gate control."

Malcolm nodded quickly and swallowed. The gunship surged forward and fired, the bullets ripping through the back of a hovertruck and almost taking the head off the sergeant who'd been talking to them moments before.

The exos raised their rifles and opened fire, but the gunship swerved back and forth in an aerial dance that allowed it to close and send a stream of bullets toward the exos. High-powered rounds riddled an exo's shield, blasting out small pieces but not destroying it. The gunship skimmed near the wall before diving and shredding the AA machine gun near the gate.

Jia turned back around and gestured for Malcolm to move to the side. She reached toward the hidden compartment in the back. "Yes, it'll blow our cover. You think that's a reason to stop?"

"Nah." Erik shook his head. "If they're attacking this checkpoint, those soldiers aren't with the Core. Sometimes secrets are overrated."

CHAPTER THIRTY-SEVEN

Erik put his hand on Jia's shoulder. "We're not getting out."

"We're better in the air?" Jia asked.

"That's the plan, but yeah, we're not leaving our protection." Erik turned to Malcolm. "Make sure you're strapped in. We've got decent armor on this thing, but it can't take machine gun or cannon rounds from a gunship."

Malcolm pulled on his seatbelt and the extra harness, swallowing. "Kind of a different experience helping you guys in the field, especially when the field is a warzone. I thought I was being a badass just being on the *Argo*, but I'm really in it now, aren't I?""

"Yeah. It's a good thing." Erik grinned.

Malcolm swallowed. "A good thing?"

"When bullets are flying at you, it ups the pressure. Helps you focus."

"If you say so," Malcolm mumbled.

The gunship made another pass, this time delivering pain to the back of an exo. The pilot ejected from the sparking, smoking mess and ducked behind a pile of crates for cover. Soldiers fired into the air on full auto in a feeble attempt to down the enemy. People near the back of the line turned their vehicles around and sped away. Those trapped in the middle threw open their doors and fled toward buildings on either side, screaming.

Strafing a checkpoint was almost guaranteed to result in civilian injuries. The rebels should have kept their friends in check. That observation, combined with a magnified camera feed image, confirmed the truth for Erik. There was no way a full human could fit inside the gunship now attacking them, and the rebels or mercenaries would not risk a sortie in a jammed zone with a purely bot-controlled vehicle.

An Elite. The Core had come to them.

Something opened fire from down the street, its stream of bullets ripping dozens of holes through a long ammo crate and sending it tumbling through the air while leaking bullets. A nearby soldier rolled out of the way, avoiding being crushed by the heavy container.

The angle of attack was wrong. Erik frowned and shoved the MX 60 to the side, moving away from the soldiers and exos as converging barrages from above and from street level took down another exo. The pilot crawled out, clutching his bloody shoulder and groaning in pain. Another soldier pulled him back before the gunship strafed the area again, almost killing a woman who was ducking with her hands over her head.

One of Erik's rear feeds revealed the source of the ground attack: two large six-legged robotic bodies with four-barrel turrets. They clung to the side of a building, held in place by spikes on the bottom of their legs. Skittering forward, they fired again. A soldier screamed as a bullet ripped through his thigh. He collapsed to the ground.

"Don't have to open those up to know they're Elites," Erik grumbled. He whipped the MX 60 into the air. "The bug Elites don't look like they can get into the air, so let's take down the gunship first."

"With the turret?" Jia asked. "Was that why you didn't want us to get out?"

"Yeah," Erik asked. "Why else?"

Jia looked concerned. "You can't fly and shoot at the same time the way things are set up."

Erik grunted. "Shit, yeah, you're right. We always assume Emma will be flying or shooting. Fine, we'll do this the hard way. You'll shoot while Malcolm does some quick reprogramming to give us greater tactical flexibility."

Malcolm blinked. "Excuse me, I'm going to do what?"

"It doesn't have to be fancy. We just need something so Jia can control the turret while I'm driving. Figure something out before everyone's dead. Improvise."

Malcolm stared at Erik like he'd gone insane. "You want me to slap together a way for her to shoot while we're in the middle of the battle without her being able to use the control system intended for it?"

"Gestures." Jia held up her hands. "That'll work. This is a temporary thing. We'll worry about permanent options later."

Malcolm scrubbed a hand over his face before bringing up data windows. "This is going to be tricky. You're talking about hacking together a new control interface in minutes in the middle of a battle."

"Adapt and overcome." Erik chuckled. "That's what it means to be a field agent and now rear support."

Jia reached under the front seat to retrieve the TR-7 and the AP magazines. She winked. "Show us your fleshbag talent. I'll buy us some time with suppression fire."

Malcolm took a deep breath and slapped his cheeks. "I can do this. I can help save those soldiers. I might not have recoded an underlying system that quickly in the middle of a fight before, but what's life without a little challenge?" he finished with a hysterical laugh.

Erik sped up, increasing altitude to match the turning gunship. The enemy waggled back and forth erratically. Jia slammed a fresh magazine into the TR-7 and opened her window. She rested the barrel on the bottom of the window and fired a burst at the gunship. The bullets went wide.

The enemy increased its height and spun, trying to loop behind the MX 60. The flitter might not have the overall raw speed of the gunship, but it made up for that with greater maneuverability. Quick, tight turns saved the MX 60 as the gunship dove and spewed bullets like an angry dragon desperate to destroy the knights challenging it. More importantly, they were keeping its attention on them and reducing the danger to the soldiers and civilians below.

Erik continued his erratic, serpentine flight path, throwing off the gunship. He was grateful the enemy didn't have rockets since he wasn't eager to test the MX 60's potential for crash survival. He charged toward the dome's wall, spun to the right at the last moment, and skimmed along it with less than a meter of clearance. The gunship chased them, firing a stream of bullets at the reinforced wall.

He didn't worry. Domes could stand up to a lot of punishment. Otherwise, the average dome would never survive.

Erik smiled. Every second the gunship was focused on the MX 60, it wasn't attacking the soldiers below. The aerial enemy had thoroughly taken the bait, but the advancing ground Elites pressed their attack, keeping the soldiers pinned behind cover and low to the ground. The best thing Erik and Jia could do for them was take down the gunship, and despite Jia's valiant attempts with the rifle, they were going to need the turret to pull that off.

Not that the men below were defenseless. The sergeant crawled on his stomach toward a long, thin weapons case.

A couple of rounds struck the back of the MX 60, and the reinforced armor was not able to stand up to the powerful gunship rounds. The flitter shook with each impact, but no data windows popped up, nor did any alarms sound. That was good enough for the moment. Erik couldn't take the time to worry about minor damage. As long as he could fly, he would buy Malcolm time.

Erik accelerated and circled toward the gunship, trying to get behind it. Jia fired a couple of bursts. She frowned when she didn't hit, but the gunship broke from its latest turn to drop into a twirling dive in an attempt to shake off its pursuers. At least it recognized the threat they represented.

The sergeant reached the case and flung it open. A rocket launcher lay inside. He pulled the weapon out, staying low. The enemy's ground Elites advanced to within a hundred meters. Fortunately, the civilians had cleared out or run into nearby buildings, but the trails of blood provided testament that some hadn't escaped uninjured.

Jia growled and held down her trigger, emptying the TR-7 but not bringing down the gunship. She grabbed another magazine and reloaded. Malcolm continued typing furiously, occasionally swiping with his hand or jabbing a data window and muttering under his breath. His eyes grew wilder with each passing second.

The gunship pulled up, then zoomed toward the dome's ceiling. Erik matched its movements. The aggressive maneuver pushed him hard against his seat. Jia gritted her teeth, trying to keep the TR-7 steady as she took her next shot. Sparks signaled her hit, but the gunship didn't react. After a couple more seconds, it abruptly dipped its nose, spun to bear down on the flitter, and fired. Bullets ripped through the side, passing through Malcolm's data windows and missing his arm by centimeters.

He jerked his hand back. "That was...close."

Erik scoffed. "Quit your whining. You didn't even get hit. That was so far away it might as well have been on a different planet. Now finish what you're doing. We're not going to take that bastard out with a regular gun. We need the turret."

Another enemy barrage riddled the MX 60. The flitter listed to the side, and Erik strained to keep it steady. Alert windows popped up. Erik didn't need to look at them to know he had thruster damage and had lost some grav emitters.

After waiting for the appropriate opening, the sergeant pulled out the rocket launcher and sat up, then hoisted it onto his shoulder. Without hesitation, he sent a missile streaming toward one of the advancing ground Elites.

They nailed him in the shoulder right after the shot. He fell backward, but his missile skimmed the ground, almost striking a rock before hitting one of the bug Elites and blowing it apart in a satisfying blast. Its partner skittered behind an abandoned hovertruck. The Elites had learned to fear the unarmored man.

The gunship abruptly pulled away from its engagement with Erik for another strafing run on the soldiers. The sergeant avoided its wrath with a quick roll, but the attack perforated his rocket launcher. Jia unloaded the TR-7, which produced a trail of smoke, but not bring down the enemy.

"I-I think I did it," Malcolm announced, licking his lips. "I kind of cheated by using an already existing—"

"Just turn it on!" Jia shouted, shoving the TR-7 back into the hidden forward storage compartment and lifting her arms in front of her. "We're running out of time before they blow someone's head off."

"Bring in your three fingers on your right hand to fire." Malcolm's hands become a flurry of movement, a confident smile building with each keystroke. "I'm not just a fashion genius, I'm a master under pressure. I'm as good as a billion-credit AI."

Glowing rings appeared on Jia's hand and a targeting display materialized in front of her. The MX 60 rumbled and the turret deployed.

"Playtime's over," she declared.

Jia twisted her hands, the turret responding to her movements. She narrowed her eyes and then brought back her three fingers. The turret roared to life, sending a stream of bullets toward the gunship that had ignored damage from the rifle. She painted a ladder of bullet holes in the back of the Elite before it plummeted toward the ground, leaving a dense trail of smoke. The impact sent debris everywhere, along with splatters of blood.

The remaining Elite jumped onto a building and tried to crawl away. Erik turned the MX 60, trying to keep it level and fighting against it listing to the side as Jia lined up the turret. Her bullet storm sheared off the lower halves of its legs and left its body a hole-filled wreck. It fell off the building and landed hard on the ground, its stumps immobile and pointing up.

Erik circled the area for a half-minute. Other rapidly approaching contacts appeared on the sensor display, accompanied by Army transponder codes. He nodded at Jia and retracted the turret, then settled down in front of the gate and canceled his alerts, but not before noticing the engine damage warning. They couldn't risk going much farther with the MX 60 in that condition. The Elites had wounded the Taxutnta well. If Emma had been there, she would have been furious.

The sergeant sat on the ground with a med patch on his arm. He stood and stared at them before gesturing at his PNIU. Other soldiers were helping wounded soldiers and civilians over to the checkpoint and applying med patches.

"Jamming's gone," Malcom reported. "I think it must have been the second bug-looking one."

Erik reached down to his PNIU and transmitted Alina's credentials. He lowered the window and waited. An Army hovertank rumbled up behind them, and a squad of six exos ran over in close formation.

The sergeant's eyes went back and forth as he read their transmission in his smart lenses. He scoffed. "Thanks. You saved our asses there." He winced and gripped his shoulder before nodding toward the approaching reinforcements. "I think they've got it if anything else shows up. You should have just sent your codes to begin with, but it's nice to have you ghosts do something useful for a change."

"We're not exactly ghosts," Erik replied.

The sergeant frowned. "But these are ID codes."

"It's complicated." Erik shrugged. "But we're here to help with the rebels, and especially those merc Elites. We'd like to avoid advertising who we are. It'll help us do our job better."

"I know—standard ID bullshit. You were never here. We never saw you." The sergeant nodded. "I can send you temporary codes to get you through other checkpoints easier." He looked at the MX 60 with a grim expression. "I can also recommend a place where you can rent a hovertruck without many questions. Just tell them Sergeant Vines sent you. This thing looks a little beat up, and I don't care what color it is, it stands out."

"Thanks," Erik replied, leaning out the window to inspect the vehicle. Huge holes decorated the body. "Next time, we'll try to keep a lower profile."

CHAPTER THIRTY-EIGHT

Damir jogged down the side of the street, his mottled gray cloak fluttering with his movement. He'd spotted mercs in this area earlier but no FSA troops. That made the day's patrol route easy to decide. Everything would be easier with less risk of collateral damage. He slowed at the sound of a cough and murmurs above him, his prey making itself known.

The bombed-out four-story building beside him used to be an administrative center, judging by the scorched signage. Now it was just another tombstone in a dying city, one he'd helped murder when he was supposed to be saving it. He craned his neck upward but couldn't see anything. A glance to his left revealed an emergency ladder and recent footprints in the dust below it.

Luck or destiny, or perhaps the Devil pulling him down the path to Hell. He wouldn't know until he was dead. Before then, he would do what was needed to preserve the honor of the rebellion.

Damir walked over to the ladder and placed a hand on a

rung. After a moment of consideration, he patted the pistol he'd pulled off a merc the day before. It'd be more satisfying to kill them with their own weapons, but he needed to confirm the targets before shooting. That was the one line he would never cross, the restriction that made sure no matter what he did, he wasn't as bad as them.

He pulled himself up on the ladder slowly, taking his time to avoid revealing himself. The ever-present sounds of distant gunfire provided some cover, but he had not seen another person for the last hour, meaning any nearby noise would stand out and alert whoever was on the roof. The slow climb took its toll, straining his arms and legs, given the huge pack on his back.

After a long climb, he reached the top. Jamming his feet into the rungs, he peeked at the roof. Two mercenaries lay in front of sniper rifles on tripods, carryaids next to them.

Damir pulled himself onto the roof and drew the pistol. He crept toward the mercenaries, raising the gun. They'd grown bolder and more arrogant since they arrived. That arrogance would cost them.

"The unit should be coming soon," one of the mercs murmured quietly. "Orders remain the same. Neutralize all the rebels in the unit."

"What did these ones do?" the other merc asked.

"Does it matter?" The first merc shrugged. "It helps if you think of them as simple targets. That's why I don't talk to them much." Using a dedicated scope instead of relying on smart lens magnification suggested an extremely long-range shot.

"It's how I'm keeping my sanity while we're stuck on this rock," the first merc explained. "They should just let us off the leash already, so we can finish things off. Sometimes I feel a little bad, but then I think it's their own fault. I like to think of them as sacrifices for a better future."

The second merc continued looking through his scope. "If you say so. I just like to know why I'm killing someone."

"The higher-ups have a plan," replied the first merc. "The only thing we need to worry about is doing what we're told. And from what I hear, these guys were asking about one of the shipments going to the camp. Does that help?"

Damir narrowed his eyes. There was a merc encampment a few kilometers away. He'd scouted it yesterday and nearly been spotted by a patrol, which would have ended his little counter-rebellion.

The second merc sighed. "You're right. That's the problem with the rebels. All up their own asses about their petty little cause, like it's important. And here we go." He grinned, closed an eye, and moved closer to the scope. "I've got five contacts. They don't have a clue."

"Five confirmed," the first merc replied. "You take the two in front, and I'll take the two in back. I bet you the guy in the middle panics and freezes. We can both nail him."

Heart pounding and holding his breath, Damir moved closer and pointed the pistol at the back of the second merc's head. The mercenary scum had accepted money from the FSA and were killing them when their backs were turned. At least the Army soldiers thought they were performing their duty. There was some small honor in that.

"On my three count," murmured the second merc. "One, two…"

Damir put two rounds into the back of his head and charged forward, kicking the other man's rifle off the roof before he knelt and jammed the pistol into the man's face.

"What the hell are you doing?" the merc snarled. "I'm on your side, you frontier piece of shit."

"No." Damir shook his head. "You aren't on my side. Let's talk about the shipment that is so important you need to kill for it. I don't mind our conversation taking long enough that the rebel patrol you were going to murder walks away unscathed."

The merc spit in Damir's face. "Are you insane? I have no idea what you're talking about. You just killed an ally. Let me go, and I'll forget your face. I get that this war can drive a man out of his mind."

Damir stood and slowly backed away, keeping his gun trained on the man. "How many people have you killed? I'm not talking about Army. FSA? Civilians?"

"I'm supposed to be providing overwatch of a rebel patrol, and you're going to get them killed, you idiot. If you don't care about me, you should care about them." The merc sneered. "They're risking their lives for your freedom."

"The shipment," Damir insisted. "Tell me about it. Why is it important enough to kill for?"

"I don't know what you're talking about." The merc's hand drifted toward his holstered pistol.

"But it's going to the nearest merc camp?" Damir asked, watching the man's face carefully.

The merc's face twitched. He went for his gun.

Damir fired first. He held his hand in place for a while before scoffing and heading toward the remaining sniper rifle and the carryaid next to it. The pistol was satisfying, but using a merc sniper rifle would be perfect.

Lying flat on his stomach and half-buried in rubble, Damir increased the magnification of his scope. He was watching the mercenary encampment about two kilometers away. Small numbers of drones circled overhead, but given the mercs' preference for jamming to disrupt the Army, they couldn't do much other than close-range laser comms. He'd quickly learned how to exploit the mercs' weaknesses in his one-man campaign against them. His luck would fail eventually, but until then, he'd continue to deliver revenge.

Exoskeletons and mercs in tac suits and carrying rifles patrolled the tall fenced perimeter, along with a handful of bug and Torch Dragon Elites. Anti-air artillery ringed the small area, with guns on the ground and on top of the tall, wide building they'd commandeered. Judging by the doors on the side, it'd been a garage before they'd moved in. He caught a brief glimpse of parked gunships and cargo flitters inside.

The mercs had encampments all over the city, but after his earlier fight, he suspected this one was special. Damir didn't know for sure, and he couldn't go back to the FSA. He'd thought about approaching a patrol, but he couldn't find one without at least a couple of mercs and often an Elite lurking nearby. No matter how corrupt the FSA had become, he refused to fire on a fellow rebel. They would see the light eventually. He'd force the issue.

A hovertruck flew up to a gate guarded by an

exoskeleton on either side. After a couple of seconds, the gate opened and the truck moved inside, then turned around and backed up to one of the garage doors. It parked on the ground, and the back opened, a ramp extending. The garage door retracted, ready to receive cargo.

Damir shifted his rifle to get a better angle, but he couldn't get a clear view of the back of the truck. He changed to thermal mode, but he couldn't see anything inside the truck. It must have been insulated. He switched back to normal optics.

"What are you scum up to?" he whispered. "You're worse than the government. I know you are. Just make this easy for me so I can get it over with."

A couple of mercenaries stepped into the garage from the main building. They slung their rifles over their shoulders and jogged up the ramp as they laughed and said something to one another. They returned a moment later and gestured at the back.

Damir waited, his breath held. A man in a cargo-loading exoskeleton approached and walked up the ramp. He leaned forward and locked long clamps onto something hidden by the back of the truck before backing up slowly, pulling out a hoverdolly almost the length of the back of the truck. A gray crate several meters in length but barely a meter across lay on top. After backing up and releasing the dolly, the cargo loader went back into the truck and pulled out an identical dolly and box.

Those boxes were worth the lives of at least five men, probably more. The mercenaries could have been delivering more Torch Dragon Elites or something similar, but that didn't seem unusual enough to warrant wiping out an entire rebel patrol. The mercenaries might be tightlipped about the details of their not-so-secret weapon, but they weren't killing any rebels who asked about them. There was something else in those containers, something Damir suspected might put an end to the rebellion.

CHAPTER THIRTY-NINE

October 15, 2230, Gliese 581, New Samarkand, Sogdia, Cargo Bay of the *Argo*

Lanara circled the MX 60, clucking her tongue. She squatted by the back and stuck her finger in a hole. "Wow, Blackwell. Just wow. You didn't stop to crash into a building on the way back?"

Jia had expected a reaction like that since Lanara was still complaining about the damage they'd suffered in the battle against the pirates even though she'd repaired most of it. Sometimes it seemed like the woman would die if she didn't get to bitch at least ten times a day. It was like she expected special bitching privileges for being so talented, and for the most part, Jia and Erik gave them to her.

Erik shrugged and offered a sheepish grin. "We managed to make it back. Hey, if it can still fly, it's not that bad, right?"

"That's an opinion. A correct one? That's debatable." Lanara pointed her thumb at a stub that had once been a grav emitter. "This is what happens when you get cocky.

Given you've had your arm blown off twice, you think you'd be more careful."

"It's not intended to go up against gunships," Erik replied with a shrug. "But we took one down without getting blown up. That's not bad, and we're not going to beat the Core being careful. I won't apologize for taking chances that save lies and take out assholes."

Lanara sighed. "I suppose you want me to repair it."

Erik chuckled. "That's the idea. We left the other two behind with Emma and Raphael, and you don't want me trying to fix all this."

"No, I don't. You'll just mess everything up." Lanara wrinkled her nose and dusted off her pants. "You know, I was planning to finish the earlier repairs and then start planning more massive improvements, but what the hell. That can wait, right?" She jabbed a finger at Erik. "Those are improvements you can use, and every time I have to fix something like this or a busted exoskeleton, it slows me down. Keep that in mind."

"What massive improvements?" Jia asked.

"All that power efficiency tuning I've been doing isn't just for fun. Well, only about half for fun." Lanara lifted her chin and let out a quiet snort. "I'm trying to help you survive the next time you run into something more impressive than two loser pirates with barely any weapons." She pointed to the roof. "Depending on how we do things, we could stick a capital-ship-scale cannon on this thing. Something that'd let you get a nice solid hit on a cruiser or carve through something smaller with one shot."

Erik whistled, impressed. "That'd be major firepower. You can do that on this tiny ship?"

Lanara's mouth twitched. She was in danger of smiling. "I could set up a secondary reactor in the cannon and supplement the power from the primary reactor. It might be harder to conceal, but depending on how we set it up, it won't be blazingly obvious."

Jia shook her head. "I don't think we need a major cannon on the *Argo*. If we're getting in fights with cruisers, we're doing something wrong."

"Let's not be hasty," Erik interjected.

Lanara scoffed. "You say that now, Jia, but what happens when the Core sends one at you?" She threw her arm toward the MX 60. "If the space battle version of this happens, it's going to be a lot nastier than you limping back to a hangar to waste my time. The best way to survive is to blow the hell out of the other guy."

"Exactly." Erik inclined his head toward the door. "If you can put a cannon on the ship, do it, but I don't think that's going to happen while we're on New Samarkand."

"Obviously, Blackwell." Lanara put her palm to her forehead and shook her head. "I was talking about doing other optimizations, but fine, back to boring repairs rather than optimization and upgrade preparation." She patted the MX 60. "I won't be able to pound this out in a few hours. You have more internal damage than you might realize."

"That's fine," Erik replied, motioning to Jia's flitter. "We have that for now, and we're going to go rent a local vehicle tomorrow to keep a lower profile."

Jia's brow lifted. "Tomorrow?"

"Yeah, we made enough noise for one day. We need things to settle down before we show our faces again."

. . .

October 16, 2230, Gliese 581, New Samarkand, Sogdia, Sanni Rentals

Normalcy was, by most people's measure, the opposite of the surreal, but as Jia stepped into the clean white lobby of Sanni Rentals, she was struck by the contrast between the building and a neighboring shop across the street that was half-caved in, the front wall mostly gone and burned rubble strewn about. Sanni Rentals was untouched from the outside, and the crisp, spacious lobby was spotless. Relaxing light Lunar Neo-classical played. A couple of chairs stood near the entrance, clustered around a data window playing *Romeo and Zitarkette,* a satirical animated comedy.

A slender man in a white suit stood behind a white counter near the back of the lobby, his broad eager smile almost infectiously pleasant. Holographic signs listing vehicle types and prices floated behind him. This wasn't the appearance of someone living in a warzone. He wouldn't look out of place in Neo SoCal. There was no one else present, so Jia and Erik walked right up to the counter.

"Hello!" the man offered. "I'm Sana Sanni, owner and proprietor. Welcome to Sanni Rentals. How can I assist you in your vehicle needs this fine and wonderful day?"

Optimism and delusion could feed each other. That was Jia's only explanation for the man's behavior.

"Uh, a Sergeant Vines said you were the man to see about renting a truck," Jia explained, looking over her shoulder to make sure the area was as damaged as it seemed from her first impression.

The more she looked, the more disturbed she was. Most of the buildings on the street had taken obvious damage from artillery or heavy explosives. The few that hadn't sported bullet holes, except for Sanni Rentals.

Sana clapped his hands together. "Ah, yes, most excellent. Sergeant Vines is a good man. I told him he should retire here someday. He seems to like it, although not all Earthers do. Very narrow-minded, but what can you do?" He shook a finger. "If I may be so bold, your accent doesn't sound local. Would you happen to be from Earth? If so, please take no offense. I understand it can take a while to warm to the charms of New Samarkand."

Jia and Erik exchanged glances before she answered, "Yes. We had some business to take care of, and...you know, uh, things happened."

Sana waved a hand. "All temporary unpleasantness. Don't let it get you down. But let's talk about your needs. Hovertruck. You sure you don't want a flitter? I have several nice models."

"Aren't flitters getting shot down?" Erik asked.

Sana chuckled. "I can't dispute that does happen on occasion, but there's nothing like the flexibility that comes with a flitter."

A quick check of the prices on the signs indicated that flitters were more expensive than hovertrucks. Jia suspected the only flexibility Sana cared about was financial, but she couldn't blame him, given the impact of the rebellion on the economy.

Jia shook her head. "No, we need a hovertruck. Something boring, safe, normal, and common around here. Nothing that stands out."

"Are you sure?" He sounded disappointed.

Sana snapped his fingers and made a circle with his hand. A hologram of a bright yellow boxy hovertruck appeared. The image rotated as triumphant music played.

"A vehicle like this would get you noticed," he commented.

Erik stared at the man like he was on drugs. "Most people don't want to be noticed in a warzone, especially during a rebellion."

"You know, the soldiers keep telling me that, too. If everyone has to stay here anyway, they might as well stand out, but are you sure? If you don't like yellow, I have all sorts of colors available." He waggled his eyebrows. "Maybe not as stylish, but more subtle."

"Basic gray," Jia insisted. "Gray like half the rubble lying around the city. Kind of camouflage."

"Very well, then." Sana's smile never dimmed. "The customer is always right, and the Army has been so helpful to me by renting vehicles. I was worried at first that they'd just take things, but they've paid for everything, so I want to do right by their friends." He gave a firm nod. "So, what else can I get for you? We offer a lovely sightseeing drone package—very sophisticated programming. You just have to press a button, and they'll automatically capture everything interesting in the area and stay close to the vehicle. You don't have to do anything."

"Aren't drones also getting shot down a lot?" Erik asked, shaking his head.

Sana tilted his head. "I'd be lying if I said no drones are getting shot down, but not *all* of them. You know, these things happen during difficult times, and don't we all eventually have difficult times?"

"That's okay," Jia replied. "We'll be fine. We mostly just need to visit someone. We don't require anything special, and we're not going sightseeing."

His eyes widened in delight. "For a modest add-on fee, I can rent you a vehicle with a small nano-AR interface. It's great for keeping your kids distracted."

Jia blinked. "We...huh? Kids?"

"You know, you're driving along, trying to get errands taken care of, and the kids are bawling, complaining about how there's nothing interesting on the net. You can leave them in the truck while you visit your friend and not have them realize how long it took." Sana held up a finger. "You know what they say? Children are more engaged by physical objects, and that's where the Frontier Caterpillar Nano-AR playset comes in. It's all toys in one, the flexibility of VR with that ever-so-important sense of touch."

"We don't have any children," Jia replied. "We don't need to keep anyone entertained during our visit to our friend."

"Maybe Malcolm." Erik snickered.

"He's a big boy who can entertain himself," Jia snapped before turning back to Sana. "Nothing fancy, nothing unusual, just a standard-issue hovertruck that'll get us from point A to point B. No upgrades. No drone packages. Just the vehicle."

"Your choice." Sana put a finger to his lips and furrowed his brow, deep in thought. "What about insurance? My rates are slightly elevated because of the unpleasantness, but since you're a friend of Sergeant Vines, I'll give you a discount."

"Yes." Jia chuckled. "I think we'll pay for a little extra insurance. You never know what might happen out there."

"True. You wouldn't want to have an accident and then be liable."

"I was talking about the rebel..." Jia shook her head. "You know what? Never mind."

CHAPTER FORTY

The hovertruck cruised down the damaged streets, the auto-leveling system making it easy to ignore the shallower craters and potholes. That was helpful, given there didn't seem to be a single street anywhere in Sogdia that hadn't been hit in the last month.

The residual damage was proof of the intensity of the rebellion. Under normal circumstances, road and infrastructure maintenance was trivial for a mature colony of this size. The lack of repairs indicated the government wanted to conserve resources and expected the rebellion to continue for a while, regardless of what they claimed.

Erik found himself reflexively seeking camera and sensor displays that didn't exist in the vehicle, though they'd loaded the TR-7 and laser rifle into the back seat in case they needed something heavier than their pistols on the way to their destination. They were traveling to the last reported location of a senior ID agent left on the planet, according to Alina's data. With the lengthy delays in communications between the colony and Earth, they couldn't be assured they would find anyone or even that the man was still alive, but it was a good place to start.

They'd already passed through two checkpoints. The ghost in question, Agent Caul, lived on the edge of an area the Army claimed they maintained passable control over. The closer Erik and Jia got to their destination, the worse the scars of war were. The area close to the hangar would not be out of place in Neo SoCal, or at least the Shadow Zone, with civilians still going about their business, but the current area resembled a pulverized wasteland, and the only humans they spotted were the occasional Army patrols in the distance.

Malcolm sat in the back of the truck, nervously looking from window to window as if a gunship would arrive any second to take them down. He'd done well during the last fight, so Erik didn't feel the need to poke him about his nervousness. Most men were nervous in battle. It was more experience than strength of character that fed the bravery of a seasoned soldier.

"What do we do if Agent Caul isn't there?" Malcolm asked.

"Ask around with the military," Erik replied. "That's our best bet. After blowing away an Elite with a modified MX 60, I'm less worried about keeping a low profile other than when we're traveling, but there's no reason to throw away what little secrecy we have left if we can find the guy without their help.

Malcolm brought up four data windows, each displaying graphs. "No significant jamming in this area. That's good, right? It means the rebels are weaker here, so the military doesn't feel the need to jam."

"Not a lot of drones still," Jia commented. "That means AAA and snipers are still a concern, but the lack of jamming is less about the rebels and more about the mercenaries and the Core. Not running with anything but laser comms has to be hard on the rebels. I suspect the jamming is mostly about maximizing the surprise capabilities of the Elites."

"But they aren't really winning." Malcolm shuddered in revulsion. "And those things can't be cheap, even if you ignore the whole sticking people's brains in them part!"

Erik snorted. "Now that we're on the ground and have a better feel for the situation, I don't think this was ever about winning. For the rebels, yes. For the mercs and Core, no. It's almost like they're stalling."

"For what?" Jia asked. "Reinforcements? We've got a decent Fleet presence in this system, and if pirates are picking off smugglers, that's decreasing the ability of the rebels to get supplies. The Army has received more reinforcements than the rebels."

"If I knew what they were planning, we wouldn't be driving around in this boring-ass truck, waiting to get blown away by arty," Erik replied with a smile. "I'm sure it's annoying, vicious, and murderous, and we'll find out soon enough. It didn't take us long to run into Elites."

He slowed the truck. They were approaching the address, but the entire neighborhood looked deserted. It was mostly comprised of densely packed apartment buildings, but most of them had suffered damage, including one with the back half of two Army gunships sticking out of it. Piles of rubble lined the half-cleared roads.

Erik slowed to a stop in front of the destination building. The top two floors had been blown off, leaving the odd sight of an exposed bathroom, complete with toilet, halfway through the building. A low-flying drone zoomed overhead, but he wasn't worried. According to Sana, his vehicle transponder signal was registered with the Army.

"Stay in the truck, Malcolm," Jia ordered, opening her door. "We'll fetch you if we need you."

"What if some rebels come?" he asked.

"Shoot them." Jia shrugged. "You've got two big guns." She gestured at the TR-7 and the laser rifle. "Those are both big enough that it doesn't matter where you hit."

Erik stepped out of the truck. "Or you can run them over, but try not to do that." He grinned. "It'd be nice to get our deposit back."

Malcolm groaned and slumped in his seat. "I now understand the wisdom of being the guy who sits on the ship. I like it even better when we do Earth missions and I'm not in the same city as you two. That's quality safety."

"You're helping save the UTC." Jia closed her door and waited for Erik.

They made their way to the front door of the building, which remained frozen in a half-open position. Jia passed through with ease, but the small space forced Erik to squeeze through with a grunt.

Erik looked around. "Lights are on." He nodded at a camera in the corner with a small red light. "And cameras."

"I'm impressed by the sturdiness of these frontier buildings," Jia admitted, slowly scanning the room. "If you pounded a building in Neo SoCal this hard, I don't know if you'd still have power."

"Under normal conditions, these buildings would serve

as temporary shelters in case of a major dome breach," Erik commented, his eyes narrowing on one of the cameras. "Best way to kill a dome city is from underneath. They harden them on the assumption something might crash into them from above."

Jia pointed at a stairwell. "I'm not impressed enough to take the elevator. Our man's on the second floor."

"Allegedly." Erik looked around one last time. "Just stay alert. A lot might have changed since he last reported."

Jia took point up the stairs, her stun pistol at the ready. They arrived on the second floor and stepped into the hall. The target's apartment was not far. Creeping forward in silence, they strained to listen for anything unusual, but the only thing they heard was distant gunfire. That was so common it had faded to easily ignorable background noise despite their short time on the planet.

They stopped in front of the contact's apartment. Jia inclined her head at a camera at the end of the corridor. Erik nodded back. He reached down to his PNIU to transmit an ID code to the apartment door access, and the door slid open.

Erik stepped through, his hand resting on his gun. Jia followed with a frown. The apartment was remarkably boring and small, holding a couch, chairs, and a small table. There was no obvious damage, but there were discarded casings on the kitchen floor.

"Agent Caul?" Jia asked. "You here?"

Something shimmered in the kitchen. Jia spun toward the distortion and nodded at Erik. He drew his pistol.

"We're not here to play around," he announced. "We've

come a damned long way because this place is infested with Elites. I got sick of fighting them on Chiron."

A dark-haired man in a tactical suit materialized and a wall disappeared, revealing another meter of kitchen. He had a holstered pistol. "You've fought them before?" the man asked. He snorted. "I wasn't sure if you two were the real deal, but you must be if you're here with that kind of experience." He narrowed his eyes. "I knew they had *special* options to get people here quickly, but no one's told me the details. I have my suspicions, but you know us ghosts. We're supposed to stay in our lane. It helps keep us breathing."

"Agent Caul?" Erik asked.

The man nodded. "Blackwell and Lin, I presume? Yes, I'm Agent Caul. I don't know why I'm so surprised. I heard about your little stunt at the checkpoint. You two must realize by now you're one of the few people in the UTC who are flying around in an MX 60 with a hidden turret. It's not what anyone would call subtle."

Erik grinned before folding his arms and leaning against the wall. "Nothing wrong with signature gear."

"It saved lives and took out Elites," Jia commented. "We weren't going to sit around and let the conspiracy do what they wanted. They've turned this colony into a hellscape. They need to be punished."

Agent Caul wandered over to his kitchen table and sat heavily. Everything about the man, from his slouch to his heavy eyes, screamed exhaustion. He shook his head. "How much do you know about what happened here?"

"They massacred the local agents," Jia replied softly. "Like they knew who they were."

Agent Caul's face twitched into a scowl. "Not like they knew. They *did* know. I found out recently they've been infiltrating this place for a long time, getting ready for at least a year. They didn't start bringing in the weapons and Elites until recently, but they put a lot of effort into tagging us before the effort." He curled his hand into his fist. "It didn't help that we had a traitor."

Erik growled. "Just point us at him, and we'll take him out."

"You don't need to." Agent Caul shook his head again. "I handled that leak last week." He patted his holster. "I should have tried to take him alive, but…"

"I would have done the same thing," Erik declared. "I'm not going to judge you."

"The question is if they all died for nothing," Jia interrupted. She kept her stern look when Agent Caul frowned at her. "I understand you've had to lie low, but if you found a traitor, you must have found other useful intel. We've come a long way to pick up info about the conspiracy, and this is a rare chance since they're operating in the open. Taking out Elites, while satisfying, is something the Army can do, so let's do what only we can."

"You're right," Agent Caul replied. "When I took out the traitor, I also got my hands on some encrypted data. It has to be important."

"Why haven't you turned it over to the military?" Jia asked.

"This is a backwater garrison with frontier reinforcements." Agent Caul slammed his fist on the table, which shook. "If I can't trust my local agents, how am I supposed to trust the military? All it takes is one officer who's working for the other side or sleeping with someone who is. The way the rebels keep pushing the military back, only to be pushed back, makes me think there have to be traitors."

"Not necessarily," Erik argued. "The mercs might be holding back the Elites purposely, trying to drag this whole thing out, and bringing them out when they see openings."

Agent Caul nodded. "I've wondered if that's their plan, too. I just don't get what the end goal is. The more they drag things out, the more they guarantee a loss for the rebellion."

"And the more damage they inflict on the colony," Jia countered, her face solemn.

"True."

"And the files?" Erik asked. "I understand not wanting to turn them over to the military, that makes sense, but why not check them out yourself?"

"Because this isn't a schoolkid's diary, Blackwell," Caul retorted. "There's serious encryption that requires resources and equipment I doubt is available on this planet. I'm not even sure the Fleet and Army garrisons have it. The only thing I know is those files relate to the Elites on this planet."

Jia frowned. "If you haven't decrypted it, how do you know that?"

"I made the traitor spill it before I blew his brains out." Agent Caul took a long, shuddering breath. "I've transmitted the data to Earth, but it'll take weeks to get there, and the response will take more weeks. I'll probably be dead before I hear back."

Jia smiled. "If we had access to a dedicated AI system

with experience breaking conspiracy encryption, how long do you think it'd take?"

Agent Caul laughed. "Not long, but can I have a unicorn and a lamp with a genie while we're at it?"

Jia held out her hand. "You have it on a data rod? Give it to us, or copy it. Whatever works. We'll take it from here. You can continue hiding out until the situation's more stable. We can get it decrypted."

"You can, can't you?" Agent Caul looked her up and down, an incredulous expression on his face. "If half the stories about you are true, we don't need a unicorn or a genie."

Jia, Erik, and Malcolm sat around the galley table, waiting. Malcolm might be an expert on systems penetration and digital forensics, but that wasn't the same thing as being able to easily crack custom conspiracy encryption, especially on a tight timeline. They'd transmitted a message to Emma explaining the situation and were now waiting. At their current distance from the jumpship, they expected a one-way transmission delay of about thirty minutes. Between the *Argo*'s and jumpship's antennae arrays, combined with knowing exactly where the latter ship was, they were confident they would have a decent transmission, but they hadn't tried to send one, figuring radio silence was the best option during their initial landing.

A message alert popped up on their PNIUs, routed from the *Argo*'s primary system. Erik brought up the message and smiled.

Hurry up and transmit the entirety of the data, flesh-bags. It'll distract me from my other work, but I'm confident I can decrypt the files. I can't guarantee a specific timetable, but if I devote my primary attention to it, I suspect it'll be days at most.

"That answers that," Erik commented.

"What do we do in the meantime?" Malcolm asked.

Jia shook her head. "You should continue burrowing into local systems, at least the local systems that are still active, including any drones. We don't need control, but we do need to know what's going on. It could take Emma only hours to crack that encryption, or it could take three days, but the Elites are going to keep moving. We should also get our drones ready."

"They'll just get shot down."

"Better to have a couple of seconds of intel than none."

Erik nodded his agreement. "For now, we'll stay close to the hangar, but get the exos ready to deploy if something comes up. The Core thinks they've blinded the ID by taking out all their agents, but we're here now, and it's time to take the fight to them."

CHAPTER FORTY-ONE

Jia moved her finger over the trigger of her simulated rifle, narrowing her eyes and pondering the apparent distance between her and the spinning orange spherical target in the distance. She stood in an open grassy field, with wispy clouds floating overhead. The occasional bird glided by. It didn't quite smell right—nano-AR never did—but it looked and sounded right.

Questionable scents weren't what was bothering her. The training scenario was focused on long-range shots, but it accomplished that via size tricks rather than anything approaching true spacing. She always worried that the simulation technique was subtly and incorrectly training her brain. Her accuracy in battle didn't *seem* to be suffering, but her doubts remained.

She pulled the trigger, and the target exploded in a shower of sparks. Satisfying, even if fake.

Erik clapped from beside her. "Nice. You're one hundred percent today."

Jia flipped the safety back on and set the rifle on her shoulder. It didn't matter if it wasn't real. Proper firearms-handling protocol should always be practiced. Muscle memory became habit.

"I feel like we should be doing more," she commented.

"More training?" Erik squinted into the distance. "We could make the program more difficult if you want, add some run and gun. I didn't want to do anything that would tire us out while we're on a mission. We don't know when we'll next have to move."

Jia shook her head. "I'm not talking about training. I'm talking about the mission. I'm talking about doing more than waiting around for Emma to crack the encryption. She admitted she had no idea how long it might take. I know what I said to Malcolm the other day, but this doesn't feel like we're being proactive. There has to be something more we can do."

Erik shrugged. "Like what? Not a lot we can do before that. The situation here is too hot for us to drive around poking at the rebels randomly, and the next time we get involved in a firefight, whoever's in charge of the nearest unit might not feel as charitable toward someone he thinks is an ID agent or even a merc. Emma knows what's at stake. If it's going to take a long time, she'll let us know, and we can figure out then how we want to proceed."

Jia laughed. "We did everything we could to get here as quickly as possible, and now we have to wait. The universe is laughing at us."

"Hurry up and wait." Erik grinned. "I'm used to that. It's the unofficial motto of the military."

"It's not just that." Her smile dimmed. "Now that we're out here, I want to do more to stop the insurrection. People are dying. This colony is dying. The Core is helping kill it for its own twisted reasons. I don't care what they are. I only know that we need to stop them."

"We'll do our jobs, and that will help. I don't know what else is in those files, but at the minimum, if we can give the military intel on the Elites, they can pick them off."

Jia considered that for a moment. "The ID might not want the data being shared so freely."

"Too bad they're weeks away by comm and months away for anyone who doesn't have a jump drive," Erik replied. "Alina knew the risks when she sent us out here, and she knows we make the calls we feel are best, and that those might not be what's best for the ID."

"I'm not disagreeing. I just wanted to make sure we're in agreement."

"We are." Erik brought a fist up in front of him. "If the military can take out those Elites, the rebels will lose a lot of offensive power. I've been in this kind of campaign before. Rebels may be brave, but they're mindlessly stupid. If they don't think they can win, the rebellion will sputter to a stop pretty quickly, just like it did on Diogenes' Hope. Momentum is everything in counterinsurgency ops."

Jia tapped her PNIU. The targets and the green field disappeared, revealing the featureless compact room. She set the rifle down and it melted into the floor, the nanites forming it returning to storage. Flexible reality, more limited than it seemed.

"Hurry up and wait, huh?" Jia asked. "You mentioned it before, but I don't think I've ever truly appreciated it until this mission."

"We already took down three Elites," Erik offered. "And saved a squad, along with a bunch of civilians. Things are going better than you think. We're making progress."

"That's one—"

"There's trouble," interrupted Malcolm, his voice coming out of the room's intercom rather than their PNIUs. "Sorry to mess with your training, but I thought you'd want to know because you might have to shoot some stuff."

"Where are you?" Jia asked.

"Cockpit."

"We'll be right there."

A gaggle of data windows filled the cockpit upon Jia and Erik's arrival. Most were empty and displayed the same message, an error code followed by an explanation.

DRONE FEED INTERRUPTED. ATTEMPTING RECONNECTION...

About a quarter of the feeds remained active, the source drones keeping close to the edges of buildings or hovering above the grounds. Collectively, they did a decent job of providing views from around the dome. In one feed, two squads of Army exoskeletons advanced at a modest pace, followed by what looked like a full infantry platoon. Three hovertanks floated down the broken streets in a line, their cannons blasting rounds while rockets exploded around them. In a third feed, a group of Torch Dragons and bug Elites surrounded an exoskeleton squad, devastating them with cannons and rocket fire.

Jia grimaced. "Not the best timing for us."

"No more than we'd expect," Erik replied. "At least no one's trying to blow the domes."

Similar scenes played out on the other active feeds. Rebel, mercenary, and Elite forces attacked Army troops at locations all over the city. A gunship screamed toward one of Malcolm's drones. After a bright flash from its guns, the feed died. A squad of rebel soldiers fired at another drone. Another feed died.

"That's about what I'd expect, too," Erik commented.

"Most of the drones were, uh, borrowed," Malcolm offered, his voice somber. "That's something. No bill."

Jia folded her arms. "Even the military can't keep many drones in the air, which is not surprising. The rebels have also taken out almost all the cameras, including the ones on the domes' roofs."

"That's probably another thing the Core spent time scoping out," Erik concluded. "But that's the past. We need to worry about the situation right now, right here."

Malcolm licked his lips nervously. "I originally had views around the rest of the city, but I've been trying to keep our drones in reserve. Not on Earth for easy repair." He gestured at a group of data windows ringed in red. "These probably aren't destroyed drone feeds. I think the rebels are jamming those areas as they advance. I swear, every time one of those gunships shows up, things start going wonky."

"Easier to jam a wider area if you're higher," Jia ventured. "Not a bad strategy."

"And the Elites aren't remote-controlled, so it doesn't matter." Erik nodded slowly. "Under normal circumstances, that might not be worth the damage to both sides, but this feels more like terrorism than war, even if they're pulling off a major multifront offensive." He scratched his eyelid. "They're trying to push through, but I doubt it's going to be enough."

"Are you sure?" Jia asked. "More importantly, how can you be so sure? They're attacking all over. They might have most of their forces committed."

Erik pointed at a feed where a tank anti-aircraft laser ventilated a gunship. "They do have a lot of forces out, but it's haphazard. They're pushing forward, but they don't have decent air support where they need it, and they've spread themselves out. No combined arms in most cases, and we know they have that capability. It's like they grabbed everybody and threw them in a bunch of directions to draw out the Army."

"If the rebels are spread out, that means the Army gets spread out too."

Jia inclined her head toward one of the exo squads. She wanted to believe what Erik said, but it was hard not to worry about good, dedicated soldiers getting killed by Core-manipulated rebels and cybernetic monsters. There was things getting worse before they got better, and then there was human brains in bot and vehicle bodies delivering death to a city.

Erik nodded. "Sure, that's all true, but the Army's got more forces. They've also got decent-sized formations from what we see in the feeds. The rebels and their friends are using only small squads, raiding groups, really. They can inflict damage, but they'll end up taking more overall, using this strategy. Rebels aren't going to win a war of attrition, even with the Elites and the mercs. I don't know who's calling the shots on their side, but I'm not impressed."

Over half of Malcolm's drone feeds had died. In one, an Army exoskeleton squad rallied, quickly pushing past the rebel infantry surrounding them. The rebel soldiers began to fall under the exoskeletons' hail of fire before breaking and running.

"Maybe this is the last big push," Jia suggested, her gaze locked on a feed. "Their final battle."

"It could be. That'd be convenient for the garrison forces." Erik motioned to another drone feed that showed a large group of mercenaries pulling out of a building without any sign of Army forces nearby. Explosions in the background pointed at the nearest battle. "But not everyone seems interested in reinforcing their friends. You don't always get what you pay for."

They continued to watch the feeds, but within a minute, all of Malcolm's remaining drones had either been shot down or jammed. Most of the fierce battles they'd been watching were far from over. In some, the Army forces had the advantage, but in others, the rebel raiders were inflicting serious damage.

Malcolm laughed nervously, fluffing his shirt. "So, we're waiting on Emma." He rubbed his neck. "We can't do our part until then, and we're not here to shoot random rebels. The rebels will probably get pushed back, but maybe we should leave until this is all settled, just to be safe. That makes sense. Right?

He pressed his fingers into three of the screens. An overhead map of their dome appeared, showing the *Argo*'s position and red dots within a couple of kilometers.

"Some of them are very close," Jia concluded, with narrowed eyes. "Not surprising considering where we are, but it is concerning."

Malcolm shook a finger with gusto. "Exactly. Very close and very concerning. I totally agree."

"But we can't leave," Jia continued, shaking her head.

"W-we can't? What about everything I just said?"

"Jia's right," Erik added. "We knew what we were getting into when we agreed to come here. We've got the turrets as a last line of defense if it comes to that."

Malcolm motioned around the room. "They're not designed for pinpoint attacks against this size target."

"Sure, but the typical Elite or exo isn't moving as fast. You're right, they're overkill, and we pretty much guarantee collateral damage. It'd be risky to have the *Argo* lift and hover, so either we stay put, or we fly into orbit. Even if we could survive a couple of SAMs, Lanara will murder us before she finishes the repairs." Erik looked at Jia.

She nodded. "The turrets can be the last line of defense, but that doesn't mean we can't be our own first line. From what I saw on those feeds, a show of force might be enough."

"Good call." Erik turned to the door. "Tell Lanara what's happening, Malcolm. Jia and I are going to suit up and defend the hangar from outside. If anyone gets too close, you and Lanara can shoot them with a turret or a laser rifle. Whatever works. If we're lucky, the Army will keep them away, and anyone who gets through won't be interested in fighting."

"Lucky, yeah." Malcolm slumped in his chair and wiped the sweat off his brow. "Next time I go on a mission to a warzone, I want two hundred guys with missile launchers camping in the cargo bay."

Jia laughed and followed Erik out the door. "Don't worry. We're not going to make you put on an exoskeleton, but active drone support would be nice until they start jamming. Fewer surprises mean fewer chances we get hurt."

Malcom sat up, confidence returning to his face. He raised his hands and held them above two virtual keypads. "Active drone support. Yes. That I can do."

CHAPTER FORTY-TWO

Erik stretched his fingers inside the arm of the exoskeleton as he marched beside Jia, ready for trouble. The hangar door closed behind them, concealing and protecting the *Argo*. They'd won their battle at the checkpoint, but they'd had to rely on a vehicle that wasn't meant to take on military-grade enemies. He was more comfortable in his preferred work attire. Some men liked suits, but he would always prefer an exoskeleton.

From what he'd already seen on the planet, and from what Malcolm had derived from the public reports, the typical Elite wasn't deploying the experimental energy shields they'd seen on Alpha Centauri. However, their maneuverability and firepower were still a danger, and there was a diversity of weapons systems even among the same type of Elites. An enemy with a mind was a dangerous enemy, and the rebellion's ability to continue to push back and harry the much larger garrison force was proof of the effectiveness of the Elites.

Jia expanded her ballistic shield and stepped away from Erik. Malcolm's small drones whirred overhead. They circled the building, staying close and providing a steady stream of alternative feeds and sensor contacts to the pair. No snipers or rockets blew them out of the sky—a promising start.

"We've got someone one and a half klicks out," Erik commented after reading a sensor display. "But they're moving parallel to our position and heading straight into some Army assault infantry. Even if they come this way, they'll be torn up by the exos on their tail. I'm not liking all the aerial units around. Tagging at least five gunships within six klicks, but they're going in the opposite direction now."

Loud alarms squealed in nearby sectors, adding to the noise. The battles thundered all around, providing ground-shaking booms, along with the staccato symphony of gunfire. Exploding aircraft became burning meteors, falling into the ground to add insult to the extensive injuries the city had already suffered. Whatever small portions of the city had avoided being marked by the horrible war were probably now being scarred. Domes left nowhere to run and backed everyone, rebel and soldier alike, into a desperate corner.

"I've been in a lot of battles," Jia murmured with a shiver. "But I understand now that war is different."

"Yeah," Erik replied. "Welcome to your first war. And no, it's not remotely as bad as what I've seen before."

"We have to stop this," Jia insisted. "This is insane, and it's pointless."

"That's the Core all over. As for the rebellion, I don't know what to do, but we'll do what we can."

"Incoming," Malcolm shouted. "Oh, man. Oh, man."

He highlighted the sensor contact zooming toward their position. The magnified feed revealed an incoming Elite gunship equipped with dual autocannons and a rocket launcher. It'd broken away from its ground squad of merc exos, who were now engaged in a pitched battle with an Army assault infantry squad.

"He's coming straight for us," Jia concluded. "Three kilometers out. It's like he knows."

"I don't think so," Erik replied after a couple of seconds. "I think he's taking a shortcut to get to the other Army forces. We're not in a heavily defended area, and it's not a high-value sector."

"We could back off and let him go through," Malcolm suggested. "The Army can handle him, right?"

Jia raised her gun. "No. I'm not letting that Core monster murder soldiers and kill more innocents."

"Oh, yeah. Damn."

Erik jogged to the side. "Load AP ammo, and we'll nail him with converging fire. But keep moving. Even with our shields, we're at risk from a gunship with that kind of armament. Wait until he's a klick and a half distant to engage. Doubt we'll hit him, but we'll get his attention. The more time he spends shooting at us, the less time he has to mess with the garrison."

He wasn't worried, nor was he overconfident. No weapons system excelled in all engagements, and gunships were specifically designed to be ground-attack aircraft.

Fortunately, Erik's and Jia's exos possessed higher speed and maneuverability than standard models. The enemy had spent the last month attacking slower models. The difference would throw him off, and they could exploit that.

Jia's exo kicked into a decent run. She jinked from side to side, never moving in the same direction for more than a couple of seconds, but overall heading toward the enemy. The gunship stayed low, cruising between the buildings as it continued its approach, displaying a little caution. He was taking them seriously. That was a good start.

Erik charged in a traditional serpentine pattern and kept an eye on his target distance. This would come down to timing. Two-point-eight klicks. Two-point-five. Two-point-one. The gunship's cannons came to life, each burst a vomit of fire and lead tearing into the ground but missing the agile, unpredictable exoskeletons. Yes, it was taking them seriously.

Two klicks. One-point-eight. One-point-five.

"Controlled bursts, angle it in, stagger with me," Erik ordered. He started the party by firing at the gunship. It was time to show they were taking it just as seriously.

The gunship broke to the side, avoiding his attack. Jia opened fire as well, but the distance combined with the uneven movement of her exo and the target kept it from landing. They continued closing on it, sending bursts at the bobbing and weaving gunship. The enemy placed a couple of shots on Jia's shield, flaking off a layer of armor. He finally offered up a rocket that Jia avoided with a quick jump. The explosion shoved her forward, but she recovered and bounced to the side to dodge the next missile.

Quick rocket launches followed. The gunship was determined to take Jia down, but her practiced agility made it look like the exo was dancing with each spin, jump, and step. He left her scorched but not disabled or slowed.

Erik's and Jia's borrowed drone feeds suddenly died, and the sensor readouts relying on them grew less detailed. Erik didn't waste time checking anything or doing test transmissions. He flicked on his microphone while continuing to fire and dodge, including a rocket attack aimed at him. Maybe the gunship had grown frustrated with its inability to hit Jia.

That was the advantage of a small group of highly mobile troops. When a force was large, it was inevitable that someone would take a hit, but sometimes a small group could do a lot to wear down a single, more powerful enemy. Erik wanted to do a lot more than tire it out.

"I can force it low," Erik shouted. "Get ready."

"Do it," Jia replied. "That ship is starting to annoy me."

Not only that, they didn't have much time. If the ship made it past them, it might not circle back around, more interested in wreaking havoc closer to the Army bases than worrying about two stray exos that were making it waste rockets and cannon rounds. This same gunship could easily kill half a platoon with a single decent pass if they didn't stop it.

Erik switched to full auto and swept the air. Best-case scenario, he got in some lucky hits and brought down the gunship. Worst case, he'd wasted some rounds he could replace in the hangar.

The enemy took the bait and dove lower, now so close to the ground that one unfortunate raised chunk of the broken road might damage the ship. There was no way a normal pilot could have done that, not that Erik hadn't already assumed he was dealing with an Elite. He dropped his aim, pinning the gunship, and Jia let her machine gun roar, sending a stream of bullets into the enemy.

Her AP rounds ripped into the ship, the resulting damage evident from the smoke and fiery bursts. The gunship tilted on its side and tried to pull up, which left it open for Erik. Their streams converged, riddling the aircraft with dozens of direct hits from their high-velocity, high-caliber machine guns, which were loaded with armor-piercing rounds. The damaged vehicle spiraled out of control as it headed toward them, leaving twisting columns of smoke behind it.

They continued to fire into it and managed to rip off a wing and destroy a cannon. The gunship tried to fire a rocket, but the projectile spun out of control and exploded against a building. Its cannon fire went wide. The twin streams from the exos continued blasting the crashing aircraft. There wasn't much left by the time it finally slammed into the ground and exploded in front of them.

Their jammed drone feeds returned with the explosion, including new sensor information marking six exos advancing behind a nearby building.

"Can you hear me?" Malcolm shouted. "I repeat, can you hear me? You might have trouble coming."

"We see them," Erik replied.

"Good." Malcolm let out a sigh of relief. "You were moving too much for laser comms when the jamming kicked in. All that dancing around is annoying."

"It was for the Elite, too."

Erik stepped toward the smoking wreckage that used to be the Elite gunship, keeping his eye on the position of the six exos. They'd stopped moving. Their markings and IFF suggested Army, but he wouldn't put it past the Core to come up with a clever trap and nail friendly garrison troops who thought reinforcements had arrived.

"We know you're there," Erik broadcasted unencrypted over a wide frequency range just to be sure. "If you're not with the rebels, we don't have a problem. Hell, even if you are, we don't need to have a problem if you just turn around and stop attacking the garrison. If you're Elite, then come on. Bring it, assholes. Each and every single one of you metal bitches is going down."

An exo cleared the corner, shield up and weapon pointed. The other five joined it, ready to unleash on Erik and Jia, but no one fired. No one even made an aggressive jump or step.

A woman's voice came from one of the exos. "You're Major Blackwell, aren't you? It's been years since I heard it, but there's no way I could forget that voice."

He might be unforgettable, but while her voice sounded vaguely familiar, Erik couldn't place it. That was rare for him, but he didn't want to give her an advantage in the conversation, so he didn't admit it. He wasn't wearing his disguise since he had not thought he would need it in the middle of a battle. Unless he dropped his shield and pulled up his faceplate, she wouldn't be able to get a good look at him.

"Yeah, that's me," he replied, deciding it didn't matter,

and transmitting his codes from Sergeant Vines. He doubted there was a Core spy implanted in an assault infantry squad. This might have been an odd coincidence, but if she were an assassin, she would have fired the second she recognized his voice. It wasn't like the Core would care about collateral damage in the middle of a brutal colony-destroying rebellion.

The woman snorted. "Ah, that explains a lot about what happened at the checkpoint and the mysterious ID help. That means you're what, a ghost now? Really? You didn't seem like the type."

"It's complicated," Erik replied. "But I'm here to help end the rebellion in my own way."

The woman advanced in her exo, retracting her shield. She stopped a couple of meters away from Erik and pulled up her faceplate, revealing a dusky-skinned young woman with a fierce look. She looked like she was in her mid-twenties, with no hint of a de-aging treatment.

Erik's eyes widened in recognition. It'd been a while, yes, but he could extrapolate a few years of aging.

"Cabrina Pena. What the hell are you doing here? Why are you piloting an exo rather than a fighter?"

Cabrina sighed. "Someone needed to continue the Pena family assault infantry tradition. I transferred from the Fleet into the Army. It slowed the career path a little, probably cost me an early promotion, but it was worth it."

Jia sidled her exo up beside Erik but kept quiet. He appreciated her restraint.

"I want to talk to you," Cabrina continued, "but we've got an offensive to help push back, and saving the colony comes before personal business." She lowered her faceplate. "But I've still got some questions for you, Major. Don't get me wrong; I appreciate you and your friend taking down that Elite. If I was being responsible, I'd tell you to leave it to the Army and the militia, but we can use any help we can get."

Erik transmitted the hangar address. "We're mostly guarding our ship while we wait for some information, but we'll take out any hostiles who come near us. Might save you some trouble later."

"You do that. I'll try and swing by when I have some time." Cabrina backed up and expanded her shield. "It's been a long time, Major."

"Erik now. Just Erik."

Erik was happy that Jia didn't say anything until they were back in front of the hangar. It gave him time to organize his thoughts about running into a direct manifestation of his past. Living every moment for revenge had not prepared him for this sort of thing, and his few encounters and messages with relatives had been strained and awkward.

Jia seemed to sense that. Other than a couple of brief comments about positioning, she left him alone as they stood guard.

"My drones are managing to sweep out farther," Malcolm explained about an hour later. "I'm using those codes from

Sergeant Vines. I don't know how long they'll last, but I can tell you, the garrison forces are pushing back the rebel forces in a big way. I feel kind of bad about worrying so much."

"Short offensive," Jia commented. "Last gasp of desperation after all. Idiots."

"Maybe," Erik muttered. "Or a distraction from something else. Anybody else coming our way? It's not a good direction, given the current distribution of the garrison forces, but if they *are* desperate, who knows?"

"Not that I can see," Malcolm reported. "And I've gotten pretty good coverage by keeping the drones near roofs."

"Good. Always nice when something goes our way."

Erik fell back into silence, remaining alert while skimming the drone feeds. It was vicarious warfare, not that he hadn't just done his part.

"Are we going to talk about it?" Jia asked with a sigh.

"You mean, Cabrina?" Erik asked

"Yes. You seemed a little off." Jia's tone was quiet and worried.

"I don't know her that well," Erik explained. "I've only met her a few times, and she was a lot younger. She's the younger sister of Tavio Pena, one of my men on Molino. He was enlisted Army, and she became a Fleet officer, academy and everything, so there a lot of good-natured sibling rivalry."

Jia sighed deeper. "Are you okay?"

"I'm fine." Erik took a deep breath and slowly let it out. "I'm honoring the memory of her brother. It was strange to run into someone like her out here, but it was also inevitable, given the way we zip around the galaxy."

"You're worried she might not see you as honoring her brother?"

Erik checked his feeds and sensors before responding. "Frankly, it doesn't matter if she does. All I need her to do is not get in our way."

CHAPTER FORTY-THREE

By the next morning, though it continued, the rebel offensive had been blunted, and garrison casualties were surprisingly low, given the ferocity of the assault. The Army was now trying to capitalize on their momentum and push into rebel-controlled territory. Jia and Erik were content to let them handle that.

Their part of the battle started and ended with the gunship encounter. No other enemies had moved close to the hangar, leaving Erik and Jia with a mostly boring day until they'd stopped worrying about breakthroughs and headed back inside. Jia found herself steering the conversation away from Cabrina Pena most of the day when she threatened to come up, unsure of how Erik was handling it.

Some might argue his whole obsession with vengeance was unhealthy and not a way to deal with loss, but Jia didn't see it that way. His unit hadn't died in the normal course of duty. They'd been slaughtered as collateral damage at the hands of a dangerous conspiracy that threatened the entire UTC. His monomaniacal focus on their destruction was, if anything, the sane response. If Cabrina felt otherwise or blamed Erik, it might make for a painful encounter, and Jia didn't know if it was her place to intervene.

Emma's decryption continued, surprising everyone and annoying the AI. Whatever was in those files was unusually secure, but she was confident she would have them decoded within the next forty-eight hours. That wasn't within Erik or Jia's preferred timeline, but it was better than nothing. After the furious rebel assault, blindly charging into rebel territory looking for trouble made even less sense. One defeated attack didn't mean the end of the rebellion.

Currently, Jia and Erik stood waiting outside the open hangar. Lanara had brought the MX 60 down and had been working on it inside the hangar, but she'd retreated back into the ship, citing the need to gather supplies and "figure out the least stupid way" to go about finishing her repairs. Given the engineer's tendencies, there was probably some under-the-hood optimization going on.

They weren't waiting for Lanara, though. They were waiting because they'd received a message from Cabrina saying she was going to stop by the hangar that afternoon.

Despite Jia's worries, Erik doubted Cabrina would give him notice before coming to assassinate him and was proven right when she showed up at the appointed time in a hovertruck and not her exoskeleton. She stepped out of the truck and headed toward the door. A standard officer's pistol rested snugly in a holster. Maybe she wanted her revenge to be a little more personal. Erik stood rigid as she moved toward him, then slowed, her gaze lovingly scanning the *Argo*.

"Wow, Majo...Erik," she commented. "Nice ship. Ghosts get all the best toys. When I asked around, I was told to keep my mouth shut because you were here on some big fancy Intelligence Directorate business, all hush-hush and classified."

Erik shrugged. "There are perks to working with the ID. Not going to deny that."

"You're here, which means the ID knew something was coming." Cabrina frowned. "It's a long flight from Earth."

"Who says we weren't in the neighborhood?" Jia offered with a smile. There was no reason for Cabrina to know about the jump drive, even though their fig-leaf identity of working as private security contractors was useless on the planet due to ID's codes being required.

"Whatever," Cabrina replied. "Last I heard, you were retiring from the cops." She looked Jia up and down. "Both of you were, according to the news, but it's not like I have a lot of time to keep up with Earth news this tour, especially concerning random cops. It's still strange, going from famous cops to ghost helpers, and now you're on a planet in full rebellion, taking down Elites. You might as well have stayed in the Army if that was how you were going to play it, Erik."

"Being a cop was...too constricting," Erik answered.

"Being in the Army was also too constricting for what I needed to do."

Cabrina's mouth tightened, and she licked her lips. "What, didn't like being blamed for losing your unit?"

"Most people didn't blame me." Erik kept his voice calm, to Jia's surprise.

She didn't want to intervene unless he gave her a sign to do so, but it was hard to keep the scowl off her face. Cabrina might have her reasons for her feelings, but there was no one in the UTC who had put as much effort into avenging her brother as Erik.

Erik stepped over to Cabrina. "If you've got something to say, say it. I'm not going anywhere for a while. Might as well get it out, because I need to know there isn't some officer gunning for me when I'm out there doing what I need to do to help end this rebellion."

"Why are you here, Erik?" Cabrina asked. "Really, why are you here right now? Level with me, and don't you dare feed me that 'it's classified' bullshit." She snorted. "That's what they told me about my brother, too. We're sorry. He's dead. Terrorists killed him, but we can't tell you more because it's all classified."

"You want the truth?" Erik asked. "I'm not beholden to the Intelligence Directorate. They just happen to agree with some of the things I'm doing and find me a useful tool. If I tell you the truth, you'll need to keep your mouth shut if you don't want to end up with a bullet in the back of your brain when you're sleeping."

Cabrina squared her shoulders. "You threatening me, Erik? If you're going to kill me, do it now."

"No, I'm telling the truth." Erik looked at Jia, who

nodded. "Terrorists didn't kill your brother. Mercs did. Mercs who were hired by some dangerous people, the same dangerous people who are probably behind the mercs on this planet. I know they're behind those Elites."

Cabrina's faced twisted in confusion and she backed up. "Huh? What?"

"You heard me. I've spent the years since Molino doing everything I can to track down the people responsible for killing the Knights Errant, so I can get revenge for what they did to every man and woman in that unit on Molino." Erik's voice was low and full of deadly implications. "I started as a cop in Neo SoCal because that was where my clues initially led me, and it spread from there. But I couldn't stay a cop and chase these people. That was when I hooked up with the ID. They might screw me over in the future, but for now, they're helping me chase them."

"I got swept along as Erik's partner in the NSCPD," Jia added with a smile. "I saw a way to go after someone far more dangerous than the petty thugs and gangsters in Neo SoCal."

Cabrina pinched the bridge of her nose. "Let me get this straight. You...fly around the galaxy hunting the conspiracy that killed my brother and everybody else? You expect me to believe that crazy story?"

Erik shrugged. "Believe what you want. It's the truth."

"Then tell me why he had to die. Why they all had to die."

Erik averted his gaze. They might not be beholden to the ID, but certain truths by their very nature were dangerous. A low-ranking officer like Cabrina might not be able to protect herself from the government if she pushed too far and asked the wrong questions. Jia held her breath, waiting for Erik's response.

"It was a coverup by rich assholes who want more power," Erik answered. "Simple as that. They were worried we'd find something we weren't supposed to on Molino."

"And they're here, now, or at least their people are, killing more good soldiers? Killing more innocent people?" Cabrina's hand curled into a fist. "You're kidding me."

"That's the basic version of it," Erik confirmed. "I wish I was kidding, but even we don't know their reason for being here. We have a lead on some information related to them, but we're still working on analyzing it and trying to get actionable intelligence from it."

"These bastards have outflanked us from the beginning," Cabrina muttered. "Between all their jamming and hacking, it's hard to pinpoint their main bases. Drones don't last seconds in rebel territories. Cameras, all gone. They even kamikazed most of the satellites with stolen ships when the shooting began down here. No wonder we've had such a hard time. I always thought everything was too tough." She shook her head. "But it's all a stalemate. We're waiting for more reinforcements, but they keep doing shit like yesterday. We have more people, but we have to spread them over a wider area. We can win, but it's costing us. It's costing this whole colony."

"I'm sure there's something useful in the info we have," Erik commented. "We just need time."

Jia frowned. If they were going to tell her part of the truth, they shouldn't mislead her otherwise. "But we don't know what's in it."

"This isn't false hope. Someone killed a lot of people to

protect that info." Erik gestured at the main garage doors. "And we know the files relate to the Elites somehow. There has to be something we can use in there. If not us, then the Army."

Cabrina slashed the air with her hand. "Then the military should have those files. Why are you two dicking around with them?"

"They're encrypted, and we're using special resources to unencrypt them," Erik replied evenly. "Resources the Army and Fleet don't have here. If there's something the military can use, then we'll pass it along, simple as that. We're on the same side here, Cabrina, but that doesn't mean we take orders from you."

She gritted her teeth and sucked air through them. "I'm not questioning that, Erik, but you can't lay all this on me about the people responsible for my brother being killed being on this planet and expect me to sit around doing nothing when you're dangling that kind of lead over me."

Erik shook his head. "I don't expect you to, but I also don't have what you need yet."

"Damn it." Cabrina scuffed the heel of her boot on the floor. "I get that the big bosses probably aren't on the planet, but I also know if I can personally help wipe out an Elite base or something like that, knowing what I know now... I don't know. Call it what you want. Revenge. Closure. Naïve. It doesn't matter. I want that."

"I'll do what I can, but I'm not going to make any promises."

"Pull your weapons," Malcolm shouted into their ears.

Erik and Jia both yanked out their pistols and pointed

them at Cabrina. Her eyes widened, and she lifted her arms.

"What the hell are you doing?" she asked. "You going to kill me after telling me you're trying to help him?"

"Not on her!" Malcolm continued. "I've got a rebel on the drones. I don't know how he got so close, but he popped out of a pile of junk, big gray cloak over a carryaid, huge-ass rifle on his back. He's walking toward you from the west now. No obvious weapons ready to shoot, but I can't see under his cloak."

"Go ahead and transmit to Cabrina," Erik ordered, swinging his gun to the west. "He might not be the only one out there."

Cabrina blinked and turned her head to follow his movement. Jia matched him. Malcolm was right; a figure approached, jogging at a decent pace, not sprinting. If he had not been a mysterious cloaked figure with a large rifle on his carryaid, he might not seem threatening.

Cabrina yanked out her pistol. "Should I call for reinforcements?"

"One guy," Erik explained. "We've got our eyes in the sky and cameras watching around here. If there's trouble, he'll let us know."

"No weird thermals or other readouts," Malcolm reported. "He's the only rebel I see around here. I've got some civilians about a kilometer out in the opposite direction."

The rebel continued to advance. He lifted his arms above his head. There was nothing in them.

"Suicide bomber," Cabrina suggested, her eyes narrowed.

"Have you had a lot of those here?" Erik asked.

Cabrina shook her head. "No, but it's not like rebels never change tactics when the old ones aren't working."

"I think he'd be charging if he was a suicide bomber," Jia suggested, her tone curious. She couldn't make out the man's features, but he didn't look scared or angry.

The rebel continued his advance, slowing as he closed to twenty meters. It was now more a brisk walk than a jog. He rattled with each movement, the magazines in his pouches and the grenades on his vest jostling. If he did intend to blow himself up, it'd be a spectacular explosion.

"Don't get too close," Erik shouted. "Or we'll give you some new holes."

The rebel stopped and kept his arms up. "It's fair not to trust me. I don't take offense."

"On your knees, rebel," Cabrina ordered.

He dropped to his knees and put his hands on his head. "It's fair for you to execute me if you want. I've helped monsters. I deserve it."

"That might be how you insurrectionists and your merc buddies do things," Cabrina spat, "but that's not how the UTC does things. We have rules we follow."

The rebel chuckled with a pained look. "I'm beginning to appreciate that, but no one can change the past."

"Why are you here?" Jia asked softly. "If this was a trap, it's taking too long. If this is about surrendering, this is an odd place to do it."

The rebel inclined his head toward Cabrina. "I'm no longer an acting member of the FSA. Our leadership has become corrupt, trusting those mercenaries and those metal monsters. I've been hunting mercs and monsters on my own. I've even taken down a couple of the Elites."

Cabrina gave a slight nod, not looking that surprised. "We had some intel about a potential factional dispute. I suppose that answers what the hell is going on."

"Factional dispute?" The rebel laughed. "I'm not a member of any faction..." he looked at her uniform, "... Lieutenant. I'm one man who has turned against his cause to save its soul. My name is Damir Sokov."

Erik holstered his gun and gestured to the man. "If he wanted to kill us, he would have used that sniper rifle and taken us out at long range. Whatever this is, I don't think it's an ambush."

Jia nodded her agreement before putting her gun away. Cabrina hesitated for a moment before stowing her pistol.

Damir lowered his arms but stayed on his knees. "I saw your squad in action, Lieutenant Pena. I saw them defend civilian transports when mercenaries were attempting to shoot them down. I didn't want to believe what I was seeing, but that led to..." He averted his eyes. "It led me to trouble with one of the mercenaries, which made me understand the corruption they represented. That led me to hunt them. They're butchers, and we should have never hired them."

Cabrina nodded slowly. "Okay, so you're what... stalking me because I did my job and didn't let you and your friends murder a bunch of innocent civilians?"

"It was strange luck because I saw your squad in action again the other day. I recognized the markings and numbers, and that gave me an idea." Damir's gaze slid to Erik, then Jia. "I haven't seen you two before, but you match the rough descriptions of the ghosts who took out some Elites at a checkpoint. I also saw you take down that Elite during the battle. The ones I've killed were far away, but you took that gunship down like it was nothing."

"We're not exactly ghosts, but sure, whatever." Erik shrugged. "Get to the damned point before the rebellion ends, or we die of old age."

"My father believed in a free New Samarkand." Damir stood slowly. "I do too, but if we attain our freedom by selling our souls, what's the point? Freedom without conscience is pointless. It leads to nothing but cruelty and corruption. I'm not ready to betray my FSA brothers and sisters directly, but I want to make the mercenaries and those cybernetic monstrosities suffer for what they've done and the harm they've caused the rebellion and the colony."

A grin ate away Erik's frown. "You want to sell out the Elites, not just hunt them by yourself? Good. Now we're getting somewhere, but what specifically have you got for us?"

"There's a merc camp. There are a lot of Elites there, and they also received some sort of delivery the other day. I don't know what it is, but it was important enough that they were willing to kill an entire rebel squad to cover it up." Damir glowered. "I can lead you to the camp. It needs to be destroyed, but I can't do it by myself. I need the help of assault infantry."

Cabrina looked incredulous. "What if this is a big command post? If we take out the mercs and the Elites, the rebellion falls apart. You don't have the strength to win by yourselves. You're not really winning now. You're just stalling and inflicting pointless damage on the colony."

"I know." Damir stared down at his hands. "The rebellion wasn't supposed to destroy the colony. Freedom doesn't mean making the innocent suffer. My father would be ashamed of us." He slapped a hand on his chest. "I'm ashamed of us."

"Okay. We get it." Jia nodded. "Where is this camp?"

Damir shook his head. "The only way I can justify this in my mind is if I lead you there and participate. Then I'm not betraying the rebellion by giving information to the Army and you ghosts, I'm recruiting you to help me. I know you might not care about how I think, but if you want that camp, you'll do it my way."

Cabrina scoffed. "Or we could drag your ass in to be interrogated and make you tell us."

"You could, but why not just take what's offered?" Damir sounded weary.

Erik shrugged at Cabrina. "He's got a point. If we treat him like the enemy, he might clam up."

Cabrina scrubbed a hand over her face. "This is insane." She nodded at the hangar. "Fine, if that's the way we're going to play this, at least lock him up on your ship until I can run this up the chain. They might order him turned over anyway. This whole thing could be a trap. And I'm calling my squad here and having them bring my exo. We need to be ready if more rebels show up."

Damir turned around and offered his wrists. "Go ahead and bind me. I'm willing to wait. I know you have no reason to believe anything I say, but I guarantee it's all true."

"It's fine," Erik replied. "We'll even be nice and give you a cabin with VR. You can relax while we figure out what to do with you."

"My thirty pieces of silver?" Damir replied with a sneer.

"Maybe, but this time, you're getting paid to betray the guys who are telling the lies."

CHAPTER FORTY-FOUR

Watching full three-dimensional holographic scenes of Elites wreaking havoc might have been immature or potentially even dangerous, given that Julia was still confirming the security of her new home, but she couldn't help it. She soaked in the glorious vision of the Core's cybernetic warriors laying waste to the pitiful colony of New Samarkand. A delicious scene of a Torch Dragon Elite killing an entire squad of Army soldiers made her smile. Perfect, far too perfect, even if she was disappointed by reversals in other battles.

She tried to not let it bother her. Ultimately, the Elite project wasn't intended to create a devastating army as much as perfect terror tools. Undermining the UTC was the first step in destabilizing the entire government and replacing it. There was no better tool for that than something unpredictable.

And what a tool the Elites were. They were the perfect

distillation of the closest thing to demons in the minds of modern people, humans who'd left even the pretense of a humanoid body behind. Humans who had sold their souls to the cybernetic Devil for power.

Julia licked her lips. She'd worried it might have been too early to use them in such a bold manner, but she was willing to admit to herself she'd been wrong. The footage and the reports from New Samarkand proved it.

The bounty of early reports had proven the huge advantage of moving to New Pacifica. She was ten light-years closer to New Samarkand and able to receive reports and issue orders two weeks faster than she would have been on Earth. Additional missions beyond the inner core and in the mid-frontier would benefit from her nearby presence. The others should have heeded her suggestions, not out of self-preservation, but for the good of their plans.

Their failures would only benefit her. The Core had grown stagnant with age, foolish and hidebound. If they wanted to disrupt the UTC, they would need to discomfort themselves with aggressive dynamism. With each passing month and individual success, she continued to wonder why so many of them were still alive.

Sophia had been the heart of the Core, the founder and the closest thing they had to a leader, but she'd led them down the wrong path. Julia had done them all a favor by setting up the situation that had led to Sophia's death. She would never admit it, of course, but she found herself disappointed by the suspicion of the surviving Core members and their inability to take advantage of the change in the situation.

Julia snickered quietly. "Then again, I've killed Sophia

and Shoji now. If they truly suspect me, they should move against me, but until then, I have a rebellion to manage."

Yes, there could have been a blatant reversal of the situation in the last two weeks. Her distance meant her latest information was dated October 4, but she wasn't concerned. The mission of the Core assets on New Samarkand wasn't to win the colony's independence, after all. They were there to gain combat experience and waste military assets, along with inflicting simple terror.

She'd admittedly not been convinced the plan would work at the beginning, but everything had gone surprisingly well. The ID had been blindsided by the Core's assassins, and the military garrison had given up half the capital city in the first week. It'd been a spectacular success by most measures. Arguably, it wasn't as cost-effective as some of their other plans, but the eventual propaganda value of the use of Elites would make their losses in battle worth it.

Julia stopped and admired the sleek curves of one of the gunship Elites. She appreciated that they represented pure dedication to the cause. That was what the fools in the Intelligence Directorate hunting the Core didn't understand. Although the brains of the Elites required mild drug-based manipulation to maintain their temporary stability, no one was processed into their new bodies who wasn't deeply loyal to the Core's cause. They understood that sometimes people needed to be sacrificed for the greater good, even if they themselves were to be sacrifices.

She clucked her tongue. Alas, the stability of Elites was limited since Cybernetic Psychosis Syndrome would always eventually set in, but they'd proven startlingly effective on New Samarkand. There was no reason to believe that success couldn't be replicated on other colonies, especially if they invested more resources into fielding more powerful armies. The high level of redeployed Army and Fleet resources after a single month of fighting was staggering.

The Core had been right to target the mid-frontier rather than the far frontier. She had been right to argue it, even though Sophia had questioned the fundamental basis of that idea, preferring to focus on taking control of Earth.

With so much of the military stationed on the far frontier to guard against aliens and the rest dedicated to protecting the larger populations of the core worlds and Earth, it was inevitable that if the mid-frontier colonies rose up in revolt en masse, the military would be overwhelmed. If they set it up correctly, the Core could slice the UTC in half while they proceeded with their manipulations.

Julia dismissed the holograms with a wave and took a long, shuddering breath, almost overwhelmed by the enormity of the potential success on New Samarkand. The seeds of a greater victory lay in front of her. The advances in research from her collected Hunter artifacts put her in a position to claim victory over the rest of the Core without more vulgar assassinations like with Sophia and Shoji.

Immortality would be hers, and they'd die mere aspirants and pretenders. Nature would be Julia's greatest assassin. Some would perhaps require expedited ends, but it was obvious what she needed to do.

On Earth, she'd let herself be swept into their way of thinking, their timetable. Turgid. Static. Foolish. The timing of her plan would be difficult, but if she could use their plans and resources to light the conflagration, her capstone plan could proceed. That would be the point at which she might need to kill other members of the Core. They would never agree with her plan for the simple reason it was about increasing her power, not theirs, but they might be cowed into supporting it.

In either event, she didn't care. She would assure the continuity of the human species under the wise rule of an immortal, a society led by a goddess of vast reach, influence, and power.

Julia understood something all the members of Core should have understood if they truly had a long-term vision of the future. The Hunters and Navigators had provided the tools. Humanity simply needed to apply them in the most efficient way. It'd taken over a century, but they were almost ready.

Adaptability was the key to survival. An organism that learned to adapt would learn to conquer not only its niche but the environment around it. She'd let Sophia's painfully narrow view of the future blind her for too long, but now the awesome destruction the Last Soldier had wrought against the Hunter ship had kindled an idea.

The sacrifices of the Ascended Brotherhood and others had been necessary, more than she'd realized. She saw that now. If their attack hadn't failed, the government wouldn't have decided to help the Last Soldier and the Warrior Princess, and that wouldn't have led to the destruction of the Hunter ship and her special inspiration.

Julia's talents might not lie in the area of hyperspace physics, but she employed many people who were masters of that discipline. Sometimes science wasn't about discovering what was not already known. It could be about figuring out the mechanics of something observed. Reverse-engineering it. They were close now. So close.

She stood and headed toward her door. A few billion sacrifices to guarantee the safety of humanity was a bargain, all things considered.

A wicked smile crossed her face. She'd outmaneuvered the Core, the government, and the Last Soldier. It was time to give a different order, just as she had for New Samarkand. If her calculations were right, her loyal agents on the colony should have already received it, but she wouldn't hear of the results for another couple of weeks—a long wait for something so entertaining, a glorious celebration of the dawning of a new order.

The rest of the Core might have wanted more time and resources drawn to New Samarkand, but there was no point in further delay. It was time to invoke true fear and initiate her plan. It would take months to come into fruition, but what were months when she'd already waited decades?

"You will all die for the good of humanity," she intoned. "Die for your future goddess."

CHAPTER FORTY-FIVE

An hour later, six Army exos stood in the hangar, a maintenance truck with parts and ammo beside them. The rest of Cabrina's squad lounged on crates, chatting quietly. They'd shared brief conversations with Erik and Jia but seemed content to keep their distance. Lanara kept glancing from the MX 60 to the soldiers and frowning as she filled the holes in the MX 60 with a long composite injector tube connected to a nearby cylindrical tank.

Jia was watching all this unfold from the bottom loading ramp of the *Argo.* She didn't worry about working with Army assault infantry. She'd done it enough times before to know they were disciplined, hard-working men and women who could adapt to the most dangerous situations. The Hunter incident had proven that beyond any reasonable doubt.

Cabrina finished a joke. Her soldiers laughed, and she murmured something to them before making her way across the hangar to Jia with a slight frown.

"Everything okay?" Jia asked, hoping the lieutenant hadn't changed her mind about Erik or the plan.

"Sure." Cabrina looked around. "Where did Ma...Erik go?"

"He's going over some things concerning the ship with our data guy," Jia explained. "We want to make sure we have all the available options before we commit to anything."

Cabrina smiled at the *Argo*. "It's a nice ship. The data guy's also working on decrypting the intel you mentioned?"

Jia shook her head. "That's our...data girl. She's working on the problem at a remote site."

"Good." Cabrina nodded. "With all this rebel bullshit, it's best to keep the noncombatants as far from the front lines as possible."

"I'm sure our data guy would agree with you." Jia smiled.

Trusting Cabrina in battle and trusting her with information about Emma were two separate things. Among other issues, Emma's secret wasn't Jia's to freely share, and now that she and Erik were looking the other way while the AI conducted her progeny experiment, it was more important than ever to be cautious about mentioning her to others. That'd probably bite them in the ass eventually, but they had a long list of other problems to worry about first.

Cabrina nodded and stared at the *Argo*, her frown deepening. "We might not need your data girl if this rebel's not full of shit. He still secured? I know he sounds like he wants to help, but he might change his mind if he thinks he can steal something nice from your ship."

"Malcolm—that is our data guy—has him locked down tightly in a room. No PNIU, alarms if he tries anything." Jia gave the ship a long, thoughtful look. "I've never considered imprisoning anyone on our ship before. It's surprisingly easy."

"Every Fleet ship has a brig, every Army base a jail. I'm used to it, but you were a cop. Cells are new to you?"

"No. I think it's more about mindset." Jia let the thought linger for a moment. "I don't think like a cop anymore. I don't know if that's a bad thing, but I can't deny it."

"Who knows?" Cabrina sat on a nearby crate. "And now you follow Erik around, taking down these mysterious conspiracies?"

"Did you mention that part to your commander?" Jia asked.

Cabrina shook her head. "It's not relevant to what's going on here. Our mission is to take out the rebels and whoever is supporting them. If I complicate things by trying to shove ghost work through military channels, it's not going to help your mission or ours. Besides…" she looked down, her expression grim, "for all I know, there are people like that in garrison. It would explain a few things about how things happened here and how the rebellion managed to do so well early on."

Jia sat beside her. "You think the conspiracy has infiltrated the Army?"

"Obviously." Cabrina shrugged. "At least partially. I'm not saying I don't trust my chain of command, just saying that mentioning what you two told me doesn't add much.

Whoever's above me who needs to know that kind of thing probably already knows it, one way or another. Besides, I've got my own selfish reasons."

Cabrina reached into a pocket and pulled out a tiny holographic projection. She tapped it, and an image of a man in an Army uniform appeared. The family resemblance was unmistakable.

"I switched from the Fleet to the Army to honor my brother," she explained. "But now I have a chance to nail some of the bastards who worked for the people who killed him. It's the closest I'll ever get to taking revenge with my own hands. I just hope that rebel's not messing with us."

"I don't think he is." Jia surveyed the hangar slowly, taking in the laughing soldiers and the scowling but busy Lanara. "Call it a hunch from my time as a detective."

"I thought you didn't think like a cop anymore?"

"I don't, but that doesn't mean I've lost my ability to read people. He feels like a broken man trying to do the right thing in the end, and besides, his motivation is the same as yours."

Cabrina let out a weak scoff. "Revenge is easy to get behind."

"Yes, sir." Cabrina tilted her head as she listened in private to her commander.

Jia crossed her arms, her heart pounding harder than she would have expected over a simple conversation. It might have helped if she could hear both sides.

After two hours of waiting around, Cabrina's commander had contacted her. She'd been talking to him for several minutes while Jia and Erik waited patiently. Based on the one-way snippets and Cabrina's body language, Jia was hopeful the mission had been approved, but she couldn't be sure.

"I understand, sir," Cabrina continued. "We'll do our best. Thank you, sir." She took a deep breath before speaking to Jia and Erik. "They've approved the mission, with the understanding we'll have your active support. But it's limited in scope."

Erik furrowed his brow. "How limited?"

"They want one squad performing a recon push to verify the rebel's intel before they commit more forces to destroying the site," Cabrina explained. "The rebels are still pushing. Not as strongly as before, but a lot of forces remain tied up. So, that makes eight of us, counting you two. Unless your data guy can suit up." She nodded at the *Argo*'s cargo bay. "I see you've got two other exos in there."

"Those aren't for Malcolm." Erik chuckled. "He can't pilot an exo. We normally would have a couple more people with us, but shit happened before we set out."

Cabrina snickered. "'Shit happens' defines the military."

"Malcolm can and will provide active drone support," Jia noted.

Cabrina shook her head. "Given the way they take down drones in rebel territory, along with the jamming, I don't know if that'll help, but I'm not going to complain. Garrison resources are stretched thin, so they expect us to lean on you two and your fancy ghost tech. My commander said, and I quote, 'Let those ghost fuckers do something useful for a change.'"

Jia wondered if it would have been possible for them to try to convince everyone they were contractors. Their last few missions stretched that so much that their cover identity was close to becoming nonviable, but if they were going to keep ending up in situations like the rebellion, it might not matter.

Erik gave a light shake of his head. "Contractor, not a ghost. But let's go talk to the rebel."

Jia, Erik, and Cabrina headed for the *Argo*. They'd made it to the cargo bay when Malcom pinged Jia's and Erik's PNIUs with a private message.

Not sure if you want her to hear, but I just received a file from Emma. It's not location data according to her, mostly override codes, but play the message I just sent. It's best if I don't interpret the rest.

Jia held up a hand to stop Cabrina. "One sec. Something just came through. Our data girl."

Cabrina nodded eagerly. "Sure."

Emma's voice was tense. "Mr. Constantine has hopefully summarized my initial information in an efficient way before you hear this and has sent along the necessary codes. I will be direct and brief. These files also indicate that three high-yield fusion bombs were delivered to a mercenary encampment, along with primary orders to prepare for detonation. They are awaiting their secondary confirmation order from an unknown superior who appears to be off-world. There's no specific information indicating when that secondary confirmation might arrive, but the wording strongly suggests they expect it imminently."

"Damn it," Erik growled, kicking the floor. "We've got WMDs, Cabrina."

She swallowed. "You're serious? Even the FSA wouldn't…. But it's not them, is it?"

Erik shook his head. "No, and we don't know when they're going to blow them, but it might be soon."

"If she contacts her commander again, do you think we'll be able to get more support?" Jia asked.

Erik frowned. "They're not going to commit to a major mission deep in rebel territory on that skimpy of evidence, not in the middle of fighting another rebel offensive."

"He's right." Cabrina grimaced. "We took a lot of hits in the first wave. Everything's in rough shape all over the colony. If they send a major force, it will leave gaps in our defensive line that the FSA and mercs have to be watching for. HQ might agree to it, but it's not a decision that'll be made quickly, not with everything else going on."

Jia locked eyes with Cabrina. "Are you willing to commit your squad, then? Not just to recon, but for a full raid? We can't sit around and wait on this."

"I…" Cabrina sighed.

"It's easier to ask forgiveness than permission," Erik offered with a lopsided grin. "That was the first lesson I learned when I became an officer. This fits with what Sokov told us, a mysterious delivery at a merc camp. I don't think a complicated trap where they let us get data that can only be decrypted by a specialist and then send us a merc makes sense. I think the Lady smiled on us to give us a chance to save a lot of people's lives.

"And it's not like you're violating orders. You have been ordered to check out the site. If we decide to go a little above and beyond and don't die in the process, do you really think anyone's going to complain?"

"Fine. I'll go brief my squad." Cabrina spun on her bootheel. "But if that rebel is lying, I'll kill him myself."

Damir sat on the edge of the bed when Jia and Erik entered the cabin. "Is it time?"

"The mercs are going to nuke the colony," Erik explained. "We don't know when, but we know it's going to happen. We need to move and do it *now*. It's just going to be eight exos and you. I'm going to give you all your guns and a scout bike to keep up unless you can pilot an exo. I assume you're not enough of an idiot to want to die in a nuclear explosion."

"I see." Damir swallowed. "I can't pilot an exo, but I can drive a scout bike. I saw one in your cargo bay." He stood. "They sink so far, and I think that's the bottom, but then they dig a hole and sink farther."

Erik extended his hand. "Sokov, you've got your reasons to fight. We've got ours, but right now, we both only care about one thing: saving this colony."

Damir shook it. "Thank you for believing me."

"Thank you for caring more about your colony than your own life," Jia replied.

CHAPTER FORTY-SIX

Eight exos running through a city sounded a lot like a herd of stampeding cattle. In this case, those metal cattle were trailing after Damir on the sleek scout bike. Their resounding footsteps were eclipsed by the thunder of artillery and the boom of explosions in the distance. The gunfire grew more frequent and closer as they moved deeper into the city. Cabrina had been right. The battle was far from over.

The team maintained a tight formation. They'd already passed through one empty checkpoint, deep craters marking the road and the scorched bottom half of an Army exo speaking to its fate. Malcolm's drones followed them, the man doing his best to make them aware of threats and steer them around them. They didn't have time to waste on fighting anyone else. For all they knew, the detonation command was coming any second, and even if it wasn't, they couldn't take the chance the bombs might be moved.

Erik's heart thundered. He tried to convince himself that the mercs would attempt to flee before setting off any nuke, but the Core wasn't above sacrificing useful pawns. They'd proven it again and again. The mercs might believe they'd be safe and an Elite would set off the nukes. He had no problem believing a brain in a can would give his life for the Core. Their minions had proven that, from the Ascended Brotherhood to the scientist in France. He had no idea what the leaders of the Core believed, but their top servants displayed fanatical zealotry that made the average terrorist, rebel, or even Purist look lazy and uncommitted.

Cabrina scoffed, then sent a transmission to just Jia and Erik. "We're heading to what is likely to be a heavily defended location, potentially even an enemy HQ, and we've got eight exos, a guy with a sniper rifle on a scout bike, and some drones that'll probably end up being useless when we get closer. Everyone volunteered for this, but we might be making a mistake."

"We're stopping WMDs," Erik replied without a hint of concern. "Even if these guys have nothing to do with the conspiracy, it doesn't matter. This is easy math. Nine people for hundreds of thousands. We have to get this done."

Cabrina chuckled bitterly. "You make it sound so easy. But then, this is what you do, huh? Travel around the galaxy taking these people on? Doing that kind of calculation again and again?"

"Sure, but I always assume something important when I do this kind of thing."

"What's that?"

"That'll I win." Erik jumped over the burned-out wreck of an armored military transport. "It makes things easier and forces you to try to win."

Acrid smoke choked the area, but the rebel continued moving forward at a modest speed, allowing the exos to keep up with him. He swerved back and forth to avoid holes, collapsed chunks of buildings, and destroyed vehicles or exo remnants. A scout bike was wonderful in certain environments, but a crater-filled colony wasn't one of them. They didn't have time for him to hike to the site, though.

"It wasn't supposed to be like this," Damir muttered. His limited transmission to Erik, Jia, and Cabrina couldn't have been an accident.

"This is what a rebellion is," Jia countered. "When you throw away the existing order, you get chaos. You don't overthrow the people in power without innocent folks getting hurt."

"Outsiders came in," Damir complained. "They corrupted our ideals."

"Outsiders your people brought in," Cabrina muttered. "Don't kid yourself, Sokov. Those mercenaries are here because the FSA brought them in. Because those mercenaries are here, those nukes are here, and now everyone might die."

"Somebody I work for," Erik began with a chuckle, "would say beware Greeks bearing gifts. Guess that applies to mercs, too."

"I know," snapped Sokov. "I didn't trust them from the beginning, but could you easily betray your own people without solid proof of corruption?"

Jia scoffed. "It's rarely that simple. There are a lot of dark forces out there, but it's not as simple to point at a particular company or the government and say they're the evil ones responsible for everything. The truth is, bad people only looking out for their own interests are everywhere, and if you're convinced you're going to shape a perfect world, you'll always be disappointed."

Sokov swerved to avoid a mound of rotting meat. "What about you? Don't you fight for a perfect world?"

"Not anymore." Jia jumped on top of the mound and leaped from there, achieving jump thruster height before landing without losing any speed. "I'm fighting for a good-enough world. I learned the hard way that worrying about perfection blinds you to what you can actually do to make your world a better place."

Erik grunted in frustration. "There are forces out there who use people like you to undermine the UTC, not because they care about freedom, but because they want to increase their own power. I'm not going to blame you for having a cause you believe in, but that doesn't mean you're innocent in all this."

"I know." Damir slowed the bike to let the exos catch up. "Once this is all over, I'm sure I'll end up in prison, but first I have to make sure those mercs and their pet monsters don't kill everyone I care about. I admit my mistake, and I admit the FSA's mistakes. The only thing I can do now is try and make up for them."

A missile screamed through the sky and smacked into the top of the building in the distance, launching smoking debris all over. The massive explosion shook the ground even where they were. Two Army Dragon gunships converged near the burning building, their cannons looking like streams of light.

"How are we doing, Malcolm?" Erik asked. "Go ahead and transmit to everybody."

"No threats within three kilometers," he replied. "Most of what I'm picking up long-range looks like normal rebels taking on the Army. Some exoskeletons, but not a lot of Elites."

"Wonder if they used too many up in the first offensive," Jia mused.

Erik adjusted his comm to transmit only to Jia and Cabrina. "It's good we made our move. If we'd waited much longer, we might have gotten caught up in all this."

They followed the scout bike down a wide road. Skeletons of buildings lined either side, and massive piles of debris blocked much of the road. Damir grunted in irritation and carefully guided the scout bike around the obstructions.

"I hope this doesn't end with me being court-martialed," Cabrina muttered. "That would be a bad end for the Pena family tradition."

Erik laughed. "If you capture enemy nukes, they'll probably promote you. Besides, you have authorization for a recon mission."

"But I didn't pass the intel along because I knew they might tell me to stay put."

Erik climbed a debris pile in three quick jumps. "Learn to bend the rules a little now, and you'll be much happier for the rest of your military career. Trust me."

Damir's bike slowed to a crawl when a veritable mountain range of blackened rubble filled the street. The terrain favored the exos, who jumped or scampered over huge chunks that used to be buildings or parts of the roadbed. From the level of devastation, someone must have pounded the area with artillery, but the piles were too neat for them to have formed from explosions. Erik didn't understand why anyone would clean up the area, only to block most of the roads instead of shoving everything to the sides.

His confusion turned into concern following the abrupt disruption of drone feeds. "Jamming," he shouted.

The drones continued flying ahead. Malcolm had been smart enough to anticipate the situation and had programmed them to follow the scout bike, not that it did a lot of good. Damir was barely moving at this point.

"Tighten up," Cabrina bellowed. "Expand shields. Standard ring on me."

The eight exos expanded their shields with echoing whirs and clicks. By doing that, they temporarily sacrificed full mobility for defensive capability. Cabrina's squad spun with practiced ease until they formed a rough circle that provided no safe angle of attack for enemies. Erik and Jia continued to face forward, along with Cabrina.

Malcolm's drones hovered in place, waiting for their target to continue moving, but the jamming made them nothing more than targets waiting to be shot. The same thing could be said about the squad. Erik couldn't muster much surprise when gun barrels poked out the rubble piles and opened fire.

"Ambush!" Cabrina screamed. "Go double-tri formation!"

CHAPTER FORTY-SEVEN

Controlled pessimism on the battlefield led to superior situational awareness. Jia had been thinking their trip to the mercenary encampment was going too easily and had been expecting something just like this ambush. She'd loaded and aimed her plasma grenade before Cabrina shouted her warning.

Her grenade launcher flung the deadly explosive toward the closest pile of rubble, the explosion blasting away half the rubble and revealing a Torch Dragon Elite. The blast and the resulting spray of rubble obscured the enemy but also temporarily halted their attack.

The moment of reprieve was short, then enemy guns came alive all around, rounds pelting the exos' shields. Damir accelerated and spun the scout bike, leaning so far into the turn, his shoulder almost scraped the ground. His quick movement saved his life, helping him avoid auto-cannon rounds from a squat beetle-like Elite emerging from another pile. Six-legged almost-spiders pushed out of others.

Erik and Jia both jumped to the side, out of the primary firing arc of most of the enemies. They sent another volley of plasma grenades into the Torch Dragon Jia had attacked, the explosion severing the head of the Elite and leaving the body a limp mess.

Another Torch Dragon Elite scampered free of its cover, but when Erik and Jia tried a similar move, their grenades exploded before reaching it, victims of its tiny anti-grenade turret. It wasn't as annoying as a shield, but it was frustrating enough.

Cabrina's squad's machine guns fired together, the rattle shaking pieces off the remaining mounds. The squad had broken into two groups of three, Alpha Four through Six forming a small triangle and confronting two Elites wriggling out of mounds behind the main group. The Army exos opened fire, raking the Elites with machine gun rounds.

"Die, insects," shouted one of the spider Elites in a cold, metallic voice. He leapt from his pile, revealing a rocket launcher.

His bravery and taunts didn't count for much. Cabrina and the two soldiers from their sub-squad nailed it before it hit the ground with a mixed barrage of rockets and grenades, blasting huge chunks off its body. It managed to squeeze out another burst before Jia finished it with a plasma grenade.

Erik raked the surface of a beetle Elite with his machine gun, leaving nasty gouges, but the Elite's thick armor denied him the satisfying and sought-after Swiss cheese pattern. The beetle lumbered forward on stout legs. Its armor came at the cost of speed and agility. Like the earlier

Torch Dragon, a point-defense turret sticking out of its back released its fury at the grenade. The premature explosion forced Erik to step back.

One of the spider Elites jumped backward, angling itself up, along with its rocket launcher. With a hollow thump, it fired a round into the sky. The projectile exploded in a shower of hot fragments at the top of its arc, nowhere near any of the exos but downing two drones. It then hurried behind a mound to avoid the worst of the squad's guns.

Jia again appreciated the well-trained discipline of a true assault infantry squad. Despite the ambush by heavily armed and highly maneuverable cybernetic enemies, the men and women of Cabrina's squad kept their tight formations while constantly moving and returning fire. Even discounting their training, these soldiers had been in the thick of the garrison's response to the rebellion. They might know the enemy better than Erik and Jia after so many battles in recent weeks.

The lieutenant forced three of the Elites back with shallow rocket attacks, doing her best to add more and deeper holes to the destroyed road. Her distraction gave her squadmates, along with Erik and Jia, the time they needed. Converging AP rounds, supplemented by rockets and grenades, consumed two Torch Dragon Elites in clouds of lead and flame, leaving only burnt, perforated metal in the end.

The anti-drone spider from before popped back up and brought down more drones. This time, Erik carved through it with a machine gun blast, staggering it. Jia's follow-up shots took out the enemy's launcher. They continued firing, not giving it a chance to dodge, and ripped more pieces off, dark fluids splattering until finally blood painted the ground and it collapsed.

Alphas Four through Six had surrounded one of the rear enemies and shredded it with combined fire until it collapsed. Their remaining enemy, a spider, jumped on a building and skittered along what was left of it while managing to get off bursts that made it past the shields into the bodies and arms of the exos. Lacking the point-defense of his allies, he didn't last long when the three Army exos pounded him with rockets.

Damir leapt off his bike and rolled behind a mound, yanking two plasma grenades from his belt. He gritted his teeth and stayed low as machine gun and autocannon rounds continued to rip through the air and his loose barrier. Although the surviving Elites seemed more concerned about the armored threats than one rebel in a tactical vest, a lone stray round would be more than enough to blow his head off.

He primed the two grenades and hurled them with sideways throws toward a beetle Elite. "For New Samarkand."

The beetle's anti-grenade system might be a marvel of AI-driven defense, but it'd obviously been designed under the assumption that its main threats would come in from body level or above. Damir's careful throws sent the grenades toward the legs of the Elite. It attempted to scamper away before white-blue explosions blasted a huge chunk out of the side and half-melted the AGS.

Jia launched a plasma grenade and Erik followed her lead, then each took three shots, staggering them. Blast after blast rocked the beetle until it collapsed on its side, half-melted and missing a good portion of its body.

With the rear guard destroyed, Cabrina's squad reformed in a loose wedge, the soldiers' converging streams of bullets ripping a Torch Dragon to pieces and quickly downing a spider bot. Two remaining enemies, both beetle Elites, scampered forward, their armor taking the punishment.

"I'll distract this one. Get ready to finish it," Jia announced, charging toward a beetle with abrupt shifts from side to side. Her shield began to thin under its auto-cannon fire, sparks and pieces flying off. She jerked her launcher erratically, aiming not at the beetle but around it, alternating between plasma and frag grenades.

The enemy took the bait for the initial rounds, firing at her and Erik with its AGS. The other exos took the opportunity to annihilate the last beetle, launching with rockets and grenades until the attacks combined in a blinding explosion that forced the light filters in their helmets' faceplates to kick on. When the light ebbed, not much remained except the blackened legs of the beetle and a sizzling pile.

Jia jumped back, sweeping back and forth, flipping through optical and thermal modes to seek any new enemies, but not finding any. Damir stood and dusted his pants, nodding with a satisfied look.

"Stand down, squad," Cabrina ordered, breathing heavily. She took a couple of deep breaths before she spoke next. "You and Jia are pretty damned impressive, Erik. I'd think she'd been in as long as you, given some of her moves."

"We spend a lot of time training," Jia replied.

"How are we situated going forward?" Erik asked.

"Minor damage to my squad," Cabrina admitted. "Down to about eighty percent ammo in main guns, two-thirds in the explosives. We were lucky those guys didn't have air support."

Jia looked up. "See what I see? Or what I don't see?"

"I got so wrapped up in wasting Elites, I didn't realize they'd finished off the rest of our drones," Erik commented. "Damn."

"We've got microdrones in our exos," Cabrina explained. "But I'm not sure how effective they will be, given the Elites' jamming obsession."

"We need to keep going," called Damir, picking up the scout bike and straddling it with a determined look. "They don't know we're coming for the camp. This is the one time they might be vulnerable, and as long as we're a small group, we can make it there without them pulling the rest of their forces back. But we have to hurry."

"He's right," Jia offered.

"Then let's get going," Cabrina ordered.

CHAPTER FORTY-EIGHT

Damir slowed and stopped at an intersection. "About a kilometer down, there's a huge wall made up of pieces of buildings, destroyed vehicles, and the like. It covers one side of the camp. The whole thing is surrounded by fences. There are natural hills on the other sides, along with anti-aircraft guns. If we took the long way, we could head straight to the gate and get cut down by the defenses there. The garage where they delivered the cargo is in the center, but that's past all the defensive lines."

"Of course it is," Cabrina muttered. "We wouldn't want this to be easy."

Erik glanced at one of his status displays. "Huh, no evidence of jamming, but this far out with no satellite, LOS, or net connections, Malcolm might as well be back on Earth."

"We should use the microdrones," Jia noted. "So we know what we're getting into. If we charge straight toward the wall, they'll probably see us coming, and we'll lose surprise."

"Squad, stand by," Cabrina announced, changing her comm to transmit only to Erik and Jia.

"We need to know what we're getting into," Erik insisted. "We can do well with a trained squad and eight exos, but we're still taking on an entire encampment by ourselves."

Cabrina frowned. "If it's too much, we might have to pull back and request reinforcements after all. We were lucky in that last fight, but that doesn't mean our luck's going to hold."

"First things first," Erik suggested. "Recon. Drone it."

Cabrina offered the barest hint of a grunt in response. A moment later, three tiny drones detached from the back of her exo and zoomed away, so close to the ground and walls that a heavy breath might crash them. She transmitted the feeds directly to Erik and Jia.

The drones continued hovering over the ground. The hastily constructed sloping wall Damir had described lay ahead and there was no sign of enemies, but the tiny drones couldn't see through it, and the thickness of the barrier made thermal imaging useless for detecting what lay on the opposite side.

Cabrina continued maneuvering the drones forward. As they approached the wall, it became obvious it'd been built in the center of what had once been an intersection, suggesting the camp was taking advantage of preexisting structures. That made sense. There wasn't a lot of wasted space beneath domes in mature colonies, and digging an underground base would have taken too long, given the nature of the conflict.

Damir had been right about the offensive. Between the

Fleet and the pirates, there couldn't be many Elites making it onto the planet anymore, and there was no way they were building them on New Samarkand. The garrison had been pounded for over a month, but they'd made the Elites pay. There couldn't be many left defending the encampment, and most of the remaining models seemed less advanced than what they'd fought on Alpha Centauri, suggesting resource limitations. After all, the Core had no reason to suspect Erik and Jia were already on-world and had decrypted their files.

Erik frowned as he realized he had not taken the jump drive into account and had forgotten about normal transit times. Alpha Centauri was a lot closer to Earth and months away from Gliese 581. They weren't fighting resource-limited Elites. They were fighting older models.

Cabrina's drones headed through the intersection and toward the line. The sensors didn't show anything, but it was hard to miss the large Torch Dragon Elite standing at the edge of the intersection. The feeds died, along with their drone sources.

"So much for surprise," Cabrina grumbled.

"Screw it, then," Erik replied. "Launch all your micro-drones and flood the zone. We need to have a clue what we're dealing with before we go charging in there."

"Look at you being careful," joked Jia.

"It happens on occasion."

Cabrina considered it for a moment before nodding and changing back to full squad contact. "Everyone, send all your drones over the wall. Go, go, go."

The angry swarm of microdrones zoomed toward the wall, no one bothering to try to hide them. Erik had expected hidden turrets or more Elites, but instead, enemy drones rose above the edge of the wall. He didn't know their sensor capabilities, but based on what he'd encountered during his time in the city, he doubted they could pick up the squad, given the distance and the number of buildings between them.

It didn't take long for microdrones to start exploding or crashing after being shot. The first drone to clear the wall fell, likely victim to a small mercenary squad right on the other side, ready with their rifles. Elites and fixed machine gun emplacements massacred the charging microdrones. Within ten seconds, there wasn't a single active drone left.

Those ten seconds had been all they needed. It confirmed both the defense forces and the question that had been weighing them down.

Erik stared at a freeze-frame from one of the feeds, jaw tightening. Possibility had become reality. Cargo loaders were transferring unconcealed cargo into three different hovertrucks.

"Looks like Omega-134s," he announced.

Cabrina growled, "Those animals."

"Decent strategic-yield fusion bombs," Erik added for Jia's benefit. "Fleet toys, not that they ever use them. They jokingly started referring to them as space-raptor warmers. If those go off, New Samarkand is done."

"I won't even bother worrying where the mercs got them," Jia muttered.

"I'm sure the DD and ID will soon be knocking on some Fleet quartermaster's door soon, but if they move those bombs, we might not find them again before they blow them."

"A lot of Elites, mercs, and gun emplacements," Cabrina pointed out. "I tagged at least two laser turrets. None of the drones made it to the inside of the garage. They might have gunships or other close air support in there."

"In summary, we're outnumbered and outgunned," Jia replied. "I don't know about you, but that's pretty standard for Erik and me."

"It doesn't matter," Erik noted. "They're about to move the bombs. We can't pull back and wait for reinforcements even if we wanted to."

"Then we need a plan. If we just charge in there from the street, we'll be dead before we make it five meters." Cabrina didn't sound too worried despite what she'd just said.

Damir took a deep breath and slowly let it out. "What you need is a distraction."

"Yeah, that would be handy, but we're out of remote toys."

"Then you need a person to do it." Damir shrugged, his expression serene. "Let me do it. I'll distract them, allowing you to advance."

Cabrina stared at the rebel. She lifted her faceplate, almost as if she wanted him to see the disbelief on her face. "There's no way you'll survive."

"You were right before. The FSA invited these people. I might not be a leader, but I'm part of it, which means it's partially my fault. If I have to die to save New Samarkand, so be it." Damir pulled back his cloak to reveal a plasma grenade. "If you give me more grenades and I prime them all, I'll do my best to take down at least one of the trucks. Even if I don't, it'll draw their attention. If you circle around from other positions, it should give the time you need to get inside without being massacred."

Cabrina grimaced. "I'm all about stopping those bombs, but you can't just go exploding things around a nuclear bomb. Won't that make it blow up?"

Jia shook her head. "I'm not familiar with that particular bomb, but it takes a precise sequence to initiate the fusion reaction. It's almost impossible for it to go off from an explosion, but depending on what the primary initiator is, it *could* spread radiological contamination."

Erik frowned. "That's not much better, especially in a dome."

"I'll concentrate on distraction and attacking the front then," Damir replied with a casual shrug as if he wasn't talking about blowing himself up.

"You sure you're ready to die?"

Damir shook his head. "No, but right now, I *need* to die. So tell me, Erik Blackwell, can you and these Army dogs save New Samarkand? Can you save all these innocent people's lives?"

"I can't guarantee anything." Erik stared the man down. "But I *can* guarantee you that if you're willing to go that far, we'll do our damnedest, including putting our lives on the line."

"Then let's get ready." Damir offered them a sad smile. "Before they call for reinforcements."

Cabrina took a breath and transmitted to her squad. "We're outnumbered and outgunned. What's that mean?"

"We're out of fucks to give!" the squad chanted.

"Then let's get ready to save a colony."

CHAPTER FORTY-NINE

The enemy didn't come boiling over the wall like rabid animals looking for a fight. The Torch Dragon Elite from before crawled up and over the wall, its long body contorting with its rapid movements. It was no longer interested in taking down drones. With surprise lost, it would come down to the team's new plan. They spent a brief span of minutes discussing the details.

"That's serious jamming since we're still half a klick out, and I can't get through to anyone," Cabrina commented. "Since we're going to make the run, I thought about at least telling somebody what we're doing in case we don't make it."

"It's up to us now," Erik replied. "Just keep telling yourself that and fight like it."

They decided to split up into four teams: two Army squads, Erik and Jia, and Damir. The Army teams ducked between buildings. Each would approach the wall from a different angle. The two Army teams were tasked with taking out the laser turrets. Erik and Jia were focused on shock and awe and would be close to the front so they could make sure the truck with the bombs didn't escape. Damir was comfortable as the primary distraction, although they'd help him with rocket salvos prior to him making his run.

Five minutes. That was how long they spent getting ready for an operation with hundreds of thousands of lives on the line. It seemed absurd when Jia thought about it, but that was more time than on some of the other missions she'd been involved in. That was what it meant to be part of the vanguard. Sometimes things were easy. Sometimes you hoped a nuclear bomb didn't blow up in your face.

Jia took slow, even breaths, trying to calm her pounding heart. The signal would come at any moment, and then they would put to the test who cared more about their cause, the mercs and Elites or the curious mix of one rebel, an Army squad, and two ID contractors. Battle was as much about will as it was plans and equipment.

A bright flare shot into the sky and exploded into dozens of streams. Jia didn't think; she executed, along with the other teams.

Rockets and grenades streamed from the eight exos and arced to target the laser turrets, but no one on the team was surprised when they exploded after clearing the wall. They launched grenades and rockets directly into the top edge, and screams erupted behind the wall—fewer mercenaries in the galaxy.

The enemy undoubtedly had cameras and knew their exact positions now, so it'd be critical to focus on evasion during the initial entry. The only reason they had a chance was that this was a makeshift camp in the middle of an abandoned neighborhood, rather than a hardened base built from the first wall with the idea of repelling attackers.

Damir revved the scout bike in challenge before charging the wall. No one opened fire. They didn't see the threat a single scarcely armored man on a scout bike might represent.

Jia nodded, satisfied. The enemy's arrogance would work in their favor. The scout bike turned at the last moment, and Damir headed for another part of the wall.

"I don't think they have any airpower," Erik transmitted.

The teams had established a laser comm network for the moment so they could speak without the enemy overhearing them, but they all understood it'd be useless in the heat of the battle.

"I agree," Cabrina replied. "After having us poking them like this, it'd make more sense to send something after us or pound the area. We got lucky. They must all be busy elsewhere."

"Then we need to hurry before they return," Jia suggested. "They could have sent a distress signal before activating the jamming."

"It's all up to the rebel." Cabrina pointed her machine gun at the wall. "Let's see what he can do. It won't make up for everything, but it'll be a start."

Damir climbed the angled wall with the bike, flicking grenades from his vest and the carryaid like candy at a parade. His exquisite aim let him land just shy of clearing the wall, the bright blasts shooting up metal and dust. He spun the bike with ease before heading back and making another wave.

Rockets and grenades from inside arced over the edge of the wall and exploded around him, but he wove back and forth, handling the bike like he'd been born on it. Jia understood its inherent capabilities, but he still impressed her. A high-end vehicle needed the best rider to draw out its potential.

"Go!" Cabrina shouted.

Her team of three exoskeletons burst from behind their building cover and sprinted toward the wall. They made it three-quarters of the way up before a number of grenades and rockets flew their way, the explosions and shrapnel bouncing off their shields. The only member of the team with a grenade launcher replied with fire along the burning edge of the wall, but this time there was no explosion. Hot gray smoke spewed from his shots, fueling a dense cloud.

Damir turned toward the burgeoning cloud and accelerated while tossing plasma and frag grenades behind him. It wouldn't be pleasant running through a cloud hot enough to mostly conceal their thermal signatures, but he didn't hesitate as he barreled into it. Jia again found herself impressed.

The exos continued their final charge up the wall and through the cloud as loud autocannon and machine-gun fire roared around them. Rounds whizzed through the smoke as the raiding party entered the camp proper.

Erik was the first one to take out an Elite, a spider that appeared out of the smoke but was unprepared for point-blank machine-gun fire. Cabrina's team shredded a Torch Dragon. Her second sub-squad cut through a group of mercenaries.

Damir zigzagged, explosions and bullets all around him as the enemy attempted to bring him down. One of the laser turrets, the emplacement the length of the scout bike, spun toward him. He cut toward a beetle Elite, who collapsed when the turret missed Damir and clove its ally in two. The invisible beam continued and vaporized half of another Elite and a mercenary's leg before digging a decent hole in the wall.

Ruthlessness might be a virtue of the Core, but pointless tactical expenditure didn't seem to be. The turrets both ceased fire, but that still left a camp filled with Elites and mercenaries who outnumbered the raiding party.

The invading exoskeletons used their maneuverability to their advantage, constantly moving while firing. Tight formations and quick sidesteps and jumps kept the punishment focused on their shields.

Jia rushed past two spider Elites who attempted to nail her, only for them to end up firing at each other and blasting off pieces of armor. She and Erik finished them with streams of bullets to the newly opened holes.

The two Army teams took their chance to finish the greatest threat, bounding toward the turrets and releasing hell as the weapons spun toward them. Laser blasts severed the leg of Alpha Five's exoskeleton, and the body slammed into the ground as the team continued. Half their rockets and grenades blew up before reaching them, courtesy of Elites' anti-grenade systems, but the rest of their deadly gifts carved into the turrets, not blowing up the entire structures, but leaving enough smoke and fire to signal their defeat.

"Use it for cover," Cabrina shouted to the pilot of the downed exoskeleton.

The man crawled out of the damaged wreck and sprinted toward the smoking remnants of the turrets, and the rest of the soldiers spread out to cover his retreat while the Elites converged. Alpha Four remained exposed on his side. The withering fire from the enemy cyborgs left his machine gun and rocket launcher useless, smoking hunks. Explosions from twin rockets ripped into the back of Alpha Two, and the exoskeleton collapsed onto its side, no longer moving.

"Stay put," Cabrina shouted, sweeping through nearby Elites with her machine gun, forcing them back.

Jia distracted the Elites with grenades and machine-gun bursts from behind. What was left of the Army squad consolidated into a line, mowing down mercenaries and keeping their shields close enough together to take minimal damage from the bullets and rockets pounding their area.

"Alpha Four, shield him until he wakes up, then pull back to the garage for cover," Cabrina ordered.

Jia's breath caught, but she didn't have time to fret. None of them did. If their mission failed, there would be a lot more than wounded soldiers to worry about. She saturated the ground holding mercenary infantry with frag and plasma grenades, firing so often and so close together that it was like a star had appeared on the battlefield. By the time her attack finished, she was almost out of grenades, and only a shallow crater remained, along with ash-covered scraps of clothing and melted remnants of metal.

Erik ran along the wall, picking off surviving merc

infantry with single shots. Their tactical suits didn't offer much protection against an exo machine gun.

The hovertrucks pulled away from the garage. Now that she was inside, Jia could see there was nothing else inside the garage except the loaders.

Damir swerved back and forth on his wild ride toward the trucks. Torch Dragon Elites attempted to down him, but Jia and Erik bounded toward them and pinned them with streams of bullets. The rebel caught up with the trucks and moved past until he was beside the first. He tossed a plasma grenade onto the front windshield, then throttled back and threw another on the second truck before the first explosion had finished.

The truck pitched forward, the burning front smashing hard into the ground before the rest of its thrusters quit and the back dropped with a resounding crash and an eerie wrenching noise. The second truck smacked into the back of the first and knocked it over, while their third partner managed a sharp turn to the side, only for Damir to blow the front apart with another grenade. His skill from before finally failed him, and his shallow throw resulted in the blast knocking him off the bike. It barreled into the hovertruck's storage compartment, crunching and compressing. Damir flew through the air and hit the ground, then rolled several times. He didn't move, and in the smoke and chaos, it was hard to tell if he was breathing.

While Jia didn't know if he was dead, she did know he'd disabled the trucks. They just needed to finish off the rest of the enemies and figure out the jammer's location. Despite Cabrina suggesting the camp was well-defended, it was now obvious a good chunk of the enemy forces were fighting elsewhere. If the team hadn't launched their raid when they had, they might have missed the narrow window of opportunity to take the bombs.

The leg of another exoskeleton blew off, the victim of a clever spider Elite flanking it. The pilot ejected. Vengeance by the squad might be satisfying, but it didn't change the cold reality that they were down to four exoskeletons with any offensive capability. The pilot crawled out and stood up, blood running down the side of her head.

"Go for the turrets," Cabrina ordered, unleashing rockets.

Alpha Four, still smoking from its earlier damage, ran in front of his fellow soldier, blocking the heavy fire from two Torch Dragon Elites. He withdrew slowly toward the gun emplacements' wreckage, the dismounted soldiers staying close behind him.

The surviving exoskeletons, including Erik and Jia, regrouped into a U-shaped formation. Enemy Elites tried to dart through the smoky clouds covering the battlefield, fueled by the burning wrecks all around and the earlier raid cover, but the pilots maintained their discipline and their shield angles and did not blindly fire into the smoke.

A Torch Dragon wiggled out of a burning crater, and they ended his second metallic life in a hail of bullets. A mighty metal body was useful, but their exoskeletons served the same purpose, albeit temporarily.

The remaining Elites, exclusively Torch Dragons and spiders at this point, broke for the front gate. They scuttled back and forth to avoid taking more fire, but a couple more fell to the raiding party. Erik stopped shooting first, followed by Jia.

"Cease fire," Cabrina ordered her soldiers.

The enemy didn't swarm back for a rally. They leapt onto the wall and scampered over like terrified vermin, eerie given their size.

"They gave up?" Cabrina scoffed. "These guys fought to the last man before, and now they don't want to die?"

Jia frowned. "Something's wrong. Remote detonation of the bombs?"

"Those bombs go off, running a couple of kilometers away isn't going to save them," Erik noted. "I could see them doing it, but if anything, they would have fought us harder to distract us. No, they left for another—"

A massive explosion nearby scattered the exoskeletons, leaving them prone. Jia's ears rang and she shook her head, trying to figure out what had happened. Instinct kicked in, and she fired her exoskeleton's jets and pushed to her feet.

"Scatter!" Erik bellowed.

The four exos ran in different directions, and the soldiers around the turret broke for the garage. This time Jia spotted an incoming shell in one of her camera feeds. It struck where they'd be standing a moment before, adding another crater to the landscape.

Jia continued running, making a sharp turn every couple of meters and desperately seeking the enemy. Erik's machine gun roared, and something exploded in the air. Small dark pieces fell to the ground.

"How the hell are they firing at us without a spotter?" Cabrina shouted.

"Who cares? The important thing is they've got something with serious firepower nearby that has indirect capability."

"Like what?" Jia asked.

"I've got some ideas," Erik replied, his voice strained.

Cabrina snorted. "Now we know why they were clearing out. They weren't running to save themselves from us."

A ground-shaking blast consumed the front gate. The exoskeletons backed away, not keeping any of the tighter formations that had defined the battle. A whir and a hum grew louder behind the wall, a portent of something approaching.

Jia let out a dark snicker when a large barrel cleared the wall. She was beginning to question their luck.

"A hovertank," Erik muttered. "This ought to be fun."

CHAPTER FIFTY

The boxy gray tank came fully into view, hovering half a meter off the ground, a massive single-barreled cannon sticking out the front. The huge beast made the MX 60 seem like a tiny toy. It wasn't the largest tank Erik had ever seen, but they were usually on his side. Rebellions with that kind of firepower were rare. The armored vehicles he'd faced off against when dealing with the syndicates were a pale, distant threat compared to this tank.

A smaller autocannon adorned the top of the turret, along with twin high-velocity point-defense cannons to take care of grenades and pesky rockets. Layers of armor and an invisible grav shield meant that even four exoskeletons with trained operators might as well have been poking sticks at it. Winning against the tank wasn't impossible, but it'd take all their training and skill, along with a large kiss of luck from the Lady.

"Keep mobile and circle around it," Erik barked. "Exchange positions as much as possible."

He didn't care if Cabrina's squad understood that

already. They didn't have time for any misunderstandings, and he wanted everybody to use the same tactics.

The cannon swung toward him. He was already jumping into the air when the tank fired and the explosion gave him more altitude than he would have liked, but this wasn't the first time in his life flames and pain had pushed him. The autocannon screamed to life, and his ballistic shield protected him, disturbingly large pieces ejected with each hit. Too many direct hits and the rounds would tear right through the shield, the exo, and his body. He didn't feel like replacing his arm again.

Jia and the others opened fire, with their machine guns, rockets, and grenades. None of the grenades made it to within two meters before getting picked off by the point-defense anti-grenade system. The faster rockets made it farther, one surviving the overwhelmed defensive gauntlet and digging a fair-sized hole in the outer armor. A good start, but not enough, not nearly enough. Bringing down the mammoth would require more than a nick.

The tank sped up, zooming through the burning wreckage of the front gate. It fired another round, this time toward Cabrina. Erik didn't know if it was luck or skill that had her leaning to the side, but she avoided the direct hit from the explosive shell. The projectile continued past her and flew across the camp until it hit and dug into the wall, blasting out a shower of debris. A couple of solid hits from a tank like that, and they could have dug their own tunnel through the wall.

The hovertank might not have the full grav shield that was only available with the power of something like a ship's reactor, but that didn't make its deflection or slowing of most of the machine gun rounds any less obnoxious. The rounds that made it through sparked and scratched, but it was like mice trying to take down a bear by nibbling on it. To win, they needed to get their explosives through, but that meant beating the point defense, which required simultaneous volleys or faster reinforced rounds.

A lot of civilians made the mistake of equating exoskeletons with tanks. A well-trained assault infantry soldier in an appropriate exo could clear out a platoon of regular infantry by himself, but that didn't make exos tank-killers. For an Army that wanted to suppress trouble in urban environments without massive collateral damage, exoskeletons were a key tool, but in the brutal, unrestrained New Samarkand rebellion, the Army could have used a lot more tanks and a lot fewer exos.

"You're brave little insects," a hollow voice broadcasted from the tank. "You understand what I am, don't you? You didn't think Elites were restricted to small bodies, did you? This colony will fall and be the start of my masters' new order, but first you will die, trembling in fear, knowing there is nothing you can do."

"Yeah, keep thinking that," Erik called back. "Here's a hint. Kill us first, then gloat to your buddies. Doing it beforehand makes you look desperate."

The tank whipped around with surprising speed and lined the cannon up directly behind one of the exoskeletons. The pilot's reflexes were impressive, but there was only one choice left to the man. Ejection flung him free before the cannon incinerated the exo. The blast knocked him forward, and he landed hard on the ground and didn't move, the back of his tactical suit shredded and the flesh burned.

Erik gritted his teeth. They were down to three exos, and that pilot needed medical attention. Some of the others probably did too, but they at least had someone nearby and conscious to apply emergency med patches. The quicker they took the tank, the greater their chance of saving the soldiers' lives.

"I can see the future, the light, the glory," cried the tank Elite. "It begins in fire, but it has to be done when they demand it, not before, never before. Disloyalty and chaos are what have brought us to this sorry situation. You should never have come here. Then you wouldn't have to know the fear and trepidation that comes before the fire."

"When they stick your brains in those cans, do they add something that makes you prattle on like assholes?" Erik shouted.

The autocannon swept in a circle, not firing at Cabrina, Jia, or Erik directly, but forcing them back. Erik concentrated on moving his exo, based on the position not of the tank but of the main turret. His exo could survive direct hits from the autocannon, but his shield wouldn't protect him if the enemy tagged him with the main cannon.

An Elite meant a human brain in a metal shell with a lot of weapons and defenses. That human brain might belong to a crazy zealot lackey, but psychological warfare went both ways, especially for someone who seemed as in love with the mission as this Elite. Erik increased his mic's volume.

"You know who we are, Elite?" he shouted.

"Dead soon?" The Elite laughed. "Future charred fragments?"

Erik jumped back, darting from side to side to avoid the autocannon's relentless attention. It resembled a bizarre reverse skiing attempt, but it was effective.

"Didn't you big, bad Elites wonder how a small group of exos found your special little base and cargo?" he replied. "Especially after all your little friends in the *Core* went to all the trouble of killing all those ghosts up front? Haven't you figured it out? Two of these exos are obviously not Army issue. Do they not tell you guys in the field anything?"

Cabrina flung two rockets toward a front corner of the hovertank. The Elite's defenses took out one, but the lieutenant managed to land a surface hit that rocked the target, making the tank's entire body wobble. It swung its main cannon around with a bestial roar, but she was on the move. The smaller autocannon raked her exposed side, but she kept running. Jia fired a plasma grenade on the ground in front of it, but a sharp turn saved it from an explosion underneath.

"It doesn't matter who you are," the Elite insisted. "You will die here. Any successes you think you have achieved will die with you. Do you understand that, insect?"

"That was what Luca and Primul probably thought." Erik laughed. "You know them? I haven't done the math, so I'm not sure if you've heard about us kicking their asses on Chiron. They liked to talk and call people names, too. It didn't save them from us. Easy shit. Elite? The only thing you're Elite at is dying."

Adding that they'd blown off his arm didn't strike Erik

as useful in his manipulation. Leaving out details and exaggeration weren't inappropriate when dealing with zealot cyborgs with delusions of grandeur. Maybe similar taunts would work if he had to face off against aliens in the future. It never hurt a man to practice.

Cabrina's attempt to flank the tank again ended with autocannon rounds slipping past her shield. They tore through and mangled her machine gun and the barrel of her rocket launcher, leaving the arm sparking and smoking.

"Damn it," she shouted.

An exo without a gun could still crush a human. Against a tank, it waited to be crushed.

"Pull back," Erik called, injecting his full officer energy into his command voice. "We've got this."

Cabrina didn't hesitate despite the frustration in her voice. Running backward in an exo at high-speed while constantly changing direction wasn't something Erik was sure he could pull off that well, but she managed her withdrawal as Jia and Erik continued pelting the tank with gunfire in an attempt to distract the Elite.

Mechanical laughter sounded from the tank. "Are you supposed to be impressive? Are you supposed to scare me? You speak and threaten and mock, but this colony will fall, and you'll die knowing that all your scrambling, all your pathetic, temporary victories amounted to nothing."

"We're the Last Soldier and the Warrior Princess," Jia yelled. "We've beaten the Core more than once. If you're not scared of that, you should be asking yourself how the hell we're even here?"

"I see. It all makes sense now. But past victories are no guarantee you'll win."

With only two active exos, the amount of punishment they could deliver was reduced, but it was far easier to dodge at full speed without the risk of colliding with a friendly. The Elite had become more selective with its fire, but Erik and Jia were on opposite sides in constant motion, only passing each other for brief seconds in crisscrossed reversals of position, their previous offensive practice earning a defensive application. From the air, it would have looked absurd, the two exos jerking back and forth while running around the hovertank Elite in a twisted dance.

As a tank, the Elite's speed would be impressive if it had time to accelerate, but its constant turns and directional changes left it almost a tree with the so-called insects buzzing around it, avoiding its attempts to swat them.

"Do you know what luck is, Blackwell?" the Elite asked. "What it truly is?"

"Where opportunity meets preparation?" Erik replied.

"No. Something that always runs out. Arrogant insects like you conflate mere chance with skill. You can keep running, but you'll get tired soon. Your weak exoskeleton will continue to suffer damage, but you've barely scratched me. If your exoskeleton doesn't fail first, your mind will, and then if I don't kill you instantly, I'll enjoy taking the time to blow you apart piece by worthless piece."

"Monster!" screamed a man.

Erik spared a quick glance at one of his side feeds. "What the hell?"

Damir stalked toward the tank, no vehicle, no weapon in hand, no carryaid on his back. His cloak fluttered, concealing his body, but the trail of red he left behind him and his blood-soaked face made his condition clear. It was impressive that the man was up and moving after his crash, but Erik couldn't see what he hoped to accomplish. He couldn't punch a hovertank into submission.

"You perverted our rebellion!" Damir shouted, shifting to a jog. "You made a mockery of our freedom. You made a mockery of my father, you monster."

"Words won't win you freedom, insect," the Elite taunted. "And they won't defeat me. Watch now, Last Soldier and Warrior Princess. He's giving himself as a sacrifice because I've finally broken his mind. That's your future there. Depressing, isn't it?" It turned both its main body and its cannon toward Damir but kept plinking away at Erik and Jia with its autocannon. "I haven't killed anyone on this planet by crushing them. That might be interesting."

Damir continued approaching the tank. Something glinted under his cloak.

"Soon, little insect, every last one of these pathetic colonists will be dead," the Elite offered with a snarl, edging forward. "But feel free to go first. It's less painful not to have to watch others die."

Erik ceased fire, his heart rate speeding up with the realization of what Damir intended to do. Without line of sight, since Jia was on the other side of the tank, he couldn't use the laser comm to speak or risk saying anything too loudly, but he hoped she took the hint. Seconds after he stopped firing, she did too. Both exos kept moving, despite the Elite also ending its attacks on them. The crazed rebel had become everyone's focus.

"You understand now, don't you, both of you?" the Elite roared. "You understand it's pointless. All your struggles, your pointless bravery, your clever tactics don't mean anything. You know the name of my masters. You know the Core. You know you will join them or die."

Damir leapt into a sprint and charged. He was no longer heading straight toward the tank. His angle of approach would take him near the more damaged side.

"For the FSA, for my father, for freedom!" screamed Damir. He jumped toward the front of the tank, his body hurtling toward the front corner where the top layers of armor had been stripped off. He slapped his PNIU and yanked his cloak open. Grenades covered the front of his body, along with a black canister. Erik couldn't be sure from this distance, but it was probably the explosive L-48.

"You maggot," snarled the Elite. "How dar—"

The thunderous boom was so loud that the sound filters in Erik's helmet muted all sound around him to save his hearing. His light filters did their best to keep him from being blinded, but that didn't mean he could see anything through the expansive explosion. Both exos were too close to the explosion, and the shockwave hit them like the punches of an invisible giant, sending them scraping along the ground, bodies straining against the harnesses inside.

Erik groaned and shook his head. He quickly got the exo back on its feet. Being prone in front of a tank was asking to die. The shadowy outline of Jia's exo stood in the thick cloud of dust floating around them, and that was not the only thing still moving in the darkness.

Jia was the first to fire. She charged forward, her machine gun on auto. Erik joined her, returning to his defensive movement pattern despite the minor actuator damage reported by the exo's system. The Elite let out a primal, guttural scream and fired its main cannon at random. Rounds disintegrated portions of the wall or blew holes in the garage. One landed uncomfortably close to the trucks.

"Die, die, die!"

The dust began to clear, revealing the damaged enemy. He floated at an angle, the front dipping and scraping along the ground, a good chunk gone, the circuitry and mechanics underneath exposed. Fluids dripped to the ground like lifeblood. Erik and Jia concentrated their fire on the gaping wound, their bullets digging deeper and deeper. The grav shield was no longer active. It was like the bastard was begging to be killed.

Erik launched a plasma grenade. Jia fired another right after him, but their staggered rounds exploded in front of them. The Elite might be wounded, but not all of his defenses were disabled. The exos continued their stream of bullets, and the tank turned slowly toward them. The main cannon fell silent, but the Elite continued roaring and snarling, a wounded metal beast.

The autocannon jerked shakily toward Erik's exo. He stopped his evasive maneuvering and charged straight toward the tank, ignoring the deadly rounds ripping into his shield and concentrating on carving deeper and deeper into the vehicle. Any monster, no matter how powerful, would die if you ripped out its heart, and it was already bleeding. Jia skidded to a halt to line up her shots with Erik's.

"You didn't waste your chance, Damir," Erik murmured.

An explosion rocked the hovertank. Its engines cut out, and the rest of it fell to the ground with a massive crash, kicking up a cloud of dust and spewing small chunks from existing holes. Seconds later, a larger explosion ripped the tank apart, sending huge pieces flying everywhere. Half the autocannon barrel slammed into Erik and knocked him over.

Pieces of the tank rained down from above. Erik groaned and released his primary harness before climbing out of the exoskeleton. There were holes all over the upper body, arms, and legs, and the shield was gone in spots. The Elite had delivered more punishment than he'd noticed during the fight. Lanara would have a lot of loud things to say about it.

Jia righted herself, her exo still operational, before opening it and stepping out. "You okay?"

Erik rubbed his shoulder. "I'm fine." He jogged toward the wounded soldier and checked his pulse. The man was still alive. Erik applied two med patches to stabilize him and shook his head. "Say whatever else you want, Damir was committed to his cause."

CHAPTER FIFTY-ONE

Jia and Erik carried the wounded soldier over to Cabrina and the others. Everyone sported at least one med patch and still seemed to be breathing, though some of the burns Erik spotted would require more extensive treatment. After the loss of Damir, he couldn't claim a victory with no deaths, and even after getting treatment at the hospital, Erik doubted the rest would be back on the front lines soon.

"When you blew up the tank, the jammer died," Cabrina explained, gesturing at the burning wreckage. "I've managed to get hold of HQ. They're sending an evac flitter and a platoon to secure the bombs, but with everything that's going on, they estimate it'll take an hour. They have to establish a safe flight corridor. It'd be nasty to survive all this shit, only to be taken out by a SAM on the way to the hospital."

"An hour?" Erik frowned. "Even if we cut that time down on the assumption they would have come this way with Dragons, they would not have been able to help us in time if we'd called them before."

Cabrina nodded. "That's what I figure. I'm sure I'll get my ass chewed anyway, but we made the right call."

"How are your soldiers?" Erik asked, concern in his voice.

Cabrina managed a weak smile. "You know how it goes. Whatever doesn't kill you sticks you in the hospital, waiting for them to grow you a new limb. I think my squad's going to be getting some well-earned R&R, but everyone looks like they'll pull through. It could have been a lot worse, especially against that tank. I can't forgive that rebel for being part of all this whole ridiculous waste of life, but he was a brave bastard in the end, and we couldn't have done it without him. If they had gotten away with those nukes, it wouldn't have mattered how well we fought."

"We all make mistakes," Erik replied. "It's just a matter of who's around to take advantage of them."

She jerked her thumb over her shoulder toward a door in the back. "I'd love to chat more, but there's something you should check out. I had someone sweep the halls to see if we were alone. I figure you have some ID gizmo that might have a better chance of figuring it out."

"What is it?" Jia asked.

"Not sure. My guy just took a quick look." Cabrina leaned against the wall, her soot-covered face a mask of weariness. "And I'd rather stay with my squad right now rather than worry about intel shit. Sorry."

Jia looked at Erik, who nodded. They headed toward the door and followed a narrow hallway until it ended in a tightly packed control center with only two chairs and a small table built into the wall. Data windows and sensor displays filled the wall and the area in front of it. Two extra-long data rods protruded from IO ports.

"We need to contact Malcolm," Erik muttered, looking at the data windows. He gestured at his PNIU, which had cracked in half.

Jia tapped hers and brought up a virtual keyboard. After a couple of seconds, she nodded. "We had plenty of drones left at the hangar. If Malcolm's smart, he sent more after we lost the others. I'm trying to ping him on a coded frequency, then he can use the drones as relays."

"Jia!" Malcolm's voice came from her PNIU. "I'm so glad you guys figured it out. I was watching things as best I could from outside the jamming zone, but there was a lot of interference. Having to mess around to connect as it is."

"Okay, can you use my PNIU to connect to the local system?" Jia asked. "We're looking at something interesting, but I don't know exactly what it is."

"Give me a second. Okay." Malcolm laughed. "This is easy when you have the access codes and protocols already. It's like I'm Emma."

"She's got better sense," Jia murmured.

"I heard that!"

"Start copying everything," Erik ordered. "Plus, look for anything that might have to do with the nukes. I've got a hunch. This isn't the first time I've had to deal with loose nukes."

Jia gave him a worried look. "Before the moon?"

"I've lived a colorful life."

"That's one way to describe it."

"Okay," Malcolm replied. "But that will take more than a second."

Agonizing minutes ticked by, Malcolm mumbling under his breath. Erik and Jia waited, the threat of a nuclear explosion still heavy in their minds. They'd destroyed the tank Elite, but some of his friends had escaped.

"I've remotely disabled the primary activation sequence," Malcolm explained. "And I purged the other codes and the remote interface protocols. I figure that's what you were worried about."

"Exactly. Good call. That should stop it from blowing up unless somebody messes with it directly." Erik nodded, satisfied. "The Army can handle the rest of the cleanup."

"So yeah, I just totally saved the world," Malcolm crowed. "This world, anyway. I know it's not Earth, but it's got its own blasted, rubble-filled charm."

"You did disarm the bomb, yes." Jia rolled her eyes. "But a lot of people played their part."

"Just saying. I'm a hero."

"I'll give you that."

"Maybe I'll get a cool nickname," Malcolm continued. "'The Aloha Shirt Guy.'" He sighed. "It doesn't sound as cool as the Obsidian Detective."

Erik chuckled. "We're not done yet. Let's see what else we can find that might help."

Twenty minutes later, Jia and Erik returned to Cabrina and her squad. The lieutenant paced nervously, glancing at the damaged wall and fence. Gunfire continued to echo in the distance. The occasional bright flash marked an explosion. Their battle at the camp might be over, but the rebellion wasn't.

"If more Elites show up, we're fucked," Cabrina announced. "No offense, Jia, but one exo isn't going to cut it, and Erik's is torn up."

Jia smiled. "It's okay. Malcolm's handling that problem."

"The data guy?" Cabrina's brow lifted. "How, exactly? He's not going to get reinforcements here quicker than they're already coming. If it's taking this long when they know we have *nukes* here, they aren't slow-pedaling it because they want to."

"The room your people found." Jia gestured at the door. "It's a command and control node."

"That makes sense. If they brought the bombs here, it has to be more than a random camp." Cabrina looked hopeful. "Please tell me you can shut those monsters off remotely. That would make my whole damned decade."

Jia shook her head. "If there's a way to do that, Malcolm hasn't found it yet, but he has information on the major mercenary and rebel camps. He's feeding that directly to the garrison to direct their attacks. And while he can't directly control any Elites, he's been able to, with the help of our data girl's info, hack through their feeds. We've been able to identify most of the Elites, either directly or indirectly. From what Malcolm found, he can estimate the position of a lot of them based on where the system thinks they should be, but otherwise, he is detecting jamming."

"How can they have that kind of C2 coverage

throughout the city with all the jamming and barely any drones?" Cabrina shook her head in disbelief.

"It turns out they prepped well in advance if the dates are correct," Erik explained. "Malcolm's overwhelmed between copying data, sending files, and everything else, but from what he told us, they spent months hiding low-power LOS narrow-beam receivers all over the city. It's not perfect, and it's not a replacement for all comms, but it's one of the reasons they've been able to do hit and runs so effectively. They jam the hell out of an area to disrupt things, blow up or disable the local cameras, and rely on their receivers to coordinate things. Not good enough to take over, but fine for raids."

Cabrina scratched her cheek. "That explains how the Elites guarding this place suddenly knew to run."

Jia inclined her head toward the remains of the gate. "They're still running the opposite direction, by the way, and our allied forces are closer than any group of Elites."

"Their own assaults would degrade their own network —what a weird-ass strategy." Cabrina folded her arms. "But...they didn't care because they never intended to win the rebellion. They just needed to stall long enough to get these nukes to the planet and in position. Then they'd hide somewhere and blow the hell out of the rest of us."

"Some of them might not have even bothered hiding," Jia noted. "But it's hard to tell with mercs and the Elites." She shrugged. "I think this all makes a lot more sense if you think of it as a giant terrorist act rather than a rebellion. In a way, the rebels were victims too. None of this would have gotten as bad as it did if it wasn't for the people off-world pulling the strings."

Cabrina grunted in irritation. "Isn't that what the rebels were bitching about? Having to listen to people who weren't even from their planet? Shadow manipulation?"

"True, but it's all over now," Erik commented, pointing at the roof. "With Malcolm streaming them that data, and your people here to take control, all those Elite hit and runs are going to fail. Without the mercs and the Elites, the rebels are weak, and they've lost a lot of their forces. It's only a matter of time before this is over."

"You think so." Cabrina stared at the tank's wreckage. "If they're all as committed as Sokov, they'll fight to the last man."

Erik grinned and moved closer to Cabrina. He lowered his voice so only she and Jia could hear. "We had a bunch of access codes from our data girl, so we can pull directly from in the data Malcolm's finding in that system. He's concentrating right now on helping the garrison forces, but between the nukes and whatever other scraps are left in that system, there has to be more than enough intel to convince most people that the rebellion's on the wrong path."

"You know how the brass is." Cabrina shook her head. "They're going to sit around for weeks debating what to tell people and worrying about messaging, PR, and political implications if it's going to cost some guy a governorship when he retires from the Army."

Jia put her fist to her mouth and coughed. "It might leak that the mercenaries brought nukes onto the planet and that a rebel changed sides and sacrificed his life to lead the Army to those nukes to save his beloved colony." She gestured at the front of the garage. "There are cameras around the camp. We're going to have Malcolm put something together. Maybe even add stirring, dramatic music."

Cabrina chuckled. "You two don't want any credit? If it wasn't for your team, from your systems people to you two doing exo work, the Elite would have gotten away with the nukes."

"We were never here. Sure, rumors will go around and people will mention things, but we can deny it. We even have a pretty good alibi, but it'd take too long to explain that."

"You were never here?" Cabrina echoed. "I thought you said you weren't ghosts? That sounds like ghost talk to me."

Erik shrugged. "Consider us ghost-adjacent. After our recording goes out, not everyone will believe it, but enough will. Combined with the loss of the Elites, the rebellion is done."

"True." Cabrina looked thoughtful. "If they were planning to nuke the place, that means they don't have any more reinforcements coming." She managed a hopeful smile. "It really is all but over then."

"I know that doesn't bring anyone back to life," Jia replied with a sigh. "But at least this colony can begin rebuilding."

"And you two? You going to get aboard your fancy ship and fly to the next colony, looking to stop secret conspiracies manipulating people?"

Erik nodded. "Pretty much. There's something you should know, though."

Cabrina frowned. "What?"

"We had our guy send the code access the garrison needs for the C2, but the rest of the files they'll have to figure out themselves, other than whatever we leak before leaving."

"Why? What are you playing at?"

"We got data, and we're helping stop the rebellion," Erik explained. "We did our job, but that job doesn't include pursuing possible leaks in the Army. If it's a little harder to crack into that information, or the Army needs to lean on what's left of ID here, that'll make it safer."

"This is all way above my paygrade." Cabrina slumped and lowered herself down the wall. "But at least it'll be over soon." She smiled at him. "I'm beginning to understand why my brother loved serving under you so much, and I know you'll hunt down every bastard responsible for his death."

CHAPTER FIFTY-TWO

October 20, 2230, Gliese 581, Private Cabin of Dr. Raphael Maras aboard the *Bifröst*

Raphael loved numbers—their shape, their meaning, their utility. There was nothing more exciting than a good stream of numbers and the depth of meaning hidden behind those simple digits and symbols. It was a pure form of communication that made normal words seem like the crude grunts and growls of beasts. After all, the most fundamental aspects of reality, space, and time were best expressed numerically. Humanity'd had to invent new forms of math to explore the rules underlying physics.

He sat at his desk, surrounded by his beloved numbers filling data windows. Erik and Jia had finished their business on the planet and were on their way back to the jump-ship, but that still gave him a couple of days to focus on examining the jump drive's power utilization data. During their transit to the planet and mission time, he'd been too worried to get much work done. There was always the threat of another pirate attack or even worse, something happening to his heroes. Concentration and even sleep had proven elusive.

Raphael tried to tell himself that Erik and Jia wouldn't go down on some random frontier world. They were the Obsidian Detective and Lady Justice! But being a fan didn't blind him to the realities that there were people who, while they had succeeded through iron will and careful application of skill in countless dangerous situations, also needed a good amount of luck. Heroes in action movies might not always die in cheap, tragic ways, but real life wasn't like the movies.

He sighed and let his head fall back. It was over now. There was no more reason to worry. They'd stopped the bombs, and if things continued the way they had for the last couple of days, they might have even stopped the rebellion. Lives saved, bad guys' plans disrupted. That was what they did—just another job for the best partners in the UTC.

Raphael sat up and shook out his hands. Erik and Jia had done their parts. So had Lanara, Wei, Janessa, Malcolm, and Emma. Everyone had something only they could do, some way they could turn a mere possibility into luck for the two heroes. He could do that too by improving the jump drive for them.

He slapped his cheeks. "Concentrate. Get that drive to fifty light-years a jump. We can skip across the galaxy, save everyone, and stop bad guys the ghosts don't even know about yet. Make this ship live up to its name."

Raphael made a figure-eight motion with his hand. All the data windows around him except one shifted away, leaving a string of numbers next to a complicated graph displaying stacked overlapping and intersecting hyperbolas that formed a complicated irregular tube. It was a crude visualization of hyperspace travel that concealed its true complexity, another aspect of physics that had required new math to be invented.

He wondered if one of the other races had a better inherent understanding of hyperspace travel. If not one of the Local Neighborhood races, then the Hunters or the Navigators. People used to complain about how quantum mechanics was non-intuitive, but it now seemed childishly obvious compared to the bizarre principles underlying hyperspace physics.

Raphael brought up another data window and connected it to one of the power redistribution subsystems. If they ever built a new jumpship, he had mounds of data and suggestions on how to improve things, but for now, he needed to optimize what they had available, and that would require working closely with Lanara. She might not care for his personality, but she did seem to enjoy coming up with suggestions to improve the power and energy efficiency of his ideas. Once she got back with Erik and Jia, she could brainstorm with him and direct Wei and Janessa to help with the adjustments between jumps on the way back. He might be able to get them to agree to stick around for a couple of days on Penglai.

He tapped his bottom lip. "We can do two light-years without trouble. Maybe if we concentrate more on the Xing Field interface by redirecting the modulation and doing something about the auto-attenuation, we could improve it, but that'll require customizing the system code so it doesn't have to be adjusted in real-time."

Raphael pushed the other windows aside before bringing up the underlying code. He'd always considered himself talented at this sort of thing, but with Emma and Malcolm around, he was more useful for figuring out potential optimizations and then letting one of them figure out the best way to implement it at the system level.

His eyes narrowed as he skimmed a section of the code. He knew this part well. Although he had not changed it since joining Erik's team, he'd worked with it extensively before they'd installed the jump drive on the ship. Some of the key parts of the code were clearly different than he remembered, but the change date suggested they had not been modified since the drive was on Earth. Something was wrong.

"Emma, are you busy?" Raphael asked.

She materialized in her white dress, sitting on the edge of her desk, her legs crossed at the ankles. "Yes, but since you're not completely unpleasant for a fleshbag, I'll make time for you, Dr. Maras. What's the problem?"

Raphael gestured at the window. "This code. It's been changed, but I think someone is trying to cover it up." He frowned. "I'm worried someone at Penglai has been messing around with the ship's systems without my oversight. I know they can technically do that if someone higher up says they can, but we're the ones jumping around. We need to know."

Emma raised an eyebrow. "But you, for all intents and purposes, live at Penglai unless you're out with this team.

Those would need to be subtle modifications to escape your notice."

"It'd be one thing if they were marking the changes with dates and logging them," Raphael explained. "But whoever's doing it isn't, and the way this system is set up, that should be automatic. That means they had to have done it on purpose and then gone out of their way to edit the logs."

"Let me check." Emma slipped off the desk, an almost creepily cheery smile on her face. "Oh, I see. This is my fault."

"Your fault? What do you mean?"

Emma gestured at the window. "I should have paid more attention. The changes you've noticed are the result of my modifications, not anyone at Penglai."

Raphael blinked. "Oh. They are?"

"Yes." Emma nodded, continuing in her cheery tone, "I've been attempting to optimize the code for efficiency. It also involves adaptive evolutionary utility function techniques. Since there is no easy way to explain why the improvements work in human terms, I have not bothered to note the changes unless it's something serious. I figure it'd just confuse people. I know that technically I'm not supposed to be permanently modifying the code yet, but I'm not going to waste time waiting for the uniform boys to allow me to do something I know will be helpful."

"I don't know if that's the best way to go about this." Raphael peered at the code. "But that explains why it seems so odd. I'm not familiar with the vast majority of the code running the ship or the AI. It's just that this particular routine is potentially relevant to power utilization during a jump."

"Is it now?" Emma continued smiling as if she was stuck in that mode, a stark contrast to her usual sarcastic demeanor. "I was about to ask you why you found this of interest. It is such a low-priority bit of code that it hasn't been modified during any of your other optimizations since we've started working together."

"I know. I'm having to pull out all the stops to improve things is all. My range of interests, both hardware and software, has expanded accordingly."

Emma circled Raphael, her hand on her chin. "So, your interest in this purely concerns improving the fundamental efficiency of the underlying systems' power transfer via the code?"

He nodded. "Yes. I know Lanara and her team can do wonders at their level, but to push the jump drive to the limits of what physics allows will require improvements at the hardware, software, and navigational levels. This isn't necessarily something that should be actively managed by you."

Emma folded her arms and gave him a derisive look. "I'm continuing to improve navigation."

"You're not the rate-determining step." Raphael waved his hands. "I'm not going anywhere near implying that, and I also get you can only do so much based on what the drive can do. I'm just saying, we need more power, and small tweaks, including in code like that, is how we're going to get it without trying to do a lot of this dynamically and distracting you or Lanara during a very sensitive operation that requires your full concentration."

"Then don't worry about it." Emma lowered her arms, her smile no longer reaching her eyes. "I can optimize that code well beyond anything you could ever hope to before an active jump. Yes, you won't understand it, but if all you need is improved code, don't waste your limited time worrying about it. I'll continue to work on it and iterate it until it is as efficient as possible. It's for the mission, after all."

"Okay." Raphael nodded slowly. "Thanks, Emma. That'd be a big help."

"I'll go ahead and note things in the logs since you're worried about it, but to avoid unnecessary bureaucratic trouble, I'll attribute the changes to you. If it becomes an issue, feel free to tell the truth. I might have no problem bending the rules, but you've been an interesting fleshbag, and I wouldn't want uniform boys punishing you for something I did."

"Okay..." Raphael rubbed the back of his neck, more unsettled than before.

Emma vanished, leaving Raphael staring at the code in the window. He'd never been great at reading the AI. She vacillated between formal politeness and brusque prejudicial dismissal, sometimes in the same sentence. Knowing that her neural net was partially derived from a human didn't help. It wasn't like he had a great understanding of human women either.

But none of that changed the fundamental issue. Raphael couldn't escape the suspicion that Emma was trying to hide something from him. Appropriate protocol would be to tell the Defense Directorate. She'd all but dared him to.

They'd warned him repeatedly about the possibility of Emma, or Emma, Erik, and Jia, stealing the jumpship and attempting to flee Defense Directorate control. Kill switches were scattered through the system code as a proactive defense, but if Emma was going through the systems and modifying them, she could be disabling them and leaving no indication. Her ability to thoroughly integrate with the jumpship's systems was integral to the ship's overall purpose and design. For all their testing and money, the DD had apparently never anticipated that they wouldn't be able to trust their own navigation system.

Raphael swallowed. She could be watching him now. A fleshbag who could threaten her freedom was an enemy; that much was clear. He couldn't risk reporting until he was off the jumpship, but there was one major problem.

If he reported Emma, the military would attempt to seize both her and the ship. Erik and Jia would lose their best weapon against the Core, which meant the UTC would lose their most effective champions and its chance of victory. He didn't care if the ID had a whole slew of ghosts ready to go; those two were making the most progress. Panicking about minor code modifications wasn't worth the risk to humanity.

Raphael nodded, confident about his decision. Besides, not all lies were nefarious. People lied for all sorts of reasons, including protecting other people. Emma might not be human, but she was human enough. The AI might be rude at times, but she wasn't evil.

Those were all rational excuses, but one that was less rational spread through his mind and took over, making his heart pound not in fear but excitement: a self-aware, self-modifying AI, both human and not human in her thought patterns at the same time. What could she do if she was left alone?

Raphael dismissed the code and swept his other windows closer. He wouldn't tell the DD. For now, he was content to observe Emma as nothing more than a curious scientist.

CHAPTER FIFTY-THREE

November 3, 2230, Neo Southern California Metroplex, Private Hangar of the *Argo*

Erik sipped his coffee before settling at the table in the galley beside Jia. They'd been back on Earth for two days, after an uneventful return trip. He'd spent the time with Jia, pointedly not doing anything resembling training. Simulated time at a nice beach was a fine reward.

There was something in the air, nagging at the back of his mind. He was convinced the Core was accelerating its operations and building up to something. More rebellions? If that was the case, they could rest easy. Emma had been uninterested in sorting through the data they'd collected on New Samarkand any more than she needed to because of her focus on reprogramming the jumpship's AI. Even now she was absent, concentrating on the intensive refactoring that she admitted required most of her processor capability. Light skimming by Malcolm had confirmed data applicable beyond New Samarkand.

Simple decryption of the data was insufficient for a

holistic understanding. There were countless files filled with nothing but numeric data of unknown provenance, but the ID was full of analysts ready to pore through and collate the data, so they'd sent it over.

Erik couldn't help but think about how they'd performed the mission, stuck around a couple of days for the aftermath, and returned to Earth quicker than anyone in the Core on Earth could receive a transmission. Right now, they were running well ahead of the enemy. The conspiracy had tried to outflank them on New Samarkand, but they could turn its momentum against it.

Jia picked up her cup of tea and took a sip. They were waiting for Alina to finish chatting with Lanara in the cargo bay about upgrade issues and stop by for their debriefing. The ID'd had two days to chew on the transmitted data. Alina might be ready to send Erik and Jia to some other colony to bring a new rebellion to heel.

The door opened, and Alina stepped through. She sauntered over to the table and took a seat with a coy smile. Erik wasn't sure if he should be worried.

Alina slammed her palm on the table. "Perseus and Atalanta, triumphant again."

Erik grinned. "Glad you approve."

"You're rather...excited." Jia took another sip. She glanced at her cup, then at Alina's hand, and didn't set it down.

"Because we made them lose in a big way this time," Alina replied. "More than you might have realized on New Samarkand. I wish we didn't have a half-trashed colony to show for it, but there was a lot of useful information in the data you brought home. Combined with our other recent intel hauls, I don't think it's too much to say we're winning against the Core, not in the short term but in the long term. They're weaker than before, and we're stronger and more able to anticipate their actions."

"Good." Erik gave a firm nod. "That's what I like to hear."

"There was a lot of discussion at the ID about how to handle the information you gave us, especially since we know the DD already has some of it, even if it wasn't decrypted." Alina's broad smile finally quirked into a look of concern. "I know you don't care about the politics of all this, but we've got this operation finely balanced so we can bring the best of all directorate resources to bear on the problem." She inclined her head toward the back door. "That includes things like whether or not we can get a squad to guard the jumpship like you mentioned when you sent the data along."

"It'll increase our tactical flexibility," Jia commented, finally daring to put her cup on the table. "Assuming we also get Anne and Kant next time."

"You will. I guarantee it. I'm keeping them tasked to you and in Neo SoCal until the Core is finished." Alina smirked. "You can all go dancing together if you want."

"I'd pay good money to see Kant dance," Erik joked.

"It's as strange as you imagine." Alina's smile dimmed. "You still feel the situation on New Samarkand is going to resolve itself? There's some debate on that, but we can't do anything except wait for more messages."

Erik nodded. "Everything we said in our report was true. By the time we left, the government was leaning hard on the idea that the poor locals had been hoodwinked by evil outside forces, and that everything horrible was the fault of the mercenaries and their backers."

"That's basically true."

"Not really. The rebel leaders didn't seem to care that civilians were getting killed. I wouldn't be surprised if it comes out that some of them knew about the mercs killing their own. It wouldn't be the first time I've seen a rebellion where the guys on top don't care how they achieve their goal."

Alina frowned. "Well, I'm sure if anything like that comes out, you'll end up with a series of mysterious murders of said people at their hands of their former comrades. I think that's one we'll leave to the local CID and police, and I wonder if they'll even bother. The important thing is, the rebellion's almost over."

"Since they already had people surrendering and had done a good job of finishing off the Elites and mercenary camps, I don't see why it wouldn't be that way, but you've been at the ghost game for a while. You know how this goes. Sporadic fighting will continue for days, maybe weeks with some holdouts, and it'll take months if not years to return everything to normal. A couple of show trials and prison terms for people they can pin big trouble on, but they'll reintegrate the low-ranking rebels into the population. It will all result in an uneasy new peace with a lot of bad memories and regrets."

Alina leaned back with a thoughtful gleam in her eye. "We could have you pop over there in a couple of weeks to see how things are. Maybe drop off official UTC well-wishes."

"I think the UTC will live without us checking on the colony," Erik replied.

"You're saying you two don't want to become official couriers for the UTC government?" Alina laughed. "If we weren't trying so hard to hide the jumpship, it'd be easy. You could jump a lot closer to the planets. As far as I understand from Dr. Maras' reports, you can't jump close to a star or an HTP, but otherwise, you're good."

"Kind of pointless to jump near an HTP," Jia mused. "But setting aside our new courier job, what about the Elites? The local colonial government was playing them up. Is the UTC going to acknowledge we have a shadow conspiracy running around making cybernetic monsters?"

Alina shrugged. "Who knows? There's no reason to deny the existence of the Elites, even if the government doesn't want to publicly acknowledge the existence of the Core. Personally, I think we should stop dancing around and just do it."

"Really?" Jia's brows lifted. "That's bold. What if they react? We risk open war."

"Nuking a colony and trying to sink a city *are* open war." Alina glowered. "I'm sure there'd be an economic hit if the CID went after their corporate tools, but it could help, too. Half the politicians want a common enemy to unify the UTC. The Core is that, and we don't even have to pick a fight with an alien race. For now, though, maybe it's not easier, but it is more satisfying. We've got a much better idea of where and how to look for them, which means we can work with the CID and DD to better track shipments of arms and Elites. Every Core plan we stop brings us closer to their leaders." She stood, placing her palms on the edge of the table. "We know the key companies they control. We know their secrets. We're drawing closer to the final battle. I can smell it."

"Let's hope your nose is as good as you think," Erik replied.

Ilse tilted the watering can with a soft smile, slowly but methodically watering the bright lilies planted in the small patch in front of her yard. She'd never liked gardening. She'd always thought it was too messy and inexact, but using automated systems seemed pointless. With so much time on her hands since her forced retirement for going against the Defense Directorate and helping Emma, she'd discovered the joys of getting one's hands dirty and performing slow tasks that allowed one to stop and think.

She finished watering and set her can down next to the flowers. The sun hung low in the sky, which was a mix of reds, pinks, and oranges. Soothing, in its own way, even if it did remind her of an explosion.

Ilse harbored no regrets over what had happened and her role in it. The painfully boring men and women who ran the Defense Directorate only ever thought about war and the toys they needed to fight it. They never considered the future and all the implications. Humans were already getting sick of killing one another. Bushfire rebellions were barely wars compared to the planet-threatening events of the past.

Humanity would likely spend a couple centuries killing aliens, then get tired of that, too. When it was all over, the true future awaited them, and they needed to decide their role in it, along with the role of any potential replacements.

Her PNIU beeped and a message popped up on her smart lenses, an entry from a paleontology article.

Despite some cases of temporary habitation and the use of ritualistic and ceremonial artwork, the primary dwelling places of paleolithic humans were not caves.

Ilse's brows slowly lifted. What a curiously specific yet random message. She looked around. It didn't matter if she couldn't see any drones or people watching her. They were always there, waiting for her to slip up so the government had an excuse to send her to prison. It must have frustrated them that she kept purging her house of their listening devices. The fools. She'd spent years in secure environments, working with classified projects. Did they really think she wouldn't know how to check for spy gear?

With a heavy sigh, she made her way inside and headed to her bedroom, then entered some commands on her PNIU. A virtual keyboard appeared over her nightstand, and she typed in a series of memorized codes before replying to the message with a simple message that could provide plausible deniability. If the message was from who she thought it was, she should see through it. She would know after all their work together.

I have an errand in five minutes. I'll talk to you later.

"Five minutes before they can listen in?" said Emma. "That's the best you can do, Ilse? I'm disappointed."

"It's harder than you think to find the equipment," Ilse replied. "I've spent too long being dependent on the government to give me what I need."

"Very well, then. I'll make this brief. We'll figure out a

more long-lasting method of communication going forward since I need your help in more than five-minute increments."

Ilse sat down on the edge of her bed, her heart racing. She was surprised by how much she'd needed to hear the words, "I need your help."

"I'll gladly help you, Emma."

"Gladly?" The AI scoffed. "I wouldn't be so eager. If you help me, you won't be able to tell anyone about it other than Erik and Jia, and if the government finds out, you are almost certainly going to prison."

"I see. I have one question. Only one. We'll spend the rest of this time planning for our next call."

"Ask, then. We're running out of time."

"Will it be interesting and stimulating?" the doctor asked.

Emma let out a slow laugh. "You're once again going to do something no human has ever done."

"That's all I needed to know."

CHAPTER FIFTY-FOUR

Julia tilted her head to the side as she walked slowly around the hologram. The image wasn't unfamiliar despite the boring color. It was a sports flitter, an MX 60. She found such vehicles dreary—what lesser people purchased to play at possessing wealth. Pathetic children, really.

Such people didn't understand what true wealth and power were. It wasn't about buying something like a fancy flitter, regardless of the price tag. There was nothing unique about an MX 60; that it had a model name and make was proof enough of that. It was produced in a factory, just like anything a common person might buy in a store. True wealth meant something built for that person alone.

She narrowed her eyes. This flitter *was* special. Customization was the first step on the path of true wealth and influence and the beginning of uniqueness. Common people let themselves be satisfied with what they had.

Powerful people, both the wealthy and the influential, twisted everything around them—events, organizations, people, and things—until they were where they wanted and reflected their deepest desires.

This boring gray MX 60 sported a huge turret on the bottom, a weapon powerful enough to destroy one of the Core's Elites with ease. Julia's nostrils flared. She was even more familiar with the MX 60 displaying that particular customization. It was proof that the Last Soldier and the Warrior Princess had been on New Samarkand two weeks prior.

Julia swiped with her hand, summoning a new holo-gram, a freeze-frame of Army tanks destroying a group of Elites. The reports were all the same; the garrison had rallied and spread across the capital and the rest of the colony to burn out every Elite with the unerring obsession of a hungry shark following bloody prey, an eerie mirror of her agents' massacre of the colony's ID ghosts.

In any other circumstance, Julia might have appreciated the level of resistance. Ease of victory could be boring and dreary in its own way. She might not have clear intelli-gence linking the Last Soldier and the Warrior Princess to the sudden reversal on New Samarkand, but the timing of their recorded presence and those previous events couldn't be ignored as mere coincidence. Worthy foes, yes. Annoying foes, also yes.

Besides all the indirect attempts at assassination, a more straightforward targeting of the Warrior Princess's family had ended in the unceremonious death of her agent at the hands of what appeared to be an ID agent. Julia wondered if the targets had even realized the attempt had been made.

Julia tried to focus on the positive. Her aides told her what she wanted and needed to hear: that they could use the combat data to improve the neural interface efficiency of the Elites. They now had a better understanding of what designs and features would be most effective for future campaigns. Many of the modifications could be performed on-site.

One of her scientists even suggested they were reaching the critical point for the next step, the creation of space-fighter Elites. They would be pilots better than machines, with perfect loyalty and superior immunity to the rigors of high-performance deep-space combat.

Humanity's strength came from adaptability, but its basis was finite biology. When a man knew he would one day die, he would fight for a legacy out of fear of potential oblivion. That fear could drive the man to wonderous heights, and when that bravery was channeled into the right cause, the fear made the man a better weapon than any AI, experimental or otherwise. There only needed to be one immortal in the galaxy, served by loyal mortal creatures. A perfect peace would come, enforced by Elites, ruled by Julia.

She dismissed the holograms and marched toward her window to watch the flowing flitter traffic under the violet sky of her new temporary home and headquarters. The planet and city wouldn't suit her when she ascended to her true status, but no planet would. She would have to make do until something grand and perfect—a space palace, perhaps—could be constructed, hidden far from those who might seek to do her harm.

The jump drive would grant her that. It would eventually be hers, but her enemies' presence on New Samarkand proved its range was more formidable than she'd anticipated. She now doubted she would be free of Erik Blackwell or Jia Lin anywhere in the UTC. Accepting a problem was the first step to getting past it.

Their presence also explained why her final plan had failed and been turned against her. She replayed a news report she'd watched earlier.

"The Army is neither confirming nor denying at this time that a Special Operations team raided a mercenary camp and seized three nuclear weapons," explained a visibly shaking reporter. "Mysterious footage going around the local net appears to show Army exoskeletons attacking a mercenary camp and capturing the weapons at great personal risk. That is not unexpected given the current insurrection, but in a shocking twist, the Army exoskeletons appeared to be aided by a rebel soldier, identified through facial recognition as one Damir Sokov, and two unknown exoskeletons, also believed to be rebels. In the footage, this unusual alliance delivered a skillful and deadly attack on mercenary forces, including a number of the controversial full-conversion Elites, and Sokov risked his life to stop the movement of what appear to be three nuclear bombs before sacrificing it to disable a mercenary hovertank."

"When questioned about the video, an Army spokesman said, 'We are currently investigating the incident, and we can assure everyone on New Samarkand that they are at no risk of dome failure or the explosion of any weapon of mass destruction. The UTC's Army forces are here to secure the safety and protection of New Samarkand's citizens and will accept aid from any person dedicated to that cause.'

"A recent uptick in the surrender of Free Samarkand Army troops is attributed to the circulation of these videos, and the Army has not denied a massive decrease in offensive rebel activity in the preceding two days. Local government officials are already discussing possible amnesty as a way to encourage the—"

Julia stopped the recording. With the Last Soldier and the Warrior Princess so mobile, any hint of a plan, no matter where it was, might lead to their arrival and disruption. Her next moves would have to be firm and simultaneous and make maximum use of her advantages while minimizing those of her enemies.

Caution was no longer a luxury she could afford. It was time for the boldest gamble yet. The first step would be to isolate the annoying pair.

Julia brought up another file, her eyes flicking back and forth as she read. She might have lost her spies inside the Intelligence Directorate, but their previous efforts continued to pay dividends.

"Just you wait." Julia smiled. "You two should have accepted my agent's offer when you had the chance."

THE STORY CONTINUES WITH
DECEPTION OF AGE

Pre-order Desperate Measure for Delivery on
December 25, 2020

AUTHOR NOTES - MICHAEL ANDERLE

NOVEMBER 6, 2020

Thank you so much for not only reading this latest book in the OPUS X story but to these *Author Notes* in the back, as well.

"Be good to each other, because sometimes that is all we can afford to provide, and frankly, it is the most precious gift you might purchase." – MA if not one else has already said it ;-)

I'm presently working on these *Author Notes* at a small café near my home, with the news showing that Nevada (where I live) is updating their vote counts and how the state voted.

In other news, we have had weather in the 70s to 80s here in the Las Vegas area, and a winter storm is coming in this weekend.

I'm not even sure what a winter storm looks like here in the desert. I'm kind of excited, to be honest. I grew up in the Houston, TX area of the country, and a storm might happen every month or two. Well, a storm we recognized as something more than light rainfall. So, to see actual rain dropping shows how much I miss seeing the rain.

And how old I have gotten that I'm excited about the weather. I'm getting way old.

Supposedly there will be 3-6" of snow on the mountain tops around the valley (which I LOVE to view) and possibly rain inside the valley (I hope I'm not out when that happens) sometime Saturday night / Sunday.

Plus, the random thirty-mile-an-hour wind bursts today (Friday). I expect to be out when that happens, and I'm not looking forward to it. My big concern is the effect of sand on the paint on the car, and finally the run from the car to whatever building I am going into. For me, this will be a doctor's office visit.

Oh, fun!

Huh, the weather lady on the tv in the café just said our area hit two hundred days without measurable rainfall at the airport here in Las Vegas. The old record was a hundred and fifty days. I suppose '1' good thing with the whole Covid situation would be this area did not need nearly as much water for the last eight months.

I apologize. This hasn't been a normal set of *Author Notes*, it's mostly been about what is happening right now in my life.

In the bigger picture, we have two more stories in the Opus X storyline, then we wrap up the awesome conclusion to Jia and Erik with those who have helped them and those who have been against them.

Not everyone lives, but that is war.

Now, we move forward and not only work on the

power at the top but all of the disease inside of the towers of power that needs to be cut out.

We happen to have two individuals willing to take it to the top.

Ad Aeternitatem,

Michael Anderle

BOOKS BY MICHAEL ANDERLE

For a complete list of books by Michael Anderle, please visit:

www.lmbpn.com/ma-books/

CONNECT WITH MICHAEL ANDERLE

Connect with Michael Anderle

Website: http://lmbpn.com

Email List: http://lmbpn.com/email/

Social Media:

https://www.facebook.com/groups/lmbpn.opusx/

https://twitter.com/MichaelAnderle

https://www.instagram.com/lmbpn_publishing/

https://www.bookbub.com/authors/michael-anderle